OKSA POLLOCK

the Heart of two worlds

**ANNE PLICHOTA
CENDRINE WOLF**

Translated by Sue Rose

PUSHKIN
CHILDREN'S

Pushkin Children's Books
71–75 Shelton Street
London WC2H 9JQ

Translation © Sue Rose 2014

Oksa Pollock: The Heart of Two Worlds first published in French as
Oksa Pollock: Le Coeur des deux mondes by XO Editions in 2010

Original text © XO Editions, 2011. All Rights Reserved

First published by Pushkin Children's Books in 2014

0 0 1

ISBN 978-1-78269-032-0

Unloveable
By Steven Morrissey and Johnny Marr
© Artemis Muziekuitgeverij B.V. (BUM/STE)
and Universal Music Publishing Limited (GB) (PRS)
All rights reserved

Undisclosed Desires
Words and music by Matthew James Bellamy
© 2009 Loosechord Limited (PRS)
All rights administered by Warner/Chappell Music Publishing Ltd

Set in 12 on 16 Arno Pro by Tetragon, London

Printed in Great Britain by CPI Group (UK) Ltd, Croydon, CR0 4YY

www.pushkinpress.com

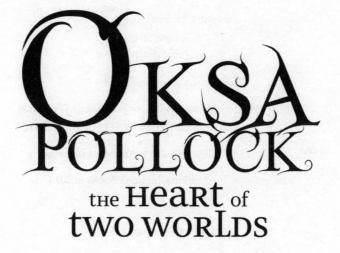

OKSA POLLOCK

the Heart of two worlds

For Zoe. Unconditionally.

PART ONE
ON THE OUTSIDE

1

FLIGHT INTO THE UNKNOWN

PAVEL POLLOCK'S INK DRAGON FLEW THROUGH THE driving rain and wind with loud, powerful wingbeats. The only light in the almost total darkness came from an octopus—the Polypharus with its eleven illuminating tentacles—held out at arm's length by Dragomira like a beacon in the gloomy night skies.

"Keep going, son!" shouted Baba Pollock, leaning forward over the dragon's crested back.

The Runaways were trying to lighten the dragon's load by taking turns to Vertifly alongside it. Brune Knut, their stalwart Swedish companion, was the next to launch herself into the air, joining Pierre and Jeanne Bellanger, who were doing their best to brave the howling wind.

"The conditions are too treacherous," warned Pavel, his voice hoarse with exhaustion. "Let me carry you!"

"No chance!" retorted Pierre, his hands shielding his eyes from the torrential rain lashing their faces.

Oksa had her arms wrapped around her gran's waist and was feeling very miserable indeed. The sudden violence of the weather seemed to mirror the terrible wrench of their departure. In just a few minutes, their lives had been turned upside down: London had been flooded after an unprecedented tidal swell had caused the Thames to burst its banks. Fate had forced the Pollock family and friends to make a run for it—they'd had no choice but to embark on a headlong flight through the turbulent darkness into the great unknown. Looking back at Gus, Oksa met his terrified gaze. Her friend was clinging with all his might to Reminiscens and his face was wet, although Oksa couldn't tell whether it was with rain or tears. Frowning, she held on tighter and caught a glimpse of Tugdual and Zoe drawing closer to the dragon, their faces strained with effort. Vertiflying in a storm was no easy feat by any stretch of the imagination... Slipping between the dragon's beating wings, they both collapsed onto its back, making the creature groan in spite of itself and slow its pace, causing a sudden loss of altitude. Oksa couldn't help screaming.

"DAD!"

Pavel was growing weaker by the minute, as were the Runaways Vertiflying alongside him. Wanting to help her father, Oksa began to slide off the dragon's back to Vertifly, but the dragon gave a roar that seemed to come from the very depths of its soul.

"NO! Stay right where you are!" ordered Pavel.

"Then we'll have to stop for a while!" yelled Oksa. "You've got to land somewhere, Dad. We'll all die if you don't!"

It took Pavel only a few seconds to face up to harsh reality.

"Mum, put the Polypharus away so that no one can see us, and sit tight, my friends!"

The Vertifliers took firm hold of the dragon's scaly hide and the creature plunged groundward through the icy downpour.

※

The dazzling beam of light nervously scanned the darkness, but the four soldiers in the helicopter were convinced they hadn't imagined it: as incredible as it might seem, they'd just come face to face with a huge winged monster in the sky. Some kind of dragon, escorted by human beings who were flying too! They'd gazed at each other in disbelief, paralysed by the shock of this unlikely encounter. The pilot's jerk of surprise had almost caused him to lose control of the helicopter.

The aircraft had yawed for a few seconds before stabilizing and the Ink Dragon had taken advantage of the brief confusion to soar to a safer altitude. Hearts pounding, the Runaways were now anxiously looking down on the searchlight, which was trying to locate them. Suddenly the beam landed on them and their blood froze. They'd been spotted! The air was filled with the din of the helicopter engine as it headed straight for them.

"They're going to shoot us!" screamed Oksa, seeing one of the soldiers positioning himself behind a big machine gun.

Instinctively, she held up her hand, palm forward, to stop the bullets. As she'd discovered before on several occasions, extreme feelings of panic tended to produce an incredible surge of power. The helicopter's engines were no match for the blast of wind that sent it spinning several hundred yards off course.

"What have I done?" exclaimed Oksa in alarm.

"You've just saved our lives!" replied Dragomira.

"Come on, let's make the most of this temporary reprieve!" rang out Pavel's hoarse voice.

The dragon spread its huge wings, banked steeply and glided wearily towards the ground.

2

TREK OVER THE MOORS

"THE DWELLING OF MY OLD GRACIOUS'S BROTHER IS eight miles from here as the crow flies, heading north-north-west," remarked Oksa's Tumble-Bawler, a small creature which looked remarkably like a bumblebee without legs. "There are two routes available to us: the main road and a footpath over the Welsh moors. The footpath is more secluded, but it will take longer than the main road, which is quicker but much busier," it continued, gazing towards the horizon.

As if to illustrate the diminutive creature's information, the Runaways became aware of the noise from the road. Even though it was barely dawn, it sounded like the traffic was already heavy, with cars moving nose to tail. In the headlights they could see birds taking flight in flocks, frightened by the blare of horns. The floods that had submerged part of England were driving people towards Wales and Cornwall in panic-stricken droves.

"Let's go over the moors," decided Dragomira with an anxious glance at Pavel.

Oksa's father was a sorry sight, bending over with his hands on his thighs, trying to recover from the punishing night flight. Although his Ink Dragon gave them a huge advantage, it was physically draining for him to share his body with another creature. He'd used up his last ounce of strength flying through the blinding rain to carry his family and friends to safety while ignoring the burning agony of his body and the anguish

14

of leaving their home. He groaned through gritted teeth. Recent events had brought his dreams crashing down around his ears. Gone was the possibility of living a *normal* life one day. It was as if everything Pavel had done to that end had been built on sand. He'd started out with such high hopes and so much faith in the future... The restaurant he'd opened with Pierre in the centre of London had been a last-ditch attempt to put the past behind them. In his mind's eye, he pictured the kitchen which was his pride and joy. Right now, it was probably knee-deep in mud as black as the misfortune about to descend on the world. *"We've got to leave... now,"* Dragomira had insisted. It wasn't the first time she'd said this, but her words had sounded so much sadder this time round, reawakening fleeting memories that filled their hearts with bitterness. Pavel shook his head as if to banish these dark thoughts. There was nothing to be gained by dwelling on the past. The most important thing now was to save his wife, Marie. She'd been a prisoner of the Felons for far too long. He straightened up as Dragomira came over and took a metal phial from her bag.

"Drink this, son," she said gently.

"Your famous Elixir of Betony?" he croaked.

"Yuck, that's revolting!" Oksa couldn't help exclaiming. "Revolting, but brilliant! It'll make you feel like a new man in no time."

Pavel smiled weakly at his daughter's enthusiasm and gulped down the contents of the phial in one.

"Blergh... it tastes like swamp water," he said, pulling a face. "It's just as well I trust you, Mum, otherwise I might think you were trying to poison me. You've really got to find some way of flavouring that disgusting concoction!"

Oksa sighed with relief. No one could match her father for teasing. But then, as he always said, mockery was simply a survival strategy for him.

"I'll give it some serious thought," promised Dragomira.

"Right, we've wasted enough time!" Pavel exclaimed suddenly, sounding much more like his old self. "We ought to get going."

It was growing lighter and the Runaways' shadows stretched over the heather as they followed the footpath through the deserted, hilly countryside. Wisps of mist clung to the bushes and leaves, creating a ghostly atmosphere. Above them, the sky was filled with British Army helicopters which roared like enraged lions and made it impossible to work any magic. They had no choice but to keep walking in silence, still dazed by the cataclysmic sights they'd witnessed in London, where they'd left behind a piece of their history.

"How are you bearing up, Lil' Gracious?"

Oksa glanced over at Tugdual. He was loping along with feline grace, tapping continually on his mobile, his wet hair hiding part of his pale face so that Oksa could only see the bottom of his jaw. She wouldn't have been able to tell if he was handsome or not, but that really wasn't the issue—more than anything, he reminded her of a black panther with his supple gait, keen intelligence and the brooding magnetism which played havoc with her emotions.

"I'm fine," she said without a great deal of conviction. "I just feel a bit... washed out. Literally as well as figuratively," she added, wringing out her sodden cotton scarf.

Tugdual gave a faint smile.

"How's the world doing?" asked Oksa, glancing at Tugdual's mobile.

"It's seen better days," he said, pocketing his phone. "Let's just say that you'll have your work cut out if you're going to impose order on this chaos!"

Oksa frowned. Today more than ever, she felt burdened by the responsibility. She was the Young Gracious, and the future of the world—of the two worlds—depended on her. She alone had the power to restore balance to the Outside, where she'd been born, and to the Inside, her family's native land of Edefia, and she had no idea how she was going to go about it.

"Don't forget we're here too," whispered Tugdual intuitively. "You aren't alone."

That was true: she wasn't alone. She could always call on the strength and support of the Runaways. The Pollocks, Bellangers and Knuts—as well as Abakum, Zoe and Reminiscens—were all nearby. But she missed her mum so much: the future would seem a lot less uncertain when she could cuddle her again. As if to illustrate her anxiety, a fierce gust of wind buffeted the walkers, driving swollen clouds over the moor. It wasn't long before the heavy rain began again.

"I'd give anything for a bit of sunshine," grumbled Oksa, turning up the collar of her jacket.

As Tugdual matched his steps to hers, she took a deep breath and fixed her gaze on the Runaways walking along the narrow footpath in front of her, two by two. Dragomira was completely hidden beneath a long canary-yellow cape, which could be seen from miles away. "That's Baba all over!" thought Oksa with an affectionate smile. The Old Gracious was leaning on Pavel's arm. They were at the head of the small group, their shoulders bowed, but their pace resolute. Oksa was proud of her father. Proud of his strength and courage, and of the decision he'd finally taken to join forces with the Runaways and support them heart and soul. He'd been very firm in his own way: "*Let me make one thing very clear, Mum,*" he'd announced to Dragomira. "*Once we've saved Marie and the two worlds, you're going to let me live my life the way I want, OK?*" Just behind him, Gus and Zoe were walking in silence, their heads hunched down into the collars of their coats. Gus was the only one who had no magic powers and he seemed to be finding this forced march along a waterlogged path in the storm totally exhausting. Brushing her blonde hair out of her eyes with the back of her hand, Zoe kept glancing anxiously at her friend and Oksa's heart constricted. It should have been her by his side, not Zoe. It should have been her encouraging him. She clenched her fists, feeling furious and frustrated. She desperately wanted to do something. But what?

"Gus?"

No one was more surprised by Oksa's shout than Oksa herself—she hadn't even realized she'd called out. Her cheeks flamed as Tugdual looked at her with a half-smile. Gus turned round, just as startled as she was by her impulsive cry.

"What?" he snapped with bad grace. Caught unawares, Oksa didn't know what to say.

"Are you OK?"

"No better than anyone else…" he replied, his features drawn.

Before he turned away, Oksa caught a glimpse of the deep pain and resentment in Gus's dark-blue eyes. He was fuming about her growing closeness to Tugdual. From the minute they'd met, an intense rivalry had developed between the two boys and they'd made no bones about it, even though Tugdual tended to resort to mockery, while Gus was just downright rude. The moody Scandinavian teenager's appearance on the scene had aroused what Oksa felt might be the stirrings of love. Tugdual now occupied a special place in her life and her heart. The downside of this, though, was that it had undeniably broken something between her and Gus. Things just weren't the same—their deep bond seemed to have been replaced by an explosive hostility which Oksa was finding hard to handle.

"Why did I call out to him?" she fumed half-heartedly.

"Because you're an impetuous Lil' Gracious who acts before she thinks and who gets a kick out of putting herself in impossible situations," murmured Tugdual confidingly.

Oksa clenched her fists. "I don't want to lose him!" she thought as she watched Gus's thin frame labouring along the muddy path. She shoved her hands in her pockets and kept walking with a scowl on her face. With the toe of her laced ankle boot, she kicked a pebble into a ditch. The distant hills disappeared under the violent downpour, and the horizon—like their future—was hidden from sight.

The Runaways had been walking for over two hours in exhausted silence when Oksa suddenly exclaimed: "Hey! Look!"

They all looked up to see a hare bounding over the moor. Dragomira gave a long sigh of relief and her eyes immediately regained their sparkle.

"Abakum…" she whispered.

The hare rapidly drew nearer, escorted by two bizarre companions: Baba Pollock's Tumble-Bawler, which was wheezing as it flew, and the Veloso, which was leaping nimbly over the vegetation with its long striped legs. When the hare finally reached them, the Runaways greeted it with unbridled delight.

"It really is you, my dear Watcher!" crowed Dragomira joyfully, kneeling down and burying her face in the animal's thick greyish-brown fur. "I was so afraid…"

They all knew that Baba Pollock had hardly ever been separated from her loyal protector. Dragomira didn't like living without Abakum by her side and their emotional reunion showed the depth of that affection. The hare allowed her to stroke him for a few minutes; then, to the amazement of the younger Runaways who'd never seen this marvel before, he changed back into Abakum the Fairyman. The old man gave himself a shake, smoothed down his grey hair, then looked at the group, as if mentally carrying out a roll call of everyone present. His eyes lingered gravely for a second on Oksa, then brightened, as though a huge weight had been lifted.

"You're all safe and sound, thank God!"

"We are, but only thanks to Pavel!" boomed Pierre Bellanger. "We wouldn't have got out of that mess without him."

Pavel looked away, embarrassed at being pushed into the limelight.

"Naftali and I saw what's been happening in London. What a terrible situation," continued Abakum, respecting Pavel's modesty. "And things can only get worse in this torrential rain."

As if to confirm his words, there was an alarming din as ten helicopters came hedge-hopping over the moorland. One of them hovered in front

19

of the Runaways and they trembled with fear. Dragomira just had time to hide her Tumble-Bawler and the Veloso under her cape before a soldier popped his head out of the aircraft, megaphone in hand.

"Is anyone hurt? Do you need any help?" he boomed.

Abakum signalled that everything was fine, thanks, and the helicopter rejoined its squadron heading for the roads out of eastern England and London, which were chock-a-block as thousands of disaster victims poured into the area.

"How did you find us?" asked Oksa.

Abakum tapped his nose in amusement.

"Leomido's house is only a couple of miles from here."

Oksa sniffed at the air and exclaimed:

"All I can smell is mud, it's so unfair!"

"I do have an uncommonly good sense of smell, sweetheart," said the Fairyman. "And it's not as if you don't have a great many talents yourself, is it?"

"Fat lot of good they are! With these stupid helicopters popping up unexpectedly, we can't even Vertifly for short distances!"

Everyone smiled except Gus, who turned his back on them with a brusqueness which upset Oksa.

"Excellent... Let's go and find Naftali then," suggested Dragomira. "It's high time we were all back together."

They set off again, their backs bowed under the beating rain but their hearts filled with renewed purpose.

3

NEWFOUND CLOSENESS

SITTING DROWSILY BY THE ROARING FIRE IN THE HUGE
hearth, the Runaways were trying to regain their strength and
composure after the turbulent events of the past few hours. Curled up
in a comfortable armchair, Oksa was desperately fighting sleep, although
she couldn't have said why. It would feel so good just to let go… She
rested her head against the padded back of the chair and looked around
at the modern paintings on the walls of the lofty converted church nave.

This house—which had once belonged to Leomido, Dragomira's late
brother—had lost none of its magnificence, but there was something
missing—its owner would never be back… Oksa took a deep breath
to stop tears welling and tried to attract Gus's attention. He was sitting
a few yards away, completely expressionless, and his poker face made
her seethe with frustration. She kept shooting glances at him, by turns
furious and pleading, her stomach churning with conflicting emotions
when, suddenly, just as she thought she was about to explode, she felt
something leave her body. The almost unbearable weight lifted as she
incredulously watched an almost invisible emanation—a transparent
figure which looked just like her—make its way over to Gus and do
what she desperately wanted to do *in her place*: lift Gus's chin with her
fingertips and force him to look at her. Gus frowned, puzzled by the vague
sensation, as Oksa avidly watched this bizarre phenomenon, feeling the
touch of her friend's skin beneath her own fingers…

"What's happening to me?" she wondered, wide-eyed. Too tired to react, Gus didn't look away and they both sat there, motionless and bewildered. For the first time in days, Gus wasn't avoiding her eyes and looked more surprised by this than anyone. Oksa held his gaze and the strange figure soon disappeared, but the most important thing was that contact had been re-established, even though it still felt a little awkward.

"Ahem, ahem…"

Two small creatures in bright-green dungarees had positioned themselves near Gus. One was podgy and the other slender, but both had huge eyes like Manga heroes, broad faces and a thin, translucent down over their pinkish skin.

"Oh, hello Lunatrixes!" said Gus.

"Our wildest compliments are to be presented to the friend of the Young Gracious," began the Lunatrix.

"Um… thanks…" muttered Gus, surprised at being addressed with such deference.

When the chubby-cheeked little creatures didn't say anything else, he had to press them:

"Can I do something for you?"

Leomido's Lunatrixes nodded frantically, pushing a third Lunatrix in front of them—their child and the only Lunatrix to be miraculously born on the Outside.

"He's so cute!" cried Oksa.

"The domestic staff of the Master-Impictured-Forever make the avowal of a request whose contents will be set forth, friend of the Gracious family… The lineage of the Lunatrixes has preserved the recollection garnished with warmth of your erstwhile consent to cradle his body and lavish caresses on him…"

Gus tossed back a strand of long black hair, revealing his handsome Eurasian face. When he'd stayed with Leomido before, he'd let the Lunatrix baby go to sleep on his lap. He'd been so angry that evening. At

Oksa and himself. Like today... He glanced furtively at his friend, who was also bound to remember that evening. She smiled at him, sharing the memory, and, dropping all restraint, gave him a wink... which he impulsively returned. Her face lit up.

"The questioning is whether the wish for a recurrence would be conceivable?" continued the Lunatrix, purple with embarrassment.

"Of course!" replied Gus, bending down to pick up the gurgling toddler.

His body was plump and soft and he was just over a foot tall. His large blue eyes shone like marbles, as he gazed adoringly at Gus. He curled up on his lap, as Gus gently stroked his back, and, a few seconds later, was sound asleep, snoring happily. Beside themselves with gratitude, the Lunatrixes bowed several times, so frantically that Gus was afraid they'd topple over.

"The friend of the Gracious family must be showered with gratitude."

"I've had enough showers to last a lifetime!" said Gus, with a wry look at the torrential rain through the window.

To the amusement of everyone there, the Lunatrixa threw herself down on the floor so violently that she slid over the waxed parquet like a penguin on ice.

"Ooohhhh! Your domestic staff is in possession of such a hollow brain!" she lamented. "Will you grant forgiveness for such a wretched declaration?"

Everyone tried their best not to laugh at the small steward's melodramatic reaction.

"It's already forgotten!" said Gus reassuringly.

"Your goodwill knows huge dimensions and our gratitude will last until the end of the world!"

This stark reminder of their perilous situation made the Runaways' blood run cold.

"*Until the end of the world*... yes, we'd almost forgotten that small detail," scoffed Tugdual.

His grandparents, Brune and Naftali, looked at him reproachfully. Tugdual loved making light of the most serious events, but those close to him knew it was just his way of bearing the unbearable. With a false smile that fooled no one, Tugdual drew himself up and stalked out with one last glance at Oksa. The silence in the room, punctuated only by the snoring of the young Lunatrix and the noise of the rain, grew heavier. No one felt like talking—the Runaways were all dazed with tiredness. Dragomira's bracelets jingled as she got up, wrapping her crimson woollen cardigan tightly around her. Brune and Naftali also rose to their feet and headed for the comfortable bedrooms upstairs, followed by frail Reminiscens and the Bellangers. Those who were left in the huge living room sat lost in their own private thoughts.

☀

Unlike the other Runaways, who were fighting a losing battle with drowsiness, Oksa felt more awake after the interlude with the Lunatrixes. She walked over to Gus, her eyes on the toddler, unable to work out why her heart was racing.

"Gently does it," murmured Gus.

She hesitated. Did he mean the hand she was stretching out to stroke the little creature? Or the way she'd acted towards him?

"I'm not a brute!" she protested.

This remark made him laugh and Oksa couldn't help joining in. It seemed like the truce he'd declared by winking back at her was holding.

"Go on then…" he said, jutting his chin at the Lunatrix, who was sound asleep and snoring gently.

Oksa lightly stroked the downy skin with her fingertips. Her gaze wandered from the chubby little sleeper to Gus, whose expression was unreadable. Only his rapidly quivering eyelids betrayed his inner turmoil. Suddenly they both started to speak at exactly the same time, drowning each other out. They burst out laughing in surprise.

"What did you say?" they both asked in unison.

Gus looked up at the ceiling, not wanting to show how amused he was.

"Um… I can't remember…" admitted Oksa.

"It can't have been important, then. No change there!" retorted Gus, gently teasing her.

"Oohhh, you should be ashamed of yourself!" said Oksa, pretending to be cross with him.

"Me? What about you?"

Oksa's face clouded over and she glared at her friend.

"I knew it wouldn't be long before the snide remarks began," she muttered.

All the merriment had disappeared from Gus's eyes. Had he been trying to hurt her or had she just misinterpreted his words? Oksa grimaced and her eyes darkened.

"Let's drop it," murmured Gus. "Look over there. What on earth do you think it's trying to do?"

Seizing this lifeline, Oksa turned round. The creature which had just come into the room, a very wrinkled kind of walrus, was struggling in vain to throw a colossal log onto the fire. Another odd-looking creature with a mane of dishevelled hair next to it was frantically dancing from foot to foot.

"Hey, dimwit! You're certainly living up to your name! Can't you see that log will never fit in a million years?" yelled the shaggy creature, jumping up and down.

The walrus turned round with an uncertain look on its face.

"I'm not a dimwit, I'm an Incompetent…"

"I rest my case!" shouted the other creature.

"What are you then?"

"A GE-TO-RIX! And unlike you, Incompetent, I've actually got some brains up here!" it said, patting its head. "That's why I said you'll NEVER fit that log in the fireplace, it's mathematically impossible!"

The Incompetent looked so disappointed at this information that Gus and Oksa burst out laughing. Coming to its aid, Oksa said:

"Incompetent, why don't you try spitting at it?"

"Spitting at it? But that's very rude!" it objected naively.

"No, go ahead, I promise it'll work."

The Incompetent obeyed with a revolting hawking noise and the middle of the huge log dissolved immediately as if attacked by a powerful acid, giving off acrid fumes. Laughing and coughing, Oksa got up to help the blissfully happy creature put the two pieces of wood in the hearth.

"You're incredible, Incompetent!" she giggled.

"Thank you, but I feel a little under the weather: I have terrible acid reflux."

"Poor thing…" said Oksa sympathetically, patting its soft head.

"My Young Gracious," broke in Dragomira's Lunatrix, "the Old Gracious has made conveyancing of the wish to benefit from your company. Would you be in agreement to follow her domestic staff to see her?"

"Er… of course, I'm right behind you," replied Oksa, slightly worried. "See you later, Gus…"

Gus gave her a small wave and she followed the Lunatrix, who was clad in a pair of spotless blue dungarees, up the monumental staircase.

4

AN UNFORGETTABLE PAST

ALTHOUGH OKSA COULD BARELY SEE DRAGOMIRA IN the gloomy room, she'd have recognized her anywhere from the plaits coiled around her head and the gold earrings bearing two tiny birds which were very much alive.

"Come in, Dushka, come in," rang out Baba Pollock's voice.

Oksa came into the room, her steps muffled by the plush burgundy carpet. She sat down in the leather armchair facing her gran in front of the hearth, relishing the comforting heat from the blazing fire. Some tiny hens were clucking with pleasure by the fireplace and enthusiastically fluffing up their speckled wings. Not far from them, a striped Veloso was in mid-air pursuit of the miniature birds, which had just taken off from the golden perches hanging from Dragomira's ears to fly over to Oksa.

"Hello, Ptitchkins!"

"It's the Young Gracious!" chirped the birds, lifting up two strands of hair to form antennae. "She's so pretty! We love her so much!"

They landed on her shoulder and rubbed their feathered heads against her neck.

"Would my Old Gracious and the Young Gracious relish the desire to lap up a fresh cup of tea?" asked the Lunatrix.

Dragomira smiled. "That would be lovely, my Lunatrix. But we'll just drink it normally, if you don't mind."

The Lunatrix bowed and left the room. Oksa leant over to Dragomira.

"I just love his use of vocabulary!"

"Well, yes…" said Dragomira, with a chuckle. "Even if his word choices do sometimes leave a lot to be desired!"

The small steward came back clutching an enormous china teapot, patterned with flowers. A few moments later, the two Graciouses were ensconced in their armchairs, sipping steaming cups of tea. Dragomira studied Oksa quizzically.

"What's the matter, Baba?"

"Something odd happened earlier, didn't it?"

Oksa blushed. Her gran had to be talking about the unusual phenomenon that had taken place between her and Gus.

"You don't miss much, do you?"

Dragomira smiled and shook her head.

"I have no idea what it was," admitted Oksa. "It sounds crazy, but it was like a part of me had taken over and was doing what I wanted to do for me."

"That's exactly what happened, sweetheart. What you're talking about is your Identego. It's something that's part of your subconscious but, unlike other human beings, your Identego can manifest itself in an intangible, yet physical, form."

"So you actually saw it?" asked Oksa in a strangled voice.

"Abakum and I were both aware of its presence," replied Dragomira. "The Identego is an extremely rare Gracious power. To my knowledge, you're only the second Gracious in the history of Edefia to possess it."

"Were you the first?"

"Unfortunately not. Don't forget that I never finished training as a Gracious… The woman with whom you share this extraordinary gift was the first Gracious of Edefia."

Oksa's heart lurched with panic. She set down her cup of tea and pressed her hands together to stop them shaking.

"Does that mean I'm the *last* Gracious? That I won't be able to restore equilibrium to the two worlds and that everything is coming to an end?"

Dragomira looked at her in amazement. "Of course not, Dushka! If there is a parallel to be drawn, I think it's much more likely that you're the Gracious who'll *breathe new life* into Edefia. I'm sure of that!"

Oksa thought for a moment, before questioning her gran again:

"How does the Identego work?"

"You'll soon learn to control it," replied Dragomira, evasively. "And I wouldn't mind betting it'll come in very handy when we have to face whatever's waiting for us around the corner."

"You mean Orthon?"

"I'm still worried about what Reminiscens said," admitted Dragomira. "If Orthon's overriding desire is to take revenge on his father, Ocious, then he'll stop at nothing. The more I think about it, the more aware I am of the repercussions of what I saw nearly sixty years ago. So many things went over my head…"

"You were still so young, though, Baba!" insisted Oksa, troubled by her gran's serious tone. "You wouldn't have been able to understand what was happening or how Ocious's behaviour would shape the man Orthon would become."

"One thing I did realize was what a cold, twisted man Ocious was—the worst possible father anyone could have."

The old woman looked up at the bare wall opposite them, focusing her Camereye on it, and various images emerged from the deepest recesses of her memory.

Orthon's teenage face appeared first. The scene was unfolding on the balcony of a high tower—the Glass Column, thought Oksa. Lush climbing plants twined about the balustrades to provide a shady canopy. Young Dragomira appeared to be playing merrily with a slender jet of water arching from the round basin of a crystalline fountain. Twirling her index finger to coax it into weird and wonderful trajectories, she was aiming the water at Orthon and Leomido, who looked around thirteen. Peals of childish laughter erupted from her when a thin stream of spinning water splashed over Orthon. His eyes wide with surprise, he nudged Leomido, who was laughing beside him, and they winked at each other before launching themselves at Dragomira, growling like big cats. What followed was the wildest tickling session ever seen. The Camereye blurred as the dark room rang with the loud laughter that still haunted the Old Gracious's memories. Suddenly, the Camereye zoomed in on Orthon, whose face fell at the sound of his father's chilly voice. It swivelled round and Ocious appeared in Dragomira's field of vision. His sturdy yet elegant figure commanded fear and respect. His dark eyes narrowed when he saw his son squatting beside Dragomira, who'd rolled into a ball to escape the two boys' "revenge". Orthon jumped to his feet, looking pale. He muttered a few incomprehensible words, which only made his father glower more fiercely.

"Why are you trying to justify yourself?" asked Ocious in a steely voice. "Making excuses shows how spineless you really are. Why don't you take responsibility for your actions, even the harmless ones? After all, you weren't doing anything wrong, were you?"

In response to Orthon's tormented silence, he added:

"Is Leomido denying anything? No. He stands by what he does. You should take a leaf out of your... friend's book," he concluded, then turned on his heel.

Now the secret about the birth of Leomido, Orthon, Dragomira and Reminiscens had come to light—Malorane was the mother of them all—this remark was shocking, hateful and perverse. Ocious was a dreadful man. Oksa couldn't help feeling sorry for Orthon, abandoned by his biological mother and despised by his father. Leomido wasn't Ocious's son and yet the man admired and respected him. Oksa understood how angry Orthon must have felt throughout his adolescence, until the love affair between Leomido and Reminiscens had caused the truth about their origins to be admitted, ruining their lives. Secrets which can't remain under wraps for ever may turn into ticking time bombs which, sooner or later, will blow up in the face of anyone who comes too close...

A different image suddenly appeared on the wall. Oksa smothered a groan as she recognized her mother's face. The shot zoomed out to show a rustic house behind Pavel, who was surrounded by many of the Runaways, all of whom looked about fifteen years younger. Pavel and Marie, radiant in their wedding outfits, were bathed in sunshine and glowing with happiness. They waltzed around the open-air dance floor gazing into each other's eyes and Oksa's heart swelled with love as her mother's laugh rang out. She was so lovely... She missed her so much...

The Camereye leapt forward in time, showing Oksa's parents a few years later, as could be seen by the decor of the Pollocks' Parisian apartment. Sitting on a sofa, his hand resting on Marie's rounded stomach, Pavel was leaning back, looking thoughtful. In front of them, Dragomira appeared to be making tea.

"What about calling her Oksa," said Marie. "That's a pretty name, isn't it?"

A shadow darkened Pavel's face. "It might be a boy..."

"I'm sure it's a girl! She'll be gorgeous and intelligent and we'll love her to bits and live happily ever after."

She gave him a tender look, then nudged him with her shoulder.

"When will you stop worrying so much? It'll be fine, you'll see."

The Camereye suddenly winked out with a crack, like a small explosion of light, ushering in a heavy silence. Oksa thought about the contrast between Orthon and herself. The love—or lack of love—from the people who'd brought them into the world had shaped their lives. It had made them who they were and had become an inextricable part of their destiny. Such an imperceptible power was both frightening and fascinating. Her heart full of resolve, Oksa turned to Dragomira and repeated Marie's final words:

"It'll be fine, you'll see."

Dragomira nodded knowingly.

"I'm sure it will, Dushka..."

5

THE NEW RUNAWAYS

THE PLAN WAS TO SET OFF FOR THE ISLAND IN THE SEA of the Hebrides the next morning.

"Let's not put it off any longer," Pavel had said, with a glance at the black skies and torrential rain.

The house was buzzing with activity. The creatures and plants belonging to Abakum, Dragomira and Leomido had been enjoying a noisy reunion—some of them hadn't seen each other since Leomido had moved to Great Britain, several decades ago. With the exception of the three Incompetents, which were content to be idle bystanders, all creatures with wings or legs were rushing about in excitement. Despite their enforced immobility, the exuberant plants were making just as much noise as their feathered and furred companions. Even the sensible, authoritarian Centaury couldn't help joining in. Oksa was listening with some enjoyment to four Goranovs talking in doom-laden tones about the Felons' abduction of Dragomira's specimen.

"Will they know how to look after it properly?" asked one.

This was followed by a piteous discussion about the different techniques for extracting Goranov sap and their respective repercussions.

"The Felons are so cruel... If they don't milk our companion, it will die in terrible, and needless, agony, that's for sure!"

"Our species is facing extinction..."

Emotions were running high and all four plants had the same reaction: they fainted, appalled by the harrowing fate of their unfortunate former companion and their own uncertain future. In another part of the house, huddled in front of the huge fireplace, the tiny Squoracles, true to form, were complaining endlessly about the terrible weather. Not that anyone would disagree… fresh disasters were spreading panic throughout the world: an abnormally hot undersea current in the Pacific was disrupting incoming tides, causing flooding along the west coast of the United States. Things were no better above ground either, as various parts of the globe were being hit by colossal tornadoes. The whole planet was suffering and the worse things became, the more damage the elements inflicted.

"I never thought it would happen so fast," murmured Abakum, his eyes glued to images of global chaos on the television. "Oh, there you are, Oksa!" he said, noticing her.

"Do you think we'll succeed?" she asked anxiously.

The Fairyman turned and looked gravely into her eyes. "We must!" he said, a hint of anger in his voice. "I can't believe this could be—"

He broke off with a lump in his throat, unable to continue.

"…the end?" asked Oksa, finishing his sentence.

By way of an answer, he put his arm round the Young Gracious's shoulders and led her into the huge living room. The Tumble-Bawler and Veloso had spared no effort in finding Runaways to join the "Island of the Felons" expedition. They'd all now arrived at Leomido's Welsh home, forming a tight-knit community that resembled a small army. Some twenty people had teamed up with the core members of the group—Abakum, the Pollocks, the Knuts, the Bellangers, Reminiscens and her granddaughter, Zoe. Although they had all led very different lives since leaving Edefia, they shared the same origins and they all had one desire: to work together to help the Young Gracious return to Edefia. She was the only one who could gain entrance to their lost land, and the future of the world and its billions of inhabitants depended on her success. Oksa walked into the lofty room followed by Abakum and all conversations immediately stopped. The Runaways who didn't see her on a daily basis jumped up from their chairs and bowed in respect. She awkwardly muttered a few words of welcome and shot her father a despairing look. Pavel smiled encouragingly, aware of the burden of responsibility his beloved daughter had to shoulder. Oksa scanned the sea of unfamiliar faces gazing deferentially at her and her gaze alighted on Gus, who was standing in the darkest corner of the room with Zoe. At first glance, Gus looked miserable, but Oksa, who knew him better than that, wasn't fooled—his downturned mouth was a clear sign of annoyance. Mustering all her courage, she began walking over to him to declare her friendship in front of everyone but, after a few steps, she came up against an invisible barrier. She glanced at Zoe quizzically in surprise. Her second cousin had raised her hand in front of her to stop Oksa advancing and, like a guardian angel, was shaking her head. Oksa blushed to the roots of her hair. Zoe was right… this was neither the time nor the place. Annoyed at her own insensitivity, she turned round and took refuge beside her father.

"We're all together at last!" said Dragomira, her voice shaking. "Oksa, sweetheart, let me introduce you to the Runaways who've just joined us."

Oksa already knew Leomido's children, Cameron and Galina. She'd only met them three times before and the last occasion had been with their father a few months ago, when the Pollocks had moved to Bigtoe Square. So much had happened since then… In his mid-fifties, Cameron had his father's gaunt face and penetrating eyes. His lean frame displayed the supple elegance of Malorane's descendants and Oksa couldn't help seeing a resemblance to Orthon. Virginia, his wife, an unassuming, delicate-looking woman, was standing quietly by his side. Although Cameron hadn't found out about his origins until late in life, he'd always suspected he wasn't like other people. Truthfulness and wariness had always been his watchwords in life: truthfulness towards his family and wariness towards the rest of the world. As a result, he'd made no secret of the Runaways' lot to his wife and sons, three young men with mournful eyes and a very *English* air of refinement.

Galina was three years younger than her brother Cameron and, due to some genetic quirk, was the image of Dragomira—a resemblance only enhanced by her sparkling blue eyes and long plaits intricately woven into a heavy bun. She'd fallen madly in love with Andrew, a handsome and intelligent minister, when still very young and, fortunately for Galina, Andrew had been open-minded enough to accept her remarkable origins. They'd married and their two daughters were now in their early twenties. Oksa remembered them as a fun-loving, slightly eccentric family with a robust sense of humour—nothing like the people anxiously studying her now with drawn faces. The Young Gracious couldn't help thinking about all the lives that had been turned upside down by the threat of extinction and their headlong flight—all those abandoned houses and unsaid goodbyes… Would she prove worthy of the Runaways' trust?

"Thank you for joining us," said Dragomira, overwhelmed with emotion at being in the same room as her beloved Leomido's children and grandchildren.

"Despite the dire circumstances, it's an honour to help you, Young Gracious," said Cameron, his eyes bright.

"Our place is here," added Galina gravely. "We're Runaways, whether we like it or not!"

"Even if some of us are only Runaways by marriage, everyone counts, don't they?" added Andrew, glaring at his sullen daughters.

"Absolutely!" agreed Abakum gratefully. "We're indebted to all of you for coming."

❁

Bodkin—the former Firmhand industrialist who had retrained as a master goldsmith in South Africa—and Cockerell—Edefia's former Treasurer, and now a banker—greeted Oksa in their turn. Making the most of the prevailing chaos, these two smartly dressed old men had travelled thousands of miles to join the Runaways by means they'd never have dared to use normally. Sheer necessity had forced them to abandon all precaution: the Outsiders were so busy coping with disaster after disaster that they were unlikely to have batted an eyelid if they'd seen someone running improbably fast or shooting through the clouds. Even if they'd been seen, what would have happened? All over the world, people had one overriding concern: to find shelter from seawater floods, erupting volcanoes and cataclysmic earthquakes. These highly respected dignitaries were standing beside Feng Li, another Runaway born and bred, and Cockerell's wife and son, Akina and Takashi. Three more pairs of dark, almond-shaped eyes staring enigmatically at Oksa.

6

THE ICE QUEEN

EVEN BEFORE DRAGOMIRA INTRODUCED NAFTALI AND Brune's eldest son, Oksa had no difficulty recognizing Olof Knut, who was as tall, solemn and charismatic as his father. Standing behind his wife—the statuesque, golden-haired daughter of two Runaways—he looked ready to brave a thousand perils. It was the striking couple's daughter, though, who gave Oksa pause for thought. Tugdual's cousin was about fifteen years old and a typical Scandinavian beauty. Dressed from head to toe in beige—jeans and baggy cable-knit jumper—her translucent complexion offset by dark brown lipstick, she was as radiant as fresh snow. Oksa immediately named her the "Ice Queen", feeling inexplicably troubled. Kukka favoured her with a chilly yet inquisitive gaze. The Young Gracious shivered, rather daunted by her startling beauty, while Dragomira was reminding everyone about the close ties between the Pollocks and the Knuts. Kukka's gaze slid away from Oksa and alighted on Tugdual, who'd just walked over. Kukka's face immediately lit up with an icy smile.

"And here's my beloved cousin," she said, straightening up.

Her clear, clipped voice cut through the air like a broken shard of crystal. Quick as a flash, she grabbed a vase from the table she was leaning against and hurled it at Tugdual, who just had time to duck to one side to avoid being hit in the face. The china exploded against the wall, shattering into a thousand pieces. Oksa screamed, while Kukka's parents cried out in indignation.

"That's some welcome, little cousin!" said Tugdual, sidling closer, hands in pockets and a mocking expression in his eyes.

Fragments of china crunched under the soles of his heavy shoes.

"I'll have you know I'm taller than you!" Kukka retorted.

She took a couple of steps forward to stand in front of him so everyone could see she was really a couple of inches taller than him, which didn't faze Tugdual at all—on the contrary.

"I wasn't talking about height, little cousin, but maturity," he answered smugly.

"That's rich coming from you!" retorted the Ice Queen, tossing back her mane of blonde hair. "Ruining the lives of your entire family is a brilliant way of showing how mature you are! Thanks a million, cousin, on behalf of all the Knuts…"

This time it looked as though her barb had hit home. Tugdual went pale and took a step back, his fists clenched. His face was gaunt and his nostrils quivered, as if he were struggling for air. Oksa would have given anything to be able to soften the blow dealt by Kukka's remark. The other Runaways filed out of the room in embarrassment, leaving the Knuts alone. Oksa was the only one who couldn't contain her curiosity. Although she reluctantly went out, she sat down on the steps of the main staircase in the shadowy hall so that she could watch them unseen.

"In case you've forgotten," continued Kukka spitefully, "may I remind you that my aunt Helena—who also happens to be your mother, remember?—struggled with severe depression after her darling son decided he was a great black magician. Ring any bells? Or that, due to the selfishness of that pseudo-magician and his dubious experiments, eight people were forced to flee a country they loved, where they were doing just fine…"

"Kukka!" thundered Olof.

"He ought to know, Dad!" spat Kukka. "It's been much too easy for him to bury his head in the sand. We had a nice, peaceful life before his nibs began having sordid dreams of glory. He put us all in danger. Because of him, none of us was safe in Finland. Do you think that's fair?

I lost everything because of him—my country, my school, my friends, everything! And what did he lose? His friends? He didn't have any... who'd want to be friends with a monster like him?"

"Kukka, if Tugdual is a monster, then we all are!" boomed Naftali.

"I'm not!" growled Kukka. "I'm *normal!*"

There was a murmur of disapproval. Oksa had a funny feeling that she didn't understand what was going on. How could Tugdual's cousin be more *normal* than anyone else? Kukka turned and glared at Tugdual.

"You don't understand anything..." muttered Tugdual tonelessly.

"I wish you'd never been part of my family!" yelled Kukka. "You ruined my life."

"That's enough!" shouted her father, losing his temper.

But a simple rebuke wasn't going to stop Kukka, who was beside herself with anger. She walked over to Tugdual, who was rooted to the spot, and angrily jabbed her finger into his solar plexus.

"Do you know where your father is now?" she asked nastily.

Tugdual staggered.

"What?" continued Kukka triumphantly, a cruel smile on her lips. "You don't know that he's on an oil rig in the middle of the North Sea. He ran away, my darling cousin. He ran away from all those secrets and all that madness. He ran AS FAR AWAY AS HE COULD FROM YOU!"

Tugdual's face seemed to crumple. They both stood there for several seconds, without moving. Kukka, bright as a snowflake, and Tugdual, with a face like thunder. Suddenly, Tugdual seized his cousin's long golden hair and yanked her head backwards, bringing his face a couple of inches from hers.

"Never mention my father again!" he hissed, carefully enunciating each syllable.

"MONSTER!" shouted Kukka defiantly.

From where she sat, Oksa could hear Tugdual's threatening strangled growl. Realizing the danger, Naftali rushed over to stop his grandson from silencing his treacherous cousin, but he was a fraction of a second too late… A flash of light blazed from Tugdual's furious eyes and Kukka collapsed senseless in Naftali's arms, as Olof and his wife rushed to her aid. Meanwhile Tugdual, paler than ever, leant against the wall and slid down to a sitting position on the floor. From the stairs, Oksa could see the pain etched on his face. Kukka had definitely scored a bullseye…

"Your boyfriend certainly has a knack of causing trouble!" Gus said loudly behind her.

Oksa jumped. Gus was bitterly eyeing her from a few steps higher. She was about to reply when a woman crossed the hall and went into the living room, carrying a little boy in her arms. Everyone fell silent, watching her as she scanned the room until she spotted Tugdual, struggling to control his anger. The toddler held his arms out towards Tugdual and cried: "Tug!"

Tugdual looked up in amazement and gasped. The woman set down the toddler and, moved to tears, went over to help Tugdual to his feet and put her arms around him.

"Hello, Helena," said Naftali, coming over.

Oksa gave a start. Helena! Tugdual's mother! Like Olof and his parents, she radiated a strange mixture of delicacy and strength. She was very tall with slender arms and legs and her pale face was framed by chestnut hair threaded with silver. Her eyes were filled with deep sorrow and she inspired both respect and admiration. She stopped hugging Tugdual and greeted her parents, Naftali and Brune. Nearby, Tugdual appeared to have regained his usual haughty expression. Only the dark fire blazing in his eyes—and no doubt his heart—belied his apparent indifference.

"Here you are at last," Naftali said emotionally to his daughter. "And you, little Till, you've grown so much!" he added, bending down towards the little boy who was clinging like a limpet to Tugdual's leg.

"I'm five now!" he declared.

Oksa looked at Tugdual in astonishment, realizing he'd never mentioned his family. Then again, she'd never asked him much about anything, which she felt bad about. In just five minutes she'd learnt so many things…

40

She smiled as she watched angelic little Till telling his brother about the Knuts' eventful journey to Wales. Tugdual replied with a tenderness that amazed Oksa and made him even more irresistible.

⁂

Things had calmed down among the Knuts. Curled in an armchair, Kukka seemed to have recovered from her clash with her cousin and was running her fingers through her long hair, looking daggers at Tugdual, who was ignoring her.

"All's well that ends well," Gus murmured behind Oksa, pretending to clap. "Prince Charming's honour has been restored. Hip, hip, hooray!"

Thrusting her hands into her pockets, Oksa raced up the steps, four at a time, then along the corridor to her room. Once inside, she slammed the door behind her.

7

A Pure, Black Heart

THE GALES HOWLING ROUND LEOMIDO'S HOUSE FOR hours had finally died down and a grey, miserable dawn was glimmering on the horizon. Oksa opened her eyes and lay quietly in bed, gathering her thoughts. She was still wearing yesterday's clothes—tatty jeans and fisherman's jumper—but someone had removed her ankle boots and covered her with a quilt. Probably her dad. She listened: the house was silent as a morgue, as if every living thing had died during that difficult night. The sudden noise of a burning log cracking in the fireplace made her jump. It was then that she noticed Dragomira's Lunatrix. The small creature was standing there with big round eyes fixed on her, like an inscrutable guard. Oksa sat up and smiled at him.

"Good morning, Lunatrix! Have you been here all night?"

"Please accept receipt of salutations from your domestic staff, Young Gracious. The answer to your question is affirmative: the Old Gracious made the entreaty that I maintain surveillance over the slumber of the Young Gracious and the eye of her servant has not met with the slightest wavering. The three Lunatrixes of the Master-Impictured-Forever have ensured the diligence of the same protection for other guests of the household."

"You mean you haven't slept all night? Poor Lunatrixes!"

"Remove all pity from your heart, Young Gracious: Lunatrixes practise obedience without suffering," replied the diminutive creature.

"You're so faithful…" remarked Oksa admiringly.

"Fidelity is contained within the spirit of the Lunatrixes, the guarantee of our faithfulness is complete."

"I know that, Lunatrix," murmured Oksa. "We're so lucky to have you here."

The Lunatrix gave a loud sniffle and went over to throw some wood on the fire. He then turned round and looked Oksa straight in the eye. "Jealousy must not lacerate your heart, Young Gracious," he remarked to Oksa's great surprise.

Gaping, she looked down.

"What makes you say that?" she asked in a whisper.

"The grandson of the friends of the Gracious named Knut lays siege to your thoughts and the frigid presence of his cousin Kukka claws at the interior of your heart."

"How can you possibly know that?" exclaimed Oksa in a strangled voice, horrified that her feelings might appear so obvious.

"Your domestic staff has performed an observation of your glances and an interpretation of your sentiments. The grandson of the friends of the Gracious invades the Young Gracious with amorous uncertainty; marmoreal Kukka fosters a relationship full of turbulence with the person who plagues the Young Gracious. Extreme electricity unites the two cousins, but their bonds are characterized by a great absence of love, so you must subtract all fear from your cranium."

Oksa shivered. The Lunatrix had just hit the nail on the head… Yes, Tugdual monopolized her every waking thought… Yes, she was jealous of his fiery relationship with Kukka… She didn't understand why, but there was no denying it.

"Is it that obvious?" she asked in a small voice, blushing.

"The Young Gracious must not be forgetting that everything residing within the heart of the Gracious is known by the Lunatrixes."

"That's very embarrassing," remarked Oksa, then added, trembling, "May I ask a question?"

The Lunatrix nodded.

"Does... Tugdual love me?"

The small creature's long, delicate lashes fluttered as he blinked.

"The grandson of the friends of the Gracious only conveys a partial surface of his character: he does not appear to demonstrate any emotion although he experiences deep disturbances and violent suffering. You should acquire the knowledge that power is arrayed with the same attraction as fire in his eyes."

"What do you mean?"

"The grandson of the friends of the Gracious encounters ambiguity: power performs the exertion of a deep fascination although he possesses no desire to put it into practice. The Young Gracious assumes the embodiment of this power coveted by many and the consequence is that a fascination for it may cause a detour towards the Young Gracious."

"Meaning that Tugdual is only interested in me because of the power I represent..." concluded Oksa, a sudden lump in her throat.

The Lunatrix's wide forehead creased in a frown.

"Nature is sometimes lumbered with complexity, Young Gracious, but you must expel all fear from your heart. The grandson of the friends of the Gracious does not operate by the same logic as other human beings. Appearances cause deception and bring about confusion because the reality is unexpected: the loyalty and love of the grandson of the friends of the Gracious admit constancy and completeness. His heart is black and muddled, but it holds purity. However, the Young Gracious must not proceed to negligence of other friends and family. Or of the annihilation of the two worlds..."

"Things are serious, aren't they?"

The Lunatrix nodded.

"Will we survive?"

"Your domestic staff can only make the gift of one assurance: your return to Edefia experiences proximity and success rests its hope on the union of the Runaways. The complete and indivisible union of all Runaways."

Oksa nervously cleared her throat, and her gaze strayed to the steely sky, split by bolts of black lightning, similar to the dark flashes that had frightened her so much inside the painting. She walked over to the window, struggling to breathe easily. From her room, she could see the small cemetery surrounded by ancient wrought-iron railings. Tugdual was there, his back against a gravestone—the same one they'd leant against when they'd talked properly for the first time, a few months ago. Tugdual didn't notice her. Could he sense her watching him? She couldn't be sure. He seemed lost in thought, his face clouded with pain and sadness. It was as if he'd let the mask drop; as if despair was all he had left. Sitting against the carved gravestone, he seemed incapable of hiding anything and Oksa was moved by his candid expression. She suddenly recalled one of Tugdual's favourite songs—'Unloveable' by The Smiths.

I wear black on the outside
'Cause black is how I feel on the inside…
And if I seem a little strange
Well, that's because I am…
But I know that you would like me
If only you could see me
If only you could meet me
I don't have much in my life
But take it—it's yours.

A few weeks ago, she'd heard Tugdual humming this song almost gaily, as offhandedly as usual. But the words were so serious, so meaningful. So clear… Oksa carefully opened the window and swung her legs over the sill. The Lunatrix watched, looking disconcerted, his long mouth stretching from side to side of his wide face.

"My Young Gracious," he sighed, "do not be forgetting my words."

"I won't. I promise!" murmured Oksa, then floated outside, several yards above the ground.

❋

Tugdual looked up in surprise: Oksa had just landed at his feet and was gazing at him with a determined expression.

"Hiya, Lil' Gracious!" he said in greeting.

"Hi," replied Oksa, sitting down by his side.

"Did you sleep well?"

"Like a log. What about you?"

"I spent part of the night here."

"Insomnia?"

"I've never been much of a sleeper, I can get by on a few hours a week. At the moment, it's even worse."

"Aren't you tired?" exclaimed Oksa, glancing at him.

"No. Anyway, I was much too uptight to sleep. I watched the sky, got my head straight and calmed myself down."

Oksa hesitated, then dared to question him.

"Do you want to talk about it?" she asked, seeing again the anguished expression on Tugdual's face earlier, as he gazed at an unconscious Kukka.

"No point."

Oksa couldn't help objecting:

"Of course there is!"

How could she admit she was dying to find out more? But Tugdual was becoming less and less talkative with every passing second, which was not what she'd intended at all. He was so complicated... She decided not to push it. Although she wasn't sure whether this was because she was afraid of making him feel worse or because she didn't want to ruin the moment. "Your mother's very beautiful... And your little brother is adorable," she said finally.

46

Tugdual didn't react at all. His hands were shaking slightly, but that could just as easily have been from the cold as from emotion. Unexpectedly, he moved closer to Oksa so that their shoulders were touching. He pulled on a thread hanging from Oksa's worn jeans and wound it casually around his index finger.

"We have to join forces and work together if we don't want to die," he said softly. "All of us."

He was being evasive again, but she didn't care. As always, whenever she was alone with Tugdual Oksa experienced a rush of exhilaration and, despite his serious words, this morning was no exception. Nothing was ever simple with Tugdual, there was always conflict, ambiguity and mystery. The complete opposite of Gus. With a long sigh of exasperation, she gently laid her head against Tugdual's.

The old cemetery was now bathed in a purplish, almost black light, as if the sky were bruised after the storms of the day before. Tugdual slipped his arm around Oksa's shoulders and they leant silently against the gravestone and gazed at the threatening sky. In the distance, Abakum appeared on the moor, followed by Leomido's two ungainly Gargantuhens—gigantic hens whose wingspan was close on ten feet.

"It's time for the call to arms," said Tugdual quietly. "We probably won't come back here."

Oksa felt a sudden surge of sadness. Everything she'd left behind was still so vivid—her school, her friends, the long evenings with Dragomira and the precious moments with her parents had not yet had time to become a distant memory. It was so hard to leave behind her life "before". She looked up and, blinking back tears, clearly recognized Kukka at one of the first-floor windows, staring so malevolently at the small cemetery that Oksa could have sworn she could feel the chill coming from her eyes. She gave a start. Intuitively, Tugdual looked up towards the arched window where his vindictive cousin's face had been just a minute ago. He immediately removed his arm from Oksa's shoulders, which confused and upset her. What did that mean? Was Tugdual ashamed? She remembered the Lunatrix's words. Why was everything so difficult? Tugdual leapt to his feet and held out his hand to help her up.

"Come on!" he remarked. "Let's go flying!"

She was tempted to refuse and leave him on his own, but he took her hands and put them on his shoulders, covering them with his, and they rose into the sky. Shielding his eyes with his hand, the Fairyman watched them take off with an affectionate smile. He was far from the only one looking: at the other end of the building, Gus rested his forehead against the cold glass, his eyes fixed on the pair as they flew over the moor. A few yards away, sitting cross-legged on a bed, Zoe gazed at Gus's hunched back and felt helpless, as she always did when witnessing her friend's obvious pain. Two rooms farther along the corridor, Kukka stalked away from the window in a rage and, last but not least, Dragomira and Pavel looked up from the vegetable patch where the creatures were doing their morning exercises and watched the Young Gracious and her melancholy friend soar through bands of purple mist. Dragomira only just managed to hold Pavel back from taking off in pursuit of his daughter, since he'd never seen her Vertifly so high.

"Have a little faith in her," she said quietly.

Oksa was oblivious to the other Runaways' reactions on the ground. Her heart filled with melancholy happiness, she surrendered to instinct, deaf and blind to the anguish of those who loved her.

8

TEARFUL GOODBYES

No one knew whether Dragomira had used her legendary powers of persuasion or a more "Granokian" method but, whatever the case, it hadn't taken the elderly fisherman long to comply with Baba Pollock's wishes and the largest trawler from the nearby port was now miraculously anchored in the creek on the edge of Leomido's estate. After much thought, given the mass exodus into Wales from the flooded areas of eastern England, the Runaways had decided to travel to the Island of the Felons by boat. It was the quickest, most discreet way to transport the thirty-one members of their group. Even though they did their best to avoid attention, the Runaways rarely went unnoticed and, despite the prevailing chaos, it was second nature for them to be cautious. Old habits die hard, after all. Even though none of them might be on the Outside in a few days…

⁂

Gathering for the last time in the huge living room with the shutters already closed, the Runaways listened gravely to Abakum's wise advice.

"Our priority on this journey is to stick to our plan and remain on our guard," he began. "The Felons have already proved they can attack first. This time, the roles are reversed: we're attacking them, but we're heading into unfamiliar territory…"

"You're forgetting your faithful informant!" rang out the voice of Dragomira's Tumble-Bawler.

"How could we?" disagreed Baba Pollock, stroking its head. "You've given us some first-rate information and we're bound to call on you again."

"At your service!" said the tiny creature, standing to attention.

"We must remember our strategy at all times," continued Abakum, "and everyone should act according to their individual abilities while keeping out of danger as much as possible. I think we should leave now. All being well, we ought to reach the Island of the Felons in about twenty-four hours, which means we'll arrive at nightfall, which would be perfect."

There was a heavy silence. This departure felt like another exile and spelt the end of the Runaways' life on the Outside. They'd all accepted that this expedition would bring them to the gateway to Edefia. That's why they were all here. But, despite this firm conviction, the Runaways' mixed feelings of excitement and sadness made it hard for them to catch their breath and brought tears to their eyes. A melody suddenly rose from the back of the room: Tugdual was sitting at the piano, the pallor of his thin face emphasized by his black clothes, playing a poignant piece which perfectly encapsulated the Runaways' melancholy. Oksa looked up in surprise. "Another thing I didn't know about him," she thought, captivated by this beautiful acoustic rendering of a familiar rock standard. Leomido's Lunatrixes were also staring at him, their huge blue eyes full of adoration.

"The initiative shown by the grandson of our friends the Knuts exerts enchantment on the ears of the domestic staff of the Gracious," murmured the Lunatrixa. "No one has practised the use of that melodious instrument since the disappearance of the Master-Impictured-Forever and the rushing emotion is a feast for the listeners, the certainty is complete."

Tugdual glanced at her unblinkingly, then shut the piano lid with a bang that contrasted sharply with his sensitive playing. He opened his mouth to say something, then changed his mind, flustered by the Lunatrixes' wildly grateful eyes and the solemn atmosphere.

Pavel suddenly broke the deceptive quiet by throwing water on the logs burning in the fireplace. Dragomira looked at him, surprised at the symbolic finality of his gesture.

"I'm probably being silly, but I'd hate this magnificent house to burn down because we hadn't put the fire out properly," growled Pavel. "For Leomido's sake."

Then he turned and strode out of the room into the hall strewn with suitcases. The Runaways trudged after him in silence and picked up their bags. Pierre and Naftali loaded themselves up with boxes of Granoks and Capacitors, as well as the two Boximinuses, and the small group miserably filed out of the house. Dragomira was the last to leave. She stood there for a moment, looking at the splendid staircase in the glow of the setting sun, then shut and locked the heavy front door. She ran her hand over the wood with a sigh.

"Goodbye…" she murmured.

Pavel put his hand on her shoulder and silently pulled her to him. Dragomira gratefully leant on the arm he offered and, supporting each other, they joined the rest of the Runaways resolutely walking towards the creek, battling the almost irresistible urge to turn back.

9

Highly Strung Passengers

THEIR BOAT—THE *SEA DOG*—ROCKED GENTLY ON THE sea, which was luckily very calm on this autumn evening. The Runaways had allocated the ten cramped cabins and some of them had already gone to sleep, exhausted by the extreme emotions of the last few hours. Oksa, however, had lost no time in joining her father in the wheelhouse.

"Where on earth did you learn to sail a 100-foot boat?" she asked in amazement, watching her father skilfully operating the ship's controls like a seasoned mariner.

"I didn't," he replied with a chuckle.

"What do you mean you didn't?"

"I've never learnt to sail," said Pavel. "But I've watched people do it."

"Well, that's comforting…" said Oksa, pulling a sceptical face.

"Some of us only need to be shown how to do something once before we can do it ourselves."

Oksa frowned at him.

"You mean like Poluslingua? You see how something is done and you can do it?"

Pavel glanced up from the control panel and smiled at his daughter. Her fears allayed for the time being, Oksa gazed out of the window with interest. Night had almost fallen and the west was already so dark that it looked like a solid barrier. The powerful lamp on the ship's prow lit up the gloomy waves a couple of hundred feet ahead, which made Oksa feel as though they were plunging into an inkwell. To the east, she could just make out the tiny clusters of lights of coastal villages perched on the cliffs. From time to time, the beam of a lighthouse swept over the waves, creating luminous strips of radiance. Suddenly the moon emerged from the thick clouds, illuminating more of the sea, and several reefs loomed out of the depths, as if attempting to bar their way. Oksa's stomach lurched, but Pavel had already anticipated these obstacles and was steering the trawler far out to sea, away from the jagged rocks of the coastline.

"Not bad, eh?" he remarked, keeping his eyes on the sea.

"Fantastic!" nodded Oksa. "Anyone would think you'd been doing this all your life!"

"Well done, Pavel! Mental focus and manual dexterity!" boomed Abakum's voice behind them. "Would you like me to take over for a bit?"

"Later on, if you don't mind, when we get to the Sea of the Hebrides. I'd like an aerial view of our *hosts'* island…"

"Good idea," agreed Abakum.

Oksa silently looked at her father, his tense broad back beneath his heavy khaki woollen jumper, his ash-blond hair and gnarled hands. In her mind's eye, she saw Pavel and his Ink Dragon flying through a stormy sky above the Felons' inhospitable rocky island. He now seemed completely in control of the creature which, only a few months ago, had been eating him up inside—after barely tolerating each other, the two seemed to have merged peacefully. The process had cost him dearly and had forced him to make some painful sacrifices, but he had come through it and here he was, at the helm of the ship, leading his family and friends towards their shared destiny.

Oksa's thoughts were interrupted by the furore shaking two of the crates piled in the wheelhouse. Dragomira's and Oksa's Tumble-Bawlers were fluttering like two large bumblebees above the jiggling boxes—the Boximinuses—from which emanated some muffled yet scandalized voices.

"Warning! Warning!" shouted the Tumble-Bawlers. "Danger of mutiny on board!"

"What, already?" laughed Oksa. "We've only just set sail!"

Abakum walked over and slipped a green scarab into the keyhole of each box. The beetles worked their strange magic and the boxes opened, revealing scores of differently sized compartments, each occupied by a miniaturized creature or plant. A loud outcry could be heard: the three Squoracles appeared to be fighting with Abakum's Centaury.

"You're creating far too much humidity!" complained Dragomira's Squoracle, reduced to a pea-sized ball of feathers.

The other Squoracles had joined their companion in the adjacent compartment and were angrily hopping up and down at the foot of the handsome plant, whose breath was coming in short, fast bursts, making its leaves rise and fall.

"I tend to sweat buckets when I'm upset..." declared the Centaury.

"Well, I'll have you know it's killing me!" said another Squoracle. "I already had to put up with the traumatic journey from my master Abakum's house and I refuse to travel another inch on board this box!"

"Do I sweat buckets?" asked Dragomira's Incompetent suddenly.

"And I refuse to travel with plants which have such pungent breath!" protested yet another Squoracle.

"Hey, hens, plants don't have breath!" broke in Leomido's Getorix. "They have fragrance."

"That's all well and good, but when you're travelling in a group, you should try your best not to upset the other passengers. You should keep yourself to yourself."

"Has anyone got any peanuts?" asked the Incompetent unexpectedly. "I like peanuts, they help me relax."

"Since when do you ever get tense?" sniggered the Getorix.

"I think I'm going to faint," remarked Leomido's Goranov, trembling from its roots to its leaves. "These overcrowded conditions... this awful din... It's so stressful."

Its leaves suddenly collapsed along its stem as Oksa watched the miniaturized scene over Abakum's shoulder. Three smaller plants near the Goranov began shaking and crying out "Mummy!" before they collapsed too. Oksa couldn't help laughing.

"Even when they're a fraction of their usual size, they're bonkers!"

"Do you have any peanuts?" asked the Incompetent, noticing her for the first time.

Oksa laughed even louder.

"For your information, we're approaching a ninety per cent rate of humidity and the temperature is almost down to five degrees outside," remarked the first Squoracle, shivering. "You're going the right way about killing us, if that's your intention!"

"You're so *égoïste!*" retorted the Polyglossiper, a little sponge no bigger than a cherry. "Do you think you're the only ones suffering? *Regardez-moi!* The rolling of the boat is making me seasick, I'm green as a lettuce leaf!"

"What do you have against the colour green?" snapped a Pulsatilla with a lush covering of leaves.

"The Polyglossiper is about to throw up!" bawled the Getorix, jumping about. "Danger! Danger!"

"I love lettuce," the Incompetent informed them. "It's very good for the digestion."

"Everyone take shelter!" added the Getorix.

When they heard this warning, the Goranovs, which had regained consciousness, began screaming:

"Help! Someone help us!"

"Uh-oh, it's time I stepped in," said Abakum, wiping his eyes.

Oksa and Pavel were also crying with laughter.

"They're completely mental," giggled Oksa.

From his holdall Abakum took a small can, which he shook well before spraying each compartment. A few seconds later there was peace and quiet in the Boximinus.

"Wow! That's amazing!" exclaimed Oksa. "What is it?"

"Fairy Gold Elixir plus a few drops of sap from the Brugmansia plant, which secretes atropine and scopolamine. When we moved last time, too many of our creatures and plants were ill, which was disastrous and very upsetting for all concerned. So Dragomira and I perfected this concoction, which combats motion sickness by distracting our companions from the cause of their suffering. We should be left in peace for a while now, I think."

"It looks like it does more than just distract them, though!" remarked Oksa, noticing the drowsy contentment of the tiny inhabitants of the Boximinuses. "It could be used as a weapon, couldn't it?"

Abakum stroked his beard thoughtfully.

"Do you remember sleepy nightshade?"

"Yes! You had some in your silo when you gave me my Granokology lesson."

"You've got a good memory…"

Abakum went over to one of the stacked boxes and slipped the beetle key into the lock. One of the sides rolled up like a shutter to reveal scores of tiny drawers. Each bore a virtually illegible handwritten label. Abakum opened one and took out a few scarlet Granoks as small as sesame seeds.

"Give me your Granok-Shooter, Oksa."

"Are you sure, Abakum?" broke in Pavel, with a worried look. The Fairyman nodded as Oksa held out her Granok-Shooter.

"You now have a new Granok," said Abakum.

"What's it called? What does it do?" Oksa immediately asked.

"It's a Hypnagogo, a Waking-Dream Granok. Nightshade is used instead of Fairy Gold, which produces a stronger version of the fluid I just sprayed over our little friends… The Hypnagogo is supposed to cause hallucinations and disorientate the mind in order to neutralize it by putting it into a sort of waking dream for several hours."

"Brilliant! Isn't that a bit like the Dozident then?"

"Not exactly. The Dozident sends people to sleep. If you're hit by one of those, you'll immediately lose consciousness. The Hypnagogo is more subtle. It goes further than the Dozident by changing your enemy's perception of reality and thereby thwarting their plans."

"I understand," murmured Oksa. "That's clever! But why did you say it's 'supposed' to cause hallucinations?"

"Because I didn't have time to do all the tests I'd have liked. Which is why your father is looking so worried…"

"What are the dangers?"

"Atropine causes hallucinations designed to make the mind wander from reality, then scopolamine and nightshade work to neutralize the mind in question and keep it anchored in unreality for a while. It's a bit like freezing an image or imposing slow motion. The problem is that I haven't quite nailed the transition between the two stages, so someone experiencing hallucinations could prove to be uncontrollable… I tested the Hypnagogo on a few Outsiders as well as Bodkin and Naftali, who're Firmhands, as you know. The Outsiders reacted just as they should, immediately being plunged into a daydream and not even realizing they were no longer seeing the real world. But trying this out on strange metabolisms like ours is a little more complicated. Bodkin and Naftali, who'd bravely agreed to act as guinea pigs, didn't react at all for a few seconds, then slipped into a kind of trance during which they believed they were experiencing a dream. However, Naftali's Werewall constitution slightly altered the effects of the Hypnagogo."

"Meaning?"

"Meaning that the images he saw didn't calm him down at all. And that made his reactions unpredictable."

"But he was harmless, wasn't he?"

"As harmless as a sleeping tiger… until it wakes up. That's the difference."

"I see," nodded Oksa. "So it works like a charm on Outsiders. What about someone who has Firmhand, Werewall and Gracious blood—would it work on them?"

Abakum looked at her dubiously.

"Wait and see, is that it?" asked Oksa.

Staring at the horizon shrouded in hazardous darkness, the old man replied:

"Yes, in every respect…"

10

Late-Night Chats

Feeling exhausted, Oksa made her way down the narrow gangway to the cabin she was sharing with Dragomira, Reminiscens and Zoe, holding on to the metal walls to steady herself against the pitching motion of the ship. Gus suddenly appeared at the other end of the gangway and leant against the wall, looking deathly pale. Concerned, the Young Gracious went over to him.

"Are you all right?" she asked anxiously.

Gus turned to look at her, although his eyes were so glazed that Oksa thought he probably couldn't see anything very clearly. His handsome face was drawn, almost distorted, as if some powerful force was exerting pressure on it from the inside. Shocked, Oksa said:

"You look like death warmed up!"

"As tactful as ever," muttered Gus, pulling a face. "I do feel awful actually. My legs are like jelly and everything's spinning…"

Oksa gnawed at a nail.

"Can I do anything to help?"

"I don't think so, unless you can stop this lousy ship!" he said, shaking his head.

"Are you seasick? Abakum has the ideal remedy for that. Would you like me to go and ask him?"

"Why would you bother?" retorted Gus sullenly. Oksa looked at him sadly, and a little exasperated.

"For three reasons: because you're my friend, because you're not well and because I know a way to make you feel better. It's hardly rocket science."

"I suppose... so what you're really saying is that you'd do the same for anyone."

Although Oksa had an almost overwhelming urge to grab Gus's shoulders and shake some sense into him, she managed to control herself, despite her irritation. She'd thought that their friendship had been getting back onto a more even keel, but she'd obviously been wrong.

"Think what you like," she sighed, in resignation. "But you're not just anyone to me. Wait there. I'll be back a minute, OK?"

"I need to lie down," groaned Gus. "I really don't feel very well."

Oksa had to admit he looked terrible. He was panting, his eyes were half closed and the sheen of sweat over his face made his skin seem waxy. He pulled the polo neck of his thick woollen jumper higher and jerkily folded his arms.

"I'll help you back to your cabin," said Oksa, taking his arm.

Gus shrugged her off, his face set.

"Don't bother! I'm sure you've got better things to do," he said, sliding back down the wall to a sitting position.

"You're doing my head in!" snapped Oksa, irritably. "Will you please be quiet and stop being so difficult!"

She pulled him up and supported his weight, surprised at how stiff his movements were. His whole body seemed wracked by terrible spasms. He groaned again, but was too weak to refuse to lean on her. When they got to the Bellangers' cabin, Gus muttered:

"Oksa..."

She looked up, a glimmer of hope in her eyes.

"What is it, Gus?" she said gently.

Gus frowned, trying to find the right words but, in the end, just replied:

"Forget it... nothing."

"You're so annoying sometimes," she muttered crossly, pulling open the cabin door and helping Gus to lie down on his bunk. He immediately curled into a ball, pulling his knees up to his chest. He stifled another agonizing moan. Oksa hated seeing him in so much pain.

"Don't move. I'll be back!"

A few minutes later she'd returned and was spraying his face with Fairy Gold Brugmansia. With one last affectionate, and anxious, look at Gus, who'd slipped into a comforting daydream thanks to the concoction's hallucinogenic powers, Oksa left the Bellangers' cabin for hers.

※

Oksa tossed and turned on her narrow bunk, kept awake by the noise of the engines and the creaking of the ship, as well as by her troubled thoughts. Their present situation didn't look any more promising than their future. Oksa was assailed by constant feelings of panic which, try as she might, she couldn't shake off. For a start, she was worried sick about her mother. Oksa had understood only too well how crucial Marie would be to the conflict with the Felons. She also suspected that Orthon would do his utmost to demoralize the people he hated: Dragomira, Pavel, Abakum and herself. He'd taunt and intimidate them, using psychological warfare to devastating effect. The thought that they might fail to defeat the treacherous Felon filled her with anxiety. She didn't think she was mentally tough enough. She was scared that she might jeopardize everything the Runaways had worked for. Her thoughts turned to her father. Would he be able to curb his impulsiveness? It was hard to know, because Pavel could be so unpredictable. Especially if the woman he loved was in danger...

As the ship neared its destination, Oksa's relief at the idea of being reunited with her mother was gradually being eroded by mounting fear, which made her feel as though she was falling apart. She desperately hoped everything would go smoothly... and, more than anything else, she hoped Marie wouldn't give up. The longer this went on, the less time the Young Gracious's mother had. Although there was a simple way to save her, it was fraught with difficulties: Marie needed Lasonillia—the Imperial Flower—a rare, invaluable plant which grew only in the territory of the Distant Reaches in Edefia and was Marie's only hope for a cure. Oksa tried to think about something else, but everything was troubling her. Gus was hardly the least of her worries—he was the personification of trouble! At least their last conversation had reopened the lines of communication, even if it had been a little tense. "That's something, I suppose," sighed Oksa bitterly. Tugdual came a close third after Marie and Gus. He made her heart race whenever he was near her… He could twist her round his little finger so easily—she adored it when he held her tightly. It made her head spin and the world drop away. Nothing could top that feeling, but she was worried she might lose herself for ever in his arms. And then there was Edefia, a land so far away and yet so close. A land crucial to the Runaways and the survival of the two worlds—another thing that made her feel as though everything was spiralling out of control…

The ship was suddenly buffeted by a violent gust of wind, which interrupted Oksa's train of thought. She held her breath, her heart pounding. She listened for a moment, gingerly standing up, her senses alert. The engine was still throbbing noisily and the ship had resumed its intermittent rolling. Oksa glanced out of the porthole: the sun was rising, revealing a louring sky heavy with swollen, ominous clouds. The sea was grey and choppy, whipped into crashing waves by the gusts of wind which were unceremoniously shaking the ship. Oksa sat down cross-legged on her bunk and pressed her face against the porthole. In the distance, she could see a pillar of water so dense it looked solid falling from a coal-black cloud and she was relieved she wasn't under it. The black-and-grey-streaked sky was filled with sinister purple clouds that created an almost supernatural atmosphere.

"Impressive, isn't it?"

Zoe had also woken up and was gazing at Oksa with large hazel eyes.

"Hmm… to be honest, I'm a little freaked out by it. Listen to that wind."

Zoe smiled gently as usual, smoothing her shoulder-length hair into a ponytail.

"After everything you've had to deal with, don't tell me you're frightened by a few puffs of wind? That's like a lioness being frightened of a mouse!" she teased.

"Some lioness…" said Oksa. "I feel more like the mouse right now!"

"Don't forget a tiny mouse can spook a mighty elephant!" broke in Dragomira from her bunk.

"Oh, Baba!"

Oksa jumped down from the top bunk to kneel by her gran's bed and kiss her affectionately.

"My dear child," sighed Dragomira, hugging her. "My little mouse…"

"Look!" exclaimed Zoe. "We're getting close to an island!"

Oksa's heart lurched, and Dragomira turned pale.

Reminiscens got up in her turn and squeezed her half-sister's shoulder comfortingly.

"We can't possibly be there already, can we?" muttered Oksa, terrified.

"I don't think so," said Reminiscens. "Let's go and ask our accomplished navigators; they'll know where we are."

11

A Fraught Breakfast

ABAKUM WAS IN CHARGE IN THE WHEELHOUSE. NEXT to him, his Incompetent was idly watching Dragomira's Getorix doing its morning exercises. Nearby, Pavel was asleep in a hammock with a Squoracle nestled in the crook of his shoulder. As soon as Oksa walked into the room he opened his eyes, ringed by dark purplish shadows, and his face lit up with an exhausted smile.

"Good morning!" said Oksa, with forced cheerfulness.

"Morning, ladies!" chorused the two men.

Reminiscens walked over to Abakum, who gave a slight start and looked shyly at her.

"Is that the island?" she asked, motioning to the strip of land on the horizon.

Her voice was trembling. Everyone held their breath, while Abakum stared out to sea.

"No," he replied eventually. "We're only halfway there. That's the Isle of Man."

Even though she knew it was only a brief respite, Oksa felt relieved. And she was obviously not alone, because everyone looked cheered by this news.

"Well, I think it's time for a hearty breakfast," said Dragomira. "Come and give me a hand, girls. You too Pavel!"

Baba Pollock obviously wanted to leave Reminiscens and Abakum on their own to talk in private. No one ever discussed the subject openly, but ever since the Runaways had found poor Reminiscens inside the painting, Oksa was convinced that Abakum was in love with her. She even had her own theory about it: inhibited by loyalty, the Fairyman had sacrificed his own happiness when young Leomido had confessed his love for Reminiscens in Edefia. Abakum's feelings had remained constant, though, and he'd never stopped loving Reminiscens. It was so clear to the Young Gracious. Now that she was experiencing the pangs of first love, she could read the signs. The intensity of Abakum's gaze when he looked at Reminiscens, the attention he lavished on her, his thoughtfulness, his jumpiness… He'd been forced to keep quiet for so long, and curb his feelings for so many years—had he ever dared to hope? Probably not. He'd stayed in the background, even when Leomido had disappeared for ever. For a second, Oksa tried to imagine what her life would be like if her feelings for Tugdual weren't reciprocated. If Tugdual were to put his arms around someone else… She'd die, she just knew it! She looked again at Abakum's slightly hunched figure as Reminiscens rested her hand on his forearm in a gesture of deep affection. With her long silvery hair tumbling around her radiant face, she looked like the Madonna. With his free hand, the Fairyman chastely pressed his beloved's hand. Dragomira ushered Pavel, Zoe and Oksa out of the cabin.

"Baba?" whispered Oksa, wanting to know more.

"The past is dead and gone but we can always improve the present," she replied enigmatically.

Oksa looked at her quizzically. She'd have liked to know more, but it seemed destined to remain a private matter, since Dragomira was already changing the subject.

"I could murder a nice hot cup of tea!" exclaimed Baba Pollock.

"I'd need several pints of the stuff to recover from last night," declared Pavel, pulling a face. "There's no two ways about it, I'm getting much too old for this lark."

"Poor old fogey," teased Oksa.

She tried to glance back into the wheelhouse, but Dragomira had already closed the door. Well, it was worth a try…

"Can you manage or would you like to lean your weary old bones on me, Dad?" she asked in the same vein.

"Come here then, you sarky so-and-so!" replied Pavel, playing along. "What about you, Zoe? Will you lend an arm to help your prehistoric uncle too? I need all the support I can get in my decrepit old age."

He tousled their hair affectionately, and the three of them followed Dragomira towards the centre of the ship.

※

When they walked into the mess room, almost all the Runaways were already sitting around a table laden with a gargantuan breakfast zealously prepared by the three Lunatrixes. The Fortensky clan was there, along with the Knuts and Cockerell's family. As soon as Oksa came through the door the room fell silent, which did nothing to put the Young Gracious at ease. She met Tugdual's deceptively casual but irresistibly intense gaze and was unable to stop her cheeks flushing bright red and her heart racing. "Well done, Oksa-san!" she thought angrily. "Now everyone knows you're crazy about him."

"Hiya, Lil' Gracious," said Tugdual, chewing on a piece of toast thickly spread with marmalade.

On the other side of the table, Kukka looked Oksa up and down, sniggering mockingly. Oksa was flustered. Kukka made her feel like a boring, stupid fool infatuated by a boy who was toying with her, like a cat with a mouse. She couldn't seem to shake off that mental picture of a mouse… Kukka haughtily tossed back her luxuriant blonde hair and her beautiful eyes bored into Oksa's. Oksa felt stung, as if Kukka had just poured vinegar into the wound she'd inflicted, and she shivered. Tugdual's face darkened when he realized that his vindictive cousin was upsetting Oksa, and he quickly intervened: with a flick of his finger, he sent the roll she was buttering with excessive care flying into the air. She gave a yell of rage and hurled her plate at him, which he easily ducked with a mocking smile.

"My respects, Young Gracious!" broke in Cameron, putting a halt to the quarrel between the two warring cousins.

In complete contrast to Kukka's haughty glare, Leomido's son was gazing at Oksa with a deferential, almost fascinated, expression in his eyes, which made Oksa feel much better. She sat down at the breakfast table and took refuge behind a huge bowl of tea.

"The honour is entire to welcome you to this refectory," said Dragomira's Lunatrix, greeting the three new arrivals. "Your domestic staff has multiplied his efforts to sheathe the taste buds and stomachs of the Runaways in satisfaction."

"I don't doubt it, my dear Lunatrix," answered Dragomira gratefully.

"Your physiognomies make demonstration of great exhaustion and strong agitation," remarked the little creature, his attention fixed on Pavel in particular.

"My thoughts exactly," agreed Dragomira, looking at the Runaways' haggard faces.

"But we all know you have a small phial hidden in the folds of your dress that will revive us. Isn't that the case, my dear mother?"

"That's my son," Dragomira said confidingly to lighten the mood. "He knows me better than I know myself… And what would you suggest, clever clogs?" she asked Pavel with a grin.

"Well, even though your Elixir of Betony is marvellous, I'd have to go for your phenomenal Fortifax Concentrate this time," replied Pavel, his tone half serious, half playful. "We'll need something strong to help us recover from the interminable night we've had."

Agreeing with his choice, Dragomira rummaged around in the pockets of her voluminous grey wool dress and produced a tiny bottle. Then, walking around the table behind the Runaways, she added a few drops of opaque liquid to their bowls, making them pull faces and wrinkle their noses in disgust.

"I feel much better already!" exclaimed Oksa, her eyes shining.

"Your gran's a real witch," added Naftali.

And he wasn't alone in thinking that. The weariness that had been etched on the Runaways' faces a few seconds ago was visibly fading: an invigorating surge of energy flooded their veins. Feeling revived, Oksa took a thick slice of brioche, then examined her father opposite. The Fortifax Concentrate had smoothed away the dark rings under his eyes, but they were still full of anxiety.

Surreptitiously, Oksa turned to look at Tugdual. He'd clearly distanced himself by stuffing earphones in his ears and turning up the volume on his MP3 as high as it would go. He looked cold and unreachable and it upset Oksa to see him like that. She knew it was just an inscrutable facade. She was desperate to go over and snuggle up against him—just the thought of it made her head reel. She remembered Kukka's scornful glance—she obviously thought she was just a stupid child and, what was worse, she might be right... And these feelings of uncertainty were chipping away at her confidence. For the first time in her life, Oksa felt unsure of herself. Her mind was seething with questions, even though she knew this was hardly the best time to be distracted by such matters. Although she didn't regard herself as all that pretty, she knew she had a bubbly personality and was quite clever. *But so were a lot of people.* Looking at Kukka, she felt as though her best qualities were dull as ditchwater. What was happening to her? She was suddenly assailed by the fear that she might not be good enough and she came out in a cold sweat. She glanced again at Tugdual, who'd retreated into his own shell, and suddenly felt depressed. The seeds of doubt, which had been sown a few days ago, began to take root. Suddenly, as if he sensed her fears, Tugdual finally looked up. A slight frown creased his forehead and a look of concern darkened his steely eyes. The next minute, he reknotted his black scarf around his neck and his face resumed its aloof expression, leaving Oksa to struggle with her inner demons in front of Kukka, who was sardonically watching the scene.

Zoe was the first one to point out that the Bellangers weren't there. At the mention of Gus's name, Oksa jumped and blanched. She was a horrible person. She gnawed her lip until it bled, appalled that she'd forgotten her closest friend. She was just about to get up and find out how he was when the Bellangers burst into the mess room with Bodkin and Feng Li. Oksa was even more annoyed with herself when she saw how dreadful Gus looked—his skin had a greenish tinge and his eyes were wild. Even Tugdual seemed shocked at how much Gus had changed.

"Good Lord, what on earth is wrong with you, lad?" cried Dragomira, jumping up from her chair and going over to him.

"He's seasick," said Pierre. "Oksa's already given him Abakum's Brugmansia remedy."

"I don't feel seasick any more, Dad," broke in Gus, holding his head.

He turned to Oksa. As if smudged by the brush of an evil painter, his eyes, which were usually so blue, looked like the bottom of a murky swamp.

"The remedy worked like a dream, Oksa, thank you," he croaked. "It's just this awful pain…"

He just had time to grab his mother's arm to stop himself from falling. Some of the Runaways cried out in surprise, others, led by Oksa, rushed to hold him up.

"What's the matter with him?" she cried, staring desperately at Dragomira.

Baba Pollock looked worriedly at Naftali and Brune who, far from reassuring her, shook their heads as if to confirm a bleak diagnosis.

"Come and eat something, Gus," she advised.

"I can't…" groaned Gus, hunching over.

"I'll take him back to our cabin," said Pierre gravely.

He walked out of the mess room supporting Gus, followed by Dragomira, Reminiscens, Jeanne and Naftali. Oksa and Zoe trailed behind at a discreet distance. The adults hurried into the cabin, leaving the two girls outside. A moment later, Abakum and Reminiscens came out again, carefully closing the door behind them.

"I think they're trying to hide something, don't you?" murmured Oksa.

"Yes," added Zoe. "And I think it must be something serious."

Oksa felt as if all her blood had drained from her body. Zoe took her hand: it was freezing—as cold as the dread gradually invading the two girls' hearts.

12

BURNING QUESTIONS

THERE WAS A STRANGE MOOD ABOARD THE SHIP HEAD-
ing north towards the rough waters of the Sea of the Hebrides.
The Runaways passed the time as best they could to mask their anxiety.
Walking the entire length of the trawler and back again, Oksa and
Zoe passed Cameron Fortensky's three sons playing cards, Andrew
the minister with his head in a book, Cockerell chatting animatedly to
Naftali in a foreign language, and Kukka sulking in a corner. Although
they'd been told nothing about Gus's worrying condition, the two
girls hadn't stopped looking for clues. Anxiously, they'd sounded
out everyone who'd accompanied Gus back to his cabin, but it was
futile... all the witnesses seemed to have signed some secret pact.
Every time, they were given the same reply: *"Don't worry, everything
will be fine..."*

"They're treating us like kids!" raged Oksa. "We'll have to find out
on our own since no one will tell us anything."

She tugged Zoe along behind her through the ship's narrow gangways
to the Bellangers' cabin. A few minutes later, Oksa was kneeling in front
of the cabin door, concentrating hard on unlocking it with the tip of
her index finger.

"See, Zoe? The door's locked. That's a bit strange, isn't it?" Zoe silently
nodded. Oksa stood up and triumphantly opened the door. Inside the
cabin, Pierre was asleep, his large body turned to the wall. The faint

light from the gangway barely disturbed him. His breathing faltered for a few seconds before regaining its steady rhythm. The girls closed the door behind them and looked around for Gus in the gloom. He was on the bottom bunk, his knees against his chest. Curled up on a pillow near him, the baby Lunatrix was snoring peacefully.

"He doesn't leave your side!" whispered Oksa sitting down next to Gus, as Zoe squeezed in beside her.

"I think he thinks I'm his father," murmured Gus, stroking the small downy head. "So what are you two doing here?"

"We've come to find out what's going on straight from the horse's mouth," whispered Oksa. "How are you?"

Gus lifted his head: he looked ghastly.

"Sick as a dog," he said, pulling a face, before adding: "That's such a stupid expression! I've never seen any dog as sick as I am right now."

"What's wrong with you *exactly*?" asked Oksa.

"No idea," replied Gus, wrapping his arms around his knees.

"Haven't your parents told you anything? What about my gran? I'm sure they know something…"

She noticed Zoe signalling to her to stop. Too late—she'd just stupidly given Gus something to worry about.

"If they haven't told me anything, then it must be serious," concluded Gus, making Oksa feel even guiltier. "Perhaps even incurable."

Zoe put her hand on Gus's shoulder in a gesture of comfort, while Oksa gnawed the inside of her cheek. She could be so tactless sometimes…

"Don't be silly, everything will be fine," she whispered, realizing she was using the same words she'd found so hard to believe when Pierre or Dragomira said them. "Do you want a little spritz from my super anti-sickness product?" she added, taking a small spray from her pocket.

Gus hesitated, then accepted.

"If magic has to be my last resort, so be it. Wait, I'll lie down."

He stretched out on his back, crossing his hands over his stomach, and Oksa couldn't help thinking of those recumbent stone figures that had impressed her so much on a school trip to Westminster Abbey. She jumped up abruptly, feeling upset, and almost hit her head on the bunk above. Zoe caught her just in time to stop her falling over.

"This will do you good, you'll see," said the Young Gracious quietly, spraying a liberal dose into her friend's face. "Hang in there, OK? We'll come back and see you soon."

But Gus was already unconscious. Before she left the cabin, Oksa turned to look at him once more. Despite the darkness, she could have sworn she saw Zoe whisper something in his ear. Unless she was dropping a kiss at the corner of his mouth… With a scowl, Oksa signalled impatiently to Zoe, who emerged from the shadows looking so solemn that Oksa immediately regretted her hostility.

With heavy hearts, the two girls made their way up to the ship's deck. The sea was rough and the sky looked ominous. The wind whipped into their anxious faces, but they did nothing to protect themselves. Oksa couldn't forgive herself for tactlessly giving Zoe the hurry-up and her remorse made it difficult to stay with Zoe. Her cousin didn't seem to bear a grudge, though, and linked arms with Oksa, who almost burst into tears.

They kept walking along the deck, lashed by the violent sea spray, until they reached the stern, where they could make out Tugdual's dark figure leaning on the rail.

"I'll go back to the cabin," announced Zoe.

"Don't feel you have to! I'm not going to throw myself at him just because he's there!" exclaimed Oksa, blushing.

"Except that you're dying to!" retorted her friend. Oksa felt embarrassed. Was she so transparent? Was Zoe disappointed in her? She mustered all her courage and glanced at her friend: Zoe was looking sadly at her, but there was no sign of a smile on her kind face. What should she do? Should she go back, when she was dying to join him?

"Go on," said Zoe quietly. "Anyway, you can't do anything for Gus at the moment."

Oksa broke down at these words. She slid to a sitting position on the deck and dissolved into tears. Zoe crouched beside her in a panic.

"Oksa! I didn't mean to upset you."

"You haven't done anything wrong," sobbed the Young Gracious. "It's me. I don't know how I feel any more… I'm upset about Gus. I can't stand seeing him in pain. I can't stand the fact that things aren't like they were before. That I need him as much as I need Tugdual. That I'm afraid and in love at the same time. That I'm acting like a psycho!"

"You're not acting like a psycho," broke in Zoe. "You're just doing the best you can. Gus has seen how much effort you've made to regain his friendship."

"Do you think so?" sobbed Oksa.

"He knows you very well and he's far from blind."

"Do you think he knows how important he is to me?"

"I'd find it hard to believe anything else."

"Oh, Zoe, how do you cope with it?"

"How do I cope with what?"

"How do you cope… with all this?"

The expression in Zoe's eyes was intense, yet resigned.

"I don't cope, Oksa."

"I'm so sorry…" Oksa spluttered, surprised and ashamed.

"Don't apologize. It's all good. Me and misery are old friends now, we can't live without each other!"

A strange smile lit up her face. She put her arms around Oksa and squeezed. Realizing that her friend wanted comfort, but wouldn't ask for it, Oksa squeezed Zoe back as affectionately as she could. Zoe gave a deep, despairing sigh, weighed down by the permanent sadness she seemed unable to offload.

"Go to him," she said, gently pulling away. "But remember, Oksa: Gus needs you. Don't ever forget that."

❊

Although Oksa had thought Tugdual was lost in contemplation of the grey waves crashing over the hull of the ship, he was actually studying the screen of his mobile, scrolling through web pages from newspapers all over the world.

"There you are, Lil' Gracious," he said, without taking his eyes off the screen.

"Seemingly…"

He glanced at her out of the corner of his eye with unsettling seriousness.

"What's the news?" she continued.

"You really want to know?"

He switched off his phone and slipped it into his pocket. Then he studied Oksa carefully.

"You look exhausted, Lil' Gracious."

"You didn't answer my question…"

"Nor did you."

"Yes, I really want to know!" she exclaimed.

"Well, in a nutshell, London is under six feet of water, as are several other major international cities. The tectonic plates are doing a good impression of figure skating, which is causing tremors in all the fault zones and the Richter scale is in meltdown. Other than that, there have been all kinds of landslides, floods, erupting volcanoes and forest fires raging out of control."

"How awful!" cried Oksa.

"Oh, I forgot! A huge section of the ice shelf has broken off after an earthquake, accelerating things further. There are 116 square miles of ice adrift in the North Pacific."

"Oh no!" gasped Oksa, her hand over her mouth.

"It's the end of the world, my Lil' Gracious," he said, sounding deceptively casual.

Oksa punched him gently on the shoulder at this show of offhandedness—aware that he'd just called her "my" Lil' Gracious for the first time.

"Ouch," Tugdual said gloomily. Oksa laughed nervously.

"I could really hurt you if I wanted to!"

"I know that," admitted Tugdual in the same tone.

He continued studying her with a sort of challenging, amused expression, which made her limbs go to jelly.

"I could also really hurt you," he said softly, as a strand of black hair fell over his face.

Oksa didn't say anything for a moment, feeling an agonizing uncertainty.

"You could, but you won't!" she retorted as firmly as she could. "Will you?"

She gazed deep into Tugdual's eyes. Just for a second, she was sure he'd hesitated, that something vulnerable had just surfaced. She found this as reassuring as it was unsettling. Tugdual had shown his weaknesses on several occasions. They melted Oksa's heart, but perhaps they were too much for him to bear? And dangerous for the others? When Orthon had infiltrated Bigtoe Square, the only person he'd tried to win over was Tugdual, as if he'd sensed that he possessed a dark power, the potential for destruction… Oksa shook her head to banish this thought. The Lunatrix had assured her that Tugdual had a pure heart and was loyal to her. There was no way he could be wrong. The words of a song by Muse floated into her head. She hummed almost inaudibly.

I want to reconcile the violence in your heart
I want to recognize your beauty's not just a mask
I want to exorcise the demons from your past…

Tugdual looked at her in surprise, then turned away. They both stared at the roaring sea for a moment, hypnotized by its powerful, ceaseless motion.

"What are you thinking?" asked Oksa, forcing herself back to the present.

"You mean when I look at you?"

"Stop answering my questions with a question!" sighed Oksa, trying not to smile.

"OK… Do you have the time?"

"Answer me instead of replying with another question!"

"You asked for it… what I'm thinking often depends on what I'm looking at and how my mind interprets it. When I look at your father and Abakum, I think of a solid white iceberg and its invisible strength below the surface. When I look at Reminiscens and Zoe, I think of a poisoned dagger secreting venom into the heart, drop by cruel drop. When I look at Dragomira and my grandparents, I think about the lightning bolts of destiny which strike without warning. When I look at the sea, I think about my father clinging to his oil rig and I want to drown myself in the same dark water…"

His voice broke. He gripped the railing, his face ashen, then continued:

"When I look at my cousin, Kukka, I think about committing bloody murder. When I look at my little brother, I think about innocence which will inevitably be lost. And when I look at *you*, I think about power and the hope you represent. And that fascinates me."

After saying this, he withdrew into himself like an oyster closing its shell. But he'd gone too far and yet not far enough, in Oksa's view.

"Is the power I represent all you're interested in?" she asked quietly, sounding choked.

Tugdual's eyes darkened.

"You know that's not true. I'm interested in everything about you. From the moment you walked into your gran's apartment that autumn evening. You were wearing pyjamas and you had wet hair and bare feet. And you were in a total panic about the mark you'd just discovered on your stomach. And, if you want to know everything," he added, raising his voice, "YES, I'm enthralled by the infinite power you represent. I know you'd like me to forget the Gracious inside you, but don't you realize that I've never been fascinated by anyone the way I am by you and everything you are? You're a Gracious and you want me to pretend that you're not! HOW DO YOU EXPECT ME TO DO THAT?"

Oksa gnawed her lip, taken aback by his words.

"Why don't you ask me what you're dying to ask?" he growled, through gritted teeth.

She was deeply moved by Tugdual's tense voice, curt sentences and set jaw. In an agony of indecision, unable to talk, she looked up at him despairingly, then lowered her eyes. Tugdual lifted her chin with his index finger and gazed into her eyes.

"Do you think I'd love you as much as I do if you weren't a Gracious?" he insisted, enunciating every syllable slowly and clearly.

His words made Oksa tremble. She didn't feel ready to deal with the answer to this question, which plunged her into a state of nagging uncertainty. She instinctively took a step backwards, but nothing could stop Tugdual.

"Well? What do you reckon?" he asked, with a cruelty that seemed to pain him too. "Would I be here, baring my soul like never before, if you were just an ordinary girl?"

He fixed his cold, feverish gaze on her. Something emanated from him that was at once completely terrifying and mesmerizing. Oksa staggered. The sky darkened with a rumble of thunder, again mirroring her emotions.

"You're obsessed by the question, but you're petrified of finding out the truth," whispered Tugdual in her ear. "So, even though I'd love to go on keeping you in suspense, I won't."

Without saying another word, he brought his lips down on hers.

13

AIR DISPLAYS

"WE'VE JUST CROSSED THE FIFTY-SIXTH PARALLEL!" exclaimed the Tumble-Bawler after lunch. "We'll soon pass the Isle of Mull, then the Treshnish Isles. After that, we just have to sail past Ardnamurchan Point and cross the fifty-seventh parallel to reach the Isle of Rum. Then we'll be able to see the Island of the Felons."

This news lifted the passengers' spirits, since the day had begun to drag terribly. Their journey would soon be over! The farther north the *Sea Dog* sailed, the more impatient they felt. Only Pavel and Abakum, who were busy piloting the ship, didn't let their concentration waver. Perched on the Fairyman's shoulder, the Tumble-Bawler proved to be just as accurate—and much chattier— than the ship's instruments and nautical charts.

"How much longer will it take?" asked Pavel, frowning anxiously.

"Five hours," replied the Tumble-Bawler, delighted to help. "We should be there before nightfall."

"Perfect," remarked Pavel.

A few of the Runaways were making the most of the break in the weather to enjoy a breath of fresh air and stretch their legs on deck, while some even took to the air and Vertiflew over the grey sea around the ship. To everyone's amazement, Reminiscens suddenly shot into the sky with remarkable grace, her long hair floating behind her as she performed some jaw-dropping spins and turns. Brune and Dragomira lost no time in joining her and the three of them looked as though they were having a whale of a time.

"Look at them go!" cried Oksa.

"Incredible!" added Cameron at her side. "Absolutely incredible! When I think how we've had to keep this under wraps for years. Such a waste…"

That was all it took for Oksa to shoot off from the deck in a fraction of a second, leaving Cameron staring open-mouthed. The Young Gracious soared into the sky to join Brune, who'd climbed above the clouds, then plummeted down in a nosedive, screaming at the top of her lungs. She stopped the right way up a few inches from the surface of the water, just as Leomido had taught her to do.

"OKSA!" yelled Pavel from the wheelhouse. Abakum put his hand on his arm.

"Don't worry. Where's the harm in it?" Pavel took a deep breath.

"There's always the risk of harm… What if another ship or a radar picked up those four idiots! We'd have the army on us like a shot and, quite frankly, we don't have time for that."

Abakum's face clouded over at this thought. Acting on Pavel's words, the Tumble-Bawler shot into the sky and made a beeline for the Vertifliers, who were pirouetting between the crest of the waves and the lowest clouds. The small creature whispered a warning into Dragomira's ear and she immediately summoned the four risk-takers. A few seconds later, they all landed on deck, applauded by the Runaways. Glancing over at her father in the wheelhouse, Oksa met his angry gaze and paled, knowing that she'd given him even more cause for concern. He shook his head angrily and she replied with a dazzling smile, which she hoped might calm him down.

"Fantastic!" remarked Cameron, coming over. "You're so talented!"

"Um… no more than any other Runaway who can Vertifly," replied Oksa.

"Are you kidding? Not being funny or anything, but your three flying companions have had decades' more experience than you. Just how long have you been Vertiflying?"

"Er... a year."

"I repeat: you're very talented!" said Cameron cheerfully.

"Can I ask you something?"

"Ask away!"

"Can you Vertifly?"

"I didn't learn until late in life," replied Cameron, "and I've never really had much opportunity to practise. For a long time, my father was reluctant to teach me and Galina. As soon as we were old enough to understand, when we were teenagers, he told us the secret of Edefia and what it meant for us. He'd decided on that course of action with all the descendants of the Fortensky family, for our own safety as much as anything. I'm sure it was the right thing to do, even though you can bet that it was really hard to accept at the time. You only have to look at the Knuts to see how much harm could be done by keeping quiet about the secret."

"You mean Tugdual?" asked Oksa eagerly.

"Yes. He paid dearly for the Knuts' decision to keep quiet about their origins. Revealing the secret so suddenly had serious consequences for the whole family, particularly Tugdual— it was like a bolt from the blue! You'd have to be incredibly strong to come to terms with something like that and Tugdual wasn't at all prepared for it."

"Do you think anyone can really be prepared for something like that? Finding out is a terrible shock, whatever the circumstances."

Cameron stroked his chin dubiously.

"You may be right... I remember I was worried sick for months that I might do something to give myself away to the Outsiders. Particularly as my father was almost obsessively afraid of that happening!"

"That reminds me of someone," remarked Oksa, glancing towards Pavel who was watching them from a distance.

"Truth is, it wasn't so dangerous once you knew. You were continually worried that someone might find you out, but as long as you were careful, there was no reason for anyone to realize we were... different."

"It sounds funny, you speaking about all this in the past tense," remarked Oksa.

"It is all in the past now," said Cameron quietly, gazing at the sea churning around the ship. "Whatever happens now, our life on the Outside is over and done with."

Oksa stiffened. Cameron was right. A wave of sadness washed over her as her mind filled with images from the past fourteen years and she lost herself in her memories.

✳

"Are you OK, Oksa? Wake up!"

She opened her eyes to see about ten people staring at her. She was lying in the hammock in the wheelhouse, which meant she must have passed out or something.

"What happened?" she asked, sitting up.

"You were chatting to Cameron and you fainted," replied her father, his face ashen.

Oksa frowned, remembering the images flashing past, her whole life condensed into a terrifyingly intense few seconds… wasn't that what was supposed to happen when you were about to die? She shivered. The person she'd been no longer existed and yet her past life still formed an integral part of the person she was now. She could never turn her back on what she'd once been—it was as if she'd died while remaining *alive*! It was a confusing paradox.

"Is that because of me?" she asked, glancing outside.

Flashes of black lightning gleaming like onyx streaked through the overcast sky and torrential rain was battering the ocean and the ship.

"Maybe," admitted Tugdual, perched on a desk.

"I really must learn to control that!" said Oksa crossly.

"You'll get the hang of it soon enough, don't worry. All in good time," said Dragomira comfortingly.

"You know, Oksa," added Abakum, "your gran was responsible for an unusually stormy microclimate over our Siberian village for several years before she managed to master her emotions."

"Really?" asked Oksa in amazement.

"Yes!" nodded Dragomira. "Take this Capacitor, Dushka, it'll do you a power of good."

Oksa took the small silvery ball from her gran and swallowed it without question. A surge of energy spread through her body, rising like an invigorating sap and making her immediately feel stronger.

"You'll have to teach me that too," she said quietly.

"Will do!" agreed Dragomira.

The storm, linked to Oksa's state of mind, passed over in the next few minutes. The sky cleared and the clouds parted to reveal the setting sun, which blazed red as it seemed to plunge into the sea.

"Ahem, ahem…"

Dragomira's Lunatrix had come over to the group and was trying to attract their attention by clearing his throat louder and louder. The old woman eventually noticed him and asked:

"What's the matter, Lunatrix?"

"The Old Gracious and her travelling companions must receive the communication that the Island of the Felons, as it has been named by the Young Gracious, is experiencing visibility for eyes that are most perspicacious."

The Runaways turned to look at the horizon, narrowing their eyes. In the distance, a tiny bump was silhouetted against the sky, stained red by the rays of the setting sun.

14

THE ISLAND OF THE FELONS

PAVEL AND HIS INK DRAGON, ESCORTED BY NAFTALI AND Pierre, approached the Island of the Felons to the rhythmic sound of the creature's powerful wingbeats. One hundred feet below, the waves were battering the dark rocks of the cliffs. An enormous full moon, mottled with shadows, cast a pallid light over the sea. The massive island was surrounded by sharp, fanglike reefs, rising from the seabed. A narrow inlet, where a ship almost as large as the *Sea Dog* was moored, seemed to provide the only safe access to the island. The Ink Dragon beat its wings more vigorously: Pavel wanted to fly over the island.

"I don't think that's a good idea!" said Naftali, flying closer to him.

"Stay there!" retorted Pavel. "I'll just take a quick look. Anyway, they know we're here…"

There was no arguing with that, so Naftali and Pierre landed on a large rock and waited.

The first thing Pavel noticed when he soared over the high cliffs surrounding the island was the magnificent sandstone building in the middle of scrubby moorland, devoid of trees or bushes. The windswept house was exactly as the Tumble-Bawler had described it: a two-floor structure bisecting the island lengthwise. Fifty yards away, a small chapel perched on the edge of the cliff kept watch over the raging sea.

The Ink Dragon flew closer to the house. Smoke was rising from the chimney and a faint light shone from several of the windows. Pavel's heart was pounding and his body was incandescent with bitter rage. Marie was being held captive behind one of those windows... A low growl, originating in the fiery pit of the dragon's stomach, rose into its throat and burst from its mouth in a threatening roar that seemed to shake the whole island. The intimidating creature circled the building several times, loudly beating its wings, then hovered a few yards from the front door. A motionless figure, whom Pavel would have recognized anywhere, appeared at the highest window of the turret that stood atop the house like a watchtower. Orthon stared in his direction. The fire inside Pavel burned higher and higher until he could bear it no longer. A long flame spurted from his throat, licking at the windowsill. Then the dragon turned and flew back to the ocean, with several measured wingbeats.

⁂

The ship moored up in heavy silence, with all its lights off. The wind had dropped, strangely, so the waves had abated and the sea was as calm as a millpond.

"The lull before the storm," murmured Tugdual, looking up at the clear sky.

"Perhaps," said Oksa in a low voice, stepping onto the tiny sandy beach which glowed in the moonlight.

One by one, the Runaways disembarked in the small inlet, relieved to arrive safely and eager to confront their enemies: Insiders and Runaways who had so much in common with them, except for one big difference—they'd chosen Felony.

"Are you OK, Oksa?" whispered Zoe, catching up with her friend.

"Um... hard to say... I think we probably arrived in the nick of time. I'd have gone mad if I'd had to spend another hour on that ship!"

"It's always better to act than to wait," declared Cockerell pompously.

"I hope so," remarked Zoe, gazing around anxiously.

The towering cliffs surrounding the inlet only increased the Runaways' doubts. Tilting back their heads, they looked up at the sharply ridged cliff face.

"Has anyone seen Gus?" asked Oksa suddenly.

"I'm here..." came a groggy voice.

Gus was sitting hunched on the sand, elbows on knees, with Dragomira and Jeanne crouched beside him, while Bodkin held up the Polypharus, bathing them in a pool of light. Hanging on to Gus's jumper, the baby Lunatrix was watching him with large gentle eyes and gurgling quietly. Dragomira offered Gus a small phial and urged him to drink. Oksa hesitated, then decided to go over to her friend, her heart racing. He looked terrible—his eyes were bloodshot, his cheeks gaunt and he seemed to be struggling to catch his breath. Bodkin moved aside to let Oksa through and handed her the Polypharus.

"Thank you," murmured the Young Gracious. Bodkin bowed and walked off.

"How do you feel?" she ventured to ask, forcing herself to look Gus in the eye.

"Like death," he replied.

Oksa couldn't help smiling: that was so typical of him!

"If you're here to put me out of my misery, then go right ahead," he went on, pretending to bare his chest for the death blow. "I'm ready!"

"Don't be daft!" scolded Dragomira gently. "This potion should ease your migraine in a few minutes."

"Have you got a migraine?" asked Oksa in surprise.

"Not only a migraine, but hellish tinnitus too," replied Gus, with a glassy stare. "The Grim Reaper's really dragging this out, the sadist..."

Oksa laughed nervously, pleased that her friend sounded like his old self but really worried about his condition. She instinctively looked behind for Tugdual, who was leaning against the cliff, casually examining his Granok-Shooter. "I love them both," she thought, alarmed at reaching this conclusion now, on the Island of the Felons.

"Perhaps it might be better if he stayed on the ship," remarked Jeanne tensely, interrupting Oksa's thoughts.

"Oh no, mercy!" groaned Gus. "Not the ship—I'd rather die on the sand."

He put his head in his hands.

"I really am a millstone," he continued. "I get myself bitten by one of those vile Chiropterans, then I get myself Impictured, and now I'm slowing everyone down with my pathetic human ailments…"

At these words, the baby Lunatrix snuggled up to him and rubbed his little head along Gus's arm, while Oksa raised her eyes heavenwards.

"It's been ages since we've had to put up with your Eeyore routine…"

Pierre, who'd been standing near his son, suddenly walked over to Abakum and Reminiscens a few yards away and the three of them began conversing in low tones. Wanting to find out more, Oksa used her Volumiplus power to eavesdrop.

"We've run out of options," said Reminiscens. "There's no time to lose. *If* they do have the antidote, it'll slow down the process and Gus may have a chance…"

Oksa stifled a cry. Gus may have a chance to do what? SURVIVE? Her heart hammered in her chest. Her horrified eyes met Abakum's— the Fairyman seemed to have realized she'd been listening to their conversation. He gave her a long stare. Following his gaze, Pierre and Reminiscens turned in her direction too. In a daze, she pretended she was looking up at the cliffs.

"Come on!" announced Pierre, going back to Gus. "I'll carry you."

"It might do me good to walk," said Gus, struggling to get up.

When he was on his feet, he had to cling to his father's arm to steady himself. He shut his eyes for a few seconds, then reopened them with a wan smile at the Runaways around him. His eyes lingered on Oksa, who was still holding the Polypharus and biting the nails of her free hand.

"See, Oksa?" he remarked shakily. "I'm in great shape! So you can stop biting your nails!"

"I just finished the last one…" she replied, smiling back at him.

"You've always been such a pig," he teased, clutching his father's arm.

"Well, I think it's time to go and meet our hosts," rasped Pavel. "Anyone who can't Vertifly should get on my back!"

He concentrated hard and they all watched as the majestic Ink Dragon rose from the tattoo on Pavel's back in the moonlight.

"Dad… you're magnificent," whispered Oksa, tears welling in her eyes, overwhelmed by the courage and kindness in the look Pavel shot her.

Awed, Abakum, Virginia, Kukka and Andrew hoisted themselves onto the back of the fantastic creature and it rose into the air with a few powerful flaps of its wings. Pierre was Vertiflying with Gus in his arms. Oksa and Zoe took flight too, followed closely by Dragomira, Reminiscens and the Fortensky clan. The Knuts, all of them Firmhands, had elected to climb the high, steep cliff bare-handed. Like enormous spiders, they scaled the sheer rock at incredible speed, taking any sharp outcrops easily in their stride. Oksa flew back and forth, fascinated by the ease with which they were climbing—particularly Tugdual, who seemed to be racing his uncle Olof. Behind them, safely carried by his mother, who was sensibly Vertiflying, little Till was screeching with joy.

The Runaways finally reached the cliff top and, suddenly, the vertiginous drop behind them into the dark sea didn't seem so frightening. In front of them, the vast moorland led towards the brooding house which held the key to the future of the two worlds.

15

OVERHEAD DANGER

A WINDING FOOTPATH CROSSED THE MOOR TO THE HOUSE in the middle of the island. With Pavel and the Ink Dragon providing an air escort, the Runaways exchanged glances. Conflicting feelings of impatience and anxiety were etched on their faces, but they couldn't turn back now…

The Runaways quietly separated into three pre-planned groups: Baba Pollock took Oksa's hand and they stood in front, flanked by Reminiscens and Abakum, with Olof and Zoe behind, followed by the Lunatrixes, Incompetents and Getorixes. The Squoracles curled up snugly in the pockets of Dragomira's long wool jacket, while the Ptitchkins settled down in the tiny gold cage she wore around her neck as a pendant. The second group, comprising the stronger members of the group—the Knuts, Pierre, Cockerell and Feng Li—raced across the moor like a pack of wolves and quickly disappeared behind the house. It had been decided that the Outsiders would wait inside the small chapel in relative safety, protected by the Fortenskys, Jeanne, Bodkin, Helena and Tugdual, who was seething in sullen silence at being put in this group. Hands stuffed in the pockets of his jeans, he fumed at his mother's side until, unable to bear it any longer, he eventually broke ranks to join the first group, ignoring Dragomira's disapproving look. Abakum turned to look at Helena, who nodded in answer to his silent question, and Tugdual officially took his place behind the Young Gracious.

"We'll be OK now," Gus couldn't help muttering. "Zorro's in pole position."

"He might make himself useful, you know," remarked his mother.

"You're probably right," sighed Gus.

"Let's go!"

The two groups set off resolutely. The bright moon bathed the countryside in a strange milky light.

"They'll see us coming!" cried Oksa in alarm.

"It doesn't matter, Dushka. Orthon and his friends would know we were here, even if we were under cover of impenetrable darkness."

"That's so annoying!"

Oksa looked up for reassurance: her father had deployed his Ink Dragon and was gliding through the sky. She waved at him, then focused again on the footpath and the house. All the windows were dark, but they knew beyond a shadow of a doubt that behind each one stood a Felon watching the Runaways' approach.

"It's so annoying," repeated Oksa.

Dragomira squeezed her hand tighter. What else could they do? The Runaways were fulfilling their destiny and they'd burnt all their bridges. Suddenly a smothered cry made everyone look round. Gus was bending over, his hands clamped over his ears, clearly in unbearable pain.

"Look!" exclaimed Tugdual, pointing at the sky.

A flock of birds was hovering above them, silhouetted against the moon. Pavel cautiously flew closer, skirting the fluttering creatures, and banked back to cover his friends with his massive wings.

"They aren't birds!" he hissed. "They're Death's Head Chiropterans!"

Struggling against feelings of panic, the Runaways immediately formed a defensive wall, bristling with Granok-Shooters. But the swarm of Chiropterans overhead didn't move. Hundreds of tiny red eyes gleamed in the semi-darkness, testing the Runaways' nerve.

"There are so many of them!" exclaimed Oksa. "We'll never survive if they attack."

"They won't attack," said Abakum. "Orthon just wants to give us a bit of a fright."

"You're right," agreed Dragomira. "It's not in his interest to attack now. We have nothing to fear."

"Those birds look a bit under the weather," remarked Abakum's Incompetent. "Have you seen how bloodshot their eyes are?"

"You're right, Incompetent!" retorted one of the Getorixes. "They're suffering from a bad bout of conjunctivitis."

"Oh, poor things," the Incompetent remarked sympathetically with disarming sincerity. "I've heard that cornflower water can work wonders for that…"

"The Fairyman has produced the gift of words sated with truthfulness," broke in Dragomira's Lunatrix. "The Runaways can fill their hearts with relief: the Death's Head Chiropterans have no premeditated belligerent intent."

"Hmm… they're not exactly out-and-out pacifists either," objected the Getorix, hopping up and down.

Feeling a little more reassured, the Runaways set off again, keeping a wary eye on the droning swarm of glittering red eyes above. Gus seemed to be getting worse as he trailed behind the group in front. Supported by Jeanne and Galina, he was struggling to keep going.

"I feel so dizzy," he groaned. "My head's… spinning… It's unbearable…"

Oksa suddenly found herself thinking back to the time when Gus had been bitten by one of those vile insects during the hot-air balloon battle between Orthon and Leomido the year before. She cast around in her memory—Leomido had said. "*Gus was injured, but the bite is superficial. Dragomira has done what was necessary and he's out of danger.*" "*What about after-effects?*" Naftali had gone on to ask. "*Chiropterans are extremely—*" But Leomido had interrupted him, saying, "*Let's not complicate matters for no reason.*"

Oksa rubbed her face, putting two and two together. Feeling horrified, she stopped dead in her tracks.

"What's wrong, Dushka?" asked Dragomira softly.

Oksa started walking again, holding on tightly to her gran's hand.

"Baba, answer me honestly, please," she whispered. "Is Gus sick because of the Chiropterans?"

"Yes," admitted Dragomira, after a brief hesitation. "The Chiropteran bite has remained inactive for months, but the poison seemed to start spreading through his veins as we drew closer to the island."

"That's terrible!" said Oksa in a choked voice. "Does being near the Chiropterans make the pain worse?"

"Yes, in a manner of speaking."

"Then we've got to get him away from here! Why would we make him go closer to creatures which are causing him such agonizing pain?"

"We don't have a choice," whispered Dragomira. "The Chiropterans are merely speeding up an irreversible process that began as soon as Gus was bitten. He has to come with us."

Oksa felt tears fill her eyes. Her nose prickled and her breath came faster.

"What do you mean an irreversible process?" she asked, sounding choked. "Is?—"

"Orthon has an antidote," said Dragomira, interrupting her.

"ORTHON?"

"He knows more about the Death's Head Chiropterans than anyone. Reminiscens is sure of that: he knows how to tame them, command them and turn them into formidable weapons of war. He can use them and, crucially, he can counter the effects of their bite."

"You mean we're relying on him to save Gus?"

"That's exactly what I mean, Dushka... Unfortunately."

This time, Oksa couldn't hold back her tears. She felt as if her heart were breaking.

"We'll sort this out, I promise," said Dragomira, squeezing her hand even tighter.

"No matter what," added Reminiscens, pressing her shoulder. "You have my word too."

Oksa wiped her tear-stained cheeks before turning to look at Gus again.

"My head's spinning…" he groaned. "I can't bear it…"

In the white light of the moon, Gus looked very weak. Oksa signalled to him encouragingly.

"Hang in there, Gus!" she called.

Although the second group was about to reach the chapel, Gus nodded to show he'd got the message. He staggered inside, with the baby Lunatrix trotting behind him, and Oksa glanced away to hide her anxiety. She eyed the Chiropterans warily; then, taking a deep breath, she let herself be led away by Dragomira and Abakum, who'd started walking again at a vigorous pace. They had to be quick. For Gus. For Marie. For the two worlds. This was no time to start having doubts. Tugdual had said as much a few days ago. She sensed him behind her, on her left, so she glanced back at him. His pale, impassive face was even more disconcerting than usual. He seemed to be looking at her, but the hair falling over his eyes stopped Oksa from reading the expression in them. Suddenly Dragomira and Reminiscens stopped. Oksa's blood froze and her heart pounded: the Felons' house was just a few yards away. It looked enormous, silent and threatening. Dragomira murmured a few words to her Tumble-Bawler, which immediately took off from its mistress's shoulder to return a few seconds later with some priceless information.

"Just behind the eight-foot-high front door is a hall twenty feet long and twelve and a half feet wide," it informed them, rocking back and forth on its rear. "A double door on the left leads into a 947-square-foot living room, divided into two equal parts. Another door on the right opens into a 452-square-foot kitchen. At the end of the hall, a five-foot-wide staircase with twenty-two seven-inch steps leads up to the first floor. Under the stairs, a six-foot door leads down into the basement. This door is concealed by a *trompe l'oeil* design and opened by a clever hydraulic system hidden in the ironwork of the banister."

"Excellent work, Tumble," said Dragomira, patting its small head in thanks. "And... did you detect any human beings?" she continued, her voice trembling.

"There are twenty-eight people on the premises," informed the Tumble-Bawler. "Nineteen Felons, six of whom are Werewalls ejected from Edefia and thirteen of whom are direct descendants, plus nine Outsiders. Without counting the Young Gracious's mother."

Oksa felt a surge of anger at the mention of her mother. Pavel, whose Ink Dragon had reverted to a harmless tattoo, hugged her, then raced off to join his friends behind the house. Oksa straightened up, looking fierce, and Dragomira began walking towards the sinister house.

"It's time to meet our destiny," she murmured.

16

An Acrimonious Reunion

A FLICKERING LIGHT WAS SPILLING OUT PAST THE DARK wooden door, which was slightly ajar. Dragomira walked up to the house, followed by the six other valiant members of this vanguard. Abakum kept Oksa by his side, escorted by the Incompetent and Dragomira's resourceful Lunatrix. Dragomira pushed open the heavy door with a loud creak, to reveal the large hall described by the Tumble-Bawler.

Wall-mounted glass candle globes bathed the room in a shifting radiance that was vaguely unsettling and the crystal pendants of the ceiling chandelier glittered in the candlelight. The draught from the opening door caused this ornate central light to tinkle and sway, covering the walls with myriad glints. On the parquet floor, darkened by the passage of years and the salty island air, they could make out a lighter geometric pattern which looked strangely familiar: it was the eight-branched star that was the symbol of Edefia—the Mark around Oksa's belly button. She rested her hand on her stomach, feeling emotional. She knew how important the star was—she'd understood its significance and all it implied, but seeing such a large representation of it on the floor reminded her of the power she'd inherited. She, Oksa Pollock, an ordinary fourteen-year-old girl, who loved rollerblading and pop rock, had an extraordinary destiny... She was here in the middle of this hall in this house on this island. At the centre of the world. She took a deep breath and lifted her head high. Deep down, and for the first time, she really felt that she was the Heart of Two Worlds.

※

The Runaways cautiously filed into the hall. Despite their apprehension, they wanted to confront their enemies and fellow Insiders. Senses alert, they took out their Granok-Shooters to give them courage and instinctively closed ranks. Oksa looked around warily, unsure what to do if a Felon suddenly appeared. Suddenly, they saw a backlit figure at the top of the monumental staircase. Its shadow stretched to Dragomira's feet and she stiffened. The elegant, regal figure slowly descended the steps, followed by two other, larger silhouettes. When they reached the middle of the staircase, the light from the candles finally illuminated their faces.

"Good evening, Dragomira... Good evening, Young Gracious," rang out a female voice that some of them recognized instantly. "You've come well protected, I see!"

"Good evening, Mercedica," replied Dragomira, suppressing a sudden surge of rage. "Allow me to return the compliment," she added, staring at the two young men beside her.

"Why, thank you," replied the haughty Spanish woman wryly. "Delighted to meet you at last, Reminiscens," she added suddenly. "After all these years... I imagine you've recognized your nephews, haven't you?"

Oksa felt Reminiscens flinch. Mercedica hadn't lost any time in opening hostilities... Reminiscens was more robust than she looked, though; she glared icily at the trio.

"Mortimer and Gregor, your twin brother's sons!" said Mercedica, looking pleased as punch.

The two young men's mocking smiles were immediately wiped from their faces by Reminiscens' retort.

"For your information, Mercedica, I feel as much sense of kinship with the young men you call my 'nephews' as this crumpled paper handkerchief in my pocket."

With this, she pulled out the handkerchief and walked over to the nearest candle sconce. There was a stunned silence as the handkerchief burst into flames. Reminiscens let it fall to the floor and crushed the burning fragments under her heel.

"Blood ties are stronger than some tatty handkerchief, my dear Reminiscens," sneered Mercedica with a forced smile. "Still, we'll have time to talk about all that later," she continued, descending the last few steps. "Do come in!"

Flanked by Gregor and Mortimer, she walked over to the double doors on the left and flung them open. There, in deathly silence, stood all the Felons who'd rallied to Orthon's cause, their eyes fixed on the Runaways.

Dragomira entered the huge living room, flanked by Oksa, Reminiscens and Abakum. The room was thickly carpeted and lit by the wavering light of oil lamps mounted on the polished sandstone walls. There were a number of worn leather armchairs arranged in a semicircle around an enormous hearth where a fire was burning merrily, while others were grouped separately around hammered metal coffee tables. The wall at the end of the room was entirely covered with bookshelves filled with shabby antique books. The luxurious setting would have been welcoming, were it not for the incredibly tense atmosphere.

Although discomfited, the Runaways were probably no more intimidated than the Felons who, despite their grim expressions, couldn't conceal their confusion at coming face to face with four people whose illustrious reputation had preceded them: two Graciouses, the twin sister of their leader, Orthon, and the powerful Fairyman. The creatures and the Runaways, whom they couldn't see but whose presence they could sense outside the house, also urged caution. Abakum, Dragomira and Reminiscens couldn't help feeling emotional at the sight of the faces before them. Some of them still looked incredibly familiar, more than fifty years after leaving Edefia. As a result, even though they'd known they'd see them on the island sooner or later, Edefia's "Elders" couldn't help feeling a little ambivalent about recognizing Lukas, the talented mineralogist, and Agafon, the former Memorarian—custodian of the Gracious Archives. None of the Insiders could have claimed they were completely prepared for this showdown in the flesh.

"Won't you sit down?" suggested Mercedica, waving a beringed hand at several sofas against the wall.

None of the seven Runaways moved. They were too busy examining the others. Oksa noticed that Mortimer couldn't take his eyes off Zoe. He'd changed so much! He'd lost his excess body weight and looked thinner, yet stronger. Turning to look encouragingly at her cousin, Oksa was surprised to see that Zoe was glaring defiantly at Mortimer with her arms firmly crossed. Oksa transferred her gaze to the other teenager, who looked as though he had to be related to Orthon: lean frame, black eyes and rigid bearing. "That must be Gregor," thought the Young Gracious, studying his hard face. "He was the one who'd dared to raise a hand to Baba and who'd stolen the Medallion and the Goranov! What a lowlife."

It was Dragomira who finally broke the stand-off. She strode over to Mercedica with a fierce expression in her eyes. The Felons looked uneasy, and several of them took up defensive stances, ready to fight. In a tight crimson wrap-over top, with expensive jewellery dripping from her neck and hands, traitorous Mercedica seemed amused by the situation and was smiling nastily. At her side, her daughter Catarina eyed the Runaways contemptuously.

"This is not a social visit," said the Old Gracious eventually. "Where is Orthon? I expect he's holed up somewhere, isn't he?"

"All in good time!" taunted Mercedica. "But, tell me, are there only seven of you? Did your friends get cold feet and turn back?"

There were a few sniggers and scornful sneers. Dragomira didn't bother to answer. Oksa was the one who replied.

"You watched us arrive!" she said, her voice shaking. "You know very well that we outnumber you!"

"My dear Oksa," sighed Mercedica, looking amused. "There may be a lot of you, but there isn't always strength in numbers…"

Suddenly there was a commotion in the hall and the door was flung open. A hideous creature burst into the living room, bellowing raucously.

"GRRR! The decrepit old shrew and her degenerate descendants! Why don't you all eat dung and die!"

"Fantastic! That's all we need," huffed Dragomira, recognizing the Abominari.

The slimy, bony creature launched itself at her, twisted claws outstretched. Dragomira put up her hand and a thin projectile of light shot from the centre of her palm to strike the Abominari head on, hurling it against the metal fireguard. It fell over backwards, its shoulder smoking, then dashed at her again, growling more with rage than pain.

"I'll disembowel you and wear your decaying guts as a stinking necklace, you scraggy hyena!"

This time Mercedica blocked its way, catching hold of the sticky limb which served as an arm. The Abominari struggled to free itself.

"I see it's just as charming as ever," scoffed Dragomira.

"Shut your putrid cakehole, vile harpy!" snarled the Abominari.

"You do not possess the right to make voicing of uncouthness in the direction of my Old Gracious!" objected the Lunatrix, who had turned completely translucent with anger.

"I possess the right to do whatever I want, pig-faced slave!"

Angrily, Oksa performed a Magnetus and the paper-knife on a desk in the corner of the room suddenly thudded between the creature's three gnarled toes, almost severing one.

"Daughter of a sow!" yelled the Abominari.

"Hey! I've had enough of this!" shouted Oksa, losing her temper.

That horrible creature had gone too far. Noticing a basket filled with wood by the fireplace, Oksa concentrated hard. A second later, a massive log dropped onto the Abominari's head and the creature staggered, then collapsed on the floor with a disgusting sucking noise.

"Tut tut tut, my friends! Is this any way to celebrate a reunion which is such an… unlooked-for pleasure?" boomed a man's voice.

The Runaways froze—they'd have recognized that voice anywhere. They stood in silence as the man walked through the wall and threaded his way between the Felons to stand in front of Dragomira.

"Good evening, Dragomira," he said, with a slight bow. "Or should I say: Good evening, dear sister."

17

OPERATION "FREE MARIE"

S TOICALLY BRAVING THE WIND AND RAIN, PAVEL AND HIS
friends were carrying out their mission in their separate ways:
Naftali, Brune, Pierre and Feng Li were scuttling across the facade like
large spiders, using the smallest crevices as footholds and handholds,
while Pavel and Cockerell were Vertiflying from window to window,
trying to look inside. No matter what method they'd chosen, however,
they were united in cause and well matched in courage.

"Marie, where are you?" muttered Pavel. Pierre signalled to him, his
face red from the icy gusts of wind. Only the strength of his index finger
clinging to the tiny cornice along the roof was keeping him pressed
against the wall. With a backflip, the "Viking" released his hold and
Vertiflew over to Pavel.

"She's here!"

In an instant, the six Runaways huddled together and had a whispered
conversation a few yards above ground. Pavel nodded, putting his hand
on Naftali's shoulder. The towering Swede plunged into the wall and
disappeared, holding his Granok-Shooter. The sound of shouting initially
gave the Runaways cause for concern but, eventually, the window opened
and Naftali popped his head out, beaming with triumph.

Gagged and bound by Naftali's Arborescens, the wide-eyed woman
watched Pavel rush over to the bed where Marie was lying. Pavel and
Marie had been kept apart by the Felons for over four months and the

indescribable relief they felt as they flung their arms around each other was almost as heart-rending as the shock Pavel had felt when he was told the terrible news of her abduction. It felt like Pavel's heart was cracking open to release all the worry he'd buried inside for so long. It was such a comfort to be reunited with the woman he loved. He took a deep breath, trying to calm his pounding heart and, cupping Marie's face in his hands, he gazed into her eyes.

"Someone's coming!" warned Pierre, his ear pressed against the door.

Pavel leapt to his feet and positioned himself defensively in front of the bed. Opposite him, Naftali was keeping the bound woman at a respectful distance. Her eyes were frightened and pleading.

"Don't hurt her!" said Marie quietly.

Pavel looked quizzically at her.

"She's done a lot for me…" she added, before the door was flung open with a crash.

Four Felons burst into the room and stopped short at the sight of the new "occupants". Against all expectation, the Runaways were proving to be a force to be reckoned with: the Knuts' imposing appearance, Pierre's and Cockerell's bulk, Feng Li's inscrutable expression and Pavel's fury only enhanced the sense of fierce determination radiating from the group.

Making the most of their assailants' brief indecision and mute amazement, Brune leapt into the air and slammed both feet against the chest of one of the Felons, who crashed to the floor, knocking over the other three. They retaliated by firing Granoks, which the Runaways managed to dodge, then some Fireballisticos, which Pavel simply intercepted, since he didn't seem to be harmed by flames, or even feel them. Pierre ended this lightning attack by knocking the four Felons unconscious with a Knock-Bong to the back of the neck.

"Watch out!" said Feng Li, standing sentry by the window. "There are more coming from outside."

"And from this way!" said Pierre, glancing out into the corridor.

Although he knew it was futile, he slammed the door and took out his Granok-Shooter. The Runaways exchanged looks, drawing strength from the intense determination burning in their eyes. Like battle-hardened soldiers, they prepared to face the ten or so Felons who lost no time in bursting into Marie's room through the walls and the window.

18

POISONED ARROWS

O KSA TOOK A STEP BACK. ORTHON WAS THERE IN THE
flesh, looking almost completely physically intact. He was wearing thick dark glasses but the Crucimaphila had clearly left its mark on his face and hands—as it must have done on the rest of his body. From a distance, his complexion looked iridescent, but as he drew nearer the Runaways could see that his skin was pitted, as if full of *holes* which had been painstakingly *filled* with what looked like… Goranov sap! Oksa couldn't help thinking about that poor, highly strung plant. She hoped it had survived. The Felon's hair was no longer deep black—it was now a striking aluminium grey. He stopped in the centre of the room and took off his glasses, revealing another change to his appearance, which amazed anyone who'd ever experienced the weight of his unfathomably black eyes. Like his hair, his piercing gaze was now steel-grey and glittered with even more cruelty than before.

Oksa felt a small hot hand slipping into hers: the Lunatrix had sensed how unsettled she was by Orthon. The Young Gracious was struggling to stay strong, assailed by all the bad memories and the dangers represented by the Felon. He'd caused her family and loved ones so much pain! After narrowly escaping death, he now seemed stronger than before, as if the change wrought by the Crucimaphila had made him more powerful. Although he looked thinner in his black sweater and charcoal-grey trousers, he radiated an aura of formidable strength. Narrowing his eyes, he curiously studied the Runaways and their creatures, then turned back to Oksa with renewed interest. When she felt his icy stare on her, the Young Gracious had the impression that she'd stepped back in time. She was hit by the same unbearable pain, like a hard punch to the stomach, that she'd experienced on the first day of school when she'd met the Felon maths teacher for the first time. Orthon looked so invulnerable. She battled to control the pain and panic, assisted by her Curbita-Flatulo, which was undulating around her wrist. Behind her, Abakum put his hands on her shoulders, and a surge of energy and confidence spread through her. She glimpsed a faint shadow of doubt pass over Orthon's face, showing that, despite his evil powers, the Felon obviously feared the Fairyman.

A few seconds later, he turned his attention away from Oksa—only temporarily, she was sure—and noticed his twin sister. Discomfited, Reminiscens stiffened and proudly braved Orthon's unfathomable gaze.

"My wonderful sister," murmured Orthon.

No one could tell if Orthon's tone was sad or ironic. Perhaps a bit of both…

"You've chosen sides then," he continued.

"There was never any doubt," said Reminiscens, her voice admirably steady. "I've followed my heart, not my family."

This answer seemed to upset Orthon.

"Why do all of you keep rejecting blood ties?" he replied, his deceptively playful tone intended to annoy them. "You can't argue with the science of genetics."

"But genes are far from the only things that bring people together!" retorted Reminiscens.

Orthon stared at her malevolently, then sat down in a heavy leather armchair in the centre of the room. After a tense silence, he continued:

"You look very well, dear sister."

"No thanks to you!" objected Reminiscens, clutching her long cashmere cardigan around her.

Orthon pulled a face.

"Of course, I forgot—the only reason you're here is because of your former devoted escort, the wonderful, saint-like Leomido! I'm surprised he isn't here with you," Orthon remarked, narrowing his eyes. "Is he afraid to face his half-brother? Or is he ashamed that he's related to me?"

The Runaways blanched. Orthon obviously didn't know about Leomido's death, and hadn't been taunting them when he'd asked the question at Bigtoe Square while possessing Zelda's body—he'd really wanted to know what had happened to his half-brother! Oksa held her breath, worried about how he might react when they told him the awful news.

"I've always known he couldn't handle the truth," continued Orthon quietly. "What a let-down. For years, he was held up as an example! And now, rather than face up to things, he's hiding like a scared little mouse. How very disappointing."

"Leomido's dead!" broke in Reminiscens, her voice trembling with barely suppressed anger.

The revelation came as a complete shock to Orthon: they saw his face change. His eyes widened and welled with tears, while his features tensed and his face went white. His hands clutched the armrests of the armchair so hard that his knuckles made a cracking noise. He didn't seem to have considered the possibility that things might turn out like this between him and the half-brother he'd always competed against. He shut his eyes to avoid the curious and apprehensive stares. When he reopened them after a few minutes, he studied the face of his twin, who was trying hard to mask her hatred.

"How did it happen?" he whispered hoarsely.

"He couldn't live with the secret," hissed Reminiscens. "He chose death. The Soul-Searcher took him."

Hearing this, Orthon stood up and went over to the fire, without a glance for anyone. Resting his hands against the mantelpiece, he stood there, back bowed, ignoring his dismayed entourage and the Runaways. Outside the wind was gusting violently, banging the shutters and shaking the walls. Since Orthon seemed lost in grief, the Runaways eventually sat down on the many sofas.

Oksa made the most of this lull in the conversation to examine the Felons. Her attention was particularly drawn by two imposing men who radiated intelligence and cruelty. "Agafon and Lukas," she deduced. "Bloodthirsty Werewalls." Although they had to be in their fifties, they were tall, well built and exuded an air of nobility heightened by their abnormally youthful looks. "Nontemporentas," immediately thought Oksa. "Pearls of Longevity!" Both men were wearing Edefia's traditional costume: a kind of dark woollen kimono with embroidered geometric motifs around the collar and cuffs. One of them bowed when Oksa met his glittering eyes and she looked away in confusion. Eventually Orthon returned to his armchair in the middle of the room and the Master of the Felons was once again the centre of attention.

With crossed arms and a murderous expression in her eyes, Reminiscens gazed at her hated twin, who looked so much like her. They came from the same egg, they shared the same cells—how could they have chosen such different paths? They'd loved each other dearly until Ocious had ordered the Beloved Detachment which was to ruin the life of the young woman she'd been and the woman she'd become. Orthon could have halted that shameful crime if he'd wanted to. Did he feel guilty at all? He must have done, before madness had claimed him... in fact, she wouldn't have been surprised to find out that it was one of the grievances he had against Ocious, their father. Subconsciously, he was probably riddled with guilt. Even though she believed that, Reminiscens couldn't bear to watch Orthon strutting around. She couldn't control the wave of bitter rage that washed over her. She rushed into the middle of the room, coming to stand a few inches from her brother, and looked deep into his eyes. The Felons immediately responded threateningly, but Orthon raised his hand to stop them.

"You'd like us to think you miss Leomido, would you?" she raged. "Why have you ruined so many lives? How many people have you killed, Orthon? How many? Do you even know?"

The Felon scornfully tilted his head to one side.

"Oh come on, you know very well that every battle involves losses! Collateral damage, so to speak…"

"And which battle are you talking about exactly?" roared Reminiscens, her hands on her hips. "You mean the petty battle you started to satisfy your pathetic excuse for an ego?"

"How dare you!" yelled Orthon.

His eyes gave off tiny sparks, which crackled ominously.

"You plotted to Impicture me for ever because you were worried I'd thwart your plans," continued Reminiscens. "You killed my son and his wife! YOU KILLED THEM JUST BECAUSE THEY STOOD IN YOUR WAY!"

Shaking with cold fury, she took out her Granok-Shooter. Orthon didn't move.

"You're no match for me," he hissed. "You can hurt or injure me, but you can't kill me."

"Not you, no," replied Reminiscens, white with rage. "But I can kill him!"

Saying that, she fired an Arborescens Granok at Mortimer, Orthon's youngest son. Immediately, everyone abandoned their efforts to maintain some semblance of peace. The Runaways' hearts were overflowing with too much anger and resentment to hold back, while the Felons were too blinded by pride and dreams of glory. The Abominari was the first to attack:

"I spit in your face, you wretched old rat!" it ranted, frothing with rage. "I'll tear your body limb from limb and throw the pieces into the sea for the crabs to feast on!"

"Yeah, yeah," muttered Dragomira, firing a Granok which sealed the creature's mouth.

"Did someone mention spitting?" broke in the Incompetent.

Seizing her opportunity, Oksa bent down and whispered in the lethargic Incompetent's ear. The next moment, the silenced Abominari, which had been rushing at Dragomira with its claws out, had skidded to a halt, astonished at the pain caused by the Incompetent's lethal spittle. Its skin blackened where it had been hit, giving off a stinking, acrid smoke, and the creature fell to the floor. Oksa rubbed her hands gleefully.

"Good job too!" she muttered.

The battle continued to rage in complete chaos. Orthon had decided to attack the Fairyman, his lifelong enemy.

"LOOK OUT, ABAKUM!" yelled Oksa, ever watchful.

Pavel burst into the room just as she was about to launch herself at Orthon, using her body as a cannonball.

"Don't you dare!" ordered her father.

"But Dad—"

"STAY HERE AND DON'T MOVE!" he shouted, dragging her behind a huge sofa.

"What about Mum... did you find her?"

"She's safe in the chapel. Stay here!"

A feeling of indescribable relief washed over Oksa, despite the fraught situation. The Fairyman was dodging countless Granoks, while brandishing the wand he'd inherited from his mother, the Ageless Fairy. A virtually invisible shield appeared over and in front of the Runaways, rendering the Felons' Granoks as harmless as grains of wheat. Exploiting the element of surprise, Pavel launched himself at the wall and began running round the room with remarkable agility. Gregor and Lukas fired lightning bolts at him from their fingertips, but Pavel was too fast. He circled the room once more and, taking a run-up from the back of the room, literally flew at Orthon. With his shins clamped around the Felon's neck in a stranglehold, he began rotating horizontally, causing Orthon to spin uncontrollably. They were so tightly locked together as they whirled in mid-air that no one dared to step in for fear of injuring their own man. Agafon decided it was worth taking the chance, though, and shouted "Orthon! Tornaphyllon!" in warning.

As soon as the Granok hit the pair, Orthon shot away with all his strength to escape the centrifugal effect of the Tornaphyllon. He landed on his feet, glaring defiantly at the Runaways, who could do nothing to help Pavel, who was caught in the vortex created by the Granok. Oksa wrung her hands, horrified at her father's predicament. She glanced desperately at Tugdual, but he was battling with Catarina who was trying to fire Fireballisticos at the Runaways. The room was filled with duels, battles and hand-to-hand combat. Oksa swallowed one of her Ventosa Capacitors and leapt towards the ceiling.

"YA-HAAAA!" she yelled.

The capsule worked its magic and her hands stuck to the ceiling as if held by magnets. She crawled closer to the fierce whirlwind, holding on to the smooth surface with all her might to avoid being swept away. The hungry vortex sucked at her hair and clothes, pulling them horizontally towards it. She unknotted her scarf, which was beginning to strangle her, and watched it disappear.

"Careful, Oksa!" shouted Tugdual, dodging a fresh volley of Granoks fired by Gregor.

Despite the danger, Oksa didn't hesitate. She plunged her arms into the tornado and freed her father by yanking him towards her. They both dropped unceremoniously to the floor.

"Ouch!" groaned Oksa, hunched over.

She might be the Gracious, but she was still human—as her body was reminding her.

"You should have listened to me!" scolded Pavel. "That was a stupid risk to take."

She looked at him, disconcerted. What had he expected her to do? Wait patiently for him to die? Her breathing quickened and her eyes darkened.

"Come now, dear nephew, your daughter simply has a highly developed sense of self-sacrifice."

Oksa stiffened: Orthon had just put his foot on her sore shoulder, the most painful part of her body. Mercilessly, he pressed harder and harder, staring at Pavel challengingly. Then, suddenly, he grabbed Pavel's throat and pushed Oksa down with his foot. She found herself flat on her back, her ribcage crushed by the Felon's heavy foot. Her eyes opened wide as she struggled to breathe. Above her, Orthon was squeezing Pavel's throat, while repelling attacks from Tugdual and Dragomira. "He's unbeatable," thought Oksa miserably. "We're all going to die!" She tried to mobilize her Identego, which she could feel trembling deep inside her. What was it waiting for? Why didn't it reduce Orthon to mincemeat? How did it work? Argh, she felt so helpless…

"ORTHON!" Reminiscens' voice rang out suddenly. "THAT'S ENOUGH!"

They all turned to look at her. She was holding up her Granok-Shooter. A slender filament of Arborescens led from its tip to Mortimer's body. She jerked it through the air as if cracking a whip and a tightly bound Mortimer was lifted from the ground and tossed in all directions. He screamed in pain and fear, unable to stop himself from smacking against the ceiling, walls and floor.

"Let them go!" Reminiscens icily ordered Orthon.

Orthon looked unimpressed.

"Are you sure you really want to go through with this?" challenged Reminiscens. "Are you really prepared to sacrifice your own flesh and blood, when family ties are so important to you?"

She shook her Granok-Shooter even harder and Mortimer screamed more loudly. Orthon blanched as Gregor clenched his fists, beside himself with rage. Behind the Runaways, Zoe was crying quietly. The atmosphere was unbearable. Neither Reminiscens nor Orthon seemed prepared to back down and this battle could easily go on for hours. Mortimer's screams were subsiding as he gradually lost consciousness.

"You wouldn't dare," said Orthon quietly, his voice quivering with fury.

"Are you sure?" replied Reminiscens, swinging her Granok-Shooter down towards the floor so hard that Mortimer's body bounced like a ball. "Perhaps I should take a leaf out of your book, dear brother... perhaps I shouldn't think twice about killing your son like you killed mine."

"Stop it!" said Orthon, ashen-faced.

He gave Pavel a violent shove, sending him crashing to the floor. Then he kicked Oksa away. She jumped to her feet and stood up straight, even though it hurt her to do so. But this was no longer a battle between clans. Reminiscens and Orthon were in a world of their own, bent on settling scores, oblivious to anything else.

"You know very well your son and his wife died in a plane crash," continued Orthon.

"A plane crash you engineered! Please don't demean yourself by playing this game. You destroyed my life by killing my son and, although I very much doubt it will hurt you as much as you hurt me, I'm going to kill yours! Do you hear me? I'M GOING TO KILL MORTIMER!"

A shudder ran through the assembled Felons and Runaways. Reminiscens looked so resolute, so pitiless... The Runaways realized that the frail, gentle old woman who'd wandered for months inside the painting and who'd become their staunchest ally was also the fiercest and most self-sufficient of them all. At that moment, Reminiscens' desire for revenge was blinding her to everything, including the rules by which the Runaways lived. The Felons, on the other hand, were seeing her as a worthy twin sister of their leader and none of them doubted she'd use her powers to do as much damage as possible with maximum cruelty. She looked unshakeable in her determination and even Orthon seemed convinced: the murderous gleam in Reminiscens' eyes left no room for doubt—or hope. She raised her arm again to deliver what would probably be the death blow when Zoe cried out despairingly:

"GRAN, PLEASE DON'T KILL HIM!" Reminiscens seemed to hesitate for a second. Struggling for breath, Oksa gazed at Zoe. Mortimer had been like a brother to her grief-stricken cousin for months and she could never forget the sincere affection he'd shown her. Zoe wrung her hands, unable to stop the choking tears from erupting.

"Don't kill, Mortimer," she sobbed. "Haven't enough people died already?"

"I'm begging you!" broke in a weeping woman, appearing from the back of the room where she'd been keeping out of the way. "Please spare my son. Killing him might avenge the deaths of your loved ones, but nothing will bring them back."

This was too much for Zoe, who hadn't seen her great-aunt Barbara since she'd left the McGraws' house on that awful day in April when her life had been turned upside down—again. Zoe gave a wail which made Reminiscens flinch and then collapsed, her face in her hands.

"Listen to them!" murmured Abakum, his eyes imploring her.

But grief was stronger than reason and, with a raging yet heart-rending sob, Reminiscens brought her arm down with a destructive resolve that nothing and no one could stop.

19

A Slow Return to Reason

THERE WAS A SUDDEN CRASH AND EVERYONE WAS DEAF-
ened and blinded by the shining gold blaze that had appeared in
the middle of the room. Instinctively, they put their forearms over their
eyes to shield them from the dazzling light.

"The Ageless Ones!" exclaimed Oksa, filled with wonder and relief.

Orthon tensed, wide-eyed, staring at the golden halo of light forming
between the Runaways and the Felons. Oksa watched him, surprised
by his amazement. "Of course!" she thought. "He's never seen them
before." A figure appeared in the light, swaying with hypnotic slow-
ness, her long hair floating behind her like seaweed at the bottom of
the sea. She hovered a couple of feet above the floor and gazed long
and hard at the two groups confronting each other. None of them
moved, sure that this strange occurrence would somehow be decisive
for their future. The figure floated closer to Oksa, causing Orthon to
take a step back.

"My respects, Young Gracious."

The Felons stared at Oksa in awed silence at those words, uttered in a
bewitching, crystalline voice. Awed, they lowered their Granok-Shooters
and focused on the Ageless One who'd greeted Oksa with a deference
none of them had yet shown her.

"The time for unity has come," the Ageless Fairy announced. "Edefia,
the World's Heart, is dying."

"What about Ocious?" interrupted Agafon, as Orthon looked on, his face unreadable.

"Ocious has done quite enough," replied the Ageless One curtly. "He and Malorane share the blame for the Great Chaos, which has led to the annihilation of the two worlds. It's up to all of you to act now. If you don't, it's the end of everything."

"What do we have to do?" cried Oksa.

"Find the strength to combine your powers," replied the Ageless One.

Runaways and Felons glared at each other sceptically.

"Nothing can ever bring us back together," objected Pavel.

"If you don't join forces, the two worlds cannot survive."

There was a heavy silence, followed by a clamour of voices in both camps.

"We can't combine forces!"

"It's preposterous!"

"Out of the question!"

"Perhaps things aren't as serious as they say," rang out Mercedica's voice.

The din was interrupted by a sudden crackle: the glowing aura around the Ageless One visibly darkened and showed cataclysmic images from all over the world. The room was filled with the sound of reporters speaking different languages, as if countless television sets had been switched on. They listened to the news reports, even though the images were enough to show the scale of the disaster on the Outside. Volcanoes were erupting one after the other, quakes were shaking the earth, tidal waves were submerging the coastline, torrential rain was flooding the land and fires were raging through cities and forests. Everywhere endless queues of people were frantically trying to escape with a strength born of hope, but it was futile because everywhere was in chaos.

"The two worlds are dying faster than any of us could have predicted," announced the Ageless One. "The equilibrium of the World's Heart, protected by the Cloak Chamber, suffered irreparable damage from the revelation of the Secret-Never-To-Be-Told. Afterwards, order was maintained after a fashion, but we're now slipping towards chaos. The wounds are deep indeed, but equilibrium may yet be restored. This recovery will entail joining forces and making compromises and sacrifices which may seem intolerable but which are essential. The future of the two worlds depends on you. ALL OF YOU."

She suddenly turned to Dragomira and wreathed her in golden coils.

"The Portal will soon appear," she declared, in a whisper that only those nearest to her could overhear. "Your Lunatrix will guide you because he is the Guardian of the Definitive Landmark. Be ready, Dragomira, because you are and remain a Gracious and, as such, you hold within your heart a fragment of the declining equilibrium."

The coils of light surrounding Dragomira continued to murmur, although she appeared to be the only one who could understand what they were saying now, then the golden light winked out, taking the figure with it.

※

The Felons and Runaways were left feeling equally stunned and dismayed. Supported by Abakum and Pavel, Dragomira was white. She looked devastated and tears welled in her large blue eyes.

"I think it's time we talked..." she croaked.

She sank down onto the nearest chair and the members of both groups hastily followed suit. Reminiscens kept her precious Granok-Shooter in her hand, still attached to Mortimer's motionless body on the floor. Reluctantly, Orthon also sat down.

"We have to face facts," began Dragomira. "Our differences are irreconcilable, but we need each other to restore the equilibrium. If we don't, then we'll all die, on the Outside and on the Inside. Is that what we want?"

There was an overwhelming silence. Everyone felt the same, despite their personal ambitions.

"Orthon, we each possess part of the answer that will allow us to enter Edefia. You have my mother's medallion."

"*Our* mother's medallion," corrected the Felon.

"Yes, that's right," continued Dragomira, narrowing her eyes. "You have *our* mother's medallion with the incantation that will allow us to open the Portal. The Portal is somewhere out there in the world, but no one knows exactly where. My loyal Lunatrix, the Guardian of the Definitive Landmark, is the only one who can tell us. So you have the key, but you don't know where the Portal is. I can find out the location of the Portal, but I don't have the key."

Orthon frowned, deep in thought. He seemed to be finding it harder and harder to decide as the seconds slowly ticked by—which some people found infuriating...

"Why don't you tell your friends why you're so desperate to return to Edefia?" said Reminiscens suddenly. "You who follow him so blindly, do you actually know?"

"No, Reminiscens," pleaded Abakum quietly. "Don't do this, I'm begging you."

The Fairyman seemed worried about the possible outcome of this conversation. The matters raised by Reminiscens were so serious and so private... Orthon's face tensed and a vicious, murderous gleam appeared in his eyes. The Felon seemed to be struggling not to destroy everything around him.

"You're hoping our father will love you at last, aren't you?" continued Reminiscens caustically. "Have you lost your mind? He's never loved anybody but himself. Himself and power. And what you've become won't change anything. You've done it all for nothing, poor Orthon!"

"Stop it, Reminiscens!" ordered Abakum, with a surprising air of authority. "This isn't the time," he added more quietly. "The reasons our enemies are doing what they are doing don't matter. What's important now is to join forces. We're running out of time."

And, as if to remind them, violent gusts of wind shook the walls of the house. A draught swirled in the chimney and stirred up clouds of glowing embers in the fireplace while outside the torrential rain seemed to have turned to heavy hail. The whole house creaked, lashed by the full fury of the elements, and they could hear tiles smashing to the ground. Suddenly the island was rocked by a tremor which seemed to come from the bowels of the Earth. The floor and the walls gave a terrible groan, as objects and paintings fell down around the occupants of the living room. They clung to each other, wide-eyed with terror. The tremor stopped just as suddenly as it had started, leaving wide cracks in the walls. Everyone was afraid, and even Orthon looked shaken. He took a deep breath, his steely gaze fixed on his twin. Then Reminiscens gently raised her Granok-Shooter. Mortimer's motionless body rose into the air, carried by the Arborescens. The old woman skilfully guided him to Barbara and placed her son in front of her. Orthon shot her one last unreadable look—it was impossible to tell whether the fire in his eyes was fuelled by resentment or gratitude. With Barbara at his side, the Felon picked up his son and headed for the hall.

"Wait, Orthon!" suddenly rang out a voice. "We need some help too."

Orthon turned round, as did all the Felons and the Runaways: drenched from head to toe, with the little Lunatrix at her side, Jeanne Bellanger was standing in the doorway of the living room.

"GUS!" exclaimed Oksa at the sight of her lifeless friend slumped in his mother's arms.

His black hair hung down, revealing the deathly pallor of his face. Abakum hurried over to help Jeanne. He pushed back one of Gus's eyelids and his face darkened. He turned to Orthon, who was looking quizzically at his potent adversary.

"The antidote," said Abakum simply.

That word and Gus's face distorted by pain were enough. The Felon's lips curved into a cruel and triumphant smile.

"With pleasure," he murmured sweetly.

20

THE ANTIDOTE

ORTHON AND HIS CLOSE ENTOURAGE—LUKAS, AGAFON, Gregor, Mercedica and Barbara—strode out into the huge gloomy hall, followed by Abakum, Gus's parents, Dragomira, Naftali, Pavel and Oksa. When Reminiscens slowly made a move to follow them, Orthon thundered:

"*She* stays here! I don't want *her* anywhere near me!"

"You'd better wait for us here, Reminiscens," said Dragomira softly. "Keep an eye on our friends, we're counting on you."

Reminiscens nodded and the small group filed out after the Felons.

Finding the hall too gloomy for her liking, Dragomira lost no time in using her Granok-Shooter to produce a Polypharus, whose glowing tentacles filled the lofty space with light.

"An eleven-tentacled Polypharus!" remarked Orthon with a whistle of admiration. "I didn't know you had one of those, dear sister."

"There are a lot of things you don't know about me," retorted Dragomira.

With a nervous snigger Orthon walked over to the elaborate wrought-iron railings of the staircase. Pressing his palm against a motif depicting a solar eclipse, he turned his wrist and the small door in the stairwell, mentioned earlier by the Tumble-Bawler, swung open to reveal another staircase illuminated by oil lamps. Orthon walked in and they all followed him in silence. The door closed again slowly, leaving just enough time for Tugdual and Zoe to slip inside behind them.

"What are you doing here?" whispered Oksa, when she noticed them. "This is really dangerous!"

"Surely you didn't think we'd let you come in here without us, did you, Lil' Gracious?" replied Tugdual, holding the baby Lunatrix in his arms.

Oksa raised her eyes heavenwards then looked away so that her two friends didn't realize how glad she was that they were there.

"Come on, let's find out what's hidden in the Felons' lair," murmured Tugdual, leading the way.

After walking down several flights of stairs, the two clans came to a wide corridor, lined with about ten doors, which seemed to lead into the depths of the island. The lights on the sandstone walls flickered and it was so stuffy that they struggled to catch their breath. However, just after the visitors appeared, a huge wall-mounted fan started up at the end of the corridor, bringing in salty sea air which immediately made it easier to breathe.

"In here!" ordered Orthon, pushing open one of the doors.

Everyone flocked in behind him and the door closed with the clatter of invisible locks. Looking around, the Runaways discovered they were in what seemed to be a giant laboratory. In pride of place in the middle of the room was an enormous still like Dragomira's and the walls were lined with shelves of bottles, test tubes, flasks and demijohns of all shapes and sizes. Crates overflowing with rocks and crystals were stacked in the gloom at the back of the room. Orthon set his son down on a camp bed and rummaged around in a large cupboard, throwing half its contents on the floor. He took out a small bottle filled with golden-brown liquid. Looking curious, Dragomira came closer.

"It's a brew of my own making," said Orthon, answering her unspoken question. "Spring water from Yellowstone National Park in which I've soaked malachite to absorb pain, a sliver of Madagascan labradorite to combat tiredness and a fragment of Saragossan aragonite to mend broken bones. Plus another key ingredient, but you'll forgive me if I keep the nature of that a secret…"

Saying this, he leant down and poured a few drops into Mortimer's half-open mouth. A few seconds later, Mortimer raised his head and looked around with wide eyes. When he saw Dragomira and Pavel, he recoiled and curled up in a ball on his bed. Barbara immediately put her arms around him reassuringly. He groaned in pain.

"A few more drops," said Orthon, holding out the little bottle.

Mortimer drank obediently, his eyes fixed on Zoe, then stretched with the obvious satisfaction of someone who's regained their former strength and vigour. He jumped up from the bed with feline grace, his face still badly bruised, surprising the Runaways with his speedy recovery.

"Stones have fascinating powers, don't they?" said Orthon.

"As do plants," replied Dragomira, irritated by his smug expression.

"If that's the case, dear sister, why don't you cure that poor lad yourself?" he said sarcastically, looking at Gus.

Although she was dumbfounded by his arrogance, Dragomira managed to restrain herself.

"Gus's condition is your fault," she said, as neutrally as possible, "and we know you have an antidote. You heard the Ageless Fairy: we're running out of time, so why on earth would I waste valuable hours concocting a remedy you already possess? And, just in case you're tempted to resort to blackmail, remember that you'd permanently endanger the future of the two worlds and, by extension, your own."

"Oh Dragomira, my dear Dragomira," sighed Orthon. "Impatience is making you foolish. How could you think I'd be so irresponsible?"

"How indeed," remarked Dragomira.

She bent over Gus, who was lying on another camp bed. His parents and Abakum had sat down on stools nearby. Jeanne was holding his hand and gazing fixedly at him, while the baby Lunatrix had climbed onto the bed and had curled up next to him.

"Would you care to tell us what's happening to him?" asked Dragomira, swallowing her choking anger.

"It's very simple," replied Orthon, sounding nauseatingly gleeful. "The poison from my pet Chiropterans is spreading through his veins. Their venom makes the body particularly receptive to all ultrasonic and infrasonic sounds produced by man, nature or machine. It's pretty formidable, I have to admit—it inspired the CIA to perfect a new generation of lethal weapons. Your little protégé is in so much pain that he preferred to lose consciousness."

"*Preferred*?" shouted Pierre, glaring daggers at Orthon.

"Give him the antidote!" ordered Dragomira. "Right now!"

Orthon sniggered evilly.

"Everything is so black and white with you, my dear sister! Do you really think I'd have created such a simplistic process? Not a chance... your young protégé is sliding inexorably towards death."

"NO!" screamed Oksa.

Jeanne buried her face in her hands and dissolved into tears, while Pierre crumpled in despair.

"Yes!" continued Orthon, relishing the effect he was having on them. "Unless, of course, I deign to do something..."

"You promised!" broke in Oksa furiously.

"I did, which is why I'm letting you choose between two solutions."

"You're so magnanimous," hissed Pavel.

"The first solution is for your protégé to continue to suffer throughout adolescence, alternating between periods of unconsciousness and unbearable pain. After reaching puberty, he'll die."

"You call that a *solution*?" snapped Dragomira.

"The second solution is for your protégé to be given a blood transfusion to allow his metabolism to assimilate the antidote. This antidote will allow him to avoid puberty, which is when the poison reaches its maximum effectiveness. That's a much better outcome, isn't it?"

The Runaways were speechless. They weren't sure how this second solution worked or what the possible implications were.

"I sense you're dubious," continued Orthon, more confident than ever. "What I'm suggesting is nothing less than a simple choice between life and death!"

"You're crazy," said Dragomira.

"Knowing you, I suppose the generous blood donor would have to be a Werewall," remarked Abakum hoarsely.

Orthon turned to him with narrowed eyes.

"There's nothing wrong with your powers of deduction, I see," he said, congratulating the old man mockingly.

"So it was true…" murmured Abakum.

"What was true, Abakum?" Oksa couldn't help asking.

21

A Shameful Pay-off

THE FAIRYMAN TORE HIS GAZE AWAY FROM ORTHON AND turned to Oksa and the Runaways.

"There were rumours in Edefia that the Werewalls had perfected a terrible weapon to force leading scientists to join their Secret Society. It was much more sophisticated than hostage-taking and involved targeting their poor children, who were bitten by a Chiropteran. The venom spread through their bodies, but remained inactive until they hit adolescence. The pain then grew so bad that the inevitable outcome was death. However, the Werewalls had a secret antidote which temporarily speeded up the ageing process during puberty, ensuring that the infected child would miss their teenage years and thereby avoid all that pointless suffering. However, there was an extortionate price to pay: both the parents and their children had to become Werewalls which, as you all know, had serious consequences."

"Come now, there are many advantages to being a Werewall," said Orthon quietly.

"Indeed," agreed Abakum bitterly, "but at what cost? Handing over other people's love to the Diaphans. That hideous sacrifice was the worst scandal ever to hit Edefia."

The Fairyman turned back to his friends:

"For years, the Werewalls coerced scientists into joining them by holding the power of life or death over their children."

"That's repulsive," muttered Dragomira.

"Why does Gus have to be given a Werewall's blood?" whispered Oksa.

"Because the antidote only works on Werewalls, little fool!" mocked Orthon.

"Why would you do that, Orthon? Why would you create something so vile?" asked Dragomira, her hand pressed to her heart.

"Adolescence is hardly the most enjoyable time in a person's life," replied the Felon coldly. "It's a period of humiliation and degradation."

"Not everyone feels that way!" retorted Abakum. "You might have been unhappy, but your own hang-ups can't justify such barbaric behaviour. Anyway, you didn't invent that nauseating process as you claim—your ancestor Temistocles did. All you're doing is exploiting your ancestor's invention with unnatural zeal."

The Felon's face set in an expression of annoyance as Abakum's barb hit home.

"Whatever the case, I'm the only one who has the antidote to save your protégé!" he sneered nastily. "I'm the only chance you've got."

Pierre and Jeanne looked imploringly at Abakum and Dragomira, silently pleading with them not to provoke Orthon further. Gus's life was in his hands and everyone sensed that things could very easily take a turn for the worse.

"If you prefer, there is a third solution," continued Orthon in a hard voice. "There are two draughts of the antidote: I have one here, in this room, and one is locked in a safe in the crystal cave where I used to live with my father in the Peak Ridge mountains. So if you can't bear to accept my help, then bring the boy to Edefia and give him the second infusion there. You should be aware, though, that he'll still have to have the transfusion of Werewall blood and he'll have to survive the agony caused by my Chiropterans. After all, he's just an Outsider, so he doesn't have our strong constitution."

He sniggered mockingly.

"Let's stop wasting time!" broke in Pierre icily. "If I understand you correctly, a Werewall has to donate his blood to Gus so that he can absorb the antidote. That will stop the pain but, in exchange, Gus will age a couple of years."

"Two or three at the most," agreed Orthon, with an airy wave of his bony hand.

"But how can an Outsider become a Werewall?" asked Oksa incredulously.

Orthon's face lit up with a treacherous smile.

"That's my brilliant great-niece!" he exclaimed. "An Outsider, like an Insider, can only become a Werewall after drinking the Werewall Elixir."

"That vile concoction made from Diaphan snot?" Oksa couldn't help exclaiming.

Orthon looked at her in amazement, then nodded grimly.

"I don't know where you get your information, but you're right. Blood won't be enough for the boy. It will keep him in remission until the elixir consolidates his new 'constitution.'"

"You're bluffing!" raged Naftali. "Blood is enough!"

"What do you know about any of this?" asked Orthon, looking him up and down.

"I never had to drink that diabolical elixir to become a Werewall," said the towering Swede. "I inherited the gene from my mother's blood when she was pregnant with me."

Orthon gave a sudden cackle of laughter, which echoed sinisterly around the locked room.

"Poor Naftali," he sighed. "Your mother was an excellent chemist, but so weak-minded… you'd certainly have been a Werewall by blood if she'd been one before she was pregnant! Didn't she ever tell you that you were born long before she became a Werewall? Didn't you know you were just a Firmhand when you were born? It was your mother who gave you the elixir that would turn you permanently into a Werewall. At my father's kind suggestion, of course…"

Naftali blanched and staggered with the shock. Abakum put an arm around his shoulder for moral support.

"She found it so hard to come to terms with her weakness," continued Orthon ironically. "And she had so many scruples, so much guilt! She didn't give him any choice."

"You mean Ocious threatened my mother?" spluttered Naftali. "He forced her to join the Werewalls?"

"Yes, and it's thanks to him that you're a man of rare strength! You should be grateful to him instead of looking so disgusted."

This was all too much for Naftali to take on board. The proud, sturdy Swede slumped, devastated.

"None of that matters now," Abakum murmured to his shocked friend.

"Anyway, my dear Naftali, coming back to your earlier remark, blood is certainly vital, but your protégé needs more than that if he's to become a Werewall. He'll only be safe after he drinks the Werewall Elixir."

"So what are you waiting for?" shouted Oksa, losing her temper.

Orthon raised his eyes heavenwards, before fixing her with an exasperated yet gleeful stare.

"Has anyone seen a Diaphan around here?" he asked the assembled Felons. "And does anyone by any chance have a fragment of Luminescent Stone from the Peak Ridge mountains which we could use to make the elixir?"

The Felons shook their heads.

"Our Young Gracious, who seems to know such a lot about the Werewall Elixir, will surely able to confirm it: no Luminescent Stone and no Diaphan, means no elixir. Isn't that right, Young Gracious?"

"Gus will only be out of danger once he's drunk that vile potion," said Oksa quietly, her heart pounding as she followed the argument to its logical conclusion. "Or rather once someone has sacrificed every last ounce of romantic love and fed it to a Diaphan…"

Orthon's eyes filled with ancient cruelty as they bored into her, then he gave a derisive hoot of laughter.

22

CONTROVERSIAL HELP

T HE RUNAWAYS TRIED TO THINK THINGS THROUGH AS dispassionately as possible. They looked anxiously at Gus, whose waxy complexion gave his face the appearance of a death mask as he lay on his camp bed. Ignored by the adults, Zoe wrung her hands in despair. Oksa was compulsively biting her nails, unable to stop her whole body from shaking.

"We have to say yes," she stammered.

Gus's parents exchanged a few words with Dragomira and Abakum, and their decision had a ring of finality about it.

"We agree," announced Abakum stiffly. "On one condition: that one of us—a Werewall Runaway—is the blood donor."

Orthon tilted his head to one side, looking surprised and amused.

"Do you think you're in a position to negotiate?" he growled. A heart-rending cry cut through the talk: Gus had just regained consciousness. He was writhing in pain on the narrow bed, his face contorted and his body bucking, as he was attacked by the venom. His parents were doing their best to stop him from getting up, but his strength seemed to have increased tenfold. He leapt to his feet and savagely scratched Jeanne's hand. He was behaving so aggressively that they all stepped back, concerned that Gus's condition was making him uncontrollable. Abakum was the only one who dared to approach him: unafraid of being scratched or bitten, he seized him securely by the waist and murmured a mysterious string of words in his ear, watched appreciatively by Orthon.

"Nicely done," remarked the Felon, pretending to clap slowly.

In the Fairyman's arms, Gus was struggling less frantically. His eyes, wide with terror and pain, rested for a fraction of a second on Oksa, who reeled as though she'd been struck by lightning.

"I volunteer!" suddenly exclaimed Tugdual, coming forward with his sleeves rolled up.

Dragomira went over to him and put her hands on his shoulders.

"It's very generous of you, lad, but I think it might be better if we chose someone whose blood is as close as possible… to its origins."

Tugdual's face darkened with disappointment.

"Thank you from the bottom of my heart, Tugdual," Pierre added. "We're so touched by your offer. However, Dragomira is right: Gus is an Outsider and we must give him the best chance we can."

"Haven't you realized yet that you're not good enough for *them*?" Orthon said to Tugdual. "Join me and you'll receive the recognition you deserve. There's still time!"

Tugdual hunched down into his black scarf and gazed at him, looking wounded and upset. Even though Tugdual had already proved his loyalty, Oksa was afraid that he'd give in to temptation. Why did she doubt him? She was ashamed of herself for thinking such thoughts. If anyone was disloyal, it was her, not Tugdual.

"We love Tugdual much more than he realizes and not just because of his invaluable powers," retorted Dragomira, much to Tugdual's great surprise.

"I'll go and get Reminiscens!" cut in Naftali.

"You refuse my help, yet ask for hers?" exclaimed Orthon. "That's ridiculous! Perhaps you've forgotten that exactly the same blood runs through our veins—mine's just as good as hers."

"Yes, but what's inside your heart isn't!" replied the Swede. "Open the door, Orthon."

Frostily, the Felon complied, without moving an inch. He merely rotated the tip of his index finger and the bolts began unlocking with a sudden clatter. The door swung open onto the stone corridor and Naftali disappeared to the sound of Gus's muffled cries.

⁂

A few minutes later, Reminiscens stalked into the large room. Without a glance at the Felons she hurried over to Gus, who was unconscious again. Tenderly she kissed his forehead and stroked his cheek. Then she rolled up her sleeve to bare her forearm and clenched her fist to make the bluish veins stand out. She pulled a dagger from the inside pocket of her jacket and was about to make an incision in her wrist when Orthon stopped her with a mocking laugh.

"Come now, dear sister, there's no need for antiquated weaponry—this is the twenty-first century, after all!"

Stung, Reminiscens looked up at her hated brother, who was wheeling over a stand hung with all the medical equipment necessary for transfusions.

"Don't touch me," she said in a low, threatening voice. Orthon stopped short.

"You're not making much of an effort, are you?" he remarked. "Annikki!" he shouted into the corridor. "Someone get Annikki!"

The young fair-haired woman arrived a few seconds later, visibly awed by the number of important people in the room. She deferentially suggested that Reminiscens lie down on a bench, then inserted a needle attached to a plastic pouch into her arm. The blood quickly filled the pouch, allowing Annikki to proceed with the transfusion. So, with a catheter in his forearm, lying there in deathly silence, Gus received blood from a woman descended from the legendary Temistocles—as well as a Gracious on her mother's side and a Werewall on her father's—a blend of dark and light representing everything that was most deadly and most powerful about Edefia.

23

FROM BAD TO WORSE

AFTER WATCHING OVER GUS'S LIVID BODY FOR HOURS, Oksa had fallen into a fitful sleep filled with bad dreams that left little room for hope. The last dream, more violent than the others, woke her. Feeling dazed, she shook her head to banish images of Gus transformed into a belligerent crow that had raked her face with its talons then swiftly taken flight towards the light of a strange horizon. She felt uncomfortable and realized with a sigh that she was starving. How long had it been since she'd eaten? Her stomach growled and she flinched, mortified. How could she think about *food* when Gus was in such a bad way just a few feet from her?

She looked round; she was alone in this small alcove with Tugdual and Zoe, who were asleep. Farther off, in the spacious laboratory, the adults were also resting. The young Lunatrix was curled up against Gus, snoring with his face buried in the hollow of Gus's neck.

"How cute that little creature is," thought Oksa, stretching out her hand to stroke him. Her eyes strayed to Tugdual. His lean body was stretched out with his legs crossed and his face, unguarded in sleep, wore a troubled expression Oksa didn't recognize. She watched him for a moment, ashamed of taking advantage of the situation, but unable to resist.

Gus groaned softly and swatted away an imaginary insect with his hand. Oksa sat up, then slumped back in her chair. False alarm... Gus seemed to be on the road to recovery—his face wasn't so tense and he was breathing more easily, but who knew what this abnormal transfusion might do to him. Oksa looked at the slowly dripping blood, then at Gus's inert body. He was her best friend and nothing would ever change that. The chimes from the big clock in the living room echoed through the house, like a sinister death knell. Six o'clock in the morning. It would soon be light. And by the end of this new day which had only just dawned, Gus would no longer be the same. He was bound to be a few inches taller and broader. His face would be squarer, his jaw stronger, and he'd look older. Would he have the confidence of a sixteen- or seventeen-year-old? Would he find it difficult being physically more mature when he still had the mind of a younger boy? Would it affect their relationship? WOULD SHE STILL LOVE HIM AS MUCH? As if she could read her mind, Zoe murmured:

"All that matters is that he survives this ordeal."

Oksa gave a start at these words, embarrassed that she hadn't realized she was being watched. Gus's survival was more important than anything, and here she was worrying that Gus might be two or three years older than her!

"What a waste of space," she muttered. "A useless waste of space."

She took a deep breath and looked at Zoe. Her friend was ashen-faced, with red eyes and lips white with worry. She seemed the worst affected of all the Runaways. She'd had to deal with so many shocks these past few months—and her reunion with Mortimer hadn't helped.

"He's changed a lot, hasn't he?" said Oksa, in a bid to start a conversation.

"Who?"

Zoe hunched down in her armchair and didn't seem keen to talk about this.

"Mortimer," pressed Oksa. "He doesn't look the same at all."

Zoe sighed. What Oksa didn't know, and what no one could suspect, was that she was eaten up inside with grief and confusion. She gazed at her friend, torn between wanting to confide in someone and her natural reticence. Oksa looked at her encouragingly—talking could be such a relief.

"I thought she was going to kill him," began Zoe in a barely audible murmur. "I was so frightened, Oksa... I realized that I don't know my gran very well and it was terrifying to see her capable of something like that."

"She's been so badly hurt," said Oksa, a lump in her throat.

"That's no excuse," objected Zoe, her voice breaking. "She was so desperate for revenge, she was so much like Orthon... I was shocked to find that out—it's tearing me apart."

Oksa watched her helplessly, as Zoe took a deep breath.

"It's like being trapped inside a vicious circle that intensifies and spreads the effects of evil. My father was killed by Orthon. It was unbearable finding that out. But it was worse for my gran. Her only son was killed by her twin brother! Her only son! And I only found out today, when she's had to live with it for months. Why did he do it, Oksa? Why did Orthon kill my dad?"

Zoe buried her face in her hands. Oksa watched her, unable to move or say anything. She didn't know how to answer that question and nor would anyone else. She could sense how deeply wounded Zoe was and she could do nothing to help. Absolutely nothing. Nevertheless, she got up and urged her cousin to make room for her. Rummaging around in the bag she wore across her shoulder, she slipped a small pouch tied with a leather thong into Zoe's hand. It was Oksa's talisman, which was supposed to chase the clouds from the sky. Zoe leant her head on Oksa's shoulder and wiped her eyes with the back of her sleeve.

"Thank you," she whispered.

Oksa smiled at her tentatively. The clouds in Zoe's sky were so much darker than hers...

"I do think Mortimer's changed," continued Zoe.

"He looks rather tense," added Oksa. "I thought he wanted to go to you, but didn't dare."

Zoe didn't reply, thinking back to the last time she'd seen him, in Hyde Park. That meeting had at least clarified things: they'd each chosen their side.

"He hasn't taken his eyes off you," continued Oksa.

Wearily, Zoe leant back in the chair. No, Mortimer hadn't taken his eyes off her, and what she'd seen had upset her—they'd been filled with resentment, fuelled by his disappointment at her rebuff. And sadness. Or had it been pity? If only she could lock and bar her heart so that nothing bad could get in. Some hope! But as she'd said to Oksa, all that mattered was that Gus survived. She loved him so much… and Gus was in love with Oksa.

❈

"The transfusion is finished," whispered Annikki suddenly, coming over.

She carefully removed the catheter from Gus's arm. He'd been so still during the procedure that they'd all assumed he was unconscious, so it was a huge surprise when he jerked bolt upright, eyes wide and pupils dilated. Annikki gave a scream and backed away, while Oksa and Zoe jumped to their feet.

"How do you feel?" cried Oksa, her heart thumping.

Gus looked at her wildly.

"Odd," he said, sounding confused. "What happened?" he added, seeing Annikki wheeling the transfusion equipment away.

But there was no time to explain anything to him, as his body was wracked by another violent convulsion of pain. He arched his back and gave a blood-curdling scream. Oksa rushed over and sat down on the edge of his bed.

"Oksa…" moaned Gus, grimacing at the relentless pain inflicted by the venom.

"Everything will be OK, you'll see," she said, her cheeks shining with tears. "We'll make you better."

"Why are you crying then?" he asked, doubled over by another agonizing spasm. "AND WHY DOES IT HURT SO MUCH?" he yelled.

Suddenly, unexpectedly, he grabbed Oksa's hand and bit down hard on her wrist. Oksa shrieked. Tugdual threw himself on Gus to immobilize him as the Runaways and Felons rushed into the alcove, terrified by Oksa's screams. Pavel lifted Oksa from where she was sitting by the camp bed, paralysed by shock, and carried her away. Her heart was racing with fear at the indescribable pain shooting up her arm and bewilderment at Gus's actions.

"Why did you do that, Gus?" she gasped. "I've never hurt you."

Everyone was in a panic—even the Felons couldn't hide their concern. The Young Gracious had been bitten by Gus, who was undergoing drastic cellular change and had huge quantities of Chiropteran venom in his system. The consequences could be fatal, as everyone realized. Filled with shame and anger, Gus was struggling, held firmly by Pierre and Abakum.

"I don't know what happened! I didn't mean it!" he yelled. "Oksa! OKSA! Forgive me!"

His head suddenly drooped and he crumpled into unconsciousness. At the back of the room a white-faced Tugdual put down his Granok-Shooter, watched in horror by Zoe, who looked a shadow of her former self.

24

DEADLY SOUND WAVES

"WHAT HAVE YOU DONE?" GASPED ZOE. "YOU'VE killed—you've killed Gus!"

Tugdual stared at her, devastated. With surprising gentleness, he tilted her head up to look at him.

"Gus is one of us," he said quietly. "I'd never hurt him. I just hit him with a Dozident Granok, to protect Oksa and to protect him from himself. You ought to have more faith in me, Zoe. I'll never be on their side," he added, glancing at the Felons.

Zoe felt icy cold. Contrary to appearances, Tugdual was much more loyal to the Runaways than she was. Had he ever been tempted? If he had, he'd never given the slightest sign of it… As if to confirm her thoughts, he murmured almost inaudibly:

"You made the right choice, you know—they'd only have used you."

With a solemn look filled with understanding, he led her over to Oksa.

Surrounded by the Runaways, Oksa was in worse pain than she'd ever have believed possible. The agony was invading her limbs and increasing with every passing second. The shock waves caused by every breath she took—every thump of her own heart, her friends' heartbeats, the ebb and flow of the sea around the island, the wingbeats of the gulls wheeling in the sky—were wreaking havoc inside her body. If she'd been strong enough to find words to describe the torture she was enduring, she'd have said that it felt as if burning acid were eating away at her brain, her lungs and every blood vessel. She put her hands over her ears to try to lessen the deadly sound waves, but to no avail: nothing blocked these infrasonic frequencies. They were spreading through her body and wouldn't stop until they killed her. Unable to hide their concern, the Felons milled around the Runaways. Orthon pushed his way through his entourage to get to Oksa, but was stopped by Dragomira and Reminiscens.

"Are you proud of the consequences of your criminal behaviour?" spat Dragomira, trembling.

Orthon flinched, his face tense with unfeigned anxiety.

"My trial will have to wait, I think," he hissed frostily, "as we seem to have a *little* emergency on our hands, wouldn't you agree? It isn't just your young protégé who needs the antidote now," he added, his eyes sliding towards Oksa, who was moaning and holding her head.

He waved a bottle in front of his two sisters, lightly pushing them out of his way. The Runaways had no choice but to let him through.

"Annikki, pass me a pipette!" he ordered. "And go and get the transfusion equipment."

Annikki obeyed immediately. A few seconds later Orthon was trickling the precious antidote between Gus's bluish lips, watched tensely by the members of both clans.

"What happens now?" asked Dragomira gravely.

Orthon waved one hand at the transfusion stand which Annikki was feverishly setting up and the other at Oksa, who was shaking with pain in her father's arms. Looking horrified, they all realized what had to be done.

"Is there no other way?" whispered Pavel, sounding broken-hearted.

Sadly, Dragomira looked at him, shaking her head. The silence was thick enough to cut with a knife. When Orthon rolled up his sleeve, though, Reminiscens sprang up with a cry.

"In your dreams, Orthon! Oksa is not going to become a Werewall with your blood!"

Orthon stopped abruptly. His eyes narrowed like a wild beast about to pounce and he puffed out his chest, seething with resentment.

"You've already donated a lot of blood," he remarked, "the transfusion has weakened you—it could kill you to give any more."

Alarmed, the Runaways looked at Reminiscens with justifiable concern. Fatigue and worry had turned her skin grey, as if her face had been smeared with ash. There were dark circles under her eyes and her straight-backed, slender figure was bowed. With superhuman effort, she straightened and declared firmly:

"I'd rather die than let Oksa receive blood from that monster!"

Shocked by these words, Zoe moaned quietly. She obviously didn't count—even her grandmother couldn't wait to abandon her. Her life was a nightmare.

"If that's what my dear sister has decided, who am I to stand in her way?" spat Orthon, looking tight-lipped. "Annikki, please do the honours."

Annikki concentrated on getting the transfusion equipment ready. A great deal depended on this fresh procedure.

"It will take a few hours for the antidote to work," announced Orthon. "Oksa and your protégé will be safe for the time being. They'll just have changed a little…"

He stumbled slightly as he delivered this last piece of information.

"Will it hurt?" asked Pavel, his voice trembling with hatred.

"Yes and no. The antidote eliminates the effects of the venom by erecting a barrier against sound waves and infrasonic frequencies, but the accelerated growth rate may be physically painful and might also cause certain emotional problems."

"Certain *problems*?" thundered Pierre. Orthon shot him a treacherous glance.

"You can't suddenly age a few years and not experience a certain amount of confusion."

"Can we please get on with it!" broke in Pavel. "There's no time for delay."

They all turned to look at him. Oksa was hanging limply in his arms, frighteningly comatose.

25

ACCELERATED GROWTH

WHEN OKSA SURFACED FROM THE DEPTHS OF UNCONsciousness, she became aware of an amazing sense of well-being. She clearly remembered her last few seconds of agonizing lucidity and the unbearable pain which had sapped her will to do anything, even survive. Was she dead? Had Gus's bite killed her? She was curled up in a ball and her body felt light, as if floating weightlessly. Her chest was rising and falling steadily with each breath she took and she could even hear her stomach gurgling! "I'm alive!" she thought joyfully. But where was she? All she could remember was the sight of Annikki sticking a needle into Reminiscens' thin arm and her father's sad, worried eyes. Although the pain had gone, the memory of it was still very much alive, lurking ominously in the background. She didn't feel afraid, though. She should have been shaking with dread, but she felt calm, confident and at peace.

In this tranquil mood, she ventured to open her eyes. The warm, shimmering mist around her didn't obscure the nearby walls of her refuge. She stretched out her hand, confirming her initial impression: her fingers were touching the inside skin of the comforting bubble-like Nascentia. The thin, veined membrane made from the placenta of twin Lunatrixes was pulsing gently like a peaceful heart, infusing Oksa with strength and encouragement, just as it had done a few months ago when she was in shock after being attacked in the science lab at St Proximus. Listening carefully, Oksa could make out some familiar sounds, as well as the voices of the Runaways. Orthon too… Although wide-awake, she wasn't ready to emerge yet. Particularly as she could feel someone else breathing against her back, another heartbeat. She twisted her body round and changed position. The Nascentia rocked and she heard cries of relief outside.

Once she was facing the other way, she found herself looking at a familiar back and head of jet-black hair. Gus! Gus was in the Nascentia with her. Of course! They'd both received the same treatment. They were in the same boat. Or almost. In principle, Outsiders' blood was compatible with Insiders' blood, but it was impossible to be sure. Oksa anxiously studied what she could see of her friend. "Calm down, Oksa," she thought reassuringly. "He's alive. We're both alive. Nothing else matters." She examined him further: Gus's hair had grown and the hand supporting his head was longer. His shoulders looked broader and the fabric of his shirt was stretched to bursting. She had to admit that her clothes felt a lot tighter too… "Yikes," she thought, hardly daring to think about the physical changes she must have undergone too.

"Gus?" she murmured. "Gus? Can you hear me?"

She stiffened when she heard her own voice, which sounded richer and more mature, and her heart began to race. The slow, steady pulsing of the Nascentia immediately became more noticeable, radiating reassurance. With the active help of her Curbita-Flatulo, Oksa grew calmer and the fear was replaced by a stoical resignation. When Gus turned round, though, it was still a shock. The two friends gazed at each other open-mouthed with amazement.

"Wow…" they chorused tremulously.

Gus's voice was soft and deep, but this was nothing compared to the other changes. His cheekbones were more prominent and the contours of his face looked firmer and stronger. Although his jawline was still delicate, his chin was squarer and dotted with faint stubble. Even the expression in his eyes was different. Although he had been no less handsome at fourteen, he was in another league now.

"This is insane!" she exclaimed. "It's you and, at the same time, it isn't…"

Gus was wide-eyed.

"Right back at you…"

Oksa looked at her hands and groaned. She carefully felt her face: her bone structure was different and her face felt thinner and longer. Her cheeks didn't seem so round and her nose felt less prominent.

"How do I look?" she couldn't help asking nervously.

"Ugly as sin," replied Gus calmly.

Oksa whimpered. Gus's face lit up in a brilliant smile which reassured the Young Gracious.

"Only kidding! You're really pretty!" he said, lowering his dark-blue eyes.

Oksa continued her inspection and gave a cry. It wasn't just her face that had altered, her body had undergone a remarkable metamorphosis too, the most unsettling change being the development of her bust. Flustered, she stopped examining herself, while Gus tactfully looked away, turning bright red—unfortunately, he realized, he still had the embarrassing tendency to blush.

"Do you think we can get out of here now?" he remarked, abashed.

"I'm scared…"

"Me too, but we can't stay in this bubble for ever, can we?"

"It's nice in here…" remarked Oksa.

"But very cramped, now we've grown. You've got to be at least five foot seven!"

"Stop it! You're making me nervous."

They sat there in silence for a moment, contemplating their new shared reality, thoughts rampaging like wild horses through their minds. Oksa was thinking about her father. He was bound to be sick with worry. And what about her mother? Her impatience to see her again was galvanizing her into action. Tugdual popped into her mind too, making her heart race. Would he like the "new Oksa"? She squirmed inside the bubble, causing it to sway from side to side. An opening appeared in the membrane and a friendly face appeared.

"Abakum!" cried the two friends.

"How are you doing, youngsters?" asked the Fairyman.

His voice and eyes betrayed his intense relief, as well as the surprise that he was trying his best to hide.

"Packed tight as sardines!" exclaimed Oksa.

Abakum couldn't hold back a grin. He looked affectionately at them, then widened the opening of the Nascentia to create a way out.

"You first," said Oksa, pushing Gus.

"You're so kind!" replied Gus, feeling nervous but glad to have the chance of showing Oksa that he was up to the task.

It wasn't easy, though, either mentally or physically. With Abakum's help, and a great deal of twisting and turning, Gus managed to climb out of the bubble. His shirt didn't survive the manoeuvre and tore across his shoulders. Once on his feet, meeting the shocked gaze of about ten Runaways and Felons who were clustering around him, he felt as miserable as a beast at a cattle market being inspected by a curious crowd. A murmur ran through the two clans.

"Good Lord…" murmured Dragomira, her hand pressed against her heart.

"Extraordinary…" remarked Orthon in a low voice.

Only Jeanne and Pierre didn't look shocked. They rushed over to their son and hugged him tightly, causing the last few seams of his shirt to give way.

"Thank God you're alive!" exclaimed Jeanne.

Gus was much taller than her now and not much shorter than his father. He let them hug and kiss him, feeling dazed and awkward. His trousers, which had been roomy and comfortable a few hours ago, were now so tight that the waistband was cutting into his stomach. All he could think about was how awful it would be if his trousers were to burst open. His shirt was already showing most of his top half… Abakum realized how embarrassed Gus was and draped his quilted jacket around his shoulders, immediately making him more at ease.

"You'd better help Oksa now," he said, to divert attention away from him. "Come on, Oksa," he said, poking his head back into the Nascentia. "Your turn!"

"I'm not sure... I want to come out," muttered Oksa.

"You don't think I'd let you get away with that, do you?" asked Gus indignantly, although he understood her reluctance perfectly. "We're waiting!"

"Who else is out there?"

"Come on!"

He grabbed her hand and they were both startled by the electrifying effect it had on them, although they tried not to show their surprise. Oksa pushed her legs through the narrow opening of the Nascentia, looked out timidly, and was overwhelmed with joy to see her mother sitting straight-backed in a wheelchair right in front of her.

"MUM!"

Oksa's head swam. Her heart felt as though it was going to burst out of her chest with pure relief. She was going to explode with happiness. Her mother was there, AT LAST! She threw herself into her arms.

"My darling," sighed Marie, burying her face in her daughter's hair.

"Mum, I'm so glad to see you..." whispered Oksa, putting her arms around her.

Without warning, the Young Gracious dissolved into floods of tears. The indescribable fear of the last few weeks disappeared so abruptly that she felt as though it had left a gaping hole in her heart. Oksa had never admitted how afraid she'd been at the thought that she might never see her mother again, but the dread had been at the back of her mind all this time. The prospect of losing her parents was more frightening than severe physical pain or extreme danger. A sob wracked her body. Finally, she wiped her glistening cheeks defiantly and, with her face buried in the crook of her mother's neck, she brought all those feelings of relief and fear under control.

"How are you?" she asked her mother. "You're not walking…"

"I'm fine, honestly. I can't walk, but I'm doing well. Anyway, I'm all the better for seeing you."

Marie did look very well. The exhilaration of the reunion had made her eyes shine and brought a rosy glow to her cheeks. She looked in better health than when Oksa had last seen her four months ago, just before her Impicturement. Her long chestnut hair had lost its shine, but her face was not so hollow-cheeked, she was moving more confidently and she looked physically more robust. Oksa found this both reassuring and disconcerting. "The Felons have treated her well," she thought. "She hasn't been locked up in a cellar on bread and water!"

"You can see we're far from heartless barbarians," broke in Orthon, as if he'd read her thoughts. "We treated our guest with all the care and attention she deserves."

"*Treated your guest?*" spluttered Oksa indignantly. "You've got some nerve!"

Marie waved her hand, dismissing the Felon's words.

"Oh Mum…" murmured Oksa, snuggling against her.

"Everything's all right now," said Marie, stroking her hair, which was tumbling over her shoulders. "You're here and you're alive—that's the main thing."

"What do I look like, Mum?"

Marie took her by the shoulders and pushed her back slightly to study her. Her eyes misted over.

"You are and always will be my daughter. Nothing else matters."

Oksa suddenly felt her father lightly stroke her cheek. Pavel was standing nearby, moved by their reunion and struggling to take in the fact that his little girl was now a young woman. Oksa threw herself into his arms and let him hug her. Her emotions were making it hard for her to catch her breath. She sensed that her body had blossomed, but she was trying to delay the moment when she had to confront her new image. Over her father's shoulder—which now only came up to her chin—she could see Dragomira and Reminiscens gazing at her in shock. Baba Pollock seemed to be crying. Orthon and Mercedica stood farther back, a superior and rather smug expression on their faces. Standing next to Dragomira and Reminiscens, Brune and Naftali were as serious as usual, but it wasn't hard to see the amazement in their moist eyes. Beside them, Zoe and Tugdual couldn't take their eyes off the pair who'd just emerged from the Nascentia. Zoe was white and wide-eyed with surprise. Tugdual was frowning, looking more intrigued than shocked. There was nothing tactless or improper about the way he was examining Oksa from head to toe, but she found it highly embarrassing. She was struggling to breathe normally, her clothes were too tight and everyone was staring at her, while she had no idea what she looked like. She hated this kind of situation.

"You look wonderful," said Pavel.

"You're only saying that because you're my father!"

Pavel sighed, raising his eyes to heaven and, taking her hand, dragged her to the back of the room where there was a large full-length mirror. On her way Oksa glanced at Gus, seeing him "fully extended" for the first time. He was so tall! And so good-looking…

"Yes, I know, I look like the Incredible Hulk," said her friend, showing off his torn clothes and his trousers, which only came down to his calves.

Oksa couldn't help laughing. Gus might have gained at least six inches, but he hadn't lost his sense of humour. It was so good to have the old Gus back!

"Shall we face the dreaded mirror together?" he asked, suddenly looking serious.

She nodded, unable to say a word. So, with their parents trailing some way behind, they nervously headed towards the huge cheval glass.

26

COCKFIGHT

BUZZING LIKE A LARGE INSECT, DRAGOMIRA'S TUMBLE-Bawler hovered above Gus and Oksa, who were standing motionless in front of the mirror, and declared:

"The Young Gracious is now sixteen years, two months and thirteen days old; she's five feet six inches tall and weighs eight and a half stone. Her waist is—"

"Enough, Tumble!" broke in Oksa, before it could tell everyone all her intimate details. "Let's move on to Gus."

He groaned, murmuring: "Mercy!"

"As you command, Young Gracious!" said the little creature. "The Young Gracious's friend is now sixteen years, seven months and twenty-eight days old. He's five feet nine inches tall and weighs nine and a half stone. Do you want any further details?"

"No, thanks, that'll do just fine," said Oksa tonelessly.

Feeling awkward, she moved nearer the mirror and touched her reflection with her fingertips—it looked both strange and familiar. It was her... and someone else. Her figure was more rounded and better-defined and there was a different, more intense, expression in her eyes. With one hand she brushed back her chestnut hair, which was now shoulder-length. Before this, she'd occasionally imagined herself older. She'd cast herself as blonde or brunette, curvy or slender, sporty or smart, as if playing a computer simulation game. But, as far back as she could remember, she'd never hoped to look like this girl in the mirror. She felt dizzy with excitement. She liked her reflection, but it was too soon to feel that it belonged to her. It had all happened too quickly. In the mirror, she smiled shyly at Marie, who was staring at her.

"You were already a babe, but now…" came Tugdual's voice behind her.

She didn't dare turn round, so she just watched him approaching in the mirror.

"We're almost the same height!" he remarked, putting his hands on her shoulders.

He was so close she could feel his breath on her neck. Still, he didn't move any closer, as if he didn't want to frighten her. Only his ardent eyes held hers in the mirror. A strange heat spread from his hands into the Young Gracious's heart. Instinctively, her eyes strayed to Gus who was watching Tugdual with cold fury.

"You're really not that tall," he said sarcastically.

"No, I'm not that tall," replied Tugdual. "But what are a few inches between friends?" he added, edging a fraction closer to Oksa.

Gus curled his lip and glared at him. Meanwhile Oksa was registering the "new" situation: it was as if Gus had caught up with Tugdual in every way within the last few hours. There was now nothing between them. In their own way, whether they liked it or not, they had the same qualities and the same weaknesses: devastating charm, a bad temper, discerning intelligence and a dark, tormented side. And they both made her heart race.

"It's all happening too fast," she muttered.

She looked like a young woman now, which was extremely unsettling. She wasn't sure what to do with those curves and that expression in her eyes. And the changes inside were even more overwhelming. Her emotions were so much stronger! The timid feelings she'd had when she was fourteen were long gone. Right now, she was battling two huge, conflicting urges: to give herself body and soul to Tugdual and to bury her head in the hollow of Gus's shoulder for ever. How could she be having such thoughts? Who was she now?

Aware that she had no control over her emotions, Tugdual dropped a feather-light kiss at the base of her neck. Immediately she blushed. It was as if every powerful feeling she'd had "before" was now ten times stronger. Her big grey eyes stared at Tugdual in the mirror with an excitement she understood and felt, but couldn't admit was hers.

"You're gorgeous, Lil' Gracious," Tugdual murmured in her ear.

The shiver that ran down Oksa's spine wasn't missed by either Gus or Tugdual, who tightened his grip, kindling what felt like a raging fire in Oksa's veins. He led her back towards Marie, who was waiting for them in the other half of the room. Oksa couldn't help looking round.

"Think very carefully about what you're doing," said Gus miserably.

The words felt like a dagger blow to Oksa's heart, severing it in two.

"And don't try pulling your old trick of starting a storm!" cried Gus, twisting the knife in the wound. "You need to take responsibility for your actions now. You're no longer a child."

27

A Blended Family

It was time to get back to the even more pressing matter of the Runaways and the two worlds. Oksa glanced out of the window at the moors in the gloomy daylight. The small group seemed to be on the first floor of the Felons' home, so there was an unimpeded view. The wind had dropped, but unsettling black streaks cut across the sky like deep scars. The sea was crashing against the rocks, sending up huge plumes of grey water. In the distance, the Gargantuhens were stretching their legs, their feathered heads ruffled by sea spray. The mood was as miserable as the landscape. Only Orthon looked shockingly pleased with himself.

"I'd urge you all to have a hearty lunch!" he suddenly remarked.

Dragomira glanced at him warily.

"He's right," said Abakum quietly. "We need to build up our strength after such a long and difficult night."

Although Oksa wouldn't have admitted it for the world, she felt as though she could eat a horse. She was absolutely starving. Her churning stomach was so hollow that it felt as though she hadn't eaten for a couple of years!

"You're my guests, when all's said and done," continued Orthon.

"Oh, why don't you give it a rest!" retorted Reminiscens in exasperation.

"Yes, enough is enough," added Dragomira sourly.

Orthon smiled mockingly and opened the door. He and Mercedica filed out into the stone corridor, followed by Pavel pushing Marie's wheelchair and the Runaways walking either side of Oksa and Gus. Their old clothes had been uncomfortably tight, so both of them had been forced to borrow things from Runaways, who were about the same size. Oksa was wearing jeans and ankle boots that had belonged to one of Leomido's granddaughters and Tugdual had insisted on lending her a black hoodie. Gus had categorically refused to wear anything owned by his rival and had gratefully accepted a khaki wool sweater and rough grey canvas trousers from Cockerell's son. Walking shakily with stiff, aching limbs, the two friends were still getting used to their new bodies. Oksa kept glancing imploringly at Gus, but he kept his distance with an exaggeratedly cool expression and flushed cheeks. His eyes were fixed on Abakum's back in front of him, and he seemed determined to keep looking straight ahead. As the group walked downstairs, Oksa felt herself getting increasingly wound up at Gus's feigned indifference. She jabbed him hard in the ribs with her elbow but he didn't react.

"Look at me!" she hissed.

"I've already said you're very pretty," replied Gus, staring straight ahead. "What more do you want?"

"It isn't that!" snapped Oksa. "Look at me. Please…"

"In memory of our former friendship, you mean?"

Oksa sighed irritably.

"Leave me alone, Oksa," Gus said at last. "I hope I'll get used to it. You have no idea how hard this is for me."

"I know…"

"No, you don't," interrupted Gus, disappearing into the kitchen.

This quiet conversation really upset Oksa. Observantly, Marie wheeled herself over and took her hand.

"Are you OK? You look a bit miserable."

"I'm so mixed up, Mum."

"It'll take a bit of time for things to work out," said Marie softly. "Both of you have experienced some very drastic changes."

"You need to stay focused, Oksa-san," added Pavel solemnly. "There are some hard times ahead and we mustn't forget that three of you now have a sword of Damocles hanging over your heads."

They were the last to enter the vast kitchen, where four tables had been laid and were groaning under the weight of steaming pies, salads, cheeses, brioches and hot drinks. Although the lavish spread was hot, the atmosphere was chilly. The two groups had taken care not to mingle and everyone was eating with feigned relish in a silence broken only by the sputtering of a large stove. When Oksa came in pushing Marie's armchair, they all held their breath. Although Gus's conspicuous entrance a few minutes earlier had prepared them, they were all startled by the Young Gracious's changed appearance. She looked round the room. Gus was studiously ignoring her, pretending to be engrossed in his mug of hot chocolate, so she didn't hesitate when Tugdual signalled to her. Without really knowing why she felt disappointed, she manoeuvred her mother's wheelchair over to Tugdual and sat down beside him.

"How's my Lil' Gracious?" asked Tugdual quietly, pouring her a huge cup of tea as black as coffee.

"Thrilled at being reunited with her mother!" replied Oksa. "Other than that, she feels very strange."

"Does it hurt?"

"Not a bit! I'm not sure how you can grow as fast as this with virtually no pain. I'm just a bit stiff and achy, that's all. The growing pains I had were much worse than this—insane, isn't it?"

"It's certainly not the type of thing you experience every day... Hey, did you realize that you're only seven months younger than me now?"

"Is that all?" asked Oksa in surprise.

"So... how do you see the future now you're sixteen years, two months and thirteen days old?"

"Honestly? It's a nightmare, particularly when I think about what's waiting for us and the dangers we'll face if we don't succeed. We'll need to find Edefia, which is like looking for a needle in a haystack.

151

And even if we find it, we have to get in, then find a Diaphan so that Gus and I can become true Werewalls—if we haven't died in agony beforehand. Then we have to pick some Lasonillia for Mum in the Distant Reaches. And that territory is, as its name suggests, a long way away and very hard to get to. Then, we have to find the Cloak Chamber before Orthon does and save the two worlds. Piece of cake!" she said sarcastically, with a frown.

"The Runaways certainly don't do 'simple'," remarked Tugdual. "And the Pollocks are the worst offenders of all!"

"You're not kidding!"

She took a large bite out of a huge sugar-topped brioche so that no one would see she wanted to cry. Around her, everyone was silently concentrating on their lunch and occasionally glancing furtively at the enemy clan. The only light relief was provided by the chirruping Ptitchkins which were flying loop-the-loops above Dragomira's head. The Lunatrixes were busying themselves at the stove, doing their bit as the "domestic help" with the assistance of the other creatures, which were desperate to show their solidarity.

"Oh, this warmth is bliss!" clucked the Squoracles, pressed up against the toaster.

"Hey, chicks, you'll singe the feathers off your wings, sniggered one of the Getorixes. "I'd pay good money to see bald Squoracles, ho ho ho!"

The Squoracles flapped their wings indignantly.

"Your words achieve the conjuring of a temperament full of jeering," remarked Dragomira's Lunatrix, squeezing oranges.

"You said it, my friend," nodded the Getorix, skipping around in a state of nervous exhaustion.

The Lunatrix suddenly stopped in mid-movement. From where she was sitting, Oksa saw him freeze, still holding a tea towel. His two puzzled companions looked at him, and the Getorix jerked on his apron to snap him out of his trance. Eyes bulging, Dragomira's faithful creature finally roused himself and shuffled towards his mistress.

"What's wrong, my Lunatrix?" asked Baba Pollock, concerned by his translucent complexion.

The silence grew even more oppressive.

"The Old Gracious along with her friends, and her enemies, must take reception of a piece of information bursting with importance," announced the Lunatrix.

He appeared to be hesitating, so Dragomira urged him to continue.

"A notification has performed an appearance in the mind of your domestic staff," said the small creature eventually. "My Old Gracious, the Definitive Landmark has made the gift of its revelation."

A low murmur rose among the ranks of the Runaways. Most of the Felons looked incredulous.

"The Portal has completed delivery of its access," continued the Lunatrix, "and your domestic staff is now in possession of the knowledge of its location accompanied by precise geographical directions."

Dragomira went white and looked so devastated that the Runaways were surprised. Oksa was more taken aback than anyone. When Abakum leant towards his old friend and gazed deep into her eyes, Dragomira nodded her head gravely. Then she stood up heavily and announced in a choked voice:

"The Guardian of the Definitive Landmark has spoken: the Portal has appeared, Edefia and the Insiders await."

28

TWELVE DAYS AND TWELVE NIGHTS

"**I**F YOU THINK WE'RE GOING TO FOLLOW YOU LIKE CRING-ing lackeys, you've got another thing coming!" thundered Orthon.

"Well there's absolutely no way we're going to let you go ahead of us," replied Dragomira. "Anyway, we share a common destiny and you know it, so why don't you stop pretending to be so hard-done-by! We'll go together and you'll follow wherever *I* lead and that's final."

Baba Pollock banged her fist on the table in front of a furious Orthon. The two enemies stared each other down for long seconds.

"I don't trust you," stormed Orthon.

"Nor I you, if you want to know the truth," retorted Dragomira. "Anyway, you have the medallion so that makes us equal."

Orthon pulled a face.

"That's as may be. But permit me to acquire an additional insurance policy!"

With these words he swiftly grabbed the Lunatrix, who turned transparent with surprise. Pavel and Naftali threw themselves at Orthon to stop him, but Gregor and Agafon were already barring their way. The Runaways immediately took out their Granok-Shooters and stood facing a serried line of Felons who'd reacted exactly the same. Impulsively, Tugdual rushed at Orthon, like a cheetah pouncing on its prey, knocking over Mortimer and seizing the terrified Lunatrix by the waist to return him to Dragomira.

"You're wasting precious time," cursed Baba Pollock, glowering at Orthon. "When will you realize there's no point fighting? We're equally matched in numbers, after all."

With that she bent down and picked up her Lunatrix, who was trembling violently, and strutted out, leaving her half-brother white with rage.

※

"Well, Dragomira? Where is the Definitive Landmark?" asked Abakum.

"I don't know yet," confessed the old woman. "But my Lunatrix will soon tell us!"

The small group of Runaways was at the top of the Felons' house, in the turret overlooking the roof. Cockerell and Olof were standing guard at the foot of the staircase leading to the small lookout tower.

"We're listening, my Lunatrix."

The small creature opened his eyes incredibly wide, took a deep breath, almost suffocating himself, and finally divulged the precious information in a whisper:

"The Definitive Landmark has broadcast the location of the Portal into Edefia. The Old Gracious and the Young Gracious, their friends, the Runaways and their enemies, the Felons, must effect a removal to the Gobi Desert, forty-two degrees north, one hundred and one degrees east. The Portal has established the fixing of its position on the west side of Gashun-nur."

Tugdual immediately began tapping on the keyboard of his mobile and, after a few seconds, provided more information.

"Gashun-nur is a lake about twelve miles south of the border between China and Mongolia. The River Xi flows into it and a small road runs around it."

The Runaways felt a mixture of relief and apprehension on hearing this information. The Portal had been located at last, but it sounded like it would be difficult to get there, to say the least...

"It's a long way from here," remarked Oksa, sounding worried.

"Four thousand, four hundred and two miles to be precise," said Tugdual, consulting his screen.

Oksa whistled between her teeth.

"Will we get to the Portal in time? And there's another thing: Lunatrix, you've said before that the Definitive Landmark, which will allow us to find the Portal, isn't fixed. Will it change position before we get there?"

The Lunatrix cleared his throat and shifted from one leg to the other.

"Edefia is at the edge of the world and the Definitive Landmark experiences mobility, that affirmation is absolute. But your domestic staff provides the confirmation: the phoenix is awaiting the arrival of the Two Graciouses at the locational exactitude indicated by your major-domo, in other words the Gobi Desert, forty-two degrees north, one hundred and one degrees east, on the west side of Gashun-nur. The phoenix will evince patience for a duration of twelve days and twelve nights. Once this time has been consumed, the Portal will cause the disappearance of the Definitive Landmark and the phoenix, like the two worlds, will experience permanent disappearance."

Pavel cursed softly. The Runaways felt light-headed with panic. The future was taking shape...

"We should probably get going then, shouldn't we?" murmured Oksa, after a long silence.

"Let's wish ourselves luck, my friends," said Abakum, speaking with emotion. "We're going to need it."

*

Clustered around Dragomira, the Runaways on one side and the Felons on the other, they all listened carefully to information that was vital for their next move.

"So we only have twelve days to travel 4,000 miles and find the Portal, is that what you're saying?" asked Agafon, breaking the heavy silence that had followed Dragomira's announcement.

The Old Gracious nodded unblinkingly.

"Don't tell me you don't know any more than that!" broke in Orthon.

"I have all the necessary details," replied Dragomira stiffly. "But I'm not going to give them to you. You'll find out when the time is right."

Orthon clenched his fists and glared at her. Then he held out his palm commandingly towards Mercedica and, without looking at her, ordered:

"The medallion, please!"

Seconds passed but Mercedica didn't move a muscle. Irritated, Orthon turned to her.

"The medallion, Mercedica!" he repeated in a steely voice.

The haughty Spanish woman jutted her chin.

"The medallion no longer belongs to you, Orthon," she said, glaring at him. "It's mine now."

29

THE CONFESSIONS
OF A FELON

"Where's the medallion?" roared Orthon. "What have you done with it?"

The Felon was beside himself with anger, his eyes burning with fury. He raised his hand with the obvious intention of slapping Mercedica, who'd just publicly defied him so insufferably, but Mercedica stopped him. Orthon's hatred knew no bounds.

"I won't ask again!" he spat, a few inches from the face of his former ally. "WHERE'S THE MEDALLION, YOU TRAITOR?"

Everyone was appalled and there was a growing sense of panic in the room. Oksa shifted nervously from foot to foot.

"Being described as a 'traitor' by the Master of the Felons sounds more like a compliment than an insult," she heard herself mutter, surprised at her own daring.

Oksa was trembling. Without the medallion, Edefia was and always would be a Lost Land. Gus and she would die a long and painful death and her mother would continue to be consumed by the disease that would eventually kill her too. And none of that would matter because the two worlds would soon be annihilated—all because of a lousy medallion and a hateful Felon.

"I've been loyal to you since the first day I met you again," Mercedica suddenly declared imperiously. "Just as I was loyal to your father for the eight years I spent within the High Enclave. But I'd like all of you here to know the reasons for my behaviour."

Mercedica glared at the assembled throng, before sitting down in the central armchair that Orthon had occupied a short while ago. He gave her a murderous look and remained standing, his fists clenched.

"You and I have always been motivated by the same desires and the same ambitions," continued Mercedica, staring at him. "Power is our driving force. When I arrived on the Outside, my lust for power was what kept me going and I used all my gifts to achieve my goals. I started off playing a leading role in the financial world, because I soon realized that, in this world, money means influence. After amassing a huge fortune with disconcerting ease, I dabbled in international relations. And I have to admit that I really enjoyed acting behind the scenes for various governments, particularly in South America and the Near East… All those conflicts resolved by signing dishonest treaties only confirmed what I'd thought about human weakness. I've thoroughly enjoyed pulling the strings for twenty years and the art of manipulation has always been central to my activities."

"No doubt about that," murmured Dragomira sadly.

"Then, by the greatest coincidence, I crossed paths with Orthon in the corridors of the CIA in spring 1978," continued Mercedica. "In my life, I've been wooed by many men, but I've only really loved two: the father of my daughter Catarina and you, Orthon."

The voice of the proud Spanish woman trembled a little. Everyone in the room looked incredulous. Orthon's eyes were like slits, which gave him the appearance of a ferocious cobra.

"Despite the ten-year age gap, I immediately fell under your spell. From that moment, I gave myself to you body and soul. Why? For love, plain and simple."

"For love of power, you mean!" retorted Orthon, tight-lipped.

"Oh, that too, I'd never deny it. But mainly out of love for you. Don't you think I had more influence working with the most powerful men in the world? Don't you think it wasn't more exhilarating, and more gratifying, to conspire with them? The most obscure and most corrupt South American governments showed me more gratitude than you ever did. And yet, for the thirty years I've spent by your side, have I ever let you down? Have I ever disappointed you? And what good has that loyalty done me? I'm now over eighty. All these years, you've never shown me anything other than ambitious self-interest in return for my love. Well, I've had enough, Orthon. You used me like you use all your slavish followers."

"That's not true!" shouted Agafon. "We follow Orthon because he shares our beliefs!"

"Maybe," retorted Mercedica frostily. "But I've had to make some really hard concessions for him: I agreed to betray Malorane first, then Dragomira and the Runaways, whom I was so happy to see again."

Dragomira spluttered with indignation at these words. Mercedica turned to her and sadness darkened her haughty eyes.

"Yes, Dragomira, believe it or not," she said quietly. "I may well have been pitiless and Machiavellian in my work, but seeing you again was one of the happiest days of my life. I'll never forget it. Orthon had finally tracked down your family a few years earlier and had sent me to Paris to make contact. It was a huge shock for me when I saw you through the window of your herbalist's shop, even though I'm not given to displays of emotion. You'd become a woman and yet I recognized you immediately. Abakum was standing nearby like the worthy Watcher he's always been. You welcomed me with open arms, of course. I was moved by your close bonds with family and friends, but it couldn't sway my inmost nature, or my love for Orthon. So I betrayed you. With some regret, but without hesitation because, I now know, there's nothing stronger than love. Or more destructive than scorned love."

There was a growing sense of unease as Mercedica fell silent for a second. Then she stood up regally and added:

"I've spent half my life waiting for you to return the love I felt for you, Orthon. I even killed for you. And what did you ever do to thank me? You used me like you use everyone else, whatever Agafon says… We'd have been so good together, you know. We could have ruled the world. You made a big mistake when you treated me as a mere flunky. But now I'm the one who has what you need. The roles have been reversed, Orthon… I'm the only one who knows where the medallion is."

"Whom did you kill?" broke in Reminiscens tonelessly.

Despite her extreme weakness after two transfusions, Reminiscens was on her feet, shakily supporting herself against the back of an armchair. Her body was trembling. Abakum and Naftali rushed over to stand either side of her, both fearing the same thing. Mercedica turned and fixed her dark gaze on Reminiscens' rheumy eyes.

"I killed your son and his wife, Reminiscens, on Orthon's orders. I DID IT BLINDLY FOR LOVE OF ORTHON!" she shouted, pointing at the Felon.

Abakum and Naftali couldn't react fast enough: quick as a flash, Reminiscens took out her Granok-Shooter and whispered a few words. Mercedica stared at her wide-eyed then crashed to the floor.

30

DISSENSION

"ARE YOU OUT OF YOUR TINY MIND?" ORTHON SPAT AT his twin. "You've just ruined our only chance of getting back to Edefia!"

Abakum and Naftali were holding Reminiscens by the arms, shocked by what had just happened. A few Felons, realizing the gravity of the situation, rushed over to Mercedica's inert body. Her heavy bun had come undone and her hair was spread out like a funeral shroud around her head. Reminiscens had fired a Stuffarax Granok at Mercedica and her face was slowly turning blue as it suffocated her. They were on the verge of disaster and Oksa, among others, began to cry. Warily, Dragomira walked over to Reminiscens and asked in a strangled whisper:

"Why did you do that?"

"She killed my son, Dragomira. She killed my son and his wife without any qualms. Imagine how you'd have felt if she'd done the same thing to Pavel and Marie... How would you have acted?"

Dragomira shivered with horror. How could she answer that? It didn't bear thinking about. She studied Reminiscens for a long time, then the Runaways. Her gaze lingered on Oksa, who looked panic-stricken.

"I understand your desire for revenge, but you've signed the death warrant of everyone here!" she gasped, before collapsing onto a chair.

"She isn't dead!" Catarina suddenly cried, kneeling beside Mercedica's body.

Orthon was the first to react. Unceremoniously shouldering his way through the Felons around Mercedica, he shoved Catarina aside and squatted down, pressing his face against that of his former ally.

"She's still breathing," he said after a few seconds. "Where's the medallion?" he demanded, shaking her by the shoulders.

"You're not going to get anywhere like that," said Dragomira, coming over. "It would be nice if you didn't sabotage what little hope we have left."

"You should have reminded that madwoman of that fact before she did anything stupid!" roared Orthon, shaking an angry fist at his twin sister.

"Out of the way!" ordered Dragomira, taking a small phial from her bag. Orthon didn't move.

"Perhaps you weren't aware that Abakum and Leomido actually designed the Stuffarax," continued Dragomira. "And, since they knew how it was made, you might have expected them to come up with a preparation to counter some of its effects..."

Orthon immediately allowed Dragomira through. Baba Pollock didn't look as confident as her words suggested, but only her closest allies would have realized this. She knelt down beside Mercedica, who was staring at her with large dark motionless eyes. Her head was cradled in Catarina's lap and Mercedica's daughter looked panic-stricken. Dragomira opened the phial and a dark plume of vapour rose from the bottle, smelling pungently of rotting plants. When it reached Mercedica's nose, her eyes rolled back in her head and her body arched with such violent convulsions that it looked as if breathing in the fumes had been fatal.

"What's happening?" asked Oksa in a low voice.

The Young Gracious wasn't the only one appalled by the scene. Tiny insects were swarming from Mercedica's nostrils and mouth, forming a seething cloud of black carapaces and wings. The swarm hovered for a few seconds above Mercedica, who was staring at it with indescribable terror, then exploded with a muffled bang.

"Just in time," murmured Dragomira, replacing the stopper on the phial.

"You mean those vile insects would have exploded *inside* Mercedica, if you hadn't done anything?" asked Oksa, wide-eyed with amazement.

"Yes. In her throat, to be exact."

Although she'd been saved in the nick of time, Mercedica looked dreadful. Her face was white with shock and every breath seemed extremely painful. It cost her a great effort to lift her hand and pull Dragomira towards her. Orthon realized she was about to reveal her last secret. He launched himself at Catarina and yanked her up by the arm. Holding her captive against him in Mercedica's line of sight, he displayed Catarina like a trophy.

"Don't even think of double-crossing me…" he snarled.

"Mercedica's dying!" Dragomira protested indignantly.

"Exactly! She has nothing to lose. Unless she wants to take her daughter to the grave with her."

"You're despicable!" hissed Dragomira. "Mercedica, tell us where the medallion is," she begged, turning to her former friend. "If not for him, then for us! In memory of all those years you spent as one of us… Please!"

Mercedica jerked. With a groan, she looked at her daughter held in Orthon's vice-like grip and opened her mouth, but no words came out. Her eyes widened, fixed on her daughter, who was struggling and crying. Then her head lolled to one side. Her chest rose, then fell as her last breath left her body and her face relaxed.

"Her heart gave out," announced Dragomira miserably. "She's dead."

31

THE KEY

THEY BURIED MERCEDICA BEHIND THE HOUSE IN A GRAVE looking out over the roaring surf. Despite the formidable Spanish woman's treachery, Dragomira and Abakum attended the brief ceremony solemnly given by Galina's husband, Andrew, who was a minister. The Runaways were all there, except for Reminiscens who'd shut herself away in a room upstairs. No one had forgotten that Mercedica had once been one of them. Nothing she'd confessed could excuse her heinous crimes, but the way things had turned out aroused her former friends' compassion, even though they'd never forgive her. Gathered around her grave covered with flat stones, they felt sorry for her knowing that she'd have hated that intensely—"Better envy than pity" had always been her motto. The only Felon who attended was Catarina, under escort by Agafon and Lukas, who'd been sent by Orthon.

"It looks like the Felons can't stomach felony," Tugdual murmured to Oksa.

She gave him a tearful look. Tugdual stroked her cheek with his index finger and smiled wanly. Unfortunately, this wasn't the first time Oksa had watched someone die, and she found it very upsetting, even though Mercedica had hurt her family so badly. Which was odd, really... She kept rolling with the punches, but how long could she keep it up?

✻

After saying a last farewell to Mercedica, they returned to the living room, where Baba Pollock resumed negotiations.

"I'll leave our travel plans up to you youngsters," she told Tugdual, Oksa and Gus quietly. "Your job is to work out a route that will enable us to reach Gashun-nur in less than twelve days. With one important condition: there are fifty-eight of us and we must all stay together."

"Consider it done!" said Tugdual, calmly taking out his mobile.

"What about the medallion, Baba?" asked Oksa.

"Let me handle that," replied Dragomira enigmatically.

The three teenagers sat down some distance from the two feuding groups, near the towering, fully stacked bookcase. "They look so grown-up now," Dragomira couldn't help thinking, with a pang.

"Anyway, back to business!" continued the old woman, looking at Catarina, whose shoulders were hunched in misery.

"I've gone through that traitor's room with a fine-tooth comb," said Orthon.

"And?" asked Dragomira. "Did you find the medallion?"

"No… but I'm sure it's in this jewellery box," he replied, holding out a chest the size of a small suitcase.

"Well, open it then!" exclaimed Dragomira. The Felon's face darkened.

"We've tried everything," admitted Gregor, Orthon's eldest son. "The lock won't respond to magic or brute force."

"I know an excellent way to find out how to open it," said Orthon, taking out his Granok-Shooter and pointing it at Catarina.

"I don't know how to do it!" objected Catarina, her eyes wide with fear. "My mother didn't tell me, I swear it, Orthon!"

"You're telling me she'd have attempted to mislead us when she was dying?" he retorted, tilting his head to one side with a baleful glare. "She was looking at you just before she died."

"Only because I'm her daughter!" cried Catarina with a long wail of terror and grief.

Orthon pretended to examine his Granok-Shooter with malevolent intent, then looked at Catarina, who was doing her best to hide her fear. Dragomira took a few steps forward, her eyes burning with anger.

"We all know that violence is your first recourse, Orthon," she said. "But perhaps it's because you haven't realized that there's a subtler, more effective way of going about things..."

Dipping her hand inside her jacket, she took out a dishevelled, extremely agitated Squoracle.

"The temperature in this room may be acceptable, but let me tell you that the weather conditions outside are abominable!" squawked the tiny hen.

Oksa looked up with a smile.

"I don't know if it's a good idea to tell it that we have to cross the Gobi Desert," she said quietly.

"Unfortunately, it's impossible to hide anything from it," remarked Gus, looking up from the atlas he was examining.

"It's going to make our life hell when it realizes!" added Tugdual, continuing to tap on his phone's keyboard.

Oksa had feared the worst when Dragomira had entrusted them with this task. She'd sat down on the sofa in the middle of Gus and Tugdual, who'd tried not to look at each other for a few minutes, and the atmosphere had been very tense. Then, given the urgency of the situation, they'd each conceded a little ground, although this lull in hostilities didn't last long.

"Can I help?" asked Kukka suddenly, sitting down next to a surprised Gus.

Oksa leant forward to look furtively at the Swedish girl, whose long blonde hair was casually brushing Gus's hand. She felt a spurt of anger—Kukka certainly had some nerve!

"Let her think she's irresistible," murmured Tugdual, noticing the Young Gracious's annoyance. "She's nowhere near as pretty as you think she is, you know."

Pressed up against Gus's shoulder, Kukka whispered a few words in his ear which made him look at her in amazement.

"If my adorable cousin wouldn't mind shelving her seduction plans for now," said Tugdual, concentrating on his phone. "We've got serious work to do."

Kukka gave a provocative giggle, which Oksa did her best to ignore.

"Let's hear what the Squoracle has to say!" she said, curbing her irritation.

Perched stiffly on Dragomira's shoulder, the Squoracle was jutting out its tiny beak at the four corners of the room in turn.

"Six degrees centigrade with a ninety per cent rate of humidity and a wind gusting at fifty-three miles per hour, that's not a temperate climate in my book!" it screeched. "You're trying to mislead me again, but it won't work—I'm not so easily fooled."

"Squoracle, we need you," interrupted Dragomira, wrapping the sensitive little creature in a ball of cotton wool.

"I'm listening, my Old Gracious. And thank you for being so sympathetic to your poor, ultrasensitive Squoracle, whose survival is continually under threat in these unfriendly climes."

"Do you know where the medallion is?"

The Squoracle burrowed down in the cotton wool for a moment, then its tiny head popped out, with all its feathers standing on end.

"OF COURSE I KNOW!" it squawked at the top of its voice. "I'm a Squoracle! I know everything, even the most closely kept secret. That's been my job since I was a tiny chick."

It began screeching with annoyance. The Felons looked at each other in surprise. The oldest members of the group hadn't seen a Squoracle since they'd left Edefia and the younger generations had heard of those tiny creatures, but had never seen one before.

"Someone's rattled its cage today," whispered Tugdual.

"It is looking a bit ruffled, I agree…" replied Oksa, with a smile.

"There's a howling draught in this room coming from the north-north-west," continued the Squoracle, while everyone listened attentively. "Didn't any of you ever consider insulating the doors and windows?"

"Squoracle," Dragomira said gently. "I asked you a question…"

"Yes, yes, I know. But I'm freezing to death!"

Suppressing a sigh, Abakum grabbed the cotton wool ball as gently as he could and went to stand as near as humanly possible to the fireplace.

"At last someone understands what I'm going through!"

"We don't have much time, Squoracle," begged the Fairyman.

"Huh!" snorted the hen. "The medallion is where the Felon Mercedica hid it."

"Priceless!" sneered Orthon.

"One woman in this room knows its hiding place," continued the Squoracle.

Orthon roared and seized Catarina's arm in an iron grip.

"It's lying!" wailed the young woman. "It isn't me!"

"Don't insult me! You know very well that Squoracles never lie for the simple reason that *they can't*. If I say that one woman here knows the hiding place, then one woman here knows the hiding place. I never said it was you…"

This made no sense at all to anyone and everyone looked around in panic. Everyone, except—

"Stop trying to open that lock!" broke in Marie imperiously.

There was general amazement. The Felons immediately stopped trying to break into the jewellery box. All eyes turned towards Oksa's mother who, sitting up straight in her wheelchair, was boldly eyeing Orthon.

"That's right, Orthon," she said. "I'm the woman who knows the secret of that chest."

"Well?" added the Squoracle, fluffing up its feathers. "Do you still dare to accuse me of lying? I demand an apology. Beg my forgiveness! Prostrate yourselves at my feet!"

Dragomira stuffed the little hen in her pocket to silence it. The Squoracle's demands slowly tailed off.

"What did you think? That this cripple without magical gifts would stay shut in her room doing nothing?" continued Marie, addressing the Master of the Felons. "Well, Orthon, you thought wrong! I may not have your powers, but I've taken advantage of these long weeks of captivity to watch, listen and learn a great many things. Particularly when I caught Mercedica stealing the medallion from you. She could be cruel and unscrupulous and she had no qualms doing the things she did, but her heart wasn't black through and through, like yours. Do you even know what a heart is, Orthon?"

The Felon clicked his tongue in exasperation. Marie turned to Dragomira and Abakum.

"Mercedica betrayed you in the worst possible way, but paradoxically she was telling the truth when she talked about her excitement and happiness at meeting you again in Paris. It was in memory of those years of sincere friendship that she told me how to reclaim the medallion if the need arose."

Orthon approached her threateningly, looking triumphant.

"Don't try to intimidate me!" said Marie, stopping him. "You don't think it's that simple, do you? Mercedica took precautions. She told me the location of the medallion, but that's not enough, as you'll see…"

"How do we open this chest?" roared Orthon.

"Shouting won't get you anywhere," said Marie curtly. "There's a password."

Orthon seemed about to explode with rage. The veins in his neck were bulging and his eyes were flashing, but he managed to maintain a semblance of icy dignity.

"Catarina, everyone called your father Rupert," continued Marie to Mercedica's daughter. "But he changed his identity to escape from the Nazis, didn't he? Only Mercedica and you know his real name."

Catarina looked at her in amazement.

"Samuel…" she announced.

Orthon immediately pronounced the name level with the lock.

Nothing happened.

"You really can be surprisingly naive," mocked Marie. "Mercedica gave me the answer, not you. SAMUEL!" she said clearly in her turn.

The chest opened, revealing a tangle of necklaces, earrings and bracelets.

"Vocal recognition," remarked Oksa, gazing at her mother in admiration. "How clever!"

Orthon plunged his hands into the glittering pile: each piece was a masterpiece, a work of art sparkling with diamonds, emeralds and rubies. The Felon smothered a cry of frustration.

"The second part of the answer is the keyword," continued Marie.

Orthon was frantically rummaging through the box, soon helped by his sons. Nearby, Agafon and Lukas were sorting through pieces of jewellery, tossing aside any that were too small to contain anything, even a tiny key.

When there was only one thing left—an ostentatious ring topped with a huge diamond—the Felon's rage reached fever pitch. He hurled a fistful of jewellery at the wall. The mood was tense and everyone stood waiting for something to happen, without knowing exactly what. Suddenly, Gus got up and went over to Marie. Despite Orthon's discouraging glare, which filled him with fear, he took hold of her wheelchair and wheeled her to one side.

"You said the answer was the *key*word, didn't you?" he whispered in Marie's ear. "The *word*?"

She nodded dubiously. Then her face lit up: she'd understood too!

"May I try?" she asked, nudging Orthon out of the way with her wheelchair. "You and your henchmen go to the other end of the room."

Orthon obeyed reluctantly. Marie hadn't given him much choice. With Gus's help, she started to search through the jewellery, examining each piece with minute care, until Gus held up a fob watch, spelling the Felons' defeat.

"That watch belonged to my father," Mercedica's daughter told the two clans. "He gave it to my mother when I was born. Look at the engraving on the case."

The Runaways studied the watch: it was a magnificent, finely worked antique watch. On the clasp, a short text from Catarina's father picked out in tiny slivers of precious stone paid tribute to Mercedica, his beloved wife:

For the woman who forever holds
The key to all my secrets.
S.

Dragomira gently pressed the word "key" and the cover opened, revealing the hands which were counting seconds with an almost inaudible tick. With her fingertip she turned them to the number twelve and there was a faint click. The face split in two, revealing a secret compartment containing the legendary medallion of the Graciouses, shining like a star.

"That's fantastic!" exclaimed Oksa. "Gus, you're a genius!"

Before he could reply, Orthon and his allies took advantage of this brief hesitation to move closer to the Runaways.

"WATCH OUT!" shouted Tugdual.

In a fraction of a second, Orthon had snatched the medallion from Dragomira. No one had time to react. The watch fell to the ground where it was smashed to pieces under the Master of the Felons' heel.

"My profound thanks, dear friends!" he exclaimed triumphantly.

With a defiant glare for Dragomira and the Runaways, he slipped the medallion around his neck.

"So, my dear sister, where were we before we were distracted by that *tiny* setback?"

Dragomira turned round and dejectedly walked out of the room.

"I may have lost this battle, Orthon," she exclaimed from the staircase of the lofty hall. "But I haven't lost the war!"

32

A Rogue Wave

THE *SEA DOG* SAILED SOUTH WITH A FAIR WIND, FOL-
lowed by the Felons' ship, the *Eagle of Darkness*. Just as Dragomira
had done on the doorstep of the house in Bigtoe Square and at Leomido's
farm, Orthon had locked the door of his grey stone house and, without
a backward glance for Mercedica's grave, he'd walked down to the rocky
beach where the *Eagle of Darkness* was moored, followed in silence by
his allies. Night was now falling around the two ships, shrouding the
jagged Scottish coastline in a sinister fog. The Island of the Felons had
vanished from the horizon, marking the start of a new chapter for the
Runaways and the Felons.

"I don't know what's happening in Ireland, but it must be serious,"
suddenly remarked Pavel, staring up at the sky.

Several squads of military planes had just roared across the sky, heading west.

"Earthquake near Dublin," informed Tugdual, who was permanently
online via his mobile. "Registering eight on the Richter scale."

"Good Lord," whispered Dragomira sadly. "Poor Ireland… poor Earth."

✳

"HOLD TIGHT!" suddenly shouted Pavel, steering towards land.

"What's wrong?" exclaimed Oksa.

With a trembling finger, Gus pointed to the stern of the ship. In the glow of the setting sun and the *Sea Dog's* lights, the Felons' ship was following hard on their heels. However, Pavel was alerting them to a much more implacable enemy than their adversaries: a massive wave was rearing up on the horizon. Despite their sturdy engines, the two boats were being sucked back by the current. The roar of straining engines rose from the holds.

"It's the earthquake," observed Gus. "It must have caused a tidal wave!"

Handing over the ship's controls to Abakum, Pavel rushed out of the wheelhouse and, unleashing his Ink Dragon, took off from the deck. Naftali and Pierre joined him immediately. He glanced anxiously at the *Eagle of Darkness*, which held one of the keys for entering Edefia. If the medallion was lost, they were doomed. A long flame escaped the dragon's throat together with a roar of fear and anger.

"Look!" shouted Pierre.

The Felons had come up with the same idea as the Runaways: about ten experienced Vertifliers surrounded the black-hulled ship, filling Pavel's heart with fresh hope. The giant wave, like a wall of water, was only a few hundred yards away. They could hear its roar. It felt like the end of the world was coming as the sky grew visibly darker.

"We have to escape!" yelled Oksa in a panic.

She was about to join her father, but Dragomira held her back.

"Baba!" cried Oksa rebelliously. "I'm a Gracious, I can help!"

"Oksa! Do as your gran tells you!" ordered Marie, in a voice which brooked no refusal.

Oksa gnawed her lip until she could taste blood. The two boats were creaking as though about to break apart at any moment under the terrible strain. Abakum was desperately working the controls, hoping against hope that he could overcome the destructive might of nature. He watched the wall of water drawing closer and closer, then looked up at the sky. Oksa and the Runaways, gathered in the wheelhouse, followed his gaze. A familiar golden light suddenly enveloped the Runaways' ship. The hull made a terrifying cracking noise causing those on board to fear the worst, then the *Sea Dog* rose into the air, lifted far above the rough surface of the sea by Pavel and his friends—the Ageless Ones were performing an emergency rescue. Behind them, fairies and a few Felons were working together to pull the *Eagle of Darkness* from the path of the wave. A few seconds later, the Runaways and the Felons watched the monstrous wave pass below the hull of their ships, which were floating thirty or forty feet above the dark water. The seething waters came crashing down and continued their relentless course towards the coastline. They could hear the wail of warning sirens in the coastal villages, as more squads of planes suddenly appeared in the sky. Which was when Pavel's fears of a few days ago were realized: four pilots, more observant than the other members of their crew, spotted the two boats suspended in mid-air, bathed in golden light. Not to mention that one of them seemed to be held in the talons of a dragon! The four planes flew closer, creating a din that was just as frightening as that of the giant wave.

"We've had it this time," groaned Oksa, seeing the huge metal craft heading straight for them. "They'll think we're extraterrestrials, who've caused all these disasters. They'll kill us, I know they will!"

They looked at each other miserably. "Goodbye, world," thought Oksa. "I don't see how we can possibly get out of this mess this time." Suddenly the baby Lunatrix stood up, his complexion so colourless that it was almost transparent, and emitted a piercing whistling noise, which produced a strange phenomenon: the seconds stretched out endlessly, like elastic. The Runaways' movements became slower, as if bogged down in thick glue. The Outsiders were affected much more severely: their movements and their thoughts were paralysed. Oksa looked at Gus in amazement. He was motionless, his eyes fixed on her. Marie and the few other Outsiders showed the same horrified rigidity, as did the pilots of the four attacking planes, which had been stopped in their tracks.

"Haaave youuuu … stopppppppped timmmmmmme?!?" faltered Oksa, turning to the baby Lunatrix, who was concentrating too hard to reply.

"Our friend is a toddler, he can't yet control his anxiety," explained Abakum, articulating with superhuman effort. "And, fortunately for us, his lack of expertise has caused this distortion of time."

"I feel weeeeaaaak…" said the Incompetent.

"Haaaaaaaaa!" came the languid voice of the Getorix.

The words were elongated, distorted by the absence of time and, despite the seriousness of the situation, Oksa couldn't help smiling.

"It's compleeeeetely unbelieeeeevable…" she whispered in slow motion, sounding groggy.

Making the most of this phenomenon, the Runaways and Felons quickly set the two boats back down on the surface of the water, with the help of the Ageless Ones. The golden halo of light vanished—the fairies had done what they'd come to do—and the Vertifliers from both clans gladly rejoined their friends. They were safe and sound, thanks to the miracle that had just taken place. When everything was back to normal, the baby Lunatrix finally relaxed. His face resumed its childlike pinkish hue as the seconds gradually regained their usual pace and they all resumed control of their bodies and minds. The four planes circled the two boats, then the pilots headed back the way they'd come, uncertain about what they thought they'd seen.

"That was close," gasped Oksa. "Thank you, little Lunatrix!" she added, scooping him up affectionately in her arms.

The small creature gurgled and laid his head on Oksa's shoulder, before toddling back to Gus, whom he followed around like a shadow.

"The domestic staff of the Master-Impictured-Forever and his descendants encounter euphoria for making a contribution of help," said the Lunatrix.

"An invaluable contribution," added the Fairyman with a grateful look. "You were incredible, young Lunatrix!"

All the Runaways applauded gratefully.

Pavel hugged his daughter, before saying solemnly:

"We escaped by the skin of our teeth this time."

"The Outside is teetering on a knife-edge," murmured Dragomira.

"All the more reason not to waste any more time," nodded Abakum. "Let's get a move on! We have a plane to catch, my friends."

33

PERCEPTIONS

O KSA WAS STRETCHED OUT ON THE HAMMOCK HUNG from the walls of the ship's wheelhouse, gazing vacantly into space. Gus was lying on some wooden chests nearby, his arms behind his head. He kept his eyes on Oksa, as did Tugdual, who was straddling a chair on casters and swivelling round every so often.

"Can't you stop spinning on that chair?" snapped Gus.

"Why?" said Tugdual.

"It's getting on my nerves."

"If you're nerves are that fragile, I doubt you'll be able to cope with what's coming."

"I might surprise you," said Gus.

"I can't wait!" replied Tugdual with a smirk.

"Don't you two get bored winding each other up all the time?" broke in Oksa.

"It's your *friend* who started it!" objected Tugdual.

"It's your *boyfriend* who's trying to pick a fight, not me!" retorted Gus.

Oksa took a deep breath.

"At the moment, there's no such thing as *friend* or *boyfriend*! Just two annoying brats!"

Tugdual began laughing, as Gus tetchily threatened to get him back. He rubbed his temples, trying to soothe the beginnings of a deep, throbbing migraine. Since his so-called metamorphosis, the terrible agony caused by the Chiropteran's bite had gone, which was a huge relief, but he knew the threat was still there. The sickness had taken hold deep within him and was lurking like a predator waiting to attack. Did Oksa feel the same? He hadn't had the time—or courage—to ask. But they were both in the same boat… He was finding that he could look at her with a bold intensity that he'd never have thought possible. She was very pretty, frowning with concentration over the notes the three of them had taken when Dragomira had given them the task of organizing the trip. He'd give anything for her to look at him the way she looked at Tugdual.

Tugdual, on the other hand, seemed cocksure and unmoved by the agitation around him. Deep down, though, he was plagued by worry. Helena, his mother, appeared to be avoiding him and, what was worse, it was perfectly understandable. It was his fault his family had been torn apart. His father had fled. He might be dead, drowned by the lethal waves wreaking havoc all over the world. The latest information he'd seen on the Internet had described some particularly destructive tsunamis in the North Sea, which had left few oil rigs standing. He hadn't said anything, but his anxiety was slowly being replaced by grief. And bitter remorse. His father was an Outsider so there was very little possibility that he could have survived the disasters. If he'd stayed with his family and friends, he might have stood a chance…

Kukka was partly to blame for Tugdual's unhappiness. He did his best to avoid his spiteful cousin, but she was always hanging around Gus, who was never far from Oksa so, as a result, they formed a strange foursome. They were joined by a silent, morose Zoe, who wasn't fond of Tugdual at all—or rather, she was too wary of him to like him. He was aware of that and understood how she felt. He had no illusions about the image he portrayed—deliberately or not—and he wasn't surprised when people didn't warm to him. He knew his appearance, demeanour and decisions weren't everyone's cup of tea and he much preferred Zoe's outright wariness to Kukka's sly remarks. His cousin managed to catch him out too often. It took a great deal of energy to harden himself to her venomous attacks. Every time, he managed not to lose face, but inside he was seething. Bottling up his feelings was souring his life and he hated not acting spontaneously.

Then there was Oksa. More than anyone else, her life was in danger. Did she know that? He'd overheard scraps of conversation between Orthon and Agafon, who feared that the Chiropteran venom transmitted by Gus's bite might prove fatal for the Young Gracious. With an astounding lack of sensitivity, the two Felons shared their fear that if Oksa died before she could enter the Cloak Chamber, their plans would come to nought. This had put Tugdual in a speechless black rage. He watched Oksa, trying to keep his face expressionless. That was all he could do. His only defence was not letting his feelings show. He saw Oksa glance at Gus, who was watching her solemnly. It was so obvious he was crazy about her… How could anyone be so transparent? Didn't he realize he was putting himself in a position of weakness? As far as Tugdual was concerned, Gus's outbursts and lingering looks were pathetic, verging on laughable. Yet, deep down, he'd have loved to act as naturally and instinctively.

"Neither of you are listening to me!" Oksa shouted.

They both jumped, roused from their thoughts.

"We have to rethink everything!" announced Oksa tensely. "The Tumble-Bawler has just told us that we can't get to Edinburgh airport."

Immediately, Tugdual began tapping on his phone.

"Do you still have network coverage?"

"Yes, it's fine," he said reassuringly.

"See what it's like at Glasgow," suggested Gus.

A few seconds later he had his answer.

"Glasgow's fine," announced Tugdual. "The flight from Glasgow to Urumqi hasn't been cancelled."

"Thank goodness for that!" exclaimed Dragomira, who'd joined them.

"Does that change the rest of our journey?" asked Pavel anxiously.

"No," replied Oksa, gazing over Tugdual's shoulder at the screen. "Once we're in Urumqi, we can catch the train to Qingshui. The journey takes about twelve hours and there's a daily service. When we reach Qingshui, we can take another train to Saihan Toroi. Then it's about sixty miles across the Gobi Desert to get to Gashun-nur."

"Well done, youngsters," Dragomira congratulated them gravely. "I hope the rest of our journey will be less eventful…"

"It's hard to plan ahead," remarked Tugdual. "The whole world seems to be in chaos. People are putting as much distance as they can between them and the coast or volcanoes. There have been a few earth tremors between Urumqi and Gashun-nur, but they haven't caused a great deal of damage. The railway lines haven't been affected. We just have to hope nothing terrible happens before we get to Gashun-nur."

"Not to mention that there may be snow in the Gobi Desert this time of year and that could slow us down," added Gus. "Let's hope the trains are running! Otherwise…"

He glanced anxiously at Oksa.

"Otherwise, we'll just have to rely on ourselves," she said, finishing his sentence. "And on magic."

34

Sorrows of the Heart

D ESPITE THE RAGING WIND AND TORRENTIAL RAIN THAT
had slowed their progress through the night, the *Sea Dog* and the
Eagle of Darkness reached the mouth of the River Clyde at daybreak.
The dismayed passengers on the two ships gazed at the coastline from
the deck or from their cabins. None of them had been able to sleep after
the frightening episode with the giant wave. Exhausted and keyed up,
the bleak sight before them only increased their gloom. It looked like
the Clyde had overflowed its banks, surprising the inhabitants in their
sleep. The withdrawing waters had left behind scenes of total devastation. The houses that were still standing had been badly battered by the
violent weather, and what looked vaguely like streets were strewn with
furniture, cars and a myriad broken, muddy objects. All around stood
formless piles stacked high with memories and ruined lives. They could
see people wandering about aimlessly like zombies, shocked at the
destructive power of the waves. Others were bustling about frantically
for no good reason.

"This is the end of the Outside…" murmured Dragomira, with tears
in her eyes.

"We'll sort it out, Baba, you'll see!" said Oksa comfortingly. Dragomira
was trembling. She raised the collar of her plum mohair jacket, hiding
part of her face, and gripped the rail with all her might.

"Are you OK, Baba?"

Dragomira turned away, as if to avoid answering. Oksa looked at her in concern.

"Your gran's just a bit tired," broke in Abakum, glancing sombrely at his old friend.

He put his arm round Oksa's shoulder and led her towards the wheelhouse.

"We'll be in Glasgow soon, sweetheart," he said. "So could you round everyone up?"

"How much do the Felons know about where we're going?"

"Not a lot, to be honest. It's driving Orthon mad."

"It must be quite a blow to his megalomaniac pride!" said Oksa.

"Indeed, and I have to admit it gives me a fair degree of personal satisfaction."

"Oh, Abakum!" said Oksa, pretending to be indignant. "A wise and honourable man like you?"

"I may be a Fairyman, but I'm still human and there are a few little pleasures I couldn't do without," confessed Abakum with a laugh. "Picturing Orthon totally dependent on us and fuming on his magnificent ship gladdens my heart."

"He must be livid!" sniggered Oksa.

Abakum gave her a knowing smile. Making the most of this moment of complicity, Oksa couldn't help returning to her gran's worrying behaviour.

"Don't forget I have a better understanding of things now I'm over sixteen. Is she frightened? Does she think we'll fail?"

"We've all had some terrible shocks to deal with in the last few days," replied the old man calmly.

Then he turned round to occupy himself with the two Boximinuses and the chest of Granoks, which he firmly strapped up: the subject was closed.

"We'll reach Glasgow in half an hour!" announced Pavel on the intercom.

Oksa took a deep breath and looked up at the louring sky. She shivered. Would the Runaways be strong enough to face the endless ordeals that fate seemed to have in store for them?

※

Glasgow had escaped the worst of the flood. Only the lowest parts of the town were still under muddy water but there was a palpable sense of panic. Long queues were forming outside shops and pharmacies, and the volume of traffic in the cluttered streets was totally baffling.

The *Dog* and the *Eagle* navigated with difficulty past countless boats adrift in Glasgow's port after the wild night. The Runaways and Felons moored their ships at one of the landing stages and disembarked onto the quay, each clan keeping themselves to themselves. Despite the rift, Annikki dared to go over to the Runaways to make sure Marie was OK and Oksa was surprised to see an expression of kindness and respect on her face, which reassured her. Annikki seemed to have made it a point of honour to protect the ailing woman, as if she were genuinely fond of her.

"Let's go, my friends," said Abakum.

None of them looked back as they headed towards the devastated town, which was in absolute chaos.

※

"We need to find a way to get to the airport," Dragomira told the Felons.

"You mean we have to catch a plane?" asked Orthon furiously.

"We have to take an eleven-hour flight to Urumqi," replied Dragomira icily. "Which leaves us barely two hours to get to the airport," she added, looking at her watch. "We don't have any time to lose."

The Felons looked furious. They weren't in charge and Orthon was finding this harder than anyone to take.

"Is the Definitive Landmark for the Portal in Urumqi?" he roared, grabbing Dragomira by the shoulder.

Baba Pollock shrugged him off, as Abakum and Pavel headed menacingly their way.

"Urumqi is the second leg after Glasgow," she said, indignantly. "Frankly, Orthon, do you think I'd tell you any more than that?"

And she turned her back on him.

"There's a shuttle to the airport in ten minutes," announced Tugdual, his telephone pressed to his ear. "The bus stop is a couple of hundred yards away."

"Well done, Tugdual," congratulated Dragomira. "You at least know how to make yourself useful!" she finished, glancing meaningfully at Orthon.

"Thanks a million, Zorro," muttered Gus. Oksa glared at him.

"Don't you get bored with harping on the same string?" she asked sullenly.

The two groups walked to the bus stop, where Gus suddenly sank to the ground. Folding his long legs under him, he put his head in his hands. A few seconds later, Oksa reluctantly joined him, assailed by a sudden pain.

"What's the matter?" asked Pavel in a panic. "Are you ill?" Oksa gave him a glassy stare.

"Splitting headache," she replied, rubbing her temples hard.

"As if you had something boring into your skull?" groaned Gus.

"Exactly!"

Immediately, Dragomira rummaged around in her bag and took out her Caskinette. She gave Gus and Oksa a tiny silvery ball each and instructed the teenagers to swallow them.

"My dear sister and her pharmacopoeia," remarked Orthon sarcastically.

"Without your ancestors' diabolical inventions, we wouldn't need it, would we?" retorted Dragomira. "And may I remind you that our future depends on the good health of these two youngsters."

"Let me die here. It wouldn't change much anyway," moaned Gus, earning himself a sharp dig in the ribs from Oksa.

"Shut up, Gus," she groaned. "Do as I do, please: suffer in silence!"

The small silvery balls gradually lessened the agonizing pain, leaving them both feeling nauseated, which made it hard to see and think straight. Meanwhile, the Runaways and Felons were impatiently waiting for the bus. Some of them were leaning against the dripping walls of buildings, others were pacing up and down, but they were all tense.

Oksa eventually stood up to stretch her legs. Glimpsing her reflection in a shop window, she felt even dizzier. "Is that really me?" she thought, going closer. With her nose virtually touching the glass, she ran her fingers over her face, fascinated and a little startled by her own image. So long as she couldn't see herself, it wasn't too hard to deal with this change—she just had to become accustomed to her new height and shape, which she definitely liked. Controlling her emotions was harder. Everything she felt was stronger, more violent, more overwhelming. When Gus was near her or when Tugdual gazed at her, she couldn't think straight. Things had been so much simpler when she'd been two years younger, a few days ago... As if to press the point home, she glimpsed Tugdual's reflection in the shop window. There was no escape! Everywhere she looked, she saw him. Fair-haired Kukka suddenly appeared between them, her perfect figure regal, oozing self-confidence. Oksa turned and saw her walk over to Tugdual. To her amazement, Tugdual did nothing to avoid his malicious cousin. "Leave him alone," thought Oksa angrily, overcome with jealousy. "Why doesn't he just walk away? He hates her!" Despondently, she went back to sit on the curb next to Gus in miserable silence, rubbing her temples in a vain attempt to banish her black thoughts.

Twenty minutes later, the shuttle still hadn't come and impatience had given way to restless irritation. Realizing there was no point waiting any longer, they were all trying to find a solution.

"Let's Vertifly!" suggested Gregor.

"And risk attracting the attention of the army again? No thanks!" retorted Pavel.

"We could easily overpower any soldiers, even if they were heavily armed," objected Gregor.

"Of course we could—but we'd also have to be devoid of human compassion to do that, which isn't really like us."

Orthon applauded sarcastically.

"That's all very well, but we won't achieve our goals with such elevated values!" he remarked.

"The bus depot is only a stone's throw from here," broke in Tugdual, with the Tumble-Bawler perched on his shoulder. "Maybe we could borrow a bus?"

They all looked at each other, open-mouthed at such a simple solution.

"Brilliant idea, Tugdual!" said Abakum. "Let's act fast, time is short."

※

The mechanic saw the group of almost sixty people walking into the bus garage, but had no time to react: Dragomira had already hit him with a Memory-Swipe Granok. The man was immobilized in front of his toolbox, eyes blank.

"What about this one?" said Pavel, indicating one of the many buses parked there. "It's big enough to take us all. Tumble, can you tell us how to get there?"

The creature nodded.

"Stay with me then, please. You can show me the way. The quicker we get to the airport, the greater our chances of catching that plane today," he added, gazing in concern at his watch.

The Runaways and Felons began climbing into the bus. Gus sat down next to Oksa.

"Has your father ever driven a bus before?" he quietly asked her.

"Er... no," she replied, smiling. "But he'd never sailed a ship either!"

"Well, I hope the Airplane has a pilot!" This reference to a film they'd enjoyed so much made both of them laugh, despite the serious circumstances, and attracted a deceptively disinterested look from Tugdual. Oksa winked at him and he ducked his head to hide a smile.

"WHAT DO YOU THINK YOU'RE DOING?" suddenly roared a voice.

A man had just appeared out of nowhere. The three Felons who hadn't yet climbed into the bus turned round defensively.

"You're trying to steal that bus!" yelled the man. "Get out right now or I'll call the police, you lousy thieves!"

The Felons smiled, intending to make mincemeat of the reckless individual, but Oksa acted first. The Young Gracious quickly opened the window and fired a Granok. The man's face immediately relaxed into a blissful smile. He walked over to Agafon, the unsmiling Felon, and embraced him warmly.

"Come back soon, godfather!" he exclaimed. "I'll make sure I have a bottle of that single malt you like so much and I'll get my revenge on you at cards, just wait and see," he chortled.

Gus looked quizzically at Oksa.

"I was hoping I'd get a chance to use my new Granok," she said.

She turned towards Abakum with a broad grin.

"Your Hypnagogo works like a dream. I love it!" The Fairyman smiled back at her.

"The road's clear, so sit tight," shouted Pavel, starting up the bus.

After a few tentative manoeuvres, Pavel soon got the hang of driving the huge vehicle and they headed off through Glasgow's congested roads.

35

A Chaotic Escape

COMFORTABLY SETTLED IN HER SEAT, OKSA RELAXED to the steady rocking of the train as it sped towards Saihan Toroi. Even though the last two days of travel by air and rail hadn't involved much physical exertion, she felt exhausted. She watched the magnificent yet monotonous landscape racing past. Nothing disturbed the tranquil appearance of the hills and plains of the Gobi Desert, which were covered with a thin dusting of snow. Everything looked so peaceful that it was hard to believe that the Outside was slipping inexorably into chaos. It felt as if this part of the world had been shielded from the disasters: the scattered towns served by the railway line seemed to be going about their daily lives as if nothing had happened; times were just as hard, but the inhabitants had lost none of their welcoming ways and beaming smiles.

The start of the journey hadn't been as peaceful. Despite Pavel's skilful driving, getting to Glasgow airport had been quite an ordeal. No one had ever seen such nose-to-tail traffic in the suburbs and on the roads out of the city centre. Fearing more floods along the coast, those who could leave were attempting to take refuge inland and, in the light of warnings from the leading specialists in Earth Sciences, no one could blame them for this exodus. In Glasgow, as all over the world, massive traffic jams were forming on the outskirts of towns at risk from tidal waves, tsunamis, volcanic eruptions, earth tremors, landslides, etc. Although the cause of some of these hazards could be traced back to human neglect and several decades of disregard for the most elementary concepts of universal ecology, there was no accounting for most of the disasters ravaging the world. The dangers remained inexplicable and unpredictable.

⁕

The traffic was so bad that the Runaways and Felons had almost missed the plane to Urumqi. Dragomira had been forced to use a discreet magical manoeuvre to clear away a broken-down car blocking the road. The bus had finally arrived at the airport less than an hour before take-off and tensions were running high. They were able to buy tickets very quickly since their destination was not very popular and the flight was far from full. However, the terminals were packed with hysterical passengers wanting to catch a plane out of danger at any cost. They had to use their elbows and, occasionally, their fists in this concrete jungle where civilized values were evaporating before their eyes. Oksa had been traumatized by a particularly nasty incident: one man had hurled himself at Marie and had thrown her to the floor to steal her wheelchair in the hope that appearing disabled might improve his chances of getting a ticket. Pavel and Naftali had immediately pinned him to the ground and had immobilized him with a Dozident Granok. Reminiscens and Zoe, still in shock at Mercedica's death, had also been easy prey for various predatory men. Someone had snatched Reminiscens' bag and Zoe had been punched in the shoulder trying to get it back. This time it was Tugdual who stepped in with magic, using a Magnetus to retrieve the bag and a Putrefactio to punish the lowlife who'd stolen it. A wave of panic had surged through the airport when the man's arm had begun to rot, giving off a vile stench.

"You certainly don't do things by halves, do you!" Oksa had exclaimed.

"You can say that again, Lil' Gracious," he'd remarked with an irresistible smile.

Remembering that scene, Oksa looked around for Tugdual. The Runaways and the Felons were sharing the same carriage on the train speeding into the heart of the Gobi Desert. Since the start of the journey, Tugdual and Gus had taken every opportunity to try to sit beside her, but neither of them had succeeded: Marie, Pavel, Dragomira or Abakum had claimed the "privilege". Still, the two rivals kept a protective eye on the Young Gracious, as did Orthon, who was never far away... the Felon hadn't stopped fuming since they'd left the island. Dragomira was a closed book: she wouldn't let any information slip about their destination. All the Felons' schemes had been thwarted by their unstinting vigilance. Even a truth potion, poured secretly into Baba Pollock's tea, hadn't allowed Orthon to achieve his ends.

"Orthon's such a creep," muttered Oksa, looking away from the Felon.

"What did you say, darling?" asked Marie.

The Young Gracious studied her mother sadly. Marie never complained about the pain, but her condition was deteriorating so obviously that she didn't need to say anything. Over the last two days her face had turned a nasty grey colour and had become deeply lined. Her body was hunched over, wasted by illness.

"I was thinking that Orthon hasn't spared our family much," replied Oksa, with a heavy heart.

"You can say that again," said her mother, blinking nervously. "How do you feel?"

"Um... like I'm crossing a crater full of molten lava on a tightrope. One false step and I'll fall! Dragging everyone else down with me—you get the sort of thing?"

"Perfectly," sighed Marie. "We'll survive this!"

"Damn right we will," said Oksa.

She focused on the sky traversed by long black streaks and the snow-covered hills, finding it soothing to gaze at such endless expanses. She watched the landscape for a while in a cocoon of lethargy, until her gaze reluctantly drifted towards Gus. He was in her line of sight, looking perfectly calm, although she was sure his expressionless mask concealed intense anxiety. Crossing the Gobi Desert seemed to bring out his Chinese side. Was he thinking about the woman who'd given birth to him and who was living somewhere in this vast country? Perhaps... unless his mind was fixed on the harsh reality of living on borrowed time.

"What are you thinking about?" she asked, going to sit next to him.

"Nothing special," he replied, moving away slightly.

"It's a long journey..." she urged.

He hunched down in his seat and looked the other way. She studied him out of the corner of her eye.

"Have I ever told you how much I love your company? You're so... chatty!" she teased.

"Hey! Don't come over here and annoy me just because you're as bored as a sloth!"

Oksa chewed her lip and stretched out her legs. Studying the seat in front intently, she scratched the worn fabric and pulled out a loose thread.

"I'm not a sloth," she said after a while.

Gus furtively glanced at her.

"Sorry."

"Forget it!" she said, relieved that he was open to a suspension of hostilities.

She waited for him to continue, but he kept quiet, his forehead lined with worry.

"Are you trying to unpick that seat?" he asked suddenly.

"Why won't you tell me what's wrong?" retorted Oksa, turning to look directly at him, her elbow propped on the headrest.

"Has it occurred to you that some of us might not be able to get into Edefia?" he asked tremulously.

Oksa looked at him wide-eyed, her chest tight.

"What do you mean?"

"What happens if all the Outsiders end up stranded at the entrance to Edefia?" continued Gus. "What happens if they're not allowed in?"

Oksa scrubbed her hand over her face. Beads of cold sweat appeared on her forehead and her head swam as she was seized by a terrible fear.

"Why did you say that? Why do you have to think such *awful* things?" Gus met her eyes. She flinched.

"I'm not the only one, Oksa. Everyone thinks the same, your parents, mine, Dragomira... You just want to bury your head in the sand. But just because something is 'unthinkable' doesn't make it any less probable."

"PROBABLE?!? But, Gus—"

The words caught in her throat. She looked around frantically. Her mother had her head on Pavel's shoulder and he was gently stroking her hair. Marie suddenly looked up and gave him a crooked smile. Oksa's heart turned over; she was suddenly convinced that Gus's fears were far from being unfounded. Oksa looked round the carriage. Olof and his wife were cuddling Kukka; the Fortensky clan were discussing something in low voices; Cockerell was clutching his wife's hands to his chest... The Felons were doing the same, she noticed: they were lavishing a great deal of attention on Outsiders. An unusual amount of attention? Her question remained unanswered; Gus had just tensed on his seat, his hands gripping the armrests. Was he having another attack? "Oh please, not another one," pleaded Oksa in her head.

"WHAT'S GOING ON?" Gus exclaimed, jumping up.

Oksa looked out of the window, as did the rest of the passengers: hundreds of animals were stampeding south, heading in the opposite direction to that of the train. Snow leopards and small horses were leading the way, followed by an unruly pack of galloping camels, running bears, sheep, goats and flocks of frightened birds. A long way behind them, enormous clouds of dust were rising from the ground, obstructing the horizon. The train slowed down appreciably, as if the driver were worried about approaching what was looking increasingly like an impassable barrier. The two Boximinuses began rocking wildly, which didn't help matters. Their occupants seemed to be in the grip of the same panic as the fleeing desert animals, which didn't bode well. The passengers were now glued to the windows, staring at the barrier of dust with appalled fascination. Suddenly the train stopped. There were loud shouts as the two drivers suddenly rushed into the carriage occupied by the Runaways and Felons.

"What are they saying?" Oksa couldn't help asking. "It's Chinese, I can't make head or tail of it!"

The members of the group with the best command of the priceless gift of Poluslingua listened hard. The panic-stricken train drivers were shouting and gesticulating wildly.

"The Great Yellow Dragon," Abakum translated finally, going white. "It's a giant sandstorm."

36

THE GREAT
YELLOW DRAGON

T HE ENORMOUS BILLOWS OF DUST WERE GROWING
nearer, roaring like a huge monster. Soon they filled the sky,
obscuring the feeble rays of sunshine and plunging the dunes into total
darkness.

"It looks very high!" whispered Oksa.

"Tumble," called Dragomira, dipping her hand into her bag.

"Yes, my Old Gracious?" said the creature, standing to attention.

"What do you know about this sandstorm?"

The Tumble-Bawler pressed itself to the window for a few seconds,
then replied:

"It's incredibly destructive. As you can see, it reaches high into the
sky, so the Runaways and Felons won't be able to lift the train over it the
way they lifted the ships over that rogue wave."

"Is it very wide?"

The Tumble pressed against the window again and concentrated.

"The sand cloud covers a surface area of about seventy-eight miles
and is moving at ninety-nine miles per hour."

"We're going to die!" cried Oksa, wringing her hands.

"It will take about forty minutes to pass through it," calculated Gus,
thinking hard.

"Forty minutes?" exclaimed Oksa, trembling. "We'll never hold our breath that long. We'll suffocate! We've got to do something! Would it help if I raised a storm? It wouldn't take much to send me over the edge…"

Everyone considered this suggestion carefully.

"Given the strength of the wind inside it, I'm afraid the sandstorm might just absorb the additional energy and that would only strengthen it," said Abakum. "Which would make matters even worse."

"What about Tornaphyllon Granoks?" suggested Oksa. "If we all fire Tornaphyllons at it, we might be able to push it back!"

"It's worth a try," said Pavel, going over to the carriage door.

All the Runaways and Felons with Granok-Shooters gathered on the snow-covered sand. Joining forces for the first time, they focused on the sand wall advancing with a roar. Oksa felt as though her brain was about to explode. She was making a superhuman effort not to give way to panic. Flashes of black light crackled above the Runaways and Felons, who were summoning all their energy.

"Together, on my signal!" said Abakum. Three… two… ONE!"

They all blew into their Granok-Shooters at the same time, saying the magic formula to themselves.

> *By the power of the Granoks*
> *Think outside the box.*
> *This twisting gale of wind*
> *Will put you in a spin.*

A transparent cylinder of wind materialized, which looked very much like a massive soap bubble, and raced at breathtaking speed towards the moving sand wall. The impact when they collided sent a few tons of sand into the air to form a hole—which closed up again a few seconds later.

"Again!" shouted Dragomira.

After two more attempts the Runaways and Felons climbed back into the train, looking undeniably anxious.

"Maybe we should turn round?" suggested Naftali.

"This isn't a high-speed train. We'd never outdistance it," said Pavel.

"The baby Lunatrix could slow down time," suggested Pierre in his turn.

"That would be an excellent solution," replied Abakum, "if it weren't for the fact that his power only works on human beings, not the elements."

"Oksa?" called Gus, his eyes fixed on the dreadful sand wall drawing ever closer. "Do you remember that video clip we saw on the Internet?"

Oksa looked at him, intrigued.

"Which one, Gus?"

"The one about the Australians who found themselves in the path of an enormous sandstorm, which was heading straight for them. Do you remember how they survived?"

"Instead of running away, they sprinted as fast as they could through it."

"Exactly!"

"But Gus," broke in Marie, sounding choked. "We wouldn't survive for forty minutes in that hellhole!"

"It's only forty minutes if we stay still. If we move too, it wouldn't take so long to pass through it," replied Gus.

"But we'll be trapped like rats by the sand…"

"Not if the Tornaphyllons create a tunnel through it for us!"

They looked at each other in amazement.

"Gus?" said Oksa hoarsely.

"Yes, Oksa?"

"You know you're a genius, don't you?"

Gus gave her a half-smile and turned away.

"QUICK!" exclaimed Dragomira. "The storm's coming!" Abakum rushed over to his chest of Granoks and handed some out to everyone with a Granok-Shooter. Then he hurried towards the locomotive, which had been abandoned by the train's drivers, who'd been just as terrified by these passengers with strange powers as by the sandstorm. He took over at the controls, while Pavel rushed outside, despite protests from his friends.

"Pavel, PLEASE DON'T GO!" yelled Marie, trying in vain to hold him back.

Watched by his companions and the other stunned passengers, the Ink Dragon reared from Pavel's back and took flight.

"The battle of the dragons," remarked Abakum, starting up the train.

⁂

Some thirty people were silently clustered around Abakum, taking it in turns to fire as many Granoks as possible through the half-open windows. Pavel's Ink Dragon was flying above the locomotive to escort the train heading at top speed for the wall.

"We're mad," muttered Oksa, shaking like a leaf.

"It will work!" said Tugdual, putting his arms around her from behind.

"GET READY!" announced Abakum, hunched tensely over the instrument panel.

The vast bulwark of sand and the train were speeding towards each other on collision course. The Runaways and Felons fought to control their mounting terror, their breath coming in short gasps. A few more yards to go, a few seconds…

⁂

There was almost complete darkness at the heart of the sandstorm. Visibility was reduced to near zero and only the train's headlamp cast a hazy yellow glow over the locomotive as it valiantly raced ahead. Ignoring the bitter cold caused by the sudden drop in temperature, the members of the two feuding groups worked together to maximize the strength of the Tornaphyllons. Large cylinders of pure energy created a tunnel through which the train accelerated. Pavel and his Ink Dragon did their bit by expelling a mighty breath drawn from deep within to drive back the onslaughts of the sandstorm. Runaways and Felons

198

alike realized how important Pavel's contribution was and they all feared for his life. If he wasn't strong enough to resist the storm, he'd be swept away... While concentrating on the Tornaphyllons, Oksa couldn't help picturing that terrible possibility. "Hang in there, Dad, hang in there!" she pleaded silently. The Curbita-Flatulo undulated continually around her wrist and she'd never needed its help more. She felt exhausted and petrified—a dreadful mix of emotions which sapped her energy.

"Thirty more miles exactly," the Tumble-Bawler suddenly informed them. "If we keep going at this speed, we should be out of the sand cloud in twelve minutes."

Twelve minutes. Twelve short minutes, which seemed like hours... Would they succeed? There was no way of knowing. They were all aware that the Insiders' fabulous powers were no match for Mother Nature. Their only hope was that today, on the threshold of Edefia, she'd be kind and offer them a slim chance of survival.

"Keep it up!" said Dragomira, her face drawn with tiredness. "The worst is over."

Despite her gran's encouragement, Oksa had a nasty feeling that "the worst" was still to come. The violent storm was intensifying and the strength of the Runaways and the Felons was waning. The train was still travelling at top speed, but it was being hit hard by the eddies of sand. All the doors and windows were closed, except for the ones in the locomotive which were only open a crack, but sand was flooding in through the smallest gaps and now lay three feet deep on the floor of the carriages. This only increased the general atmosphere of panic and despair as the added weight was beginning to slow the train down.

"Abakum? What's happening?" cried Dragomira in alarm.

The Fairyman had no time to reply: the train suddenly shuddered and seemed to rock on its rails.

"We're too heavy!" he said, going pale. "We'll be derailed! Naftali! Pierre! We have to uncouple some of the carriages!"

The two men rushed out, followed by Orthon and Gregor. It was too difficult to walk through the sand, so they lost no time in Vertiflying towards the rear of the train, watched in amazement by the passengers who'd gathered in the front carriages. A few minutes later, half as light again, the train picked up speed. Only to slow down again after a few hundred yards because of the violence of the storm.

"Come on!" encouraged Oksa, surprising herself. "We've come so far. We can't let ourselves be buried in the sand now, can we?"

Up to their waists in sand, they drew on their last reserves of strength. They had to get out of this, come hell or high water. There was a heart-rending howl from the roof. The wings of the Ink Dragon suddenly banged against the little windows of the locomotive. They rose again feebly, then collapsed to cover the front of the train, which was beginning to shake under the force of the storm. The Yellow Dragon was overpowering the Ink Dragon!

"NO!" yelled Oksa. "It can't end like this!"

It took her just a few seconds to visualize her father, lying lifeless on the cold metal, his face scratched raw by sand. The feeling of outrage provoked by this thought filled her with a seething anger that awoke her Identego with a frantic call for help. As she felt that part of her inner self leave her, she'd never been so aware of her mind and body. Dragomira watched in wonder as the miracle unfolded before her eyes. The Two Graciouses exchanged a guarded look of understanding as Oksa's Identego slipped out through the slightly open window.

37

RESCUING THE
INK DRAGON

LTHOUGH OKSA DIDN'T SEE WHAT HAPPENED NEXT,
she felt it as intensely as if she were experiencing it in person.
Her Identego elongated to spread a strong protective shield over Pavel
and his dragon, unconscious on the roof of the train. Gradually, Oksa
realized that her father's heart had started beating again beneath the
unexpected shelter she'd provided. She could physically feel the blood
flowing again through the veins of the man who'd almost sacrificed his
life for them. Her cry of triumph was echoed silently a hundred times
over by the Identego.

"Look!" exclaimed Abakum.

Was it an optical illusion? A mirage born of her wish to survive? Oksa
blinked and a wave of indescribable happiness washed over her. At last!
The sand cloud was becoming lighter! They began to see daylight and
the wind was gusting less violently.

"We're safe!"

Cries of joy rang out through the train. Most of the passengers—
Runaways, Felons and Outsiders—were crying with relief.

"Where's Dad?" asked Oksa anxiously.

She couldn't sense anything any more. Her Identego must have slipped
back inside her without her realizing. Abakum stopped the train and

extended his arms to open the door of the locomotive. Sand flowed out, forming a high mound. Oksa leapt out onto the gritty ground. She looked up.

"DAD!" she yelled hoarsely. "DAD! Where are you?"

Peace had returned. The clear sky was completely cloudless. All around, the bleak Gobi Desert stretched out for miles and miles. Strangely enough, the only sign of life was the huge sand wall disappearing into the distance, whipping up tons of yellow dust as it continued on its destructive course.

"Dad…" wailed Oksa, falling to her knees.

Dragomira and Abakum also climbed down from the train, looking worried. They scanned the sky and sand dunes, but there was nothing. As a last resort, Oksa Vertiflew into the air.

"He's here!" she cried, standing on the roof of the train. "Dad!"

Pavel was lying on his face, protected by the bronze hide of the exhausted Ink Dragon. As Oksa approached, the dragon dissolved, becoming a tattoo once more, and Pavel sat up, holding out his arms to his daughter.

"We did it…" he said, coughing and spluttering. Oksa threw herself into his arms.

"Dad! You were amazing!"

On the sand dune, the passengers were congratulating each other and enthusiastically applauding. Pavel looked at the Runaways and Felons, who had spontaneously split into two groups again.

"We were all amazing," he said with great emotion. "All of us…"

He turned away and his eyes narrowed. Oksa followed his gaze: on the horizon a vertical beam had appeared, glowing a strange colour. A colour the Young Gracious and her father had never seen before…

38

THE LAST EVENING

"**I** KEEP TELLING YOU I CAN'T SEE ANYTHING! HAVE YOU forgotten that I'm just an ordinary Outsider with ordinary eyes which can only see ordinary things? Your rotten vertical beam of light is invisible to me, OK?"

Scowling, Gus angrily kicked the seat in front.

"Ouch!" yelped Brune.

"Sorry," apologized Gus. "It wasn't aimed at you. It's Oksa's fault."

"Oh, come off it," sighed Oksa.

She looked away in annoyance and concentrated on the road. Two hours earlier, the Runaways and Felons had finally disembarked from the dusty train in Saihan Toroi. The violent onslaught of the Yellow Dragon had left the small town licking its wounds and the inhabitants were struggling to recover from the devastation caused by the fury of the elements, as was the case all over the world. A crowd of hysterical men and women, obsessed with the idea of escaping the ravaged areas, mobbed the train as soon as it pulled into the station. Saihan Toroi was the last stop on the line, and the train was then heading back south. In the north, according to the latest information, the land was being hit by continuous earthquakes. Despite the bad news from every continent, everyone was looking for an escape route—running away in the vain hope of finding safety somewhere else. It was what people had done since time immemorial.

In the general panic, no one paid any attention to the tall stories told by a few passengers about travellers with strange powers, some of whom—they swore on their lives!—could fly or turn into dragons. The Runaways and Felons took advantage of the prevailing chaos to slip away and disappear into the milling, ravaged town. Dragomira and Abakum managed to commandeer two clapped-out old buses and no one needed to be asked twice to climb on board for the journey north to Gashun-nur.

The rickety buses wheezed along the bumpy road, but the travellers were too tired to complain. Once the Definitive Landmark had appeared on the horizon, Orthon had hastily taken the wheel of the first bus. He was driving straight ahead on the only road, followed by Naftali, who was driving the other bus.

"Let him think he can gain an advantage over us," Dragomira had sighed.

Gus had also been in a tearing hurry. Not to take the wheel, but to sit next to Oksa before Tugdual did. Tugdual had initially looked a little disappointed, but had then favoured Gus with a mocking smile. As soon as the two buses had left the town, Oksa had tried to talk to Gus about the peculiar beam that was drawing them like a magnet but Gus, upset and ashamed that he couldn't share his friend's fascination, had reacted badly. Oksa tried to think about something else, but her mind kept coming back to the strange ray of light cutting through the sky, and Gus's words, which she couldn't shake from her mind. Her doubts were blackening her thoughts like indelible ink. "*What happens if all the Outsiders end up stranded at the entrance to Edefia? What happens if they're not allowed in?*" She shook her head in alarm and looked at Gus. They'd soon realized that only the Insiders and their descendants could see the brightly shining beam. No one else could see its peculiar colour, which had put Gus in a foul mood… and had made everyone more anxious. Oksa remembered what Dragomira had said a few months earlier: *"You know, of course, that objects can only be seen when the light they reflect reaches our eyes. Well, the light in Edefia draws its source from a singular beam of sunlight. This forms a solar mantle, which is totally invisible from the Outside and operates as an impassable barrier or force field. Even when Outsiders are near to Edefia, a strange phenomenon renders our land invisible and causes them to go in a different direction. The same thing happens from above: Edefia cannot be seen by the most sophisticated satellites, probably for the same reasons. Our findings suggest that these light waves move faster than ordinary light waves. Edefia's mantle is visible to Insiders: it's our frontier and our eyes have become genetically adapted to the prodigious speed of light which lends it a colour that none of us has ever seen on the Outside. An unknown colour…"* Oksa now understood what Baba Pollock had told her when she'd discovered the secret of her origins, and it didn't bode well for the Outsiders. What would happen if they couldn't see the beam and were diverted away from the Portal? Oksa shivered. She looked at Gus.

"I'm sorry," she murmured.

"Forget it," replied Gus sullenly, making no attempt to lighten his tone. "Tell me what the colour is like and we'll call it quits."

Oksa frowned. How could you describe something that didn't exist? She could see the beam of light, but it was impossible to find the right words. Oksa wracked her brains and, doing her best not to annoy her friend any further, decided to tell him exactly what she saw:

"At first it looks like the beam is rising from the ground into the sky but, if you examine it more closely, you can see it is actually coming from the sky. It's falling like a vertical ray of sunshine."

"I'm with you so far," nodded Gus. "But what about the colour, Oksa? Tell me what the colour is like."

"It isn't like anything, Gus," admitted Oksa.

"How can it not be like anything?"

Oksa glanced at him in frustration.

"I could tell you that it's a blend of all the existing colours, but that wouldn't be right. I don't know, Gus... I don't know what the colour's like."

Gus sighed noisily.

"OK, I believe you," he said, giving in.

The bus suddenly stopped. Naftali got up and stretched.

"It's almost dark, we should get some rest."

A shadow crossed Oksa's face. After travelling so many miles and enduring so many hardships, everyone should be dying to pass through the Portal, but no one seemed that bothered about reaching the beam of light. It made no sense! The Young Gracious's concern was only heightened when she saw Orthon banging on the door of the bus in a temper.

"Why are you stopping?"

"We're going to spend the night in this village," replied Dragomira, calmly and authoritatively.

Orthon glared at her.

"That's just wasting time!" he fumed.

"You can go on ahead and wait for us!" replied Baba Pollock. "We're spending our last night here together."

LAST NIGHT? Oksa stiffened. She looked at her gran in a panic, then her parents. She shakily left her seat and went over to her mother.

"Mum? What's going on? Tell me it isn't true..."

Her voice broke. Marie hugged her. She didn't deny or confirm anything, but her silence spoke volumes. The bus creaked as the Runaways got out and Pavel picked up Marie to carry her down from the vehicle. Hanging on to her mother's hand, Oksa followed, a scared look in her eyes.

"That's pretty," said Gus behind her.

The village looked abandoned. The houses were in ruins; sections of wall had fallen down to reveal glimpses of dusty interiors and toppled furniture, vestiges of lives that had been turned upside down. However, in the middle of this wreckage stood an almost intact Buddhist temple, built of grey stone and weathered wood. Small sculptures of men astride dragons dangled from the curved ends of the roof, which had only lost a few glazed tiles. The setting sun bathed this ancient building in an aura of mystery.

"No kidding," exclaimed Oksa. "It's gorgeous." Dragomira was already marching towards the temple, where she and her clan would spend the night. She climbed the few steps leading up to the entrance, took out her Polypharus, then walked inside.

"I hope there aren't any ancient ghosts of demon monks," whispered Gus to Oksa, in a ghoulish voice.

She jumped and punched him on the shoulder.

"Idiot!"

"Come on, let's take the grand tour."

Oksa smiled, grateful to him for attempting to lighten the mood. She followed him inside the temple, which felt safe and peaceful, despite being dilapidated. A brazier in the centre of the large main room, filled with sticks collected by Pierre and Abakum and lit by Dragomira's Fireballistico, soon had everyone feeling warmer. The Runaways searched the houses nearby and brought back the makings of a real feast: potatoes, dried meat, lard and nuts.

"I'm starving," admitted Oksa, greedily eyeing the potatoes beneath the embers.

"Everyone knows you're a pig!" said Gus.

Oksa looked at him, her eyes shining, torn between laughter and tears.

"And don't say you're a growing girl…"

"Well," sighed Oksa. "It does feel like I haven't eaten for days."

"Are you on a diet?" asked the Incompetent, looking puzzled. "But you're thin as a rake!"

He crunched on a walnut, spat out the shell and ate the kernel.

"You're hilarious," laughed Oksa, stroking the creature's wrinkled skin.

Everyone sat round the glowing brazier. Driven by a type of clan instinct, the families had gathered into groups: Pollocks, Bellangers, Knuts, Fortenskys… They were all drawn with tiredness and anxiety, but there seemed to be an unspoken agreement not to mention the fact that the Outsiders might not be allowed into Edefia—that would be too hard to bear. So they all concentrated on their loved ones in tormented silence, hoping against hope that everything would be all right.

✻

With a full stomach and greasy hands, Oksa laid her head on her mother's shoulder.

"It'll be fine, darling," murmured Marie, stroking her daughter's hair. "But, whatever happens, you must always believe in yourself. And in us. You have a huge responsibility and you must do everything you can to succeed, do you understand? Everything... that's more important than anything. And tell yourself that nothing is ever hopeless, there's always an answer."

Oksa choked back a sob.

"Do you really think so, Mum?"

"Of course I do!"

Marie seemed so sure! Her words cut through the gloom, touching the hearts of those who heard them.

"You aren't alone, you'll never be alone, don't ever forget that."

Oksa suddenly felt very tired. Her eyes strayed towards Tugdual, who was staring at her solemnly. If the Outsiders couldn't get into Edefia, he wouldn't be separated from anyone in his family. All the Knuts were descendants of Insiders. Except for Tugdual's father, who was already lost, swallowed up by the raging chaos that had overtaken a world fighting a losing battle.

"You ought to go and see Gus," Marie suggested quietly. "He needs you."

Oksa scanned the room; Gus was no longer there. He was standing farther away, silhouetted against the shimmering moonlight. With his back to the Runaways, he was leaning on the railing that ran the length of the temple, his black hair forming a curtain over his face. Oksa went over to stand beside him. They stayed silent for a moment, staring into space.

"Do you love him?" Gus asked suddenly.

"Who do you mean?" replied Oksa defensively.

"Who do you think I mean? Your 'Goth Superman.'"

"Oh Gus," whispered Oksa, exasperated. "Do you really think it's the right time to talk about this?"

"We may not have the chance to talk like this again for a while…"

Oksa hunched over.

"What difference would it make?" she asked.

"Oksa—it makes all the difference!"

"Well, in that case, you'll understand when I don't answer your question."

Gus turned to look at her. His blue eyes darkened.

"Don't you think you owe me that much? It's important for me to know if you love him or not."

"Oh Gus," sighed Oksa, the colour draining from her face.

"It's only natural, isn't it? Before my life is completely turned upside down, I'm entitled to know if you love someone else, aren't I?"

"Am I imagining things or are you trying to pick a fight?" asked Oksa indignantly.

Gus scowled.

"It's not like that…"

"It is," replied Oksa, warily.

She tapped nervously on the polished wood of the railing, avoiding the slightest physical contact with Gus.

"Can I ask you something?" she continued after a few minutes.

"Mmmm…" said Gus.

She coughed. The words were stuck in her throat, but she eventually managed to ask hesitantly:

"Are you in love with me?"

Gus stood still as stone. Only his accelerated breathing gave him away.

"What do you think?" he asked in a low voice, looking straight ahead. "How could someone as brilliant and brave as me be interested in someone like you? Honestly! Take a good look at yourself, you're dull, ugly, boring, thick and you have absolutely no sense of humour. Who'd want you apart from your 'Swedish crow'?"

Oksa would have burst out laughing if Gus's anguish wasn't so obvious in those bitter-sweet words. During the embarrassing silence that followed, Gus studied the abandoned village for no good reason and Oksa took advantage of the moment to put her hand on his arm. He feebly tried to shake it off. Then, without thinking, she turned to him and gently kissed the corner of his mouth.

39

ON THE THRESHOLD
OF EDEFIA

THE WATERS OF LAKE GASHUN-NUR SHIMMERED IN THE eerie, dramatic glow of the Definitive Landmark. An ominous gangrene-like darkness was gradually spreading across the sky from Saihan Toroi, while the crackle of occasional flashes of black lightning broke the silence of the desert and startled the travellers.

The sun was going down behind dark bands of thick fog by the time the Runaways and the Felons arrived at the lake shore. Orthon had been driving his bus flat out, frantic with impatience. Everything he'd been working for and had dreamt of—his revenge—was at last within reach. The minute the buses stopped, he leapt out like a big cat and positioned himself beside the radiant Definitive Landmark, ready to meet his destiny. Surrounded by the members of both clans, a trembling Dragomira approached in her turn. Oksa and Abakum took her hand. Baba Pollock and the Fairyman were crying silently and their emotions were so raw they were almost palpable.

"Old Gracious, Young Gracious, their Runaway friends and their enemy companions should receive the information that the opening of the Portal is encountering imminence," informed the Lunatrix standing before Dragomira. "The phoenix of the Young Gracious is signalling its approach. When the meeting has been accomplished, the medallion will make disclosure of the song concealed within its depths and the Two Graciouses will have to articulate the incantation with harmony to implement the opening of the Portal."

Dragomira teetered. Abakum held her up and put his arm under hers to provide more support.

"Are you all right, Baba?" asked Oksa softly.

Dragomira smiled sadly. Oksa felt giddy. Her gran suddenly looked so old...

"Here we are at last, dear sister!" whispered Orthon, triumphantly waving the medallion in the air.

Without deigning to give him a look or a word, Dragomira held out her hand for the medallion. She slowly turned it over in her fingers, examining it before gazing up at the sky, which was turning a mottled black. The medallion opened with a soft click, then a mechanism began working and some engraved words slowly appeared on the worn gold. Oksa waited for a sign from Dragomira.

"Time makes urgent expression for action," reminded the Lunatrix.

"Give me a moment, my Lunatrix," entreated Dragomira, sounding choked. "Just one minute..."

One by one, she hugged all her friends, paying particular attention to Abakum and Pavel. When only Oksa was left, she walked over to her with dragging feet, eyes brimming with tears she was struggling to hold back. She hugged Oksa hard.

"Everything will be fine," said Oksa reassuringly. "Don't worry. You're going back to Edefia, your Lost Land, Baba!"

Dragomira went to stand behind Oksa and put her arms around her. In the unbroken silence, the Definitive Landmark gradually disappeared, slipping slowly below the waters of Gashun-nur. The lake acquired an indescribable hue, which seemed to come from the bowels of the Earth.

"The phoenix..." gasped Reminiscens.

Oksa looked up. A fabulous creature with blood-red feathers was growing noticeably larger, its broad, powerful wings steadily beating the air.

"It's so beautiful!" declared Oksa quietly.

The phoenix flew over the heads of the Runaways and Felons and landed at Oksa's feet. Although its wingspan was as large as an eagle's, it was much more flamboyant, as if every feather were formed of fire and gold, and its small eyes burned with the intensity of molten lava. The delicate plume on the bird's small head swayed as it bowed respectfully. Oksa knelt down and reached out her hand to stroke the fantastic creature, her face alight with exaltation.

"What... what do I do now?" she asked softly.

Dragomira hugged her even tighter. Oksa felt her gran's heart beating hard, which scared her. Trembling, the old woman held out the medallion so they could both read the incantation appearing on it.

> *The Lost Land will be found*
> *If sworn enemies will set down*
> *Old wrongs to combine their might.*
> *The phoenix will be the guide*
> *Leading all exiles inside*
> *Through the Portal's gate*
> *That Two Graciouses unified*
> *Have the power to create.*
> *The Secret-Never-To-Be-Told is no more*
> *But the hope of two worlds lives on.*
> *Let the Portal now restore*
> *The mysterious entrance to our kingdom.*

The atmosphere was horribly tense as a few seconds ticked by. Then the phoenix suddenly took off and flew west over the dunes towards the setting sun. It slowed to turn its head round to look at Oksa and its song filled everyone's hearts as it disappeared into the twilight.

40

When Fate Knocks at the Door...

O KSA HAD PICTURED THIS MOMENT THOUSANDS OF times. Even though it was different every time, it was always filled with magic, excitement and a spirit of pure adventure. However, when she saw the Runaways and Felons being sucked randomly into an invisible void, she realized that this was nothing like she'd imagined. Screams of panic rang out until suddenly silenced by the frontier between the two worlds. She felt herself torn from Dragomira, as if her hand had dissolved in hers, and saw Orthon, Naftali, Tugdual and Gregor pass through the Portal, but none of the Outsiders. Her heart turned to ice. Her father shot her one last panicked look before he was separated from Marie and disappeared into what looked like a black hole. Then an implacable force took hold of her too.

Eyes wide, unable to control her body, she let herself be drawn inside. She saw herself pass through a golden corona of light, which reminded her of the ethereal outline of a ghost. Then, a moment later, she crashed down onto another sand dune, which looked exactly the same as the one she'd just left, except that the light was much brighter. Many of the Runaways and Felons were there, looking dazed but alive. Her father, Abakum, Naftali... they all gazed at her miserably. They'd succeeded, but the price they'd paid was unbearable.

"Mum…" groaned Oksa, her hand over her mouth.

Her whole body was trembling with shock. It was heartbreaking—everyone's worst fears had been realized: the Outsiders hadn't made it. But when Oksa saw everyone staring at something behind her, she felt a terrible sense of foreboding. She whirled round and screamed in despair.

"Baba! No!"

The golden corona they'd all passed through was still there. Despite its hazy contours, they could all recognize Dragomira's upright figure and her plaits fastened in a crown around her head. Oksa collapsed onto the sand, her heart in pieces. The corona swayed and seemed to want to come nearer. Oksa held out her hand, filled with the foolish hope that everything would be all right and she was just having a nightmare. But she knew she was awake—this wasn't a nightmare, it was harsh reality.

"Baba—stay with us, please!" she wailed.

Her entreaties and tears did nothing to alter the inevitable. Dragomira vanished in a gold mist, surrounded by the Ageless Ones, bearing her up into Edefia's stormy sky.

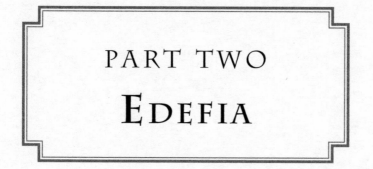

PART TWO

EDEFIA

41

THE NEW GRACIOUS

OKSA FELT AN ARM AROUND HER SHOULDER. PAVEL was sitting beside her, his eyes brimming with tears.

"Is Baba dead?" she whispered, still in shock.

"Her power as a Gracious made it possible for the Portal to open," replied Pavel, sounding choked. "As it opened, your gran's spirit left us to join the Ageless Ones."

"I'll never get over it…"

Oksa dissolved into tears, her body racked with violent sobs. She couldn't believe fate would be so cruel. She ran to the top of the dune, where the Portal had materialized and then disappeared immediately after. Edefia's pale shimmering mantle was now visible, although faint. As soon as Oksa drew near this very real frontier, she found that some kind of invisible force was preventing her from going any farther. Blinded by grief, she tried to push against it but was unceremoniously hurled back down the sand dune. She sat up. The Runaways had successfully accomplished their mission and had rediscovered their lost land, but they'd paid a heavy price for it and no one knew if this sacrifice would jeopardize the rescue of the two worlds.

Oksa lay on the cold sand, the aching pain in her heart obliterating everything that made life worth living. Everything that made life… good. Dragomira, her Baba… The grandmother who'd been with her since birth, who'd guided her and supported her. The grandmother who'd taught her everything she knew about her inner magic. How could she have disappeared like that? Oksa sensed someone beside her. It was a white-faced Abakum with Dragomira's Lunatrix. The Fairyman opened his mouth but nothing came out. He was choked with grief, unable to speak. The small creature with huge eyes put his chubby hand on Oksa's forehead to soothe her.

"My Young Gracious…"

His complexion was ashen, as if every drop of blood had left his veins.

"The Old Gracious has made abandonment of her fleshy and bony presence. Her domestic staff, reduced to the Lunatrix before you, now encounters the completeness of belonging to the New Gracious."

Oksa looked at him with red-rimmed eyes.

"You're… my Lunatrix."

She looked away to avoid crying again.

"The heart of the New Gracious is stuffed with suffering, like that of all the Runaways, their Felon companions and your domestic staff. Have you the wish to share a few words?"

Oksa shook her head.

"Grief can't be shared," she said, squeezing her eyes shut as hard as she could.

"The presence of your domestic staff is an assurance wrapped in permanence. The moment chosen by the New Gracious will for ever be in accordance with the moment accepted by your Lunatrix steward."

A heavy silence descended. All that could be heard was the quiet sobbing of clan members who'd left behind loved ones on the Outside. Oksa couldn't even picture the people she might never see again. Everything had happened so fast. Everything had gone so wrong. She gave a low moan. Eventually, her mother's face appeared in her mind's eye. She looked surprised and horrified at seeing her family and friends pass through the Portal, abandoning her on the threshold of this new life. And what about Gus? She recalled the light in his eyes as she'd brushed his lips with a kiss. He'd been on cloud nine… She thought back to the last words they'd said to each other, to Gus's desire to know what she felt for him and the harmless emotional blackmail which had felt more like unfounded scaremongering than a serious threat. Oksa imagined them eaten up with anxiety, wandering aimlessly in the middle of the Gobi Desert. Tears filled her eyes again. What would become of them? Would they be lost for ever? Would they survive the disasters? Suddenly the Lunatrix who'd been sitting on the sand, his little legs stretched out in front of him, said in a tremulous, but determined voice:

"You must hold fast to the firmly moored certainty that only death brings about the non-consolation of hearts. And no death entails no lamenting. When death has not made its selection of the living, then hope experiences survival. The remembering of this truth must never be gone from your minds."

Oksa straightened. She glanced miserably at the bleak desert stretching out around her and gave the creature a resounding kiss on the cheek.

"You're wonderful, my Lunatrix! Thank you. You're right, anything is better than death. But Baba—"

Her voice caught in her throat again.

"The opening of the Portal caused the demise of the Old Gracious, but her soul is in the magical company of the Ageless Fairies, who are now her species, and her future will elevate her towards a role full of amplitude and power."

The Incompetent waddled over to them. With its snout in the air, it was wearing its usual clueless expression, which Oksa loved so much.

"I don't understand a word that strange individual said," he said, looking at the Lunatrix.

All the creatures were clustered behind him. Although they looked sad, they were determined to show their solidarity with Oksa, who'd just tragically become their sole Gracious. A Squoracle fluttered over and gave her the small gold cage Dragomira had been wearing around her neck a few minutes ago.

"The Ptitchkins!"

Oksa released the tiny birds, while the Squoracle curled up in her hand and said:

"Even though I'm relishing the relatively balmy temperatures of this place, I must tell you, my Gracious, that I share your sorrow. But the Lunatrix is right: only death matters. Your mother, your friend and all those who were unable to pass through the Portal are stronger than you think."

"Your domestic staff makes the addition of advice garnished with importance," broke in the Lunatrix. "You must achieve the conservation of a conviction: you are the Gracious and your powers will encounter multiplication and expansion."

"The Secret-Never-To-Be-Told..." murmured Oksa.

"The Secret-Never-To-Be-Told no longer exists," objected the Squoracle.

"Thanks for crushing our hopes!" grumbled the Getorix, gesticulating wildly.

"But the Secret-That-Is-No-Longer-A-Secret may undergo evolution in the direction of a variation," added the Lunatrix.

Oksa took her time absorbing this stream of information, and her eyes widened. There was still a chance, a slim, but not insignificant, chance— one last hope. She looked at her father, his head in his hands, Abakum, Zoe, Tugdual... the Runaways and Felons devastated by the awful ordeal they'd just lived through. Then she wiped her dirty, tear-streaked cheeks furiously with the back of her hand and said in ringing tones:

"I understand, my Lunatrix: where there's life, there's hope. And the opposite is also true: life cannot exist without hope!"

The Lunatrix nodded wisely. Oksa rose to her feet and hugged him tightly. Hope was all they had left, but it was the only way they'd survive.

42

WELCOMING COMMITTEE

ABAKUM SUDDENLY JUMPED UP, LOOKING WORRIED.
Everyone followed his gaze to see a group of people rapidly
approaching in Edefia's steel-grey sky. Some were Vertiflying, others were
clinging to what looked like flying boards, as if swimming through the air.
Pavel went over to Oksa and protectively put his arms around her, while
the Runaways gathered around them, flanked by the Gargantuhens, who
had puffed out their necks and were sheltering the other creatures under
their massive wings. As for the Felons, they clustered behind Orthon,
who was impatiently scrutinizing the horizon.

"The welcoming committee didn't lose any time," remarked Abakum,
taking out his Granok-Shooter.

Everyone followed suit, including Oksa.

"That's all we need!" she couldn't help saying.

"Don't worry, Lil' Gracious," whispered Tugdual. "No one is going
to hurt you."

Oksa realized she was showing her fear.

"Not me," she added. "But they could hurt the rest of you."

"Do you really think we'd let them?" asked Tugdual, his eyes fixed
on the men who were now circling a hundred feet above them like
vultures.

Beside her, Pavel stiffened. Oksa could almost feel the tension coming
off him. He was burning up as the fire from the Ink Dragon spread

through his body in red-hot waves—it wouldn't be long before he unleashed it.

"Pavel," murmured Abakum, putting his hand on Pavel's shoulder. "It's too soon, your dragon should remain a secret. We may need it as a last resort."

"That's all very well!" growled Pavel. "But we're in such danger…"

"Lunatrix," called Oksa quietly, without taking her eyes off the flying men.

"Yes, my Gracious?"

"Please help my father."

Immediately the Lunatrix took hold of Pavel's hand and concentrated. His mysterious power allied to that of the Fairyman rapidly had the desired effect: it cooled Pavel's blood, dousing the fire raging inside him and releasing him from the fever that was preventing him from thinking clearly. The fliers were still circling above their heads, forming a funnel whose mouth was gradually nearing the ground. The leader of this intricately choreographed arrival finally landed on top of the dune, followed by around thirty men and women. They were all wearing the clothes that Oksa had seen when Dragomira had projected images of the Great Chaos on the Camereye: short baggy trousers, laced ankle boots, supple leather armour and helmet. They stared at the newcomers from the summit of the sand dune with daunting severity, before advancing together, kicking up small clouds of dust. Abakum and the oldest Runaways took a few steps back, recognizing the man at the head of the group, while Orthon stood straighter, his face glowing with renewed ferocity.

With a wave of his hand, the leader silently gave the order to surround the two clans. He examined the Runaways and their creatures one by one, then the Felons, looking amazed and exultant. When his gaze rested on Oksa, she couldn't help shivering.

She was in no doubt that this was Ocious, the terrible Werewall. Despite his grand old age—everyone knew he was well over a hundred—he didn't look like an old man. He radiated a greater sense of power and authority than the most intimidating members of his entourage. His perfectly shaped bald head enhanced a face that barely showed his years. He gazed at the Young Gracious for a few seconds in a silence thick enough to cut with a knife. His eyes were such a deep black that Oksa felt she could drown in them. His thin lips curved in a slight smile, furrowing his face with deep lines that disappeared into his short grey beard. Then he continued his inspection, before stopping at Orthon. He stepped forward resolutely holding out his arms. Orthon stood his ground, letting his father come to him.

"My son," said Ocious, putting both hands on Orthon's shoulders and scrutinizing him with intense curiosity. "I thought it was you..."

Everyone was wondering the same thing—what was Orthon thinking at that precise moment? Was he moved? Happy? Relieved? His father was alive... Even though this could complicate the Runaways' crucial mission, everything rested on the outcome of this reunion between despised father and scorned son.

Orthon was remarkably composed. His pale, slightly iridescent face remained impassive. Only his chest, which was rising and falling faster than normal, gave him away.

"Yes, Father, it's me," he finally said, in perfectly modulated tones. "And, as you can see, I haven't come empty-handed!" he added, glancing over at Oksa.

"What?" immediately hissed Oksa indignantly. "Don't imply you were the one who brought us here. That's total rot!"

Ocious turned to her, puzzled by these low words, which he hadn't quite heard.

"Oksa! Be quiet!" hissed her father.

"But Orthon's lying, Dad!"

"Listen to your father, Oksa," broke in Naftali quietly. "It's in our interest for this reunion to go as well as possible."

Oksa clenched her fists, furious at losing her temper and frustrated that she couldn't expose such a flagrant lie.

"So this is our New Gracious, is it?" continued Ocious, with a predatory smile.

"Yes, nodded Orthon with barely concealed satisfaction. "My mother Malorane's great-granddaughter, and Dragomira's granddaughter, in person! I scoured the world to find her and bring her back to Edefia."

"And it took you so many years to do it?" said Ocious.

Everyone watching this scene was dumbfounded by this unexpected taunt. Orthon blanched. His steely eyes darkened. Then he raised his head, shrugging off the implied insult. Impressed by his son's self-control, Ocious tilted his head.

"You've been away a long time," he said. "You've been much in my thoughts."

"I don't doubt it," replied Orthon, his hard eyes meeting those of his father.

Orthon's allies looked at each other in concern. Not even his most battle-hardened, loyal followers dared to move. Ocious inspected the group inquisitively and greeted those he recognized.

"Lukas... Agafon... I've always known I could count on you. Fifty-seven years, and you're still on our side."

"Our families have always been devoted to yours, Ocious," replied Agafon. "In Edefia and on the Outside."

"Ah, family!" crowed Ocious, putting his arm round Orthon, who willingly let him do so. "Is anything more reliable? Or stronger?"

"That's what I kept telling my dear sister and... our extended family for so many long and pointless years," said Orthon.

The elderly ruler reacted sharply to this statement.

"Is Reminiscens with you then?"

"Not with us, Father. With them."

Orthon waved dismissively at the Runaways. Reminiscens left Abakum's protection to stand in plain sight of the man who was her father. Ocious was clearly delighted, which seemed to upset Orthon, who frowned in annoyance as Ocious walked over to his daughter.

"Reminiscens!" he exclaimed.

"Stay right there!" replied the elderly woman frostily. "I forbid you to come anywhere near me."

Ocious paused, surprised and vaguely amused, then said:

"I still recognize you, despite all these years. Your hair may have turned white and your face may be lined, but you still look the same. I can see you're determined to make the wrong choice now, just as you did then. Isn't your gallant protector—sorry, your half-brother—with you?"

"Leomido passed away," retorted Reminiscens, tense with icy rage, "because of you! And, if you want to know, Dragomira's gone too."

Ocious looked shaken, as if an earthquake had occurred deep within him, wreaking havoc inside, but barely showing on the surface. His fierce eyes darkened with sorrow and regret, but he soon recovered.

"So you're your own brother's widow. How ironic," he said caustically to Reminiscens with his head held high.

"Leave her alone!" broke in Abakum, standing between them. "You also ought to know that she's been braver than your son Orthon ever was."

"Well, well," replied Ocious. "Abakum—or should I say the Eternal-Backstage-Lackey?"

"How dare you!" shouted Oksa, her cheeks crimson.

Ocious gazed at her inquisitively.

"Our New Gracious has a lot to say for herself, doesn't she?"

"I'm not *your* New Gracious!"

"Oh, but you are!" replied Ocious. "You're completely in my power, girlie."

At these words the Felons closed round the Runaways.

"Don't do anything," murmured Abakum to his friends. "Fighting won't do any good and will just put us in danger."

"Abakum!" objected Oksa, panic-stricken.

"We can achieve more from inside."

"The maggot in the fruit, Lil' Gracious," added Tugdual, squeezing her hand.

Curbing her blood-chilling terror with difficulty, Oksa walked forward, accompanied by the Runaways and creatures. Ocious smiled evilly at her.

"Welcome to Edefia, my Gracious!"

43

A Tempting Escape

T HE RUNAWAYS VERTIFLEW CAUTIOUSLY THROUGH Edefia's murky sky, escorted by a steadfast band of reunited Felons. The creatures and Sylvabuls who couldn't fly were perched on the back of the Gargantuhens, which were clucking shrilly as they beat their wings at a slow, steady pace. A regal Ocious led the way, accompanied by his son and grandsons.

"He's worse than Orthon," remarked Oksa, looking at the patriarch of the Felons.

"He certainly has a flair for killer put-downs," nodded Tugdual, Vertiflying beside her.

"Don't forget he's the one behind this whole mess," said Pavel.

"Orthon hasn't made his move yet," continued Tugdual. "And he's holding all the cards. It could be dangerous."

"Very dangerous."

Oksa turned away from Ocious in his leather armour to contemplate the countryside. Edefia… the lost land which had now been found. Their long-hoped-for return. Edefia was in a bad way. Bathed in a metallic light, every living thing, even the smallest blade of grass, was blanketed in a layer of dust. The atmosphere had a twilight quality and everything seemed to be in its death throes, beyond rescue. Skeletons of trees brandished dead branches like wizened claws clutching at the sky. One of these trees stood so tall in its lost magnificence that it dwarfed all the others.

"The Majestic," said Brune, very upset. "What's happened to our world?"

The Majestic? Oksa remembered the images Dragomira had shown her on the Camereye: the lush forest surrounding the cool, clear waters of Lake Saga. The aptly named tree stood a good 300 feet higher than the crests of other trees. But this desert of dust and dead plants, extending as far as the eye could see, bore no similarity to what she'd been shown. Only the bright shifting shimmer on the horizon, which looked like the Northern Lights seeping into this strange world, gave her cause to hope that some life had been preserved. Other than that, the grey, heavy sky seemed moribund. Fascinated by the sights spread out before her, Oksa rummaged in her rucksack for her sunglasses to shield her eyes from the steely glare and a few of her flying companions followed suit. Her strained muscles were protesting and her body was tense—she'd never Vertiflown for as long as this, or as... openly. Even though this limited amount of freedom was controlled strictly by the Felons, it still felt like freedom. In Edefia, she could be herself. She would *have* to be herself. She stretched her arms in an attempt to ease her aching limbs, and groaned.

"Would you like to join Abakum on the Gargantuhen?" asked Pavel in concern.

She shook her head. The constant physical discomfort was proving less of a problem than her agitated state of mind. Oksa was experiencing all kinds of conflicted feelings and had never felt worse than she did now, even during the toughest times of her life. There were so many things upsetting her that she felt paralysed emotionally, which was the only thing actually stopping her from falling apart. She couldn't do anything to make herself feel better in the short term, and her survival instinct was telling her to save her strength to deal with the immediate future. She had to be on her guard and as alert as possible if she was going to get the better of an evil despot like Ocious and his gang. There would be time enough later to tend to her wounds.

The russet Gargantuhen ferrying the creatures and Abakum was lagging behind so badly that its pace could have been described as lethargic in the extreme. However, although the giant hen was beating its wings slowly, its brain was working overtime. Erring on the side of caution, Dragomira's Lunatrix acted as a mouthpiece for the bird's plan.

"The russet Gargantuhen is making the proposal of a tactic of escapement," the Lunatrix murmured quietly in Abakum's ear, watched suspiciously by one of the Felon escorts. "Its muscular energy and its unsuspected speed may help the Fairyman dissociate himself from the dominion of the jailers."

Abakum's expressionless face revealed nothing of his excitement at this opportunity. The Squoracles placidly flying beside their enormous counterpart fluttered closer. One of them landed on Abakum's shoulder and informed him in a whisper:

"The Young Gracious's Tumble-Bawler has just told us that a group of Sylvabuls has managed to keep part of Leafhold, in the Green Mantle territory, from becoming a desert. The town, thirty-four miles from here, has a population of 348 people and the temperature is cooler than in this desert—ten degrees centigrade with an eighty per cent rate of humidity—which is terribly severe for Edefia and sensitive creatures like us. That's why we're opposed to this plan!"

"Your altruism does you credit!" scoffed Dragomira's Getorix.

"Do you think so?" innocently wondered one of the Incompetents.

※

"Pah!" spluttered the Squoracle. "Anyway, no one has ever shown *any* consideration for our species. We're going to die and no one could care less."

"That's true," sighed the Getorix.

"Are you dying?" asked the Incompetent. "That's terrible…"

Abakum raised his hand to interrupt this pointless sparring, and the creatures sulkily fell silent.

"The Squoracle is committing the oversight of one detail weighted with importance," continued the Lunatrix. "Like all people in Edefia, the final inhabitants of Leafhold are experiencing the constraint of the dominion overflowing with severity exerted by the Felon Werewalls. But resistance swells their heart. Since the Ageless Ones have procured the information that the Fairyman and the New Gracious is here, their hope has encountered exponential growth. They are preparing to provide welcome and rebellious action! If your wish encounters the choice of schism from this forced expedition, the russet Gargantuhen provides assurance that the breakaway will be crowned with success. It has the physical ability and you have the power to ensure protection. That belief may be firmly rooted in your consciousness."

Abakum was clearly torn. He gazed at the Runaways—his dear friends and their descendants—then at the horizon where he could just make out an oasis of greenery in the grey desert. Not far from the Gargantuhen, the slender figure of Reminiscens was Vertiflying ahead. She had to be exhausted… He loved her so much… He looked from Reminiscens to Oksa, who was flanked by her father and Tugdual. All he could see was her bowed back and streaming chestnut hair. Oksa was heading straight for an uncertain destiny. The Lunatrix cleared his throat: he needed an answer. Ahead, beyond the hills, Thousandeye City appeared. The capital of Edefia, shrouded in purple mist, was no longer just a dream.

"I have no doubts about our Gargantuhen's ability," whispered Abakum, barely opening his mouth. "Just qualms about abandoning the other Runaways and our Young Gracious. I know I could achieve more from outside than under Ocious's thumb, but I can't leave them, Lunatrix. I just can't."

44

The Glass Column

"I T MAY HAVE SUFFERED A LITTLE DAMAGE OVER THE YEARS, but it's still magnificent, isn't it?" asked Ocious, addressing the question to the oldest among them.

The Glass Column rose in the centre of Thousandeye City—a vast cylinder reflecting the sky's mottled clouds. Its crystal walls were supported by a complex framework of intricate steel spirals, which gave the building the appearance of a huge precious stone. The former exiles' hearts had leapt in their chests on seeing the Column rising from the dusty ground. The youngest among them had only seen it through Dragomira's Camereye, so their reaction was different, although just as strong.

The city spread out like a slumbering octopus from the base of the Column. The wood or glass structures were no more than two storeys high and all had large terraces and small plots of land which would have been attractive gardens a few years ago. It wasn't hard to imagine the abundant vegetation that must have covered Thousandeye City once upon a time. Hundreds of bare trees stood in the courtyards and lined the streets, as they had around dry Lake Saga. Only a few patches of greenery—carefully tended vegetable plots— remained on some of the terraces. There was virtually no one around. The humming, seething yet perfectly ordered activity so characteristic of a thriving city seemed to have been extinguished and it was as if almost all the inhabitants had gone to ground in their houses. Flying over Edefia, Oksa had glimpsed a few figures—a few anxious, hopeful faces turned inquisitively towards the sky. From the street, a little girl waved. "Who does she think she's greeting?" wondered Oksa. "Does she know what's happening?" The Young Gracious couldn't help waving back, watched coldly by Ocious and his guards.

"You see, Ocious, respect and recognition cannot be earned by a show of strength," remarked Naftali. "The people of Edefia will know whom to follow."

"You've always been such an idealist!" sneered Ocious. "Strength is and always will triumph over the soundest moral principles."

"That's what the cruellest dictators have always thought until they were eliminated by their people like the vermin they are."

Ocious couldn't hold back an evil smile.

"If you think your threats worry me in the slightest, you're going to be disappointed, my dear Naftali. Anyway, enough small talk—we're here."

The Felon landed at the base of the Column, followed by his clan and the Runaways. When the Gargantuhen planted its wide webbed feet on the ground, the creatures rushed over to cluster around Oksa.

"My Young Gracious encounters at last the location of her residence," said the Lunatrix, looking up at the top of the Glass Column.

"A residence which is now mine, girlie, although you are, of course, a welcome guest," corrected Ocious.

The Lunatrix looked at him with an expression of intense disapproval.

"The Glass Column belongs to the Gracious's family and no one else."

"And you would be well advised to treat our Young Gracious with the respect she deserves!" added the Getorix. "Only her closest friends and family may be so informal with her."

"Tut, tut, I've upset the menagerie!" mocked Ocious. "But, my dear little servants, you should remember that I am closely related to her: you only have to look at our family tree to see that."

234

"Machiavellian alliances are far from being true bonds," objected Abakum before Reminiscens had time to react. "Now we'd like to rest, if you don't mind."

Ocious's eyes narrowed to gleaming slits; then he turned to the main doors of the Column, guarded by about twelve men in leather armour. They stood up straighter, with chests puffed out and faces blank, as the Master of Edefia approached. When Oksa walked past, they glanced almost imperceptibly at her. Was it out of curiosity? Fear? Respect? Impossible to know. She kept walking, followed by the Runaways and the creatures. She caught a glimpse of a small cluster of people a few hundred feet away, attentively watching the scene. A cry rang out:

"Long live the New Gracious!"

The guards immediately turned to look threateningly at the group. Frowning with annoyance, Ocious gave a sign ordering them to ignore such demonstrations, then hurried into the Column. Sad and exhausted, Oksa and the Runaways entered an incredible hall paved with crystal, and the huge doors closed behind them.

✺

The Column's structure and interior design owed a great deal to the use of minerals, mainly precious stones, marble and glass. At the centre of the hall, which was filled with light, was a vast translucent staircase leading up to a cornice adorned with polished steel tracery. In one corner, water was flowing down a sloping section of wall to form a quietly murmuring water feature. The rest of the hall was left unembellished, which created a strangely harmonious effect. When Ocious's booted feet broke the silence, they jumped, roused from their contemplation of this singular place, which some of them had thought they'd never see, or see again. The older Runaways seemed very moved. Even though they'd spent decades hoping to come back, even though they'd pictured this moment so clearly in their heads, nothing could have prepared them for the overwhelming emotion of this return.

Oksa saw Abakum stagger. The Fairyman had paid such a high price to come back... Reminiscens hurried over to him and put her hand on his forearm. The old woman looked upset. Oksa found herself wondering whether Reminiscens had *really* wanted to come back to Edefia? Had she done it to avoid being alone? Was she there out of love or revenge? The Young Gracious shook her head, feeling out of sorts. Her gaze came to rest on Zoe, whose face was drawn with suffering and tiredness. Oksa met her eyes, but couldn't tell what she was thinking: Zoe seemed to have absented herself. Tugdual, on the other hand, was examining everything. The Felons, the Runaways, Oksa, the splendid decor—nothing escaped his inquisitive gaze.

"There are a few important details that my Young Gracious should know," the Tumble-Bawler broke in suddenly, fluttering above Oksa.

She held out her hand as a landing stage for the little messenger.

"The Glass Column initially rose to a height of 843 feet and had 55 floors. However, during the time of the Great Chaos, three floors were destroyed, including part of the Memorary and the Gracious's quarters."

"Why don't we save the guided tour for later?" interrupted Ocious, "Let's go straight to my private quarters."

The creatures stirred restlessly, upset by his tone, which they felt lacked the proper deference. This didn't escape the Felon.

"It's fifty-seven years since any Gracious has entered this place," he barked. "And for fifty-seven years who do you think has worked hard to maintain the splendid appearance of this residence? Who has enabled Edefia to survive? Was it any of you?"

These absurd questions startled everyone and begged some obvious answers...

"None of you was here to repair the damage caused by the Great Chaos, so wipe that indignant expression off your faces. This place is now mine by rights!" concluded Ocious.

Saying this, he waved his arm in Oksa's direction to invite her over to the glass cubicles against one of the opalescent walls. Silently Oksa did as he wished, followed closely by the members of her clan, and entered what proved to be a lift. The car immediately shot up to the top of the tower, filled with blinding light. Fear of the unknown as well as the motion of the lift made Oksa feel dizzy, so she grasped her father's hand and closed her eyes.

45

THE PAST SPLENDOUR OF EDEFIA

O KSA HAD NEVER SEEN A ROOM LIKE THIS EXCEPT IN films or her wildest daydreams. Although the years of hardship had left traces here and there, even the smallest touches oozed an understated, yet undeniable, luxury.

Stretched out on a giant bed strewn with masses of cushions and a feather-soft counterpane, Oksa was too tired to sleep. Too many emotions and too many worries to process… Lying there, she gazed in fascination at this new decor, which was so different from her usual surroundings. There was no doubt that the dark veined wood on the walls was from a precious species of tree. When she'd entered the room, Oksa couldn't help running her fingertips over it to appreciate its velvety feel. It reminded her of butterfly wings. The floor was just as lavish, paved with gigantic turquoise slabs. The furnishings were unusual: the room was designed to be a haven of rest and some of it was given over to a large pool—Oksa had promised herself to take a dip as soon as the opportunity presented itself.

In the meantime, she simply admired the hypnotic shimmering of the water on the ceiling, almost in a state of torpor. She'd been thrilled with the adjoining bathroom, though, which was entirely decorated with slate, and boasted a rosewood bowl filled with all kinds of creams, oils and soaps. Some clothes had been left out for her, but Oksa had preferred to put on the last clean pair of jeans and T-shirt in her rucksack. One whole wall of the main room was a bay window which afforded a breathtaking view of Thousandeye City and beyond. Apart from a mountain range that stood out against the horizon, everything was blanketed in dust. Sometimes massive plumes, raised by people employed in various activities, rose into the dark sky, then disappeared. Edefia no longer looked like a land of plenty.

"Would my Young Gracious like some information about what this land was like before?" asked the Tumble-Bawler.

Oksa looked at the little winged messenger, which once again had shown it had an excellent sense of timing.

"Absolutely, Tumble. Baba always talked about the luxuriant land of Edefia but… there's nothing left!" she exclaimed with a wave of her hand at the arid countryside stretching as far as the eye could see.

The Tumble-Bawler nodded vigorously.

"What the Old Gracious told you was the truth: Edefia was a paradise extending for the equivalent of 74,565 square miles on the Outside. The mountains you see in the distance occupy western Edefia. That's the Peak Ridge territory, which is hard to get to because its steep cliffs are made of a pure, almost transparent pink crystal, emerging from black rock so hard it's virtually unusable. Do you see that summit rising above the others in the southern part of the range?"

Oksa went over to the bay window and screwed up her eyes to look at the mountains.

"That's Mount Humongous," said the Tumble-Bawler. "Aptly named, since it rises to an altitude of 42,579 feet."

"But that's enormous! It makes Everest look tiny!"

"Well, Everest certainly isn't the Roof of the World. As you can imagine, the height of Mount Humongous makes it the coldest place in Edefia. You should visit the cave carved into the peak—the view is amazing and it feels as though you could almost touch the sky. You leave by riding hollowed-out logs down vast slides carved into the rock, it's great fun."

"I'm sure I'd love that," said Oksa, engrossed in the Tumble-Bawler's descriptions.

"At the southernmost point of this territory, lapis lazuli cliffs glow with remarkable brilliance. From the neighbouring region of Thousandeye City, you can see them lit by the setting sun—it's a sight no one could ever tire of. There are countless cascades in the Peak Ridge mountains. The two most spectacular waterfalls, which plunge more than 16,500 feet, are the Silver Cascade and the Glitter Falls. I don't know if they're still there, given the drought here, but from what I know of the Outside, there are no waterfalls as high as these."

"That's for sure. What about Green-Mantle?" asked Oksa.

"Green-Mantle was Edefia's lungs. It was nothing like that desert we flew over to get here... There were abundant dense, bushy forests. The most spectacular were the forests of gigantic Parasol trees, whose trunks could grow to a diameter of 160 feet and a height of 1,640 feet. Even the tallest American sequoias would have looked like shrubs beside them. These trees derived their name from their large parasol-shaped leaves. A single leaf could shelter forty people from the sun! When chewed for a long time, their bark would allow you to jump as high as the kangaroo in Australia. It was also used as a repellent for sugar-loving insects like ants... and the smallest ants here were on average three inches long."

Oksa pulled a face, fervently hoping she'd never have to encounter one of those abnormally large specimens.

"There were smaller trees farther north in Green-Mantle: Majestics, for example, had very sturdy clover-shaped leaves. They produced beans weighing as much as six pounds each, which contained Zestillia, a substance used to make Gorgelettos."

"Gorgelettos?"

"A mouth-watering invention by one of Edefia's greatest ever gastronomers, a brilliant culinary inventor. These were ice creams that would acquire your favourite flavour, anything that set your taste buds tingling. If you fancied a passion fruit Gorgeletto, you merely had to think about wanting it and your Gorgeletto would taste like passion fruit. If you decided to change the flavour, the Gorgeletto would adapt to whatever you wanted."

"Excellent!" exclaimed Oksa, imagining a raspberry-flavoured Gorgeletto.

"Another ancient species was the Broad-Leaved Ball tree with foliage shaped like a huge sphere. This was very popular with nesting birds and some Broad-Leaved Ball trees could house over 500 nests! Not far from Green-Mantle was the territory of the Distant Reaches, which was the home of wild animals like the fearsome blue rhinoceros with its nine-foot-long horn and the highly venomous black-and-white-striped zebra snake. But one of the most spectacular animals was the twenty-foot-long silver tiger, whose extraordinary pearly-white pelt was highly sought after a few centuries ago. The species is now on the verge of extinction, although the tiger still kills scores of reckless hunters keen to possess this legendary fur which is still believed to have magical properties."

"Amazing," whispered Oksa. "Do you think the Distant Reaches still exists?"

She wasn't really interested in blue rhinoceroses or black-and-white-striped reptiles. No. Oksa was only concerned about the mysterious territory of the Distant Reaches because, according to Abakum, it was the one place in Edefia where Lasonillia, the Imperial Flower, grew. Marie had remained on the Outside, but that flower was still the only remedy that could cure her and Oksa wasn't about to forget it.

"Of course," replied the Tumble-Bawler, aware of her unspoken thoughts. "I could carry out a reconnaissance flight to see what the situation is, if you like."

Oksa nodded, unable to speak because of the lump in her throat. The little creature respectfully stayed silent for a moment before continuing:

"To the east and west of Green-Mantle, vast lakes surrounded by lush vegetation were the main centres for fish-farming and seaweed-farming.

The Insiders were very fond of seaweed, you know. Around and beyond those lakes were areas devoted to growing cereals, such as Golden Pearl, which is like corn, except each grain is as big as an apricot."

"Just imagine the size of the popcorn!" quipped Oksa.

"What a funny thought," laughed the Tumble-Bawler. "They grew the same varieties of vegetable as the Outsiders, but they were fresher, more plentiful and bigger. A rich soil and a warm temperature that never got too hot—twenty-five to thirty degrees centigrade—are always conducive to farming. The carrots were three feet long, the potatoes a foot and a half in diameter and the strawberries weighed at least a pound... each strawberry, I mean. And no chemical fertilizers or pesticides were used! Energy was exclusively green: giant windmills on the plains, solar panels on all houses, and widespread use of geothermal and hydraulic energy. None of the vehicles, machinery or factories used polluting fuels. Just sunshine, wind or water."

"Brilliant!" cried Oksa. "And... what about the people? I know there were four tribes..."

"That's right, Young Gracious. The last census carried out before the Great Chaos recorded 16,245 people effectively spread across the four main tribes: Firmhands, Sylvabuls, Long-Gulches and Ageless Fairies."

"Not to mention the Diaphans," added Oksa.

The Tumble-Bawler couldn't help shivering at the mention of the fifth tribe, which struck such fear into the hearts of Edefians and was the source of such shame.

"As in all societies, a small minority of people chose to live on the fringes or opted for a life of crime. Disagreements could also arise. However, the whole system was based on notions of self-sufficiency and the idea of matching need with available resources. And the Insiders lived in complete harmony—everyone got on well with each other, even though each tribe had its own characteristic features. As you know, the Firmhands have highly developed senses, like animals, particularly birds of prey. In Edefia, they're renowned for their great physical strength, which means they tend to gravitate towards the building trades, architecture, manufacturing and the processing of metal and glass, as well as stonemasonry. They are experts in science, chemistry and engineering: over 600 years ago, they discovered how to use solar energy to power flying machines, machinery and tools."

"Better than Leonardo da Vinci!" exclaimed Oksa.

"Oh, but that inventor of genius was a great source of inspiration for the Firmhands. The Glass Column was governed by Gracious Laure-Amée at this period. Her Dreamflights often took her to Italy, to the studio of that brilliant visionary, and she made a few inspired suggestions to the best Firmhand engineers who carefully put da Vinci's plans into action, using their own technology. But they were not only gifted in the fields of science and engineering, they also worked in mineralogy—they developed and perfected a body of remedies using stones 1,500 years ago, which has been such a useful addition to the Sylvabul pharmacopoeia. I don't know how things are today but, before the Great Chaos, the Firmhands tended to live in the Peak Ridge territory in huge troglodytic dwellings in the cliffs, fashioned from precious stones."

"They must have been magnificent!"

"They were, yes," confirmed the Tumble-Bawler. "But the Sylvabuls were not to be outdone. They'd miraculously managed to build their houses in the trees, creating incredibly beautiful aerial cities that were moulded to fit the branches. Even now, their abilities and nature-loving sensibilities predispose them to work the land, even though it's dying. The Sylvabuls possess the power of Greenthumb: their touch makes the vegetables, fruit and cereals grow more vigorously than when tended by any other Insider."

"I know," interrupted Oksa, her eyes suddenly misting over.

A wave of nostalgia washed over her at the mention of this power. She thought back to a few months earlier, when her father had shown her the French Garden, the restaurant he'd been so proud of creating from scratch. She'd been celebrating her thirteenth birthday at the time. She hadn't seen her mother for a while and she'd been missing Marie unbearably. Like today… with the huge difference that she might never see her again. She shook her head to banish all thought of this awful possibility which she'd do everything in her power to prevent.

"Do you think I have the power of Greenthumb?" she asked, trying to take her mind off these things.

The Tumble-Bawler rocked from right to left on its rounded behind.

"Yes… and you'll certainly need it to rebuild Edefia, when equilibrium is restored."

Oksa imagined plunging her hands into the depleted soil and causing thousands of plants and trees to grow. That really would be magical. She couldn't wait to get started—she'd love doing that!

"Tell me some more about the Sylvabuls, please."

"That tribe monopolized any activities connected with food, as well as pursuits less well known on the Outside, like seaweed-farming, flower-growing, the breeding of creatures and Granokology, of course."

"That's one discipline that's certainly less well known!" exclaimed Oksa impishly. "What about the Long-Gulches?"

"The Long-Gulches live mainly in Thousandeye City. They're citizens and have an innate feel for structure and system design at all levels, whether it concerns road networks, town planning, education or the legal system. You could call them Edefia's organizers."

Oksa studied Thousandeye City spreading out around the Glass Column. The city was badly damaged, but many parts bore witness to its glorious past. The size of the houses and the materials used to build them, the terraced design of gardens where nothing was growing now—everything pointed to bygone days of splendour.

"Thank you for all this information, you're a great help," she said pensively.

"I remain at your disposal, Young Gracious," concluded the Tumble-Bawler, fluttering around her.

46

THE EXTRAORDINARY COUNCIL MEETING

O KSA FLOPPED OVER ONTO HER STOMACH WITH HER chin resting on her hands. She had a pounding migraine and was really hoping she wasn't about to have another attack—this was neither the time nor the place. Ocious had given the Runaways a few hours' respite before they had to attend what was bound to be a tedious summit meeting. Each of the "guests", allies or adversaries, had been allocated a room. The Glass Column was huge, so there was space for everyone. Pavel's quarters next door were smaller but just as sumptuous, and there was an interconnecting door between the two rooms. However, like all doorways, it was guarded by a forbidding, and rather strange-looking, sentinel: a six-inch flying caterpillar with a blue abdomen and dangerous-looking hairs, called a Vigilian. When Oksa had tried to go to see her father, the caterpillar had suddenly positioned itself in front of her and had ordered her to step away.

"What! Aren't I allowed to speak to anyone?" she demanded, feeling nauseated by the insect, whose cilia were spinning at top speed like the rotor blades of a helicopter.

"Everyone is to be confined to quarters until after the council meeting," declared the caterpillar. "Those are the Docent's orders."

"Who's the Docent?"

"The Master, if you prefer."

"I don't prefer anything… what happens if I disobey?" grumbled Oksa, despite her loathing for the insect.

"My stinging hairs are not deadly, but they can cause a very painful paralysis."

"Fine," sighed Oksa, with a grimace.

She threw herself onto her bed again, feeling worried and annoyed, and resigned herself to the interminable wait.

※

"Young Gracious… Young Gracious…"

Oksa opened her eyes. She'd finally dozed off for a few seconds, but just as she felt herself slipping into deep unconsciousness she heard a voice speaking softly in her ear. When she saw Annikki bending over her, she flinched.

"Don't be afraid, I don't mean you any harm," said Annikki. "I've just come to fetch you for Ocious's council meeting. We've a little time to spare so perhaps you'd like to eat something? You must be so hungry."

Oksa was tempted to say no, just to be difficult, but the sight, and especially the smell, of a newly baked round loaf was too hard to resist. She reached for the tray at the foot of the bed and pulled it closer. A slab of fresh butter served with small cubes of cheese, figs and grapes overcame her reluctance. Annikki was right, she was starving. She buttered a piece of bread and devoured it, keeping her eyes fixed on Annikki. The young Felon's face was drawn and pale, and her blue eyes were red-rimmed. Oksa suddenly realized she wasn't the only one who was missing "absent" loved ones: Annikki's husband was an Outsider. Like Marie, Gus and some of the others, he'd been left behind on the threshold of Edefia. Oksa's gaze softened. Annikki came nearer and squeezed her hand. Oksa's initial reaction was to pull away, but finally she accepted Annikki's gesture in compassionate silence.

"I'm a Felon and I realize you're wary of me," murmured Annikki. "But you should know that I took great care of your mother while she was with us on the island. Despite the situation, we got to know each other well and developed a mutual liking and respect. She's a brave woman, whom I admire deeply. She helped me understand a great deal about other people in my clan, and about myself."

She turned away, her face strained: a Vigilian was buzzing near the bed, keeping a close eye on them. Oksa shivered.

"Will you please allow the Young Gracious to finish her meal?" exclaimed Annikki hoarsely.

The caterpillar hovered in the air.

"The Docent is waiting," it said.

"Don't worry, it's OK," replied Oksa, eating one last grape.

She looked warily at Annikki who, while pretending to tidy Oksa's hair, whispered:

"Trust me…"

Then she shoved her imperiously towards the door, which did nothing to reassure the Young Gracious. The Vigilian moved out of the way, then followed the pair closely to the glass lift, which enclosed them in gloomy silence.

※

The massive Council Chamber was filled with unsmiling faces, which made the stuffy atmosphere feel even more oppressive. The space was flooded with light from a single source: a vast cylindrical shaft, descending through some ten floors from the top of the Column, which cast a bright milky light over the assembled throng. The circular design of the chamber perfectly mirrored the shape of this cone of light. On a small podium, Ocious and around twenty inscrutable men and women were sitting in dark leather chairs arranged in a semicircle. Only four of the chairs were unoccupied. Facing the podium was seating intended for the Runaways. Flanking this central section sat the Felons who'd been living on Orthon's island. Above their heads, a few Vigilians kept guard.

When the glass lift opened and Oksa emerged at the top of the tiered seats, all eyes turned in her direction. Absolutely everyone was there, and she cursed herself quietly for arriving late. There was little doubt that Ocious had deliberately summoned her after the others. The layout of the room showed that the man liked putting on a performance. The Runaways stood up, their shoes noisily scraping against the turquoise paving slabs. The Felons followed suit, some of them reluctantly, more to emulate Ocious, who was standing with arms open wide, than to show any respect for Oksa.

"Here's our Young Gracious at last!" Ocious thundered. "Come nearer, don't be shy."

With a wave of his hand he indicated the seat in front of him with its back to the Runaways. Oksa hesitated, intimidated. The way the seats were arranged reminded her of a courtroom in which she was the accused, facing her judges alone. Her Curbita-Flatulo was undulating constantly and her heartbeat eventually slowed to the steady pace set by the small creature's regular movements. Oksa looked up. The central aisle was lined with familiar, loving faces. Her father, Abakum, Zoe, Tugdual... the Lunatrixes... They were all studying her intently, their eyes anxious but full of strength. She could count on them, they were there for her. Not behind her, as Ocious wanted to symbolize by his unsettling arrangement of chairs, but by her side—come what may. So, escorted by Annikki, she walked down the steps less hesitantly than she'd feared, drawing courage from the eyes of the people she loved.

Ocious was staring at Oksa with a certain amount of curiosity as she took her seat and she caught herself wondering what he was thinking. What did he see? On the Outside, she usually passed for an ordinary teenager in jeans and trainers, an unaffected, impulsive schoolgirl, but that formidable, lavishly dressed old man obviously saw something different in her and his piercing eyes were making her feel ill at ease. Challenging herself not to lose face, she forced herself to tolerate his scrutiny. Suddenly Ocious switched his attention to Orthon and his sons, who were standing with the "newcomers".

"My dear son and grandsons, we're all here together at last. Who'd have thought such a miracle was possible? Please, come and sit by my side!" said the old man, indicating the four unoccupied seats on the rostrum. "You too, dear daughter," he added, with a glance at Reminiscens.

The pale old woman glared defiantly at her father without moving a muscle, while Orthon strode up to the stage triumphantly, followed by Gregor and Mortimer. All three sat down to the applause of the Felons and Werewalls. Oksa felt bitter: three generations of the worst Felons to walk the two worlds had been reunited. They could savour this happiness while the Pollocks and Runaways had been parted from the people they loved. It was so unfair...

Oksa gnawed her lip, feeling raw inside, and watched the Felons and Werewalls congratulating each other with almost obscene exuberance. Only Mortimer didn't seem to share their exhilaration. Despite his brawny appearance, he looked lost and alone. Of course, Oksa suddenly realized. Mortimer's mother, Barbara McGraw, was an Outsider! Oksa remembered that frail woman and her deep love for her son. From what little she'd seen, Oksa could understand Mortimer's sadness today.

Orthon was unlikely to concern himself with anyone but himself. He was overjoyed at being officially recognized by his father. He was Ocious's son, worthy to sit at last by his side. That had been his lifelong dream—a dream that was soon shattered by an unexpected revelation when, after lengthily embracing Orthon, Ocious turned to a tall, thin man standing on his right. In his early fifties, this latter was wearing a charcoal-grey suit with a high collar and an impassive expression.

"Orthon, my son," began Ocious, "our reunion wouldn't be complete if I didn't introduce you to Andreas. Andreas is my youngest son from my second marriage after your... departure to the Outside."

This was devastating news: the dream of holding the coveted position of the only son of the absolute ruler of Edefia had just been dashed. The Runaways were appalled. This was the worst thing that could have happened. Would Orthon tolerate direct competition? Abakum scrubbed his hand over his face. He looked miserably at his clan. How would all this turn out? No one knew. Sitting on her own out in front, Oksa stiffened, realizing the significance of this announcement. Wide-eyed, she watched the two half-brothers greet each other coldly. Orthon looked like he'd accepted the situation, but Oksa was well placed—in every sense—to know that the Felon had just been dealt a heavy blow. It was obvious from his clenched jaw. Ocious was watching this meeting between his two sons, and Oksa could have sworn that she detected a nasty glint of pleasure in his dark eyes, which didn't bode well for the future. Ocious sat back down, followed by everyone else, and began to speak in ringing tones:

"It's been sixty-two years since Gracious Yuliana, the mother of our late lamented Malorane, appointed me First Servant of the High Enclave. It's not always been an easy job…"

A few of the Runaways almost choked on hearing this and made no bones about showing their irritation with much coughing and spluttering. Annoyed by these interruptions, the Vigilians threateningly flew closer to the troublemakers, their stinging hairs erect on their repulsive bodies.

"Fortunately, despite the hard times that have afflicted our poor land since the Great Chaos, I haven't had to face any of these terrible ordeals alone. There are some whose loyalty has never faltered, no matter what."

With an expansive wave of the hand, he indicated the men and women sitting beside him.

"My friends and my son, Andreas, who have provided such invaluable help for almost thirty years."

Sitting motionless on Ocious's left, Orthon was controlling his every move, every blink of his eyelids, every line at the corner of his mouth. The only thing he couldn't control was the pallor of his face, which showed anyone with eyes to see that he was seething with bitterness and resentment at discovering that he had a half-brother.

"My family is now reunited, and we'll be able to work together to bring our plans to fruition."

"Your plans?" asked Naftali flatly. "If you mean your age-old desire to conquer the Outside, let me tell you it's too late. You may not know this, but the Outside, like Edefia, is dying."

Ocious paused to digest this information, which disturbed him more than he'd have liked to admit. Taking advantage of any sign of weakness in the enemy camp, Abakum rammed the point home:

"Why do you think we came back?" He deliberately allowed the painful silence to linger before he continued: "I won't deny that, ever since our departure from Edefia, we've been feeling homesick for our land and longing for the chance to return. But in fifty-seven years, we've all made lives for ourselves on the Outside. We became integrated as Outsiders, then grew to love that imperfect land with its extremes of good and evil. As you might imagine, our return has forced us to make some painful sacrifices: we've turned our back on what's become our new homeland and which, for most of us, is and will remain our land of choice. Furthermore, we've left behind loved ones and you can appreciate what a wrench that is, you who value the importance of family ties so highly."

Ocious was listening intently, still as stone.

"Why do you think we're here?" repeated Abakum. "Why, Ocious?"

There was a ripple of agitation among the Werewalls sitting on the rostrum. Only Orthon and his sons remained inscrutable. Too proud to ask him to continue, Ocious waited, keen to know more but determined not to have to ask. It was a woman a few seats away who broke the silence.

"It's useless trying to toy with us, Abakum," she declared imperiously. "Spit it out!"

"We had no choice but to come back," said Abakum. "However, contrary to what your son would like you to believe, we're here of our

251

own free will. He didn't bring us back to Edefia. We'd have come, with or without him. The Outside is dying and there's very little time left."

Everyone was holding their breath.

"So Orthon hasn't told you anything?" continued Abakum, careful not to look at the Supreme Werewall's son.

Ocious gazed at him with narrowed eyes, then slowly turned to look at Orthon.

"Is the Outside really dying?" he asked finally.

"The Outside is in its death throes, Father," said Orthon. "Like Edefia."

Ocious blanched, then suddenly banged his fist on the table. Everyone jumped and Oksa gripped her chair in the front row. Orthon was staring at her with a tight smile, causing Oksa to feel even worse—she knew what was coming next, it was inevitable.

"The girl in front of you, Father, is the New Gracious you've spent nearly sixty years waiting for," said the Felon, his voice resonant with renewed confidence. "There's no doubt she could allow you to achieve what you've always wanted to do, what our ancestors have worked so hard to do for centuries: leave Edefia to conquer the Outside. However, since the two worlds are dying, leaving here will accomplish nothing."

Ocious gave a cry of anger. He could kiss his life's ambition, the legacy of his powerful ancestors, goodbye—everything was collapsing around his ears like a house of cards. Orthon paused for a few seconds, delighted to be back in control.

"Our dear friend Abakum has, however, provided part of the solution," he continued, with obvious satisfaction.

Ocious looked up, listening hard.

"Why didn't you have a choice, Abakum?" thundered Orthon. "WHY?"

Abakum didn't speak.

"Because she is our only chance of surviving the catastrophe and of restoring equilibrium in Edefia and on the Outside!" declared Orthon, pointing at Oksa. "And despite what Abakum says, it's because of me and only because of me that she's here."

A scandalized buzz rose in the ranks of the Runaways, which didn't appear to worry the Felon.

"Do you know what her family called her when she was born?" continued Orthon. "The Last Hope. They had no idea of the significance of that nickname... but they couldn't have chosen a better one, could they?"

At these words Ocious's face lit up with a malicious smile. The future was no longer bleak—it beckoned once again, full of the promise of bringing ancient schemes to fruition.

"The Last Hope," he murmured, his eyes glittering.

He gave a ringing laugh which bounced off the room's curved walls and struck despair into the hearts of the devastated Runaways.

47

The Spurned

His breath coming in short gasps, Gus looked out over the shimmering waters of Lake Gashun-nur, which reflected the dark mottled sky. He could still feel the pressure of his father's firm grip on his hand. His parents had disappeared, yelling his name. Oksa, Dragomira, Abakum, Zoe… they'd all vanished. In the space of a few seconds, everyone had been sucked through the Portal by an invisible force. Everyone except the unfortunate native Outsiders.

"What's happened?" he croaked.

He studied the surface of the lake, where the Runaways and Felons had vanished into thin air. He walked over to the water's edge, attempting to look beyond the emptiness, beyond the invisible Portal which had shut him out, in the hope of seeing something, some sign, that might give him hope, but it was obvious that all hope had gone. Eleven of them had been refused entry to Edefia and were still in shock at being parted from their loved ones. Locked in misery, they sat on the sand, frozen in what seemed like dignified restraint—it had all happened so fast that they were lost for words. Only Kukka was sobbing uncontrollably.

"Why is she still here?" wondered Gus in amazement. "Her parents are Insiders…"

Suddenly Kukka sprang to her feet and rushed into the lake.

"Please!" she yelled. "Whoever you are, let me in. I want my parents!"

She was up to her waist in icy water when Andrew, the minister married to Galina, rushed in and prevented her from going deeper. Kukka wept and struggled, beside herself with terror and despair.

"I want to be with them! Don't try to stop me!"

Andrew put his arms tightly around her and carried her out of the water.

"All you're likely to do is catch a nasty dose of pneumonia," he said breathlessly, setting her down on the sand. "Don't forget we're only human. Which is why we've been left behind."

Gus sat down on the sand near Marie, who was staring blankly at the lake. He buried his head wearily in his hands.

"It was obvious that we wouldn't all get into Edefia," whispered Marie, her hands clutching the armrests of her wheelchair. "It was such a slim hope…" Her voice cracked. Gus looked at her in agony. What was there to say?

"Do you think… they're OK?" he asked hesitantly. Marie looked away.

"We can't afford to doubt it," broke in Andrew, coming over. "They're strong, supportive and determined."

"Everything we're not," remarked Gus, taking stock of their unfortunate situation.

There were as many Runaways as Felons in the ranks of the "Spurned" and they'd lost no time in gathering in their clans, even though they were all in the same boat. On one side were Gunnar and Brendan—the husbands of the twins Annikki and Vilma—with Sofia and Greta—the wife and daughter-in-law of Lukas, the mineralogist. Slightly farther away sat Marie, Gus, Andrew, Kukka, Virginia Fortensky, Cameron's wife, and Akina Nishimura, Cockerell's wife. Only Barbara McGraw didn't appear to have chosen a camp. Sitting despondently with her arms around her knees, she looked like a doe terrorized by a pack of hunting dogs.

Everyone was staring blankly at each other, registering very little. Gus studied the Spurned, one by one, as he struggled to control mounting feelings of panic. They looked a sorry sight and he was probably no better. They were just pathetic human beings. Pathetic human beings who'd shared their lives with a group of *extraordinary* people while being far from extraordinary themselves. However, despite being all too aware of their weaknesses, they'd grown accustomed to living close to magic and had become proud, loyal, steadfast Runaways. Life hadn't exactly been restful—they'd experienced times of happiness and great danger, they'd been manhandled and sometimes separated, but even when he'd been Impictured, Gus had never felt as heavy-hearted as he did now. A definitive line had been crossed: the link between the two worlds had been broken. They were all exactly where they belonged.

The waters of the lake churned as the ground was rocked by another earth tremor; then, to add insult to injury, a sudden icy downpour began pelting the Spurned.

"Run for shelter!" shouted Andrew, seizing Marie's wheelchair.

They took cover from the raging storm in one of the two clapped-out buses. Barbara McGraw was the last to climb inside, soaked from head to foot. Virginia seemed to hesitate for a minute before making up her mind; rummaging around in her backpack, she held out a towel and a sweater to the frail wife of the much-hated Felon.

"Thank you," said Barbara softly.

After a few minutes Gus got up from his seat, tense as a bowstring.

"We have to do something!" he said forcefully, his shaking voice betraying his anxiety. "We can't stay here for ever."

"What if they come back for us?" said Kukka tremulously. "We should stay right here."

Andrew looked at her sadly.

"It shouldn't be any harder to leave Edefia than to get out of a painting, should it?" she shouted hysterically.

"It took our friends over three months to be Disimpictured," replied Andrew steadily. "So, even if there's a chance they might come back from Edefia, we must remember that we're in the middle of the desert. We could easily die of cold and hunger here."

"Andrew's right," said Marie, "we won't survive long here."

"We won't survive long anywhere!" cried Kukka angrily.

"All the more reason to give ourselves a fighting chance, even though the odds are stacked against us," insisted Gus.

Since this conversation had started, he'd been trying to answer one crucial question: what would Oksa do in his shoes? It was hard to think about her, but it was also the only way that Gus could reason things out effectively. If Oksa were here, in this dire situation, she'd turn to him and, gazing steadily at him, she'd say: "C'mon, Gus! Use your head. Show us what you're made of!" He'd taken what had proved to be some pretty sound decisions in the past—so why was this any different?

"I think we should go home," he said quietly, his cheeks on fire.

"WHAT?" shouted a few of the Spurned in surprise.

"What do you mean?" asked Virginia.

"I mean that if our families did manage to get out of Edefia, then they'd look for us at home," continued Gus. "That strikes me as the most sensible thing to do."

"What if our homes aren't there any more? What will we do then?" asked Brendan.

"We should stay together somewhere we think would be easy to find," suggested Andrew.

"That's very subjective," retorted Brendan, who seemed irritated by the minister's suggestion.

They all considered their prospects carefully. Outside, the rain wasn't letting up. Night had fallen and their attempts to find a solution hadn't allayed anyone's fears.

"I think you're both right," said Greta, Lukas's daughter-in-law. "But the alliances we've forged make us enemies. We can't travel together, our outlook is too different."

"Can't we join forces like the Runaways and Felons must have done?" exclaimed Andrew.

"Did they *really*, Andrew?" asked Greta, tossing back a thick mane of white-blonde hair.

"It doesn't matter whether they did or they didn't!" retorted Andrew, his eyes shining. "Are we doomed to be the victims of ancient alliances? Do we have to be slaves to this endless clan war?"

Greta sighed. "You're a man of faith, Andrew. Your view of human nature is idealistic."

"You're wrong, Greta. I'm far more clear-headed than you."

They both sat there scowling. Gus leant over to Marie and covered her with the fleece blanket that had slipped down from her shoulders during the discussion.

"That's a very good idea, Gus," she murmured. "Let's go home. And wait."

Gus looked at her in surprise. Wait? That word implied there was still hope... He was finding it hard to be hopeful about anything in that freezing-cold, dilapidated bus, stuck in the middle of the Gobi Desert as earthquakes shook the land. The only thing he could hope for right now was to find the strength to survive this chaos.

48

DIFFERENCES OF OPINION

B Y THE TIME THE SUN ROSE BEHIND THE HILLS IN THE east, Gus had made up his mind. Despite feeling depressed and disillusioned, he was unexpectedly determined to survive this nightmare. It had nothing to do with hope, it was just a burning desire to prove he was capable of shouldering responsibility. The one person he'd have liked to see this "new" Gus wasn't there and the grief was choking him. He knew Oksa wasn't far away, and yet she wasn't just somewhere else: she was nowhere, by Outside criteria. Obviously, he'd miss his parents too, but he was sure they'd watch out for his friend the way they'd watched out for him over the past fourteen years, which had suddenly become sixteen, after Orthon's evil *conversion*…

In a spirit of acceptance, he wiped away the condensation forming long frosted trails down the bus window and examined his reflection. He still wasn't completely used to his new appearance. His hair hung to his shoulders and his cheekbones were more prominent, which made him look more… enigmatic. Which was just as well. He hated being an open book to everyone.

The terror of the day before, along with the grief and the unexpected shock, had turned to exhaustion and sleep had eventually claimed the Spurned, like a snake devouring its prey. At daybreak Gus had surfaced from a restless slumber and had sat there thinking. On the seat beside him, Marie turned over. It was so cold that her breath formed small puffs of icy vapour above her. Her face was ravaged by grief and disease and her body was shrivelled, like an autumn leaf. Her pain ran very deep and Gus was more aware than ever of the burden of his new role.

"OKSA!" Marie suddenly shouted in her sleep.

Several of the Spurned sat up in alarm. Gus shifted closer to his friend's mother. She was tossing and turning in the grip of a bad dream. However, since their current circumstances were probably no better than the dream in which she appeared to be fighting someone, Gus decided not to wake her up.

"Come over here, lad," called Andrew softly.

The minister, Virginia and Akina had gathered at the front of the bus. Kukka was a few seats away, her legs drawn up against her chest, looking distractedly at the window. Gus glanced furtively at her, but she gave no sign that she'd noticed him.

"Are you OK, Gus?" asked Virginia. "Are you coping?"

"This is by far the worst thing I've ever gone through," he admitted, rubbing his arms, chilled to the bone.

"Yours is the best suggestion," announced Andrew, coming straight to the point. "We're going to head back to London."

"Do you think we'll get there?" asked Akina timidly.

In her bright-pink padded jacket, the small Japanese woman with her lined face, framed by long jet-black hair, resembled a battered doll. Gus looked down, tormented by the same unanswerable question.

"We're going to try going back the way we came," declared Andrew.

"Such relentless logic!" commented Greta, Lukas's daughter-in-law.

"No one's forcing you to do the same," retorted Virginia Fortensky. "You're all free to go where you want."

All the Spurned were now awake. When Marie tried to sit up, Barbara McGraw hurried over to help her, beating Gus and Andrew, then sat down in silence beside her.

"May I come with you to London?" asked Akina, almost inaudibly.

"It would be an honour," nodded Andrew. "Gus? Marie? Virginia? You'll join our party, won't you?"

All three nodded vigorously. The minister diffidently murmured his thanks and turned to Kukka, who was still miserably hunched in her corner, muffled up in a baggy beige wool jacket.

"Kukka? I'm hoping you'll come with us. However, even though you're not yet an adult, you don't have to do the same as us."

A shadow passed over Kukka's face and she made herself even smaller on her seat.

"I'll go with you," she muttered offhandedly.

They all turned to look at the five Spurned who hadn't yet spoken. Greta stepped forward and said bossily:

"We'd rather stay here."

"But how will you survive?" cried Virginia. "It's almost winter and there's nothing to eat or drink. How long do you think you'll last?"

"We're planning to find accommodation in the last inhabited village we passed, about nine miles back along the road that led us here," said Gunnar, Annikki's husband.

"We'll leave directions at the lakeside, so that those who went into Edefia can find us," finished Greta confidently.

"See, Greta, you're a woman of faith too, in your own way," remarked Andrew, with a penetrating look.

"You're mad," said Gus softly. "What makes you think they'll ever come back? You're going to spend the rest of your life in this desert, clinging to false hopes."

Gus had never been much of an optimist, but he now felt like an out-and-out defeatist. The Spurned gazed at him, some annoyed by his words, others saddened.

"If we don't want to abandon hope, that's nobody's business but ours, is it?" asked Gunnar flatly.

"No, it isn't. But, personally, I'd rather abandon my illusions," cried Gus, surprised by his own daring and his flat refusal to keep hoping.

"This time, it's a matter of life and death! And I don't want to hold on to a fantasy that will never come true," he added, his voice breaking suddenly.

"Hope isn't a fantasy, Gus," objected Andrew, squeezing his shoulder. "But no one can blame you for feeling so angry."

"I'm not angry!" yelled Gus. "I'm just being sensible."

"Stop it!" suddenly wailed Kukka. "I can't take it any more—you're driving me mad!"

And she burst into tears. Virginia sat down and put her arms around her, rocking her like a baby. Just as she would have done with her children, the three strong, loving boys she'd probably never see again. Virginia stifled a sob, her hot tears soaking into Kukka's hair.

"What about you, Barbara?" asked Marie, trying to catch her eye.

Barbara McGraw shrank into her seat, as if frightened by what she was about to say. Her lower lip was trembling slightly, when she finally uttered the words.

"I'd like to come with you. To London. If you'll let me join you…"

Greta gave a shout of rage.

"Barbara! How could you?"

"I want to, Greta. I want to go back to London," she declared firmly.

Andrew looked at his friends. The women seemed unsure, torn between compassion and distrust. Gus couldn't make up his mind about Barbara. All they'd seen of her until now was a meek woman terrified by the ordeals they'd been through. However, she was still Orthon's wife. He may not have been the man she'd thought he was when she married him, but she'd lived with him for years and had borne him two sons. She probably didn't know all her husband's secrets—his origins, his ambitions, his deeply ingrained psychoses—but she couldn't have been completely in the dark either. Gus studied her again, unable to work out whether she really was the sensitive, vulnerable woman he saw before him or someone different. Someone totally different. Someone dangerous.

"Gus?"

They were all waiting for his decision, as if it really mattered. Gus blushed and felt flustered. It was hard to feel that his opinion might count for so much! He hated this type of situation. He glanced over at Marie, who was nodding almost imperceptibly.

"I'm happy for her to come with us," he heard himself say, with the horrible feeling that he might be making a big mistake.

49

Strong-arm Tactics

THINGS WERE UNBELIEVABLY TENSE IN THE LARGE CIR-
cular Council Chamber. Oksa would have given anything not to be
there. She felt more trapped than ever, glued to her chair facing Ocious
and his Werewall clan.

"So you're the one who's going to restore equilibrium," said the powerful old man, fixing her with his piercing dark eyes.

"…and who's going to permit you to leave Edefia at last!" added
Orthon, his voice quivering with pride.

He couldn't help glancing defiantly at Andreas, whom he'd had to
accept as his half-brother, but who had turned out to be his worst
rival.

"Wonderful!" crowed Ocious, keeping his eyes on Oksa. "Would you
come up here, please."

Instinctively, Oksa turned round to look at the Runaways for reassurance. She felt so alone in front of these people who were examining her
hungrily with hostile, inquisitive eyes. To everyone's surprise, Abakum
and Pavel stood up and started descending the steps in the hall, followed
immediately by Tugdual. Orthon was about to send them back to their
seats when Ocious stopped him, looking amused, the way only someone in perfect control of the situation can. Ignoring a score of buzzing
Vigilians flying ominously near them, Pavel went to stand beside Oksa
and took her hand.

"Don't worry, Oksa-san," he murmured quietly. "You're the one with the power, not them."

Abakum stood behind the chair with his hands on Oksa's shoulders. She immediately felt comforted by his nearness. Tugdual went to stand on the other side of her chair and glanced at Oksa.

"Don't let them rattle you," he whispered. "They aren't stronger than us."

Oksa was trying to convince herself that her father and Tugdual were right, but she was terrified by the occasion and the Werewalls' jubilation. Orthon muttered a few words to his father and Ocious immediately looked over at Tugdual.

"So you're Naftali and Brune's grandson, are you?" he said. "Did you know that your great-grandmother was one of the staunchest allies of our Secret Society?"

This was too much for Naftali, who leapt from his chair and hurled himself with all his might at the rostrum where Ocious was sitting. Everyone watched him shoot over their heads like a missile packed with explosives. The Werewalls tried to ward off the attack by firing Fireballisticos and Knock-Bongs, but they couldn't stop the towering Swede, whose resolve was unshakeable. Followed by a swarm of Vigilians, he landed just behind Ocious and caught the Felon in a neck hold. He patted out the flames licking at his trousers, then declared belligerently:

"My mother was never one of your staunch allies. She was forced to join you!"

All the Werewalls had their Granok-Shooters trained on him. The tension was unbearable. Oksa could sense that her father was seething with rage and it wouldn't take much for the Ink Dragon to put in an appearance. "We'll all be killed," panicked the Young Gracious. Naftali tightened his grip, white with rage. Ocious tensed.

"And I forbid you and your lot to go anywhere near my grandson!" thundered Naftali in his enemy's ear.

"They've got no chance of winning me over to their cause," rang out Tugdual's firm voice.

Oksa turned to look at him. At first sight Tugdual looked unflappable, his face as expressionless as if made of wax. The only sign of his inner agitation was a throbbing vein that could be seen through the pale skin at his temple. Suddenly noticing a Vigilian dangerously close to Naftali, he fired a Fireballistico, reducing it to ash with a small burst of flame.

"And yet you'd be very welcome," added Orthon, attempting to provoke him further.

Tugdual pretended to spit on the ground at this offer and eyed the Felon icily.

"Now, Ocious," continued Naftali, "you're going to tell us exactly what the situation is in Edefia. Spare us your boasts and charades and bear in mind that I have nothing to lose. I won't hesitate to break your neck if I have to, nothing could be easier and nothing would give me greater pleasure."

"But you won't, because you need me," said Ocious with a grimace. "You all need me!"

"Are you so sure of that?" asked Naftali sceptically, tightening his hold. "Don't overestimate your power, or you'll wind up dead. You're nothing but an old man with overweening ambitions. What have you achieved with your life, Ocious? You caused the Great Chaos, which has now brought the two worlds to the brink of destruction, you have two sons who hate each other as much as they hate you, and your powers are limited to the terror you instil in other people."

The Werewalls stiffened around Naftali, quivering with indignation. From the seats in front of the rostrum, a Felon fired a Granok at the Swede, but the Runaways were watching. Quick as a flash, Brune diverted the Granok with a flick of her index finger, defying anyone to attack her husband. Nimbly she leapt in front of the Felons, on the alert for the slightest move. Cameron and Pierre joined her as backup.

"Malorane was to blame for the Great Chaos, not me," began Ocious hoarsely.

"Malorane shares the blame, certainly," admitted Abakum, "but her plans were not as evil as yours. Her only mistake was her naivety in not realizing what kind of man you really were. If you hadn't influenced her as you did, the Secret-Never-To-Be-Told would never have been revealed. The Supreme Entity would still be here and the Great Chaos would never have happened."

"If it hadn't been me, someone else would have put pressure on her," retorted Ocious. "I wasn't the only one who wanted to leave Edefia. As soon as Malorane began showing her Dreamflights to the people, most of us wanted just one thing."

Abakum and the oldest Runaways had to corroborate Ocious's remarks. Those who'd known Malorane well knew that she'd been an idealist, a gullible reformer unaware of the voracious appetites of some of her peers. Despite its fragility, Edefia's secret had been safeguarded for centuries by the Graciouses. It had kept them safe by maintaining the Insiders in blissful ignorance or by misleading them about the supposed dangers on the Outside. Malorane had wanted to overturn this ancient precept by showing them what the Outside was really like.

"You're conveniently forgetting that it was you who encouraged her to make her Dreamflights public!" exclaimed Reminiscens, pointing her Granok-Shooter at her father.

Ocious glared daggers at her.

"You don't know what you're talking about!" he raged. "You all think Malorane was so innocent and so easily swayed. Well, I'll have you know that she was a lot more stubborn than any of us here: she had a deep inferiority complex and was obsessed with standing out from earlier Graciouses. She wanted to ring the changes and introduce a different type of reign that everyone would remember."

"Well, she certainly succeeded there," muttered Oksa.

"That's as may be," broke in Abakum, "but you have to admit her character suited you down to the ground! You exploited it unscrupulously, but then manipulation has always been your weapon of choice, hasn't it?"

"Is it my fault Malorane couldn't resist me?" said Ocious, unable to hold back a twisted smile. "And things didn't turn out that badly, whatever you say. After all, we did have our amazing twins!"

A mocking laugh erupted into the stunned silence. Reminiscens stiffened as Orthon jutted his chin proudly, yet scornfully. Zoe hunched even smaller on her seat, her heart filled with one desperate desire: to disappear for good. As if she could sense her cousin's dark despair, Oksa turned round and looked at her, clenching both fists in a sign of support. A gesture which didn't escape Ocious...

"Twins who've given us some wonderful descendants, despite a few improbable liaisons," he added, before Naftali tightened his arm around his throat.

"Yes, why don't we talk about that! Descendants who didn't hesitate to murder their own flesh and blood!" burst out Reminiscens, white with rage.

Orthon's self-control had reached its limits. A dense flash spurted from his fingertips and hit his twin sister in the throat. Jeanne and Galina immediately fired a Knock-Bong at Orthon, flattening him against the wall, although it was too late.

Abakum rushed over and Reminiscens collapsed in his arms. The impact had created a dark circular hollow on her delicate skin, and her eyes were wide with fear. The Fairyman knelt down to lay her on the floor. He took off his fleece-lined jacket and folded it into a pillow which he placed under the wounded woman's head. When Dragomira's Lunatrix—now Oksa's—waddled over, some of the Felons couldn't hold back their surprise: the Lunatrixes hadn't set foot in the Glass Column for nearly sixty years.

"The family of my Old Gracious must not allow life to perform abandonment of her body," said the small creature, taking Reminiscens's hand. "The Lunatrix domestic staff cannot allow him who shares your twinship to experience the satisfaction of watching you encounter death."

"I didn't mean to kill her," objected Orthon, in a steely voice, "I just wanted to silence that annoying windbag!"

"The strength of the blow received may however carry the kin of my Old Gracious towards death," replied the Lunatrix, examining the injury. "The accumulation of years and ordeals aggravates the injury and prevents speedy recovery."

"Orthon," sighed Ocious, although he didn't look all that bothered, "what have you done now?"

He was addressing him the way a father would scold a child for something stupid.

"I'm doing what you do, Father," replied Orthon, straightening his clothes with shocking offhandedness.

Jeanne and Galina's Knock-Bong had barely affected him and he seemed stronger than ever.

"Father and son develop identical cruelty in their hearts," the Lunatrix said to Reminiscens. "But this cruelty does not reside in your blood. Perform the accompaniment of my gaze, that is my counsel."

The old woman tried to keep her eyes on the large blue eyes of the creature, which were slowly spinning in their sockets. At the same time, the Lunatrix put his chubby hand on her burnt throat and hummed a few incomprehensible words. She began breathing more steadily and her eyes gradually lost the glazed stare of imminent death.

"Good!" said Ocious happily. "Now my daughter is out of danger, perhaps we might continue?"

Disgusted by this behaviour, the Runaways focused on Ocious, while remaining clustered around Abakum, Reminiscens and the Lunatrix.

"Edefia entered a state of unstoppable decline after the disappearance of the Supreme Entity and the advent of the Great Chaos," continued the Werewall. "First the light faded, causing a drop in temperature. The climate remained mild, but nothing like before. Gradually plant life adapted, which is to say it became sparser. Crops failed and the harvests dwindled every year. Ten years ago, the first water shortages began to make themselves felt. We started water-rationing, which became more rigorous every year, but despite our precautions things got worse. For five years, we've been suffering from a terrible drought. The desert which bordered Green Mantle at the start of the Great Chaos suddenly gained ground, swallowing up the forests and plains which were once so fertile. The lakes and rivers have dried up, the reserves of drinking water are almost depleted and the temperature drops every year. Edefia is heading for disaster and nothing can stop it."

He fell silent. It was impossible to know if he was pausing because he was overcome with sadness or whether he was simply, and perversely, doing it for effect. When he continued, everyone was riveted: even with Naftali's strong arm around his neck, Ocious obviously relished the odd theatrical flourish.

"Then, a few days ago, I realized that Edefia's tragic destiny was about to change: the New Gracious would soon appear among us."

"How on earth could you know that?" asked Naftali.

"Oh! It's very simple: the Cloak Chamber reappeared…"

"WHAT?!" exclaimed Abakum. "And you waited until now to tell us?"

"Just saving the best for last!" sneered the Master of the Werewalls. "Yes, in the Column's deepest catacombs, directly below the centre of this hall, the Chamber is preparing to welcome our New Gracious. It should only be a matter of days."

50

Uncertain Conclusions

AFTER THAT DIFFICULT COUNCIL MEETING, THE Runaways had gone back to their quarters feeling drained. Naftali had agreed to release Ocious, despite his burning desire to break his neck. The Runaways aren't killers, he'd said, as he athletically leapt from the rostrum to rejoin his clan. They'd each been escorted back by a Felon or Werewall, as well as a few enthusiastic Vigilians.

"It's a bit stupid," Oksa had groused, loud enough for Ocious to hear. "The equilibrium of the two worlds depends on me entering the Cloak Chamber, so I'm hardly going to run away, am I? I'm not stupid!"

"None of us have anything to gain by jeopardizing Oksa's enthronement," Abakum had added, his arm around Reminiscens' waist to support her.

But the Master of the Werewalls would not be swayed: the Runaways were to remain confined on the second-to-last floor of the Glass Column.

"We could do without the praetorian guard, you know."

Oksa was still fuming: a few zealous, enthusiastic Vigilians were buzzing in front of the door. Farther away, two helmeted, leather-clad Werewalls were guarding the lift.

"Can I at least see my father?" Oksa yelled in their direction.

One of the two Werewalls left his post and disappeared down the corridor. A few seconds later, Pavel appeared.

271

"Dad!" exclaimed Oksa. "Get out of the way, you," she shouted at the Vigilians, who parted to allow Pavel through.

She slammed the door and snuggled against her father. The Lunatrix came over, his mouth stretching the entire width of his moon-like face.

"The father of my Young Gracious makes the contribution of exultation filled with relief."

"Damn right!" said Oksa, finding it hard to hold back her tears. This was the first time they'd been alone together since their harrowing arrival in Edefia and Oksa felt on the verge of cracking up. Pavel led her to the sofa facing the vast bay window.

"I miss them so much, Dad," she wailed, unable to stop thinking about her mother and Gus.

"I do too, Oksa."

"Do you think they're OK?"

"I'm sure of it."

But his eyes betrayed his doubts and he didn't know what to do or say for the best. Unable to comfort Oksa, he remained silent, merely hugging her tightly. Oksa had never felt so weary. They clung together, tormented by similar feelings of powerlessness and grief, until Oksa slipped into a troubled sleep, her head on her father's shoulder.

❊

She was woken by the noise of the door opening: a young woman in a tightly buttoned leather waistcoat had just come into the room. Silently she put a tray laden with steaming dishes on the hammered-metal coffee table. Oksa studied her curiously, unsure whether to thank her or not. Despite her expressionless face, she looked the same as her but, then again, what did she expect? The Werewalls, Felons and Runaways were all human…

"Although you wouldn't think it the way some of them behave," she muttered.

"Did you say something, darling?" asked Pavel in surprise.

"No, Dad."

She waited for the young woman to leave the room before examining the tray, because she had to admit she was ravenous. As if prepared by someone who knew just what she liked, the meal was perfect: pasta, mixed cooked vegetables—without a leek in sight!—warm rolls, cheeses and jams, served with cold water and fruit juice.

"Look! It's just like we have at home," she declared.

"Did you think they'd serve lightly grilled Abominari steak?" teased Pavel.

Oksa punched his arm gently.

"I just hope it isn't poisoned," she said, spearing some buttery tagliatelle with her fork.

"I'd very much doubt it, having seen how fond Ocious is of you."

"Oh, Dad! I hate that self-important fossil, who thinks he rules the world!"

"Self-important fossil, eh? No one can accuse you of pulling your punches, can they?"

They ate in silence until they could eat no more, feeling their strength return as the tray emptied. The Lunatrix had joined them, warily at first; then, throwing caution to the wind, he'd devoured several small rolls covered in sunflower seeds and a large piece of smelly cheese.

"My stomach conveys happiness beyond all comparison!" he said, his belly distended.

Oksa smiled at him.

"I'd never have thought you were such a greedy-guts!" she teased gently.

She looked at her father, who was standing by the window, staring out blankly at the vast landscape. The future had never been so uncertain. She walked over to him.

"What's going to happen to us?" she whispered.

"You heard Ocious, didn't you? As soon as the Ageless Ones give the sign, the Cloak Chamber will admit you. You'll then become the Gracious and your first task will be to restore equilibrium."

"But how am I going to do that? I have no idea what to do!" Oksa felt lost.

"Don't forget what Abakum said: the Ageless Ones will guide you," reminded Pavel. "You must trust them."

"Dad, can you tell me who or what the Supreme Entity is?"

"If the father of the Young Gracious will offer the gift of assent, your Lunatrix will undertake an initiative of enlightenment," broke in the small steward.

Pavel nodded.

"The Supreme Entity was the embodiment of the equilibrium of Edefia, the Heart of the World," said the Lunatrix.

"Of the two worlds!" corrected Oksa. "But where is this Entity now?"

The Lunatrix paled slightly before continuing:

"It was wreathed in disappearance along with the Secret-Never-To-Be-Told, the Chamber and the life of Gracious Malorane."

"That's terrible…" remarked Oksa. The Lunatrix nodded.

"Has the Entity been reborn?" asked Oksa.

"Perhaps there's a new one," suggested Pavel. "Lunatrix, do you know?"

The Lunatrix opened his eyes incredibly wide.

"Your domestic staff cannot deliver words without possessing certainty."

"Oh, don't worry about that!" exclaimed Oksa. "Tell us, even if it's only a guess."

The Lunatrix shook his head and repeated:

"Your domestic staff cannot deliver words without possessing certainty."

"Oh! That's a pity," sighed Oksa.

Her slate-grey eyes clouded with worry.

"I wonder what it will be like. I'm scared, even though I can't wait for it to happen."

Pavel got up and tiptoed over to the door. He pressed his ear against it to listen, then came back, with his finger to his lips.

"Your enthronement will be an enjoyable, magical experience," he murmured. "It's only afterwards, when you're a Gracious, that things will get complicated. Ocious will do everything in his power to make you open the Portal for him."

"But Dad, I'll have to open the damn Portal!" said Oksa, trying hard to keep her voice down. "Mum and Gus need us. Otherwise, they'll die…"

The words caught in her throat.

"The problem is, Oksa, that we don't yet know what will replace the Secret-That-Is-No-Longer-A-Secret. Or what new rules will be imposed on you in the Chamber. None of us is sure that the Portal can be reopened… without you losing your life."

A wave of dizziness and fear washed over Oksa as her breathing accelerated. The Lunatrix put his small podgy hand on hers.

"Before the Great Chaos, the Graciouses were the only ones possessed of the secret of the opening of the Portal, to the exclusion of all Insiders. Some performed visitations to the Outside, for example there existed Graciouses who practised the encountering of Confucius and Galileo. However, the population of Edefia was conserved in ignorance. The drastic change occurred with the accompaniment of the Great Chaos when the knowledge of the secret was made public. Since then, the Portal has experienced two openings and each time it has claimed the life of the Gracious who held possession of that power: Gracious Malorane and the Much-Loved Old Gracious."

Oksa groaned at the still-vivid memory of Baba Pollock fading as the Portal appeared.

"The only thing that matters to Ocious is reaching the Outside once I've restored equilibrium," she stammered. "He won't bat an eyelid if I die opening the Portal…"

The Lunatrix glanced at Pavel, worried that he'd said too much, but Pavel nodded: everything he had said was the truth, however hard it was to hear.

"Let's wait and see what you learn in the Cloak Chamber," he said, trying not to show his unease. "And trust us: we won't let anyone put you in harm's way, on my word as a Runaway."

Oksa gave him a weak smile, then lay back on her bed, her heart pounding in her chest.

51

A Comforting Visit

THE YOUNG GRACIOUS'S MOOD WAS AS DARK AS EDEFIA'S louring sky now her father had been escorted back to his quarters by a close-mouthed Werewall and two zealous Vigilians. Still, it had been comforting to have a short chat in private, despite the pessimistic overtones of their conversation. At least she had her father—Gus was all on his own.

"Don't think about Gus… Don't think about Mum…" she groaned, squeezing her eyes shut.

Ever loyal and conscientious, the Lunatrix got up from his armchair and went over to Oksa. Since he'd become her personal Lunatrix, he was never far away and remained continually attentive to her every need. Oksa looked round, then knelt down so she was at eye level with him—she'd suddenly had an idea.

"Lunatrix! I'm sure you can tell me how they are!"

The small steward gazed at her with his customary kindness and shook his head.

"The frontiers of Edefia possess great opacity," he said regretfully. "Your domestic staff is thwarted, his cerebral access to the Outside experiences unfitness."

Oksa's face clouded over.

"But if you will turn your gaze in that direction," continued the Lunatrix, pointing to the bay window. "A friendly visit is imminent…"

Unnoticed by the pair of Vigilians keeping a watch on things outside the Column, two tiny golden birds were tapping on the glass with their minuscule beaks.

"The Ptitchkins!" exclaimed Oksa, immediately covering her mouth with her hand.

Suppressing her impatience, she casually stood up and went over to open the window, as if she fancied a breath of fresh air on the balcony. The Ptitchkins were chasing each other back and forth in front of her, as if playing. Becoming bored by their looping flight, the Vigilians eventually stopped watching. The Ptitchkins then swooped down and hid beneath Oksa's hair just before she went back inside and slammed the window shut.

"Young Gracious!" they chirped in her ear. "It's wonderful to see you!"

"Where were you, Ptitchkins?" she asked, turning her back on the sentinels.

"In Abakum's quarters with the Squoracles and the rest of the menagerie."

"Is everyone OK?"

"So-so," replied one of the tiny birds. "Anarchy reigns, as always... the Squoracles are complaining about the weather, the Incompetents are doing everything at half-speed and the Getorixes won't stay in one place for a second. I won't even mention the Goranovs, which are making themselves ill..."

"Why?" asked Oksa.

"They're afraid the Werewalls are planning to extract their sap in industrial quantities."

Oksa couldn't help smiling. She'd always felt a sincere, if amused, sympathy for the Goranovs.

"Poor things, they must be in a real state."

"The Getorixes told them stress was more likely to kill them than the Werewalls," added one of the Ptitchkins.

Oksa laughed. This visit from the tiny golden birds had really improved her mood.

"It must be pretty lively there," she remarked.

"It's total chaos."

"Where are Abakum's quarters?" asked Oksa.

She was longing to see the Fairyman.

"Opposite yours, on the north-east side of the Column, between the rooms occupied by Naftali and Tugdual."

At the mention of Tugdual's name, Oksa looked up and asked tremulously:

"How is he?"

"He has a message for you, that's why we came to see you."

Oksa felt a thrill of excitement.

"Our jailers are watching the exits, but they're not guarding the inside of apartments, except for yours, which is being kept under closer watch than the others," chirruped the tiny bird, very quietly. "Some of the Runaways with Werewall powers have managed to pass from room to room without anyone noticing."

"Fantastic!" murmured Oksa.

The Vigilians were pressed against the bay window, watching Oksa closely.

"Tugdual suggests you launch a campaign of destruction against those vile insects that are watching every move you make."

"Because he'd like to visit you," finished the second tiny messenger.

This thought gave Oksa courage, and made her shiver with anticipation. She turned to look at the diabolical insects, which were watching her intently. They were so revolting that she had no qualms about killing them. Initially, she considered a Fireballistico. The one Tugdual had fired during the council meeting had been very effective, instantly reducing the Vigilian to ash.

"What if I miss though? I'll be in big trouble then," she muttered, chewing a nail.

What about a Granok? That could be the answer, but which one? And how could she be sure that Granoks would work on the hideous blue caterpillars?

"Come on, Oksa-san, stop prevaricating," she scolded herself. "Act!"

One option appealed to her more than the others. She got up and resolutely opened the bay window. The Vigilians moved out of the way as she leant against the balcony railing, but remained nearby.

"What are you doing?" they asked when they saw her take out her Granok-Shooter.

They were buzzing with agitation, hairs erect, ready to attack.

"I'd like to use a Reticulata to look at the mountains, if that's OK with you?" replied Oksa, not allowing herself to be distracted by her revulsion at the two insects or by the painful consequences of possible failure.

The Vigilians seemed to hesitate, then hovered just above Oksa, as she'd hoped. She spoke the appropriate magic words in her head and, looking up unexpectedly, whispered into her Granok-Shooter which was pointed at her sentinels—who were hit head-on by a Hypnagogo.

"Didn't you mention a trip to the Distant Reaches?" asked one of the two caterpillars.

"Oooh, yes!" replied the other, with a pirouette in the air. "Why don't we go now? There are some flowers there with un-belie-vable pistils. You'll love them!"

And the two caterpillars took flight, disappearing into the distance before Oksa's amazed eyes.

"That was effective!" she exclaimed. "I love this Granok."

"Bravo, Lil' Gracious!" remarked a familiar voice behind her.

Her whole body was suffused with warmth, reminding her just how much she loved him. Despite tragedy. Despite her doubts. Despite everything. She turned round, eyes shining.

"Oh, there you are," she said, pretending to scratch her head nonchalantly. "You took your time!"

"I was just waiting for you to get rid of your winged chaperones," replied Tugdual, poker-faced.

Simply dressed in black T-shirt and trousers, he was leaning against a column in the middle of the room, hands in pockets, his face framed by black hair.

"Are you OK?" stammered Oksa, disconcerted. "I hope the walls weren't too... thick?"

They both laughed nervously at this odd question, feeling relieved and happy.

"Abakum, my grandparents, the Bellangers, my mother and Till send their love," said Tugdual.

"Gosh," said Oksa, giving a whistle of admiration, "you covered some ground getting here!"

"Did you really think you'd be able to keep this sumptuous apartment all to yourself?" he replied, looking around the vast room. "It's the largest and most comfortable suite in the place, they're spoiling you."

"One of the advantages of being a Gracious," she retorted.

Tugdual suddenly strode over to stand just a few inches from her, taking her by surprise. He cupped her face in his hands, gazed intently at her, then dropped a feather-light kiss on her lips.

"One of the advantages of being me," he murmured.

She nestled against him and they gently rested their foreheads together, a simple gesture that best expressed their emotion at seeing each other again.

"Come on," he said, suddenly taking her hand and pulling her towards the door. "I've got something to show you."

52

SUBTERRANEAN TOUR

STANDING FACE TO FACE IN THE GLASS LIFT PLUMMETING into the depths of the Column, Oksa and Tugdual gazed at each other. The pair had made short work of the sentries: a simple Dozident Granok fired by Oksa had plunged the two Vigilians into a deep sleep, while Tugdual had neutralized the one guard with a tightly knotted Arborescens.

"He didn't know what had hit him," remarked Oksa.

Tugdual just smiled. His eyes were shining with their usual chilly brilliance and his face bore no trace of the ordeals they'd been through, as if he were untouched by time and tragedy. However Oksa knew that wasn't the case. She could now recognize his mask, even if she wasn't always sure what it was hiding. Unable to help herself, she brushed away a strand of hair concealing part of Tugdual's face. As in the Council Chamber, the only visible indication of his inner agitation was the fast beat of his pulse under the skin of his temple. She pressed it gently with her fingertips to show Tugdual that she knew and that she was there for him. He covered her hand with his, pressing it against his face, then kissed her palm. Oksa could have stayed like this for hours, but the lift reached its destination and the doors slid open to reveal unusually transparent rough stone walls. Oksa looked at Tugdual, without daring to say a word.

"We're in the Column's first basement, Lil' Gracious," Tugdual said.

"The lift doesn't go any deeper, but there are seven more levels below this."

"How do you know?" asked Oksa in surprise. Tugdual gave a small smile.

"Let's just say that a few of us decided not to waste our Werewall gifts... they have to be good for something, don't they?"

He pulled her along a wide passageway, whose steeply sloping floor made it difficult to walk slowly and carefully. After twisting her ankle hurrying down the incline, Oksa clung onto Tugdual's arm, but they soon decided it would be faster to Vertifly. The stone walls glowed with a light that seemed to come from nowhere, bathing the two intruders in a milky radiance that had an almost magical quality. For the first time since she'd arrived in Edefia, Oksa felt free and happy. These minutes spent flying beside Tugdual felt like a short reprieve from the waking nightmare which had become her life. For a short time she forgot everything before reality regained the upper hand.

"Where does this light come from?" wondered Oksa, admiring the shimmering glow.

"It comes from the bowels of the Earth and is reflected thousands of times over by the transparent stones," remarked Tugdual. "Did you notice how they were cut?"

"Like precious stones," replied Oksa, stroking the perfectly geometrical facets.

"That enables them to intensify the light endlessly. It's even brighter now than when I came here before."

"But how can there be light coming from below us?"

"That's what you're about to find out, Lil' Gracious."

"And, of course, you're going to make me wait so that I can see for myself..."

"You're getting to know me well," he admitted, sounding amused.

At the end of the passageway, they came to a flight of stairs. After descending the fifty steps, holding on to the walls, they reached another passageway, about a hundred feet long. Although the light barely diminished as they forged deeper and deeper into the Glass Column, the tunnels grew narrower, making it impossible to Vertifly. Oksa wondered how many hundreds of feet below ground they were now.

"Shut your eyes," said Tugdual, when they came to the seventh passageway.

Oksa shook her head firmly.

"This is no time to play games!" she objected.

"Shut your eyes."

Reluctantly she did as she was told, cautiously shuffling along as he led her by the hand. The ground had levelled out, but the ceiling was very low and they could touch both walls by stretching out their arms to the side. Tugdual went to stand behind Oksa, his hands on her shoulders, and guided her to the end of the last passageway.

"We're here," he said. "You can open your eyes."

Oksa didn't need to be told twice and gasped in surprise at the breathtaking beauty surrounding them: she was looking at a vast domed chamber, lined with brightly coloured translucent stones scattering the light in myriad directions. The air was mild, if dusty and slightly oppressive. A sort of glittery ash on the ground muffled their footsteps and rose in small sparkling plumes whenever Oksa and Tugdual moved.

"Amazing!" Oksa exclaimed. "Do you think they're precious stones?" she asked, running her hand over an impossibly blue wall.

"Probably," replied Tugdual, peering through the transparent stone.

"Oksa!" suddenly yelled a familiar voice.

Oksa whirled round.

"ZOE!!!"

They ran to each other, kicking up clouds of sparks, and hugged affectionately.

"Oksa! Are you OK?"

"I'm fine! But you don't look so good…"

Oksa was delighted to be reunited with sweet, sensible Zoe, her best friend as well as her second cousin. She looked terrible. Her large brown eyes looked enormous in her gaunt face. She seemed to have lost a lot of weight and her T-shirt was hanging off her.

"Things aren't brilliant, but we're all in the same boat, aren't we?" remarked Zoe, looking down. "We're all coping as best we can."

"What about your gran?" asked Oksa simply.

"She's resting. She'll be OK, she's a tough nut!" said Zoe, with a short laugh.

"I know," nodded Oksa. "She's incredible! What are you doing here anyway?"

"Tugdual had the idea of using our Werewall gifts to do a little… 'sightseeing'. I have to admit some of the walls weren't that easy, but he's a very good teacher."

She gave Oksa a long look, as if to press home the point that she could be objective about Tugdual, despite her previous warnings. To her great surprise, Oksa found this more reassuring than she'd ever have imagined.

"Shall we show her?" Tugdual said to Zoe.

"Show me what?" asked Oksa immediately.

"THAT!" chorused Zoe and Tugdual.

Oksa followed their gaze to discover a strange phenomenon on one of the walls on the left-hand side of the chamber: a door was appearing in the stone; its outline and handle could be seen clearly, but its entire surface was glowing, as if pulsing with inner fire. Small bluish flames were escaping from the hinges fixing it to the stone wall. Fascinated by the rhythmic, hypnotic ripples of light, Oksa edged closer, followed by her friends. With each step she could feel the heat growing fiercer—it was as though the palpitating air was living breath and she reckoned that it could be horribly destructive. When she was about four yards from the door, she could go no farther—her progress was impeded by an invisible force.

"We tried really hard, but we couldn't get any closer," said Zoe.

"What is it?" asked Oksa, her eyes fixed on the door. "A secret passage?"

Zoe and Tugdual looked at her doubtfully.

"No, Lil' Gracious, it's much better than a secret passage," said Tugdual eventually. "I think we're standing in front of the Cloak Chamber."

53

DISAPPOINTMENT

"**O**F COURSE!" EXCLAIMED OKSA, SMACKING HER PALM against her forehead. "It has to be! Wow… the Cloak Chamber…"

She pressed her face against the invisible barrier and felt it give a little. "Hey!" she said. "I think I might be able to go a bit farther."

Pushing hard, she managed to take another step forward, but that was as far as she got.

"Remember what Ocious said: the Chamber isn't ready," reminded Tugdual. "It's only a matter of days."

Oksa's heart gave a lurch. Gus was usually the one who helped her reason things out, convincing her to sit tight and not be too impulsive. She took a deep breath, as unsettled by this strange place as by the horrible reminder that, like every other human being, she had very little control over her life.

She'd often been told that life is a matter of choice and she liked thinking that she was in relative control: even though fate set the rules—and Oksa was sure about that—she believed that the power of free will trumped everything and was the ultimate deal-breaker. But now she was beginning to have her doubts: the theory didn't stand up to scrutiny. The proof of this was that she'd been separated from people she loved without being able to do anything about it, and that she was here, in the depths of a dying world, shouldering a heavy burden of responsibility—when she should have been sitting in a maths or history lesson. She felt completely at the mercy of fate, without any room for manoeuvre. Unless… She turned round, a new gleam in her eyes.

"I've got an idea!"

Zoe and Tugdual couldn't help smiling at her triumphant expression.

"I'll hide until the Cloak Chamber is ready! I'll be enthroned without the Werewalls realizing; then, when I'm the Gracious, we'll all go back to the Portal, I'll reopen it and we'll go and find Mum, Gus and the others!"

Tugdual and Zoe didn't look all that impressed.

"It's very tempting," said Tugdual, "but you're forgetting a few important little details. It's much more complicated than that, Oksa, sorry to be a wet blanket."

Oksa stared at him, surprised that he'd just called her by her name. Like Zoe, he looked very serious again.

"No one knows if it'll be possible to leave Edefia again or, if we can, what price we'll have to pay. If you're going to die doing it, then it's out of the question: we'll all stay here."

Oksa aimed a kick at the ground, clenching her fists in anger.

"And I'd have to spend the rest of my life hiding in some dump, so that Ocious can't find me. What a great prospect…"

"Ocious won't live for ever," ventured Zoe.

Oksa glanced up suddenly, struck by the feeling that Zoe could be just as implacable and determined as Reminiscens, when it came to helping her clan.

"Yes—but he's not the only one with big ambitions for the Outside," objected Tugdual.

"That's true," admitted Zoe. "But we can fight…"

Tugdual nodded. Zoe might look fragile, but she had the heart of a warrior.

"The second objection is that you're living on borrowed time, Oksa," he continued. "You need Ocious so that you can take the Werewall Elixir, otherwise—"

He fell silent, his forehead creased in a frown and his eyes anxious.

"Otherwise, I'll die," whispered Oksa, finishing his sentence.

She sat down cross-legged on the ground and began drawing lines in the glittery dust with her fingers. She felt a little foolish at not having thought about all those things before opening her mouth. Her body might have grown, but her mind was still as ungovernable.

Tugdual was still standing there with his hands in his pockets, watching her. Zoe knelt down beside Oksa, her back hunched but her eyes bright with understanding. Farther away, the door to the Chamber shone with such piercing supernatural radiance that it looked like it could dissolve any object or life form. Was there no other choice but to toe the line without batting an eyelid?

A movement caught their attention. The light had become so blinding that at first they couldn't see anything. Then Tugdual suddenly threw himself at Oksa, pinning her down with all the weight of his body. She cried out in fright and surprise as Zoe grabbed fistfuls of dust and threw them into the air. Unlike her two friends, whose Firmhand and Werewall origins had just undeniably proved their worth, Oksa hadn't spotted the swarm of Chiropterans flying into the subterranean dome. The bat-like insects circled just below the ceiling, wheeling in slow, sinister formation, then gradually drew nearer. Their beating wings were making a terrifying clicking noise. A wave of nausea mingled with panic and disgust washed over Oksa and she broke out in an acrid sweat. Her heart was pounding so hard it felt as though it would burst, but it was nothing compared to the unbearable pain welling up inside her. She pressed her hands over her ears in what she knew was the futile hope of stopping the waves of sound mercilessly boring into her body. The infrasonic noise felt as if it were entering every pore of her skin, spreading like poison. It was destroying everything on its way, frazzling her nerves, crushing her organs and subjecting her body to the worst possible torture.

Tugdual fired some Fireballisticos to keep the Chiropterans at bay, helped by Zoe who was frantically using every weapon she had at her disposal: Granoks, Magnetuses, handfuls of dust... Three Chiropterans managed to evade these attacks to position themselves three feet above Oksa's head. The Young Gracious stared at them in panic, eyes bulging and her body arched in agony. The nearer the Chiropterans came, the worse the pain. With a cry of rage, Tugdual managed to incinerate one, while Zoe grabbed the other two, smashing them against each other with surprising violence, then matter-of-factly dropping their mangled bodies on the ground. Suddenly Oksa noticed the dark figure of a man flying through the dome. She saw Tugdual look up and make an attempt to prevent the Vertiflier from reaching them. It was no use—two feet clad in black ankle boots landed just beside her, a few inches from her strained face. She felt Tugdual collapse on top of her, before she herself slipped into unconsciousness.

⁂

Her head was such a jumble of images that she couldn't tell whether what she was seeing was real or a product of the nightmarish coma she knew she was in. She wasn't in pain any more, which wasn't necessarily a good sign. Did the absence of pain mean she was far from consciousness? Too far? In a place of no return? No. She wasn't in pain, but she could still feel things. She was fairly sure someone was carrying her. She could hear hurried footsteps, muffled voices, several people walking beside her. The face of the man who'd appeared for a fraction of a second just before she fainted popped into her mind at the same time as the image was obscured by a dark fog. She felt as though she were moving restlessly, but the fog spread, preventing a return to full consciousness.

⁂

Orthon hadn't been surprised to find Oksa and her two friends beside the Cloak Chamber. What a bonus… When he'd met the lethargic Vigilians coming to alert Ocious to the Young Gracious's "escape", he'd immediately realized that he could make good use of this so-called breakout—no one could get out of Edefia at the moment, anyway. And there was nowhere to hide, since Ocious and the Werewalls knew this land better than anyone—every corner, every cave, every underground passage...

"Don't disturb my father," Orthon had ordered the Vigilians. "I'll take care of this."

The sentinels had hesitated to impart any vital information.

"The Docent gave us an order—"

"To do *what*?" Orthon had interrupted brusquely.

"To alert him or his son immediately about any problems, and no one else."

Orthon had taken a deep breath to calm himself and to convey an impressive sense of authority.

"And who am I?"

The Vigilians had been perturbed by this question.

"You're the Docent's son."

"That's right!" Orthon had answered gleefully.

"But the Docent meant his son Andreas."

"Of course he did! But you're not neglecting your duty by giving me any information you want passed on to him. I'm Ocious's elder son, the son born long before Andreas. Which gives me superiority, wouldn't you agree?"

The Vigilians couldn't argue with this irrefutable logic, so they told Orthon what had just happened within the walls of the Glass Column.

⁂

Orthon was feeling very smug. He carried the unconscious Young Gracious back up the seven levels to the ground floor of the Column, then decided to Vertifly to the top floor where her father was billeted rather than take the lift. Such a conspicuous entrance would spread panic among any of the Runaways who saw him fly past with a lifeless Oksa. That would show everyone that he, Orthon, was the real master here, not Ocious or that imposter Andreas. Oksa was in a bad way, but she wouldn't die. Not right away. Not while he had the situation in hand. Despite what everyone thought, his intelligence and poise made him the only person in Edefia with a smidgen of self-control—and it was only a short step from self-control to supreme power, a step which the Felon was happy to take. Spurred on by ambition, he emerged from the Column watched with concern by the guards standing on the square in front of the main doors. Gazing fiercely at the summit, he took off and soared upwards.

54

STATES OF COLLAPSE

WHEN PAVEL SAW ORTHON FLY PAST THE BAY WINDOW of his room, he thought at first he was having a bad dream. He rushed out onto the tiny balcony and craned his neck, scared that what he'd seen might be real. The Felon immediately flew back again, his chest puffed out with pride, and Pavel gave a shout of rage: his enemy was holding Oksa in his arms, her head lolling and her body motionless.

"What have you done to my daughter?" he yelled.

Orthon merely gave him an evil smile and shot up to the floor above. This was more than Pavel could stand: the Ink Dragon awoke and took flight, blazing with flames and giving a roar that could be heard as far as the suburbs of Thousandeye City. The city's inhabitants and those living in the Column rushed to the windows to see the incredible creature circling the Gracious's residence with a strength born of despair. A dense swarm of Vigilians soon gave pursuit, buzzing menacingly. However, thirty or forty caterpillar-sentinels were powerless to stop the dragon, maddened by the wound inflicted by Orthon, and none of the insects escaped a summary cremation. A shower of charred Vigilians pattered onto Ocious's balcony as he gazed at the scene from his private penthouse apartments.

❋

When his son burst in with the Young Gracious in his arms, the Master of the Werewalls managed to look far more unruffled than he felt. Orthon's landing had been undeniably stylish—he certainly knew how to make an entrance, a quality he'd clearly inherited from his father. Ocious knew how much theatrical flourishes could influence a situation or people's perception of events, but he didn't think this was really the time for ostentatious displays when Oksa—their key asset—looked in such a bad way.

"Father, our Young Gracious tried to escape," began Orthon confidently. "I found her by the Cloak Chamber."

"Why wasn't I told about this?" snapped Ocious, an annoyed frown deepening the groove between his eyes.

"I took the initiative of acting without delay," said Orthon curtly, his expression colder. "Before any damage was done."

"She wouldn't have got far anyway," objected his father.

Looking injured, Orthon deposited a deathly pale Oksa on one of the many divans. At that moment there was an almighty din. The window panes shattered and the furniture near the windows was flattened: Pavel and his Ink Dragon had just unceremoniously burst into Ocious's spacious living room and were skidding over the onyx floor tiles. It took an iron will to transform the creature back into ink—Pavel hated the two men clutching their Granok-Shooters in front of them with all his heart, and would happily have burnt them to a cinder.

"Bravo, Pavel! Bravo!" applauded Ocious, putting away his Granok-Shooter. "You're so strong!" Orthon shot his father a hate-filled look, which didn't escape Pavel, despite the complex situation.

"Oh, you didn't come alone," continued Ocious. Pavel turned round in time to see Tugdual and Zoe land beside him. Their clothes were torn, their hair was tangled and their worried faces were covered in dust. Zoe rushed over to Oksa.

"Oksa! Wake up, please!" she groaned, shaking her friend.

Pavel pushed past Orthon, who was trying to block his way.

"Have you still not grasped how much danger we're ALL in if you continue to persecute her?" he growled, leaning over Oksa.

"I'll have you know that it's your daughter's own fault she's in this state," retorted Orthon, his face hard. "If I hadn't got there when I did, who knows if she'd still be alive?"

These words infuriated Tugdual.

"You must be joking! If you hadn't got there with your revolting Chiropterans, Oksa certainly wouldn't be in this state!"

"You exposed her to Chiropterans?" broke in Ocious, with a disapproving glare at his son.

Orthon's face darkened, but he didn't lose his composure. He stared defiantly at his angry father without saying a word. The relationship between the two men didn't seem to be improving, which didn't bode well. It was clear to the three Runaways—and Ocious—that Orthon had wanted to flaunt his own importance by portraying Oksa as a pawn over whom he had power of life and death. It was a brutal way of showing his father who was really boss.

"You're playing with fire," said Ocious simply.

The old man turned round and went over to Oksa. He seemed as worried by this sudden realization as by the Young Gracious's condition.

"Settle your scores later," said Pavel, gritting his teeth. "This is an emergency!"

Orthon kept his distance, his eyes gleaming with satisfaction.

"Oksa has to drink your vile elixir so that the antidote can take permanent effect," Pavel told Ocious.

"That goes without saying," replied the Werewall.

"You really are a psycho!" muttered Tugdual.

His icy fury was shocking. Pavel and Zoe had never seen Tugdual so angry. Worry and rage were written all over his face and, for the first time since they'd met him, he was showing his vulnerability.

"Where is it?" suddenly shouted Tugdual. "WHERE'S THE ELIXIR?"

"It's a long time since a drop of Werewall Elixir has been seen in Edefia," replied Ocious coldly.

"WHAT?!" gasped the three Runaways, while Orthon shifted nervously.

"Don't forget that the Great Chaos took place nearly sixty years ago," continued Ocious. "And for all those years, we've never stopped hoping we could leave."

"And you knew damn well that your foul elixir wouldn't be any use!" raged Pavel. "It wouldn't help you leave…"

"I will not permit you to judge me!" thundered Ocious. "You've never had to deal with conditions like the ones we've endured here."

"You're nothing but a damned sorcerer's apprentice!" hissed Pavel.

"That's as maybe, but I'm the only one who can make the elixir again, so I'd be obliged if you'd lower your voice and treat me with a little more respect."

"Do you even have the necessary ingredients?" snapped Pavel, interrupting him.

Ocious looked at him, almost amused.

"The cube of Luminescent Stone isn't a problem, nor is the blood of our Young Gracious, which seems to flow in abundance, despite her unfortunate condition. The last Goranov plant died out in Edefia a decade ago, but I believe you succeeded in keeping several seedlings alive. As for the Diaphan…"

The Master of the Werewalls stopped and rubbed his chin, looking suddenly sombre. The Runaways were in agonies.

"These have been difficult years and the Diaphans have gradually died out due to a reduction in the light which guaranteed their survival in the Retinburn territory."

Pavel groaned, while Zoe and Tugdual exchanged a look of despair.

"But who do you think you're dealing with?" continued Ocious. "Do you take me for a complete amateur?"

Pavel couldn't contain his exasperation.

"Get to the point!"

"The last Diaphan in Edefia lives in a specially equipped cave that I personally authorized," announced Ocious triumphantly.

Pavel closed his eyes as indescribable relief washed over him.

"It's going to be OK," breathed Zoe, her cheeks shining with tears.

"Yes," confirmed Ocious, "but only on one condition."

Zoe shivered violently. Tugdual made a move to go over to the sofa where Oksa was lying, but Zoe put up her hand and said, almost inaudibly:

"Stay away…"

Tugdual stopped. His dark pupils dilated, consuming the piercing blue of his eyes. Orthon looked intrigued, while Ocious seemed bewildered. He was missing something.

"The Diaphan will only give us what we need in exchange for its favourite delicacy," said the Master of the Werewalls.

This time, Zoe couldn't stop Tugdual: he went to sit on the edge of the divan where Oksa was lying and put his head in his hands. Then he took Oksa's fingers, which were clenched with pain, and kissed them.

"You shouldn't have done that," whispered Zoe, looking upset.

Tugdual gazed miserably at her, then gently shook his head. He was finding it hard to breathe. He allowed his hair to fall in front of his face to conceal his agitation and clutched Oksa's hand even tighter. Her fingers moved slightly and her eyelids fluttered like the wings of a butterfly trying to fly. She eventually opened her eyes, looking dazed, and tried to sit up.

"I really thought I was done for this time," she stammered, before slumping back on the divan.

Ocious came into sight, just behind Tugdual, who was looking at her more intensely than ever before. Realizing where she was, she began to remember what had happened.

"This is like a bad dream…"

"We'll get you better, sweetheart," said Pavel. "You've just got to keep strong!"

"I'll do my best, Dad," she replied, alarmed by everyone's serious expressions.

"You'd better do, Lil' Gracious," whispered Tugdual, resting his cheek against hers. "You'd better…"

55

SACRIFICE FOR LOVE

O CIOUS HAD SUMMONED HIS STAUNCH ALLIES AND HAD reluctantly agreed to the presence of the older Runaways. It had been heart-rending for Abakum and the Knuts to enter the lavish suite of rooms that had belonged to Gracious Malorane in happier days, and seeing Oksa there only made their memories more poignant.

Oksa was still trying to come to terms with the idea that her time was running out and she couldn't stop thinking about the Outside, and her mother and Gus, who also had a sword of Damocles hanging over their heads. They had to be in a great deal of emotional, as well as physical, pain. At least she could hope for a speedy recovery. The Werewalls and Runaways were exchanging bitter words some way off and Oksa couldn't muster enough concentration to hear what they were saying. Her ears were still buzzing, transforming all sounds into an indistinct din. Despite being unable to make out the details, though, she'd realized what was going to happen and was trembling with fear.

"The things you have to do to stay alive," she murmured ironically, in a bid to stop herself crying at the thought of drinking that elixir.

Sitting on the ground, with their backs against the sofa where Oksa was lying, Zoe and Tugdual turned to look at her and she was surprised by how worried they were.

"It'll be a breeze," said Tugdual hoarsely. Zoe remained silent, unable to utter a word.

They both went back to following the agitated discussion between the adults a few feet away. Oksa was worn out. She fell back against the cushions and watched her two friends. They seemed to have buried their differences, which would have pleased her in any other circumstances. But they seemed to be colluding over something she couldn't make out, which had brought them closer, and that bothered her. Surprised at her own spontaneity, she rested her hand on Tugdual's head and ran her fingers through his silky hair. She'd never have dared to do that a few weeks ago. Tugdual leant back against the sofa, moved by her gentle caress.

"We have to summon all the young people in Edefia!" suddenly rang out Ocious's voice. "We're bound to find a few young men or women in love."

The Master of the Werewalls looked concerned, which didn't bode well at all.

"What's he talking about?" asked Oksa in a low voice. She was finding it hard to hear.

"About the Diaphan," replied Zoe, before Tugdual could say anything.

Oksa saw Abakum pacing up and down, looking preoccupied. They were all lost in thought. Except for Orthon, who kept his eyes fixed on the three teenagers.

"That will take too long! We have to find another solution," declared Abakum in response to Ocious's suggestion.

When Orthon pointed triumphantly at Tugdual, Oksa suddenly realized what the Felon was plotting.

"No way! Not that," she whispered, her face crumpling.

"Why complicate matters?" said Orthon.

Oksa felt as if she'd just been stabbed through the heart. For the space of a terrifying second, she imagined the Diaphan sucking every scrap of devotion from the man she loved, which is exactly what Orthon had in mind.

"Why scour Edefia to find someone who's passionately in love," continued the Felon, "when there's a young man perfect for our needs right here… Or at least, perfect for the Diaphan, which will save our Gracious's life!" he added with a sardonic snigger.

"Out of the question!" objected Naftali, white with rage.

"You're mad!" hissed Abakum.

Lying motionless on the sofa, Oksa felt as though her blood had drained away. This was the worst solution imaginable. She'd already lost her gran, her mother and Gus. If she had to lose Tugdual's love too, she knew she'd die.

❋

Tugdual hadn't moved. He sat there with his head tipped back towards Oksa, studying the veins in the blue marble ceiling. He looked a million miles away, lost in thought, even though his body was there. Orthon, on the other hand, was in seventh heaven.

"You should have joined us while you had the chance," declared the Felon to Tugdual.

To everyone's surprise, Tugdual raised his head and eyed him with icy calm.

"Don't kid yourself! I'd never have followed you, NEVER!" he remarked. "I've always taken responsibility for my actions, both good and bad, even if I've sometimes made the wrong choices. And I accept full responsibility for the decision I'm taking now and its consequences."

He paused briefly, which some of them read as a hesitation and which gave others the hope they'd be proved wrong for believing the worst. Then Tugdual stood up, trembling uncontrollably despite himself. He turned away from Oksa to face Ocious, ignoring Orthon completely.

"You can take me," he said breathlessly. "I'm ready to… *meet* your Diaphan."

Oksa wanted to protest, but pain and lack of comprehension made it impossible to speak. Her sight blurred by burning tears, she saw Naftali go over to Tugdual, who abruptly pushed away the hand held out by his grandfather.

"No, Tugdual, we won't let you do this!" stammered Brune.

"We don't have a choice."

"Think about Oksa," added Naftali.

"That's exactly what I'm doing," retorted Tugdual. "She's all I think about. DO YOU WANT HER TO DIE?"

"Let him do what he wants," snapped Ocious. "He's old enough to make his own decisions."

The Master of the Werewalls didn't try to hide his satisfaction. He'd just killed two birds with one stone: not only had he found a way to save that scatterbrained Young Gracious but he was also getting his revenge on the Knuts. Those two stubborn individuals would have made powerful allies if they'd chosen the right side… Today, their cool-eyed grandson would pay for their mistakes, despite his incredible potential.

"You're fooling no one," Zoe suddenly said in a shaky but determined voice.

"Zoe, stay out of this," warned Tugdual.

"Tugdual's love is a sham," continued Zoe. "He used his considerable skills to seduce Oksa, he tricked her into caring for him and now he has her wrapped around his little finger. But the only thing he's really interested in is her power."

Tugdual tried to silence her by firing a Knock-Bong, which she avoided by leaping to the other side of the room with the agility of a cheetah. Her face hardened and her eyes filled with a cold glitter that surprised everyone, briefly reminding the Runaways of Reminiscens when she'd fired the deadly Granok at Mercedica. Zoe's face wore the same determined, and pitiless, expression.

"Why would he sacrifice himself then?" asked Ocious sceptically. "Getting up close and personal with a Diaphan is no picnic for a young man."

"Tugdual's always been fascinated by Beloved Detachment," replied Zoe. "He was totally captivated by the story of my gran and that of the fifth tribe. He's always been obsessed with the idea of meeting a Diaphan."

Oksa looked from Zoe to Tugdual. She was appalled by Zoe's revelations, which felt like dagger blows to her heart. Tugdual kept silent, his fists clenched, his eyes fixed on Zoe to the exclusion of everyone else. Oksa felt as though she didn't exist for either of them any more. Or worse, she felt like some pawn in an implacable game: she was being used by a power-hungry Tugdual or by Zoe, who was desperate for revenge. Or for the truth… it didn't matter. Either way, Oksa's heart was shattered into a thousand pieces.

"Anyway, he knows he's got nothing to fear by putting himself forward because he isn't in love with Oksa," concluded Zoe, just as icily. "It changes nothing for him. But it makes a huge difference to us: Beloved Detachment won't work and the Diaphan won't be satisfied."

The Werewalls and Runaways looked shaken at this potential spanner in the works.

"I do know someone with enough love in their heart to save Oksa, though," announced Zoe to her perplexed friends and enemies.

"Who's that, my dear great-granddaughter?" whispered Ocious, intrigued by Zoe's self-possession and charismatic personality.

Oksa distinctly heard Tugdual murmur: "No, Zoe…" which confused her further, then he threw himself out of the broken window that had been shattered by the entrance of the Ink Dragon and soared into the dark skies over Thousandeye City. In a whisper, Zoe said:

"Me."

56

CONFUSION

OCIOUS PUT A FIRM ARM AROUND ZOE'S SHOULDER AND silently led her to one side, watched by the devastated Runaways. If the Master of the Werewalls and his son Orthon had felt any qualms about taking Zoe up on her offer—she was family, after all!—it didn't take them long to overcome them. Presenting a united front for the first time since their reunion, they both looked over the moon; it would have been very satisfying to take their revenge on the Knuts, but it was much more gratifying to strike such a painful blow at Reminiscens—the unworthy daughter and hostile sister who'd traitorously turned her back on her family and friends. Until now, Reminiscens had overcome all the ordeals she'd faced and had begun to appear virtually unassailable, but this would bring her to her knees at last!

"Why, Zoe? Why you?" Abakum suddenly asked in a cracked voice, gazing sadly at her.

Zoe looked at the Fairyman, then Oksa, before answering, her head bowed:

"I'm in with love someone who loves someone else," she said, with disconcerting honesty.

Ocious looked puzzled.

"Is that… all?"

The Knuts and Pavel harrumphed indignantly. Oksa suddenly realized why Zoe was doing this and everything fell into place.

"This person has a great deal of respect for me," continued Zoe, sounding more determined than ever. "But he'll never love me. And I'd rather lose all feelings of love than spend my life hoping for something that'll never happen. Beloved Detachment will be a blessing for me."

Oksa shook her head, struggling to catch her breath. Zoe loved Gus, she'd known that for such a long time. But she hadn't known that Zoe loved him so much that she'd willingly sacrifice any chance of love in the future.

"But Zoe... you can't be sure of anything," said Oksa quietly, drawing glares from Ocious and Orthon. "You don't know how things might turn out, you don't know... what your life will be like! There are other fish in the sea—Gus isn't the only one!"

Zoe looked up, her face haggard with emotion.

"Gus? Who said anything about Gus?"

Oksa couldn't help giving a yelp of surprise. Was Zoe in love with Tugdual? If she was, she'd played her cards very close to her chest. The Young Gracious tried to consider this possibility, but her thoughts were all over the place. She didn't understand what was going on. Had she been misled? She quickly thought back over the main stages in their relationship and, the more she thought about it, the more likely it seemed that Zoe was in love with Tugdual. Oksa was shocked to her very core.

"Zoe, think about yourself, about your future," broke in Abakum, sounding overwhelmed with sadness. "You're only fourteen, you can't contemplate a future like this!"

"I may only be fourteen," replied Zoe, "but it doesn't mean I haven't gone through a lot or worked out what life is about."

"A life without love is a life half lived," added Abakum.

Oksa shivered. She knew the Fairyman was in a good position to warn Zoe: Reminiscens could feel affection, tenderness and sympathy... but she'd never feel passion for anyone again. Including Abakum.

"Well, it's not as if you'd die from it!" exclaimed Ocious, sounding shockingly callous.

"Well, as Tugdual said, we don't really have a choice," continued Zoe flatly. "If Oksa dies, we all die."

Zoe tentatively walked over to Oksa. Her eyes, so hard a few seconds earlier, were now filled with their customary kindness and suffering. Oksa took a step back as she came nearer. She'd thought of Zoe as her best friend before this awful episode, but who was the real Zoe? And what about Tugdual? She thought she'd answered those questions a long time ago and had drawn a line under her doubts, but now she realized in horror that her certainties were built on shifting sand. It was all so distressing. Zoe hugged her with disarming sincerity and Oksa let her.

"Don't believe anything I've said," murmured Zoe.

And she pulled away to join Ocious, leaving Oksa standing stock-still and incredulous. What shouldn't she believe? What was true and what wasn't? Oksa was confused. To make things worse, fresh waves of sound were assailing her ears, causing acute pain to spread through her nervous system. She couldn't help grimacing, then groaning, terrified by the intensity of this attack. Her sense of balance deserted her, as the walls and floor seemed to recede, and every sound in the room echoed inside her body, amplified a million times over: blinking eyelids, heartbeats, microscopic mites crawling over skin… everything produced a hideous din which was becoming a weapon of destruction targeting every cell of her body. Oksa swayed towards her father and clung to his arm to stop herself falling. The Runaways surrounded her helplessly, watched by the Master of the Werewalls, whose smile was devoid of kindness.

"I think it's time we paid our saviour a visit!" he declared loftily.

Pavel swallowed down the acerbic retort on his lips and kept quiet. There was nothing to be gained by talking now. He walked over to the window and went out onto the balcony that had been damaged by his landing. It took only five seconds for his Ink Dragon to emerge from his back, watched by an impressed Ocious and Orthon.

"Oksa! Abakum!" he called. "Climb on!"

The Young Gracious and the Fairyman obeyed, while Naftali and Brune Vertiflew either side of the creature. Keen to stay in charge of the expedition, Ocious and Orthon positioned themselves in front, Zoe between them with two pairs of Werewalls as escort. Then they soared off like jet planes, followed by the powerful dragon bearing Oksa towards a new chapter in her uncertain destiny.

57

HOPE AGAINST HOPE

THE PEAK RIDGE MOUNTAINS LOOMED STEEP AND INHOS-
pitable. The strange group flew over gorges so deep they appeared
bottomless and past peaks towering so high they beggared belief. From
time to time, a tremor rocked the depths of the Earth with a terrifying
rumble. Stones broke loose and disappeared into the dark abysses, making
the travellers even more jittery.

Keeping Zoe under close surveillance, the Werewalls escorted the Ink
Dragon and the Runaways through the narrow canyons, taking care to lose
no one on the way. Orthon was Vertiflying beside his father. Although the
Felon's severe, slightly mocking expression was unchanged, his pleasure
at winning favour with Ocious could be seen in his steely eyes and by the
jaunty tilt to his head. He was the worthy son of a hypercritical father
he envied, idolized and hated. Their relationship was clear proof of his
superiority. Bursting with pride, he jutted out his chin and glanced at his
father's eagle-like profile. The Master of the Werewalls was flying with
powerful elegance through the mottled sky, his arms pressed flat against
his sides. Orthon was proud to be his son. One day, very soon, he'd succeed him. And no milksop like Andreas was going to stand in his way...

Thirty or forty yards behind the Werewalls, Oksa was clinging to
the dragon's neck and gazing in fascination at the imposing landscape.
The present might be grim and the future uncertain, but for the first
time since she'd come to Edefia she couldn't help feeling excited by the

prospect of becoming the ruler of this world. The signs of its decline were clear for all to see: forests had been replaced by deserts, rivers no longer flowed and the tallest mountains were crumbling. Life was gradually, and relentlessly, ebbing away. Oksa thought about her gran—she would have been so sad to see what had become of her lost land if she'd been allowed to return. However, despite the dark clouds and arid land, Oksa couldn't help sensing a powerful spirit of rebirth—potential abundance and harmony—lurking just below the surface. Oksa had to believe that. Around her, the vividly coloured mountains shimmered endlessly as she flew by, despite the waning light. She could make out blades of grass and mountain-top flowers blooming on the slightest incline. And although the thin trickle of water—probably one of the legendary endless waterfalls—flowing from the top of a lofty outcrop was little more than a dribble, it could also be regarded as a symbol of hope. It all depended on your point of view. It was the theory of the glass half full or half empty that her parents had so often argued about. Like her mother, she tended to choose the "half full" option. And if life was a matter of choice, that was hers.

"I'm such a bad person," she murmured, suddenly horrified by her own optimism.

How could she be hopeful when things were so bad? Her mother probably wasn't feeling so optimistic now, given her present situation. Her glass had to be completely empty... As if annoyed with herself for believing in the future, Oksa's heart clenched painfully as she thought about Gus, the last time she'd seen Dragomira, the confusion Tugdual made her feel, and Zoe's bleak prospects. Hope? Hope for what? Wasn't it all... futile? Absurd? She felt trapped by her destiny, which resembled the ring of crumbling mountains around her.

She gazed despairingly at the shimmering rocks stretching endlessly into the distance. At the intersection between two sheer corridors, she thought she glimpsed a familiar figure and immediately thought of Tugdual. A thousand new questions assailed her. Had he betrayed her?

She couldn't believe it. She didn't want to believe it. Everything they'd shared since they'd met was too strong not to be real. She couldn't have got it so wrong. But, as soon as Zoe had forced his hand, he'd taken off. He'd run away without a word or look. Had he felt that his behaviour was indefensible? Was it? She was desperate to know and understand. But, she realized, no amount of uncertainty could be worse than thinking that Tugdual might be lost, tormented and in danger. She loved him so much—even though she was longing to know the truth, she would wait until she heard his explanation before passing judgement. Patience wasn't her strong point, but Tugdual was worth making an effort for. And if it turned out that he'd really betrayed her, well…

She felt a hand on her shoulder. Abakum, who was also finding life hard at the moment, could sense her agitation. Her lack of balance made it too precarious for her to turn round and see the reassurance in his eyes, so she simply put her hand on top of his and pressed her body against the dragon for warmth. The creature roared. A flame escaped from deep within its body and licked the glittering stone of the mountains, raising a swarm of insects hiding in the cracks and crevices—which only served to remind Oksa that life still existed, even in that loathsome guise.

At the curve of a gorge, the dragon suddenly reared up and stopped, beating its wings to hover in the air and ward off falling stones, while Brune and Naftali circled. Opposite, on the sheer face of the highest mountain in the chain, a score of caverns had been hollowed out of the mountainside. A dense, shifting light spilt out of them, projecting a myriad multicoloured reflections onto the rock face of precious stone. In front of the largest cave, whose mouth was about thirteen feet high, they could make out a figure, who was easily recognizable as Andreas. Oksa and her escort were expected. A few people also appeared at the mouth of the other caves. Pavel swore; the Master of the Werewalls' retinue hadn't wasted any time and most of the core members were there. In a few seconds, the dragon and the Runaways were surrounded. Everyone seemed eager for the close encounter with the Diaphan.

58

ENCOUNTER WITH
THE DIAPHAN

H ELPED BY NAFTALI AND ABAKUM, OKSA SHAKILY
climbed down from the back of the dragon, annoyed at appearing
so weak in front of all these Werewalls, who were watching her intently.
Ocious's loyal supporters were all there, some twenty men and women
gathered around their Docent and his two sons, Andreas and Orthon.
After the euphoric journey through the Peak Ridge mountains, the latter
considered his half-brother's presence there as a downright insult. His
mood was also not improved by the fact that the Runaways had obviously guessed how he was feeling and made no bones about it showing
it: Naftali favoured him with an ironic stare, while Abakum gazed at him
with intolerable pity in his eyes. To pay the Runaways back for witnessing his disappointment, he grabbed Zoe by the shoulders and held her
tight with a vengeful smile.

Oksa was seeing her second cousin's face for the first time since they'd
left the Glass Column. Zoe looked surprisingly calm, almost serene,
her features relaxed after her heartfelt revelations. How could she be so
composed a few minutes before an awful procedure that would change
her life for ever? Zoe looked at her and Oksa gave a start when she realized that Zoe was holding the talisman she'd given her a couple of weeks
earlier, on the Island of the Felons. She wasn't sure how to react in such

an awful, and unprecedented, situation so, trusting to instinct, she gave Zoe a small smile of encouragement and support. Whatever happened, whatever she might have said or done, she was sacrificing an important part of herself to save Oksa's life—to save the two worlds, in fact, since Oksa was the answer to all this chaos.

"Well," began Ocious. "Let's not waste any time. Andreas, my son, thank you for taking charge so effectively and for getting everything ready."

Orthon tensed and concealed his annoyance by carefully examining the cave, following the example of the Runaways, who were amazed by their breathtaking surroundings. There was nothing antiquated about the place, which was a miracle of architecture with priceless stones studded over the harmonious curves and angles. Its high domed ceiling was tiled with countless translucent blue mosaic squares pierced by shining pinpricks of light that represented the heavens.

"How wonderful," Oksa couldn't help murmuring.

Waving his hand, Andreas pointed to the back of this first chamber, where there was a corridor.

"Welcome to the territory of the Firmhands and to this cave in Mount Humongous, the ancestral seat of the Werewalls," he said. "Let me take you to our host. He's impatient to see us."

If this remark hadn't been so cruel, the Runaways would have been struck by Andreas's voice, which they'd barely heard before. Its captivatingly mellow, almost irresistible, timbre formed a marked contrast to his hard features and severe expression. Oksa shivered. If Orthon was like a ferocious raptor, swooping down on his prey, Andreas reminded her of a snake, mesmerizing its quarry before swallowing it whole.

"I hate that man," whispered Oksa to her father. "Promise you'll never leave me alone with him."

"I promise," declared Pavel.

She took his hand and squeezed it tight, wondering which was stronger: the eagle or the snake. They were both probably as strong as each other, in their own separate ways.

"Follow me, please," continued Andreas.

Manoeuvring with great determination, Orthon managed to enter the corridor first, holding Zoe firmly.

"There's no need to cling onto me as if I'm a prisoner likely to escape," she remarked with surprising self-assurance. "I'm here by my own free will, remember?"

True to himself, Orthon replied sarcastically:

"If you're as elusive as my dear sister, Reminiscens, I prefer to remain on my guard."

"With a brother like you, it's hardly surprising anyone would want to run away!" exclaimed Oksa. "Or should I say, with brothers like you and Andreas…"

Pavel squeezed her hand so hard she winced. But it felt so good to dent the Felon's pride! From the glare he gave her before he began walking again—if looks could kill she'd be dead—she knew she'd hit home. The benefits of a good put-down! From now on, she intended to plague Orthon to death about Andreas.

"Stop playing with fire, Oksa," hissed Pavel.

"But Dad!"

"It might be tempting, but it's more dangerous than you think, I can assure you."

Oksa's face darkened. The Runaways always had to walk on eggshells—it was so frustrating! Angrily, she turned her attention to their magical surroundings: the corridor sloped gently down into the depths of Mount Humongous. Every so often it divided off into galleries identifiable by the colour of the stones covering their walls: ruby, emerald, blue topaz… The main gallery was glazed with pebbles whose fierce yet delicate brilliance suggested they might be diamonds. Andreas was walking at the head of the group, veering right, branching left, leaving the Runaways feeling confused and frightened. The den of the Werewalls was a dazzling labyrinth which provoked wonder and dread in equal measure.

After they had walked through the endless corridors for about ten minutes, the light grew so strong that Oksa, Abakum and Pavel had to shade their eyes with their hands. Only the Firmhands seemed able to withstand the blinding radiance reflecting off the stones.

"We must be here," Abakum said to the Runaways. "These must be the special arrangements that Ocious mentioned."

Oksa looked at him quizzically. Then she remembered what Naftali had said a few months ago: the Diaphans—the fifth tribe—lived close to the territory of the Distant Reaches until the Ageless Ones cast a Confinement Spell on them for pursuing young people in the Love Hunt. Since then, the Diaphans had been confined in isolation to the hostile lands of Retinburn, unable to leave that incandescent region under pain of immediate death.

The extremely strong light in that territory had kept them imprisoned there and, over the centuries, their metabolism had adapted, resulting in the features that Oksa could now see with her own eyes: the last hideous Diaphan of Edefia was standing right in front of her! Petrified, Oksa wanted to run as far away as possible from this monster and this nightmarish scene, but her strength had deserted her. A short distance away, Andreas was speaking smoothly, describing his father's ingenuity in installing a complex lighting system to save the life of the last Diaphan. Instinctively Oksa knew she should do everything in her power to avoid meeting the creature's eyes, but curiosity got the upper hand once again. Horror exerted a strange fascination.

"Delighted to meet you, Young Gracious," grated the Diaphan.

The creature was much worse than anything she'd imagined from Naftali's description. It was almost as tall as her and its translucent white skin shone with a thick covering of grease which protected it from the light. But what sickened Oksa most wasn't its opaque eyes or its melted nose, or the absence of actual ears… it was the life below the skin, an excitement that she could not only hear with her heightened senses, but also see! Everything was on view: the veins pulsing with black blood, the organs throbbing and the dark heart beating frantically.

"It's… disgusting!" she said quietly, unable to tear her eyes away.

"Come now, is that any way to talk to the creature that's going to save your life?" said Ocious with a short laugh. "Pavel, my dear great-nephew, you haven't brought your daughter up very well!"

"My parents brought me up excellently!" snapped Oksa angrily. "And, to be honest, you're hardly in a position to give any lessons, judging by your two psychopathic sons…"

She ignored Pavel's pleading glance.

"It doesn't matter. I'm no stranger to that kind of reaction," said the Diaphan in its horrible gravelly voice.

It sidled so close to Oksa that she could smell its stale odour. A nauseating blend of dust, bad eggs and garlic. She forced herself not to look away from its bottomless gaze and, to her surprise, was unable to resist as she felt herself surrendering to its will. She couldn't move in this confined space, while her limbs grew heavy and a sort of torpor invaded her mind. It was hot and stifling, she was tired and distressed, and so close to giving up, so close…

"Bravo, Ocious, you've kept your promise, the Young Gracious is going to be very tasty indeed," whispered the Diaphan, licking the edges of what remained of its mouth with a tiny black tongue. "So much passion in such a little heart!"

At these words, Abakum and Pavel stood between Oksa and the creature. Ashen, her face shiny with sweat, Zoe stepped forward.

"She isn't the one intended for you," she said breathlessly. "I am."

Oksa couldn't help groaning. Intrigued, the Diaphan turned towards Zoe and studied her at length. When it realized it wasn't going to be short-changed by her—far from it—it grunted with satisfaction. A few yards behind, Brune turned away to stifle a sob.

"This can't happen," she murmured. "How can we let such a loathsome act take place?"

Naftali squeezed her shoulder, unable to say anything. Like Abakum and Pavel, his eyes were brimming with tears. Zoe's sacrifice broke their hearts. Only Ocious and his sons, as well as the more uncompromising Werewalls, seemed happy to countenance what was happening before their very eyes and showed no remorse. The Diaphan walked over to Zoe, its webbed feet moving across the ground with a sucking sound, and sniffed. Everyone could see its heart racing through its diaphanous skin. Zoe's eyes widened; her pupils dilated, spreading a dark mist over her eyes as she was transported into another dimension, far from the real world. The Diaphan took hold of her hands and brought its vile features so close that it brushed Zoe's expressionless face. Finally, it breathed in, at first slowly, then more and more greedily until it collapsed on the floor of the cave, drunk on stolen love, a tarry substance trickling from its flaring nostrils.

59

A Damaged Heart

THE DARK HOURS THAT FOLLOWED THIS VILE ACT WERE followed by dark days, devoid of light. Oksa didn't leave her room. She wandered from bed to sofa with vacant eyes, sometimes venturing out onto the balcony. The precious stirrings of hope she'd felt since she'd arrived in Edefia had been snuffed out when the Diaphan had seized Zoe's innermost emotions. This was one tragedy too many. Her life had been saved by the vile Werewall Elixir which had overcome the poison in her system. She wasn't going to die, but she no longer felt any enthusiasm for anything. Her head was dull and heavy and her heart was just a muscle beating mechanically without any spark of emotion—it had been damaged by too much suffering.

She'd accidentally made herself feel worse when she'd finally unpacked. Right at the bottom of her backpack, she'd found her uniform tie amongst the sweaters and socks. She didn't even remember putting it in… and that small strip of fabric took her back in time, exacerbating the pain. She'd hated wearing a tie at first, then she'd got so used to it that she hardly ever took it off. It had gradually come to symbolize her friendship group and had become a link to her friends, St Proximus, happier days, Gus… With a lump in her throat, she'd loosely knotted the tie round her neck, the way she used to wear it, and had thrown herself on her bed in tears.

Concern was growing in the Glass Column. The Runaways had tried everything to rouse the Young Gracious from her worrying condition:

potions, compounds, Capacitors… The creatures wouldn't leave her side and vied with each other to find inventive ways of amusing her, or at least of making her smile. Despite looking dreadful after her ordeal, Zoe had visited Oksa's room to reassure her, but couldn't get her to perk up. Even the Nascentia proved ineffectual. The damage ran deep and all hope was gone.

The Werewalls and Felons were just as worried, because Oksa's depression had caused serious repercussions: the Cloak Chamber was still shut. Although a few days earlier it had seemed about to open, that now seemed doubtful. The seventh underground level had been plunged again in darkness, as it had been for nearly sixty years. At the same time Edefia was dying, the land was shaken by convulsions and the sky was shrouded in what looked likely to become everlasting night. Those who'd left loved ones on the Outside were finding it harder than the others, imagining the worst and knowing they were probably right. Oksa was aware of all these things. She felt guilty and was trying to snap out of it, but nothing made her feel any better.

"The Young Gracious must not deplete her heart of the hopefulness that makes it beat," the Lunatrix said one morning, stroking her hand.

Oksa looked at him wordlessly. She could hear and understand, but nothing reached her any more. She felt numb.

"Hope is the salt of life!" exclaimed the Getorix, its hair dishevelled.

"You should never add too much salt," broke in the Incompetent. "It's bad for your blood pressure."

"SHUT UP, INCOMPETENT!" shouted all the creatures together.

"Come on, Oksa, let's go out for a while, you need some fresh air," suggested Zoe, pulling her friend by the arm.

Oksa didn't resist. The penultimate floor of the Column was still under surveillance, but the two girls—like all the Runaways—could now go wherever they wanted, accompanied by a swarm of Vigilians. They descended the Column in the glass lift, since Oksa was too abstracted to Vertifly, and strolled around what remained of the Gracious's garden:

sandy avenues lined with skeletal trees. Leaning on their balconies or pressed up against their windows, members of every clan watched the two figures walking slowly in the half-light. Although they looked vulnerable, everyone knew that their frail exterior hid great strength, waiting to rise again from its ashes, like the phoenix which had been circling above Thousandeye City for several days. Oksa was the only one who didn't seem to realize and that was the problem. So, when a golden halo of light appeared in the murky sky, everyone looked more hopeful.

"The Ageless Ones have come looking for you, Oksa," murmured Zoe, releasing her hand. "They have something to show you…"

60

SUMMONED TO THE
SINGING SPRING

O KSA ALLOWED HERSELF TO BE LIFTED INTO THE AIR
within the halo of light. The Ageless Ones flew over Thousandeye
City, then headed north towards the mysterious Isle of the Fairies, then
beyond. They flew for over two hours in benevolent silence until they
spotted some unusual geometric shapes on the ground. When they drew
level with them, the Ageless Ones dived, as if drawn down by the surface
of the land, and alighted, taking care not to hurt Oksa. One of the fairies
emerged from the halo of light, revealing hazy feminine contours.

"We're here, Young Gracious," she chimed melodiously.

"Where's here?" asked Oksa, looking around.

All she could see was a vast dusty desert and a high wrought-iron gate
in an endless stone wall.

"The maze, Young Gracious," replied the Ageless Ones.

Oksa nodded. She knew all about the maze, which Abakum had
described: it was the way to the Singing Spring, the home of impossible
memories. The Fairyman had been able to see the day of his concep-
tion—which was also the day of his birth—and at last find out where he'd
come from and who he really was. But did she really want to remember
anything when it was all so painful? She preferred to keep her memories
buried—at least, that way they couldn't hurt her...

"Why is this wall so high when you could Vertifly over it or pass through it?" she asked, to distract herself.

"As you've guessed, it's symbolic," confirmed the Ageless Fairy. "It's just for appearances. Not even the strongest Vertiflier or the most talented Werewall could enter the maze without invitation, even if the wall were just a line drawn on the ground."

"Have I been invited then?"

"You have. I'll help you find your way to the Spring. Someone's waiting for you there."

"Who?" said Oksa.

For the first time in days, something broke open inside her and she felt a surprising surge of animation. Whom did she want to see most? Her mother? Dragomira? Gus? Tugdual? She groaned, shaking her head to stop the tears. The choice was impossible.

"Follow me."

Although all she could see was a golden shadow, Oksa felt someone take her hand. The gate swung open, revealing an endless labyrinth made up of walls and leafless hedges of different heights and widths. This perplexing maze was so vast that it seemed to cover the rest of the land, like the convoluted folds of a brain.

"What are we waiting for then?" murmured Oksa.

❄

The maze put up no resistance, but it was horribly complicated. Trying to take her bearings was like trying to navigate in the middle of an ocean without instruments. All the walls were built of large irregular stones and looked the same, while drought had turned the hedges into impassable clusters of dead branches, which also looked the same. This was nothing like the beautiful garden mazes in France in which she used to love wandering aimlessly a few years ago. There was so much she didn't know back then, like who she really was and where her family came from… Dragomira always reached the centre of the maze first and Oksa used to call her a "witch", which used to make Baba Pollock smile and for good cause, since it was secretly true… Oksa sighed and turned her attention back to the golden shadow guiding her onwards without the slightest hesitation.

※

An hour later, the monotonous appearance of the maze gradually changed. The passages widened, the walls weren't so high and afforded glimpses of the horizon ringed with hills. At the base of one hill a bluish light spilt out. That had to be the Singing Spring. Oksa made her way around the last few obstructions, her heart beating with renewed vigour. When she was just a few yards from the exit, she was confronted by two awe-inspiring creatures with the body of a lion and the head of a woman—the legendary Corpusleoxes! The Ageless Fairy led her forward, giving her no choice but to approach. Sitting on hind legs with their forelegs stretched out in front, the magnificent yet terrifying Corpusleoxes were about six feet tall. Suddenly they roared, tossing back thick manes of feminine hair. Oksa took a step back in fear, but the Ageless Fairy wouldn't let her retreat. One of the Corpusleoxes raised its leg in her direction and Oksa screamed at the sight of its long, sharp claws. The creature was going to tear her limb from limb! Or dislocate her shoulder at the very least… The leg came down and Oksa closed her eyes.

"We've been waiting for you for an eternity," boomed the other Corpusleox.

Both creatures roared again. Oksa opened her eyes, realizing that they hadn't meant to frighten her, but to greet her. The two creatures bent even lower, their heads bowed in respect.

"Enter, someone wishes to talk to you."

Feeling a mixture of impatience and fear, Oksa stepped forward and, passing between the Corpusleoxes, found herself in the cave that Abakum had described. The Singing Spring made the air pleasantly damp, and the pinkish waters cast shifting glints on the lapis lazuli walls. It really was a magical place. Abakum had been right, it was like being at the heart of an enormous gem. The peace and quiet immediately made Oksa feel better. She sat down cross-legged beside the Spring, tempted to drink its effervescent waters, and waited. Who wanted to talk to her?

"Is anyone there?" she called.

Her voice bounced off the blue stones, producing an echo which surprised her. Suddenly an opalescent figure appeared, walking across the surface of the water in the middle of the cave. As the figure grew closer, Oksa realized her first impression was right: the plaits pinned around the head, the regal gait, the smile she could just make out within the aureole of milky light…

"Dushka…"

Beside herself with joy, Oksa jumped into the water to make her way to her gran.

"BABA!"

61

SHOCK THERAPY

WAIST-HIGH IN WATER, OKSA HURRIED TOWARDS THE figure of her gran.

"Baba! I can't believe it's really you!"

She tried to fling her arms around her, but they passed straight through her gran's intangible body. Shocked, she took a step back.

"Are you a… ghost?"

"No, Dushka, much better than that. I've become an Ageless Fairy."

"Oh! Baba…"

She was assailed by mixed emotions—intense joy coupled with deep sorrow—at the realization that Dragomira wasn't entirely dead.

"Are you OK?" asked Oksa, her voice breaking.

Dragomira bent over as if to kiss her. Oksa felt a slight breath of air, then a delicate touch on her forehead: a kiss from beyond…

"Get out of the water, Oksa, and come and sit near me. I have things to tell you and, more important, things to show you."

Oksa joined Dragomira by the water's edge. Her clothes dried in a few seconds—what an incredible place! Oksa wanted to curl up against her grandmother, but she couldn't. What she could see of her was real, yet untouchable. However, the main thing was being reunited with her. Dragomira stretched out on the sparkling sand and Oksa did the same without taking her eyes off her. She felt her gran stroke her tangled hair.

"You knew, Baba,"

"What did I know, Dushka?"

"What would happen to you when we passed through the Portal."

Her gran sighed sadly.

"Yes, I knew, the fairies told me when they appeared to us on Orthon's island."

"That's why you looked so sad…"

"It's a great honour for me to have succeeded in getting you into Edefia. I had to pay dearly for that, and I'm no longer permitted to share the life of those I love… but it was worth it. I'm here all the same, in my fashion. I've been reunited with my mother."

"Really?" exclaimed Oksa. "Malorane is with you?"

"Yes, and not just her. There's also Youliana, my gran, and all the dead Graciouses. And just think, I have an Attendant at my beck and call!"

"Oh… one of those half-human, half-stag creatures? I hope he's looking after you!"

"He's marvellous. Just as marvellous as my Lunatrix."

Dragomira faded as she said this.

"How is he?" she asked hoarsely.

"The same as the rest of us, Baba… It's been very tough, you know."

"Yes, I know. I visited you on several occasions and I saw what happened."

"Why didn't you show yourself? It would have cheered us up to know you weren't dead!"

"I am dead, Dushka. Physiologically speaking, anyway. What you can see is my soul."

Oksa groaned.

"But I can see your body! It's just a bit blurry."

"You can only see me today because of the Ageless Ones. Since we entered Edefia, I've been invisible and I'll need quite a few centuries to appear as a shadow like them. After you leave, I'll become transparent again."

"So I won't see you again…" said Oksa sadly.

"Yes you will, we'll be together again soon, darling." Oksa opened her eyes wide in panic.

"Do you mean I'm going to die too?" she asked worriedly.

"No, Dushka! No! The Lunatrix hasn't told you anything then?"

"Wait a moment…" replied Oksa, thinking really hard. "Are you the new Supreme Entity? The one who embodies the equilibrium of the two worlds?"

Dragomira nodded.

"When you enter the Cloak Chamber, I'll be there. Even though I'm the Supreme Entity, I can do nothing on my own. We have to combine our Gracious powers to restore the equilibrium."

"As if you're a bomb and I'm the detonator," said Oksa. "Without a detonator, the bomb's harmless. And without a bomb, there's no point having a detonator."

"Similar, but much more peaceful!" smiled Dragomira.

"The problem is, Baba, that the Chamber isn't opening."

"Do you know why?"

Oksa frowned.

"Because I'm not well," she whispered.

"Exactly. You're blaming yourself when everything that's been happening is outside your control. You're beating yourself up about everything, so the Chamber thinks you aren't ready."

"But I am ready, Baba!" replied Oksa angrily.

"No, you aren't, Oksa," said Dragomira gently. "But I'm going to help you… watch."

Some images appeared on the calm waters of the Spring. Blurry at first, they soon steadied to provide Oksa with answers to the questions that were preventing her from being truly herself.

"The Camereye…" she murmured, desperate for certain assurances.

"For the first time in my life, I've Dreamflown," explained Dragomira. "And this is what I was able to see for you…"

Oksa was shocked by the first image: seven people were in a large round tent—probably a yurt. Oksa easily recognized the Runaways who hadn't entered Edefia. Marie, Akina and Virginia were snuggled up under a thick fur, while Gus and Andrew were busying themselves around the central hearth, where a good fire was burning. Their faces were drawn and they had bags under their eyes, but they seemed in good health. A few people who, by their traits and clothes, seemed to belong to one of the Mongolian nomadic tribes, were bustling about. The Camereye veered off to show Kukka, whose long blonde hair was being brushed by a young woman. There was clearly no one from the Felons' clan. Except Barbara McGraw, whom Oksa was surprised to see there. So she'd stayed with the Runaways... why did she decide to do that? There'd been other Felons amongst the Spurned, whom she could have joined.

"We're not going to spend the rest of our lives here, are we?" suddenly rang out Kukka's voice.

Oksa saw the Spurned turn to look at her. Marie seemed despairing and Gus made no attempt to hide his irritation.

"Please don't shout," he growled. "I've got a splitting headache."

"We have to regain our strength before we set off again," added Andrew. "Instead of complaining, let's be grateful to our hosts. Without them, we'd have been lost in the middle of the desert and perhaps even dead of hunger and cold already."

Another scene appeared, showing the seven Spurned in an airport waiting room packed with hysterical travellers. The building seemed about to fall down: some of the walls had ominous gaping cracks, many of the windows were broken and the ground was strewn with pieces of glass and lumps of concrete. The Camereye scanned the space and Oksa could see soldiers armed to the teeth, as well as many notices written in Cyrillic. Marie was still in her wheelchair, and Gus was standing beside her. They all looked exhausted and anxious. Suddenly, a message echoed from the loudspeakers, first in a language that sounded like Russian, then in English: a flight was announced. Immediately, a dense crowd of people surged towards the boarding gates. The hubbub was so loud that Oksa couldn't hear the destination of that one flight. Everyone was pushing and shoving—this was the ugly side of the law of the strongest. The Spurned tried to push through with Marie's wheelchair. Andrew was brandishing their tickets above people's heads and, without Gus's intervention, a hysterical woman would have grabbed them. There was growing chaos, people were becoming increasingly violent, so the soldiers decided to step in. Horrified, Oksa watched them firing into the air. There were loud screams of panic, then silence as the armed men surrounded the crowd.

"Will any passengers with tickets please make their way towards the check-in desks," ordered one of them. "The others wait here!"

Some of the crowd broke away and gathered in the appropriate area. Reassured, Oksa watched her mother's wheelchair being escorted by the Spurned and a few soldiers to the boarding gate. The Camereye zoomed in on the small group, who were congratulating themselves on surviving this ordeal. They'd all lost weight, their clothes were nothing but rags and tatters, but they looked enormously relieved to be catching this plane. Gus's face appeared on the watery screen. He studied the ceiling, looking for something. Did he suspect that Dragomira could see him? Could he sense her?

"Oh, Gus…" sighed Oksa, her heart in pieces.

It was so hard and yet so comforting to see they were coping and that they were escaping from that chaos. So long as they kept strong…

✳

Several scenes appeared in quick succession on the Camereye. Despite its severe damage, Oksa immediately recognized the Pollocks' house in Bigtoe Square. The Spurned must have succeeded in returning to London. She couldn't imagine how they must be feeling. It was awful to come back in such terrible conditions. The world was nearing its end and all they could do was wait and hope. They were all busy cleaning, repairing and tidying the house. The water had come halfway up to the first floor and had left a sticky residue of mud over everything. Gus and Andrew were working on the roof to replace the countless missing tiles. The hardest thing to bear wasn't the damage caused by the disaster, but the looting—the house, like hundreds of others in these troubled times, had been ransacked. As Oksa found out when she heard her mother talking sadly to her friends: everything that hadn't been destroyed by the elements had been stolen or wrecked.

"As if we haven't suffered enough," groaned Marie, gazing around at the desolate scene.

"We're safe and sound, that's all that matters," replied Virginia, hugging her tightly.

The Camereye paused, before showing one last scene, which really upset Oksa. Gus was in what had been her room. He was lying on her bed, his face screwed up in pain, suffering what was clearly a really bad migraine.

"It hurts so much," he murmured, "I can't stand it." A few minutes later he got up. Leaning on the sash window, he looked out at the ruined square, unhappily fiddling with his school tie. Was he thinking about Oksa the way she'd thought about him when she'd found hers? She didn't doubt it. And yet, when she saw Kukka come into the room and go over to Gus, her heart lurched.

"How dare she go into my room!" she thought angrily.

Gus glanced neutrally at the "Ice Queen", which didn't prevent her from going to stand beside him. She rested her head on his shoulder and Gus did nothing to stop her. Did he realize what that meant? Oksa gave a cry of rage. She grabbed a handful of sand and threw it at the water. The Camereye immediately winked out.

"Baba!" shouted Oksa hoarsely, still reeling from the pain caused by that sight. "Why did you show me that? WHY?"

The milky figure had disappeared.

"I'm not like Zoe, you know!" continued Oksa, clenching her fists. "I don't want him to be happy without me!" She sat there open-mouthed at the enormity of her declaration. The truth, sudden as a whip crack, had just taken her by complete surprise.

"What about you?" rang Baba Pollock's voice. "Could you be happy without him?"

"I... I can't answer that," she replied, dropping to her knees on the ground.

"Think very carefully about what all this means, Dushka... Think very carefully and use your anger wisely, without forgetting that you're central to everyone's hopes and expectations. Don't give up. Never give up. And don't leave it too long before you join me."

The voice faded, leaving Oksa in turmoil.

"If you wanted to shake me out of it, Baba, it certainly worked!" she shouted. "I'm furious, sad and upset, but there's no doubt I'm alive!"

62

RETURN TO REASON

WITH RENEWED DETERMINATION, OKSA GOT TO HER feet and paced up and down the cave. She had mixed feelings at the images she'd just seen and she felt torn between huge relief and intense frustration. Her mother and Gus were hardly on top form—as might be expected—but they'd worked miracles to get back to Bigtoe Square. There really wasn't a better solution. Andrew and Virginia seemed to have their heads firmly set on their shoulders, they were bound to take things in hand... *All* of them had a great deal of common sense so they'd be OK. It was Kukka who'd caused the most heart-searching. Why had she stayed with the Outsiders? That shouldn't have happened. Oksa immediately felt cross with herself for being sidetracked by this... tiny *detail*. Marie's and Gus's health was much more important than the machinations of that treacherous little pest, but after the shock delivered by the Camereye, she couldn't just ignore her. She wouldn't stand for it. And the physical maturity she'd gained through her forced metamorphosis wasn't helping. On the contrary, it had heightened her feelings, the way she viewed her relationships with other people and her reactions. She felt more uptight than she'd ever been.

"Perhaps it isn't mutual," she tried to reason with herself, remembering Gus's casual reaction when Kukka had put her head on his shoulder.

She remembered being very jealous of Zoe when she'd realized how much her second cousin had been attracted to Gus. How much she'd hated her... and yet, Gus had never strayed. He was in love with her. That's what he'd as good as told her before she entered Edefia. And that's why Zoe had sacrificed herself: Gus would never love her. Unless she'd got the wrong end of the stick? Zoe had really unsettled her by implying that her unrequited love was for Tugdual. And why not? It was conceivable, Zoe could be so secretive. Unfortunately, that didn't help Oksa to work out how she felt. The only advantage was that her rage at those stolen images had roused her from her apathy.

She made for the mouth of the cave, where the waiting Corpusleoxes greeted her with a searching look. One of them held out a slender chain from which dangled an unusual sphere the size of a plum. Oksa accepted the gift and examined the gem, a tiny Earth which looked like an identical copy of the real planet.

"How beautiful!" she exclaimed.

Intrigued, she whispered into her Granok-Shooter to produce a Reticulata, then gave a cry.

"Amazing! It's moving!"

As if she were guiding a satellite, she had an overview of the planet, which was both magical and terrifying. Some of the oceans looked calm but others were raging, eating into the coastline and surging inland. She could also make out the mountain ranges, rising to meet the floating clouds, sometimes wreathed in plumes of white smoke caused by the forest fires burning at their bases. A volcano erupted in the part that Oksa identified as Iceland, spewing out tiny sprays of lava. All over the world, similar eruptions were wreaking havoc. Oksa studied Great Britain closely, particularly the area around London. She was relieved to see that, unlike the Volga or the Mississippi, the Thames had subsided. That would give the Spurned some breathing space at least...

Suddenly, Oksa felt the ball quivering in her palm like a vibrating phone. She narrowed her eyes to peer through the Reticulata and clearly saw an earthquake rocking the west coast of the United States. She closed her hand, tears in her eyes.

"Those poor people…" she groaned, thinking about everyone affected by the dying world.

Thousands of people must have lost their lives because of her moods. She was so annoyed with herself right now. One of the Corpusleoxes placed an enormous foreleg on the Young Gracious's shoulder.

"You should make haste."

"What must I do… exactly?" asked Oksa, a lump in her throat.

The creature pointed to the figure of the Ageless Fairy, who'd guided her through the maze.

"Good luck, Young Gracious," said the Corpusleoxes.

Oksa went over to her escort, who was hovering a few inches above the ground.

"Let's go, I'm ready!"

She raised her head high and slipped the "Earth" around her neck. Escorted by the golden shadow of the Ageless Fairy, she rose into Edefia's fading sky. The Heart of the Two Worlds was dying and it was time for her to face her destiny and accept who she was: Edefia's New Gracious.

Coming soon

OKSA
POLLOCK
tainted
BONDS

1

A Date with Destiny

DEEP IN THE SEVENTH BASEMENT OF THE GLASS COLUMN, the door was blazing with the mesmerizing intensity of molten metal. Oksa squinted, dazzled by the blinding light spilling out from around the door frame and through the keyhole. It was time to enter the Cloak Chamber at last. Images of the past flooded her mind, reminding her of everything she'd gone through, from the moment she'd discovered her remarkable gifts in her London home to her arrival in Edefia. However, these memories only strengthened her resolve. She took a deep breath and turned round to look at everyone standing in a semicircle, staring at her intently—her father and the Runaways in the middle, flanked by Ocious and the Felons, who were glowering at her. Everyone was there. Everyone except the four people whose absence had left an aching void in her heart: her mother, Gus—who was so much more than a friend—Dragomira, her late gran, and evasive Tugdual, with whom she was so deeply in love.

Oksa screwed up her eyes to hide her violent emotions and protect her gaze from the intense glare radiated by the door. Endlessly reflected and magnified by the highly faceted precious stones lining the walls, the light was growing brighter with each passing second. Not only that, but the disagreeable stroboscopic effect created by the aerobatics of the Death's Head Chiropterans and Vigilians high above the Runaways' heads was even harder to bear. Oksa shot a disgusted glance at those revolting tiny bats and winged caterpillars, sorely tempted to put an end to the torture by cremating them with a Fireballistico.

"At last!" whispered Ocious, raising his hand and clicking his fingers to halt the frenetic comings and goings of his airborne escorts.

The imposing old man took a few steps towards Oksa. Pavel Pollock stiffened but Abakum—the wise Fairyman—caught his eye and made a pacifying gesture.

"I've waited so long for this moment," continued Ocious, blatantly exultant. "But since you've been here, my dear Oksa, those long, hard years have ceased to matter. The Cloak Chamber has reappeared; you will enter it and be enthroned, since you're the one chosen as our new Gracious, the Gracious who'll make it possible for me—for *us* to accomplish our mission."

"Your mission? You're such a megalomaniac!" protested Oksa, clenching her fists. "Anyway, you know very well I'm not here for you, I'm here to save the two worlds! You've got nothing to do with it. Nothing at all."

The Felon gave an evil smile.

"Poor child," he said. "You're so naive!"

"You fancy yourself as the ruler of Edefia," continued Oksa furiously, "but you're just an ageing psychopath without a future. You've been nothing but a curse on the inhabitants of this magnificent land, which is now dying because of you, and you continue to believe you're stronger than anyone. You're... pathetic! Can't you feel some remorse for once? There's still time to show you're a man, not a monster."

"Oksa!" implored Pavel. "Be quiet."

Beside herself with anger, Oksa was pulling at the hem of her blue T-shirt so hard that she was in danger of tearing it.

"I don't give a damn for your impertinent opinion," sneered Ocious "because I'm the one who has the power of life and death over your family and friends, until you come out again."

Ocious waved a hand and the guards in leather armour posted around the vast circular hall closed ranks, putting the Runaways under even closer surveillance. Then, with a speed that took everyone by surprise, he launched himself at Pavel and caught him in a firm neck hold. Drawing himself up to his full height, he glared evilly at Oksa.

"Now, you'll do me the great pleasure of entering that chamber, restoring the equilibrium and coming out again to open the Portal for me. Do you understand, girlie?"

Before Oksa could reply she was suddenly distracted by a movement in the highest part of the seventh basement's vaulted ceiling, covered in blue gems. A gorgeous bird with wings of fire was flying among the Chiropterans and Vigilians, which parted to let it pass. It circled above their heads with silent grace before landing at Oksa's feet. The heart-stopping solemnity of this moment caused both Felons and Runaways to hold their breath.

"My Phoenix!" murmured Oksa.

The sublime creature bowed, then stretched out its foot and opened its talons to reveal a key decorated with an eight-branched star—the emblem of Edefia, which had turned Oksa's life upside down when it had appeared around her belly button. The key fell to the ground, raising plumes of fine sparkling dust, then the Phoenix uttered a throaty caw and took off again, disappearing into the lofty dome.

"My Young Gracious is henceforth in possession of the final component," declared a small chubby creature, hurrying over to pick up the key and offer it to Oksa.

"Thank you, my Lunatrix," replied Oksa, holding out her hand. The key was surprisingly heavy and so cold to the touch that she almost dropped it. A few yards away, the door to the chamber grew larger with a roaring noise caused by the intense heat. Oksa trembled.

"The flames of hell…" she said, with a grimace.

She felt a hand on her shoulder.

"No, sweetheart," whispered Abakum in her ear. "Your date with destiny."

Turning to meet the Fairyman's green eyes, Oksa gave him a faint smile. Feeling powerful and *actually* being powerful were two different things.

339

"Will you let me give my daughter some moral support?" growled Pavel, struggling to free himself from Ocious's grip.

"If you must," retorted the elderly Felon. He released Pavel, but kept his Granok-Shooter trained on him.

Looking distraught, Pavel walked over to Oksa and held her so tightly she could feel his heart racing.

"Everything will be fine, Dad," she said quietly, as if trying to reassure herself.

Then, emptying her mind of all thoughts and refusing to look at anyone, she walked towards the chamber brimming with light.

BE ACCEPTING OF THANKS

The two authors of Oksa Pollock have hearts palpitating with gratitude. They are possessed here of the insistence to grant expression of firmly rooted gratitude to certain people:

The extremely active and loftily perched XO team; Gracious Bernard; indispensable Caroline; reassuring Edith; dynamic Valérie; imperturbable Catherine; international Florence; exuberant Jean-Paul; effervescent Stéphanie and all the men and women who labour in darkness or light.

The teams at SND and Jim Lemley for their decision and their colossal work.

All Pollockmaniacs, young and old, who continue to experience exponential growth in number and interest. Their dynamism stocks the minds of the authors with encouragement and happiness.

The booksellers and professionals in the industry of literature and books, the teachers and librarians in schools and cities who construct pillars replete with confidence which uphold this whole adventure.

The journalists who have been responsible for a circulation scintillating with sparks from the initial delight to the present endurance.

The foreign publishers whose perception, garnished with enthusiasm, will bring enjoyment to readers in all the far-flung corners of the world.

PUSHKIN CHILDREN'S BOOKS

We love stories just as much as you. Since we were very young, we have loved to hear about monsters and heroes, mischief and adventure, danger and rescue, from every time and every place.

We created Pushkin Children's Books to share these tales from different languages and cultures with you, to open the door to the colourful worlds beyond that these stories offer.

From picture books and adventure stories to fairy tales and classics, from fifty-year-old favourites to current huge successes abroad, Pushkin Children's books are the very best stories from around the world, brought together for our most discerning reader of all: you.